GAEL HARRISON was born in Malaysia and attended a boarding school on Penang Hill for three years before going home to Scotland where she attended boarding school and qualified as a teacher. She also gained a Fine Arts degree at the Open University.

With her husband and three children, she spent ten years in Singapore and Kota Kinabalu in North Borneo, where she taught in an international school as well as running her own multinational kindergarten.

In the 1980s she returned to Scotland where she and her family lived in a village overlooking the Isle of Skye. In 2001 she took up the challenge of VSO and spent a year in the Vietnamese mountains close to the Chinese border, and three further years working in the UN International School in Hanoi.

She has worked in Ukraine and Qatar and, always keen to learn about different peoples and cultures, has travelled extensively overseas. Her books reflect her particular love of Scotland and Malaysia, the two countries that have most strongly influenced her. Gael now lives with her husband in North Queensferry, Scotland.

Also by Gael Harrison

The Moon in the Banyan Tree
The Highland Games
The Highland Rocks
Where the Golden Oriole Sang
Piping for Victory, a play about Bessie Watson, the youngest suffragette

THE FISH
IN THE TREE

GAEL HARRISON

SilverWood

Published in 2025 by SilverWood Books

SilverWood Books Ltd
14 Small Street, Bristol, BS1 1DE, United Kingdom
www.silverwoodbooks.co.uk

ISBN 978-1-80042-301-5 (paperback)
Also available as an ebook

British Library Cataloguing in Publication Data
A CIP catalogue record for this book is
available from the British Library

Page design and typesetting by SilverWood Books

Thank you to all my friends in Malaysia,
in particular to Ming and Francis Frey for their wonderful insight
and as always to John for his constant support.

Prologue

It was a cruel day he had for his birth. The fields had frozen hard. A smattering of hail had whitened the heap of coal left by the shed where she'd dropped the scuttle in her haste. The pains had come and she'd bent into the wind, hurrying back into the house, her face contorted, clutching, clawing the stuff of her apron. It was too early; no one would come.

Outside, the screech of the wind threatened the roof and, wild-eyed, she scoured the forsaken fields. Another lashing of hail spattered the glass of the living room and the woman moaned low like a beast, a growl deep in her throat as she cowered over in pain. No time, no time for anything. She knelt down on all fours on the thread-bare rug. Another stab of pain and she rolled on to her side, her knees pulled up foetal-like, and she knew it wouldn't be long. Twisting her neck she caught sight of a stack of newspapers kept at the fireside, and with a heave she pulled herself up again and crawled painfully over to where they were. Trembling, she arranged the snippets of news beneath her hips, then lowering herself down she rested for a moment upon her papery nest.

The wind screamed and she heaved a final time. At a quarter to eleven on the eighth of February 1924, Francis Findlay Farquharson came into the world and was wrapped in the pages of *The Sunday Post*.

Chapter 1

The wind had been blowing for days now, bringing squalls of rain across the bleak cliffs. Edie Shariff stood dangerously close to the lip of a ledge, thrilling to the sound of the gulls and the smash of waves hundreds of feet beneath her. Glittering shafts of light streamed through the clouds and splintered on the surface of the cold North Sea. She scanned the thrashing surf, trying to make sense of the fleeting shapes. Could they be the heads of seals or the fins of cod? Edie was not much of an expert in such things. She pulled her jacket tighter around her and wondered for the hundredth time what her life would have been like had she taken a different path. She hadn't been one to reflect in the rear-view mirror, well not until now.

She had woken up this morning feeling a sense of loss, as though she'd missed something, some pull of the generations, a yearning of her genes, an unfinished longing for this land that had been in her bloodline going back through time. Lying on the worn sheets in the old house that had once belonged to her father's family, she had felt loath to get up. The room was simple. A dressing table with an embroidered runner pinned under protective glass stood against the wall at the end of the bed. Edie's hairbrush and her few bits of makeup littered the surface. A wardrobe made of plain wood, reminiscent of a coffin, stood guard on the wall opposite the window. Its mirrored door reflected the weak light through the net curtains. Edie herself felt quite at home in such a Spartan setting, never having been a woman who craved luxuries or fine furnishings. She sat up in order to see the dressing table mirror, adjusting the pillow so that she could view herself in her ancestral surroundings. She saw a woman in her early fifties, with fine skin as white and unblemished as a hen's egg. Only faint lines ran down her cheeks to her chin, almost like a surgeon's scar. It was not a face that betrayed emotion. There was no evidence of laughter she thought, nor a face that revealed the signs of care. The smooth dome of her forehead disguised any grief or tension. She flicked her thin hair, still a soft brown, but lustreless and streaked now with grey. It fell to her shoulders in wisps. Edie squinted to see her eyes. Pale, almost opaque. Blue, but not bright like a cornflower or a warm summer sky. More like a wet wash on a bit of pottery. She remembered how she had once looked, when she was a student in Edinburgh. She had only recently learnt that her husband Kamal had surreptitiously kept an old photograph of her in his desk drawer, probably to remind him of the young girl that he'd fallen for. She had been bemused that he had kept it all these years. She closed her eyes now and saw again the image of herself in a white fluffy coat that looked more like a long jacket. Her legs were long and thin as stilts and she had worn the high leather boots with the platform heels that her mother said reminded her of a dominatrix. Her head had been covered by a blue woolly ski-type hat, but her long hair fell on to her shoulders, a waterfall of soft sleek feathers. Oh well, Edie thought resignedly, I have fared all right, and here I am, lying in my grandmother's bed, still with my long thin legs, but with a bulging middle-aged spread. She ran her hands over the folds of her midriff and thought of Isobel Farquharson. Edie ran her fingers over the lumpy mattress, and imagined that it was in this bed that her grandmother had birthed her eight children.

When she finally got up, she decided to go exploring. Grabbing an apple she drove the coast road towards Dunnottar Castle. It was here that she now stood, staring down from the rugged cliffs towards the ancient stronghold, seemingly holding back not only Scotland's enemies but the full force of the North Sea. Perhaps I'll visit another day, she thought, it's so cold and I'm not acclimatised yet for such adventures. Iron grey clouds scudded overhead while a wind gust showered her with icy slivers of sleet. Shivering she hastened back to the relative warmth of her car. She had hired the vehicle yesterday in Edinburgh before making the journey north to Scotland's east coast, just south of Aberdeen, after first calling into the solicitor's office in Perth to pick up the house keys and the various papers she would need. Mr Sutherland knew a lot about the family and was eager to talk. 'You'll find yourself going into a time machine, Mrs Shariff. It will just spirit you back through the ages better than any museum could do. Now then, would you like me to give you a quick timeline of your relatives who once lived there?'

'I would, please,' she said. 'My mother refused to tell me anything about the Farquharsons, including my own father.'

Mr Sutherland had nodded, 'Well I don't know that much, just a bit about the more recent occupants, but it might help.' He looked down at his papers before continuing. 'Your grandfather Jock Farquharson and his wife Isobel owned Formylie Farm and it was there that they raised their seven sons, including your father Francis Findlay Farquharson, and their one daughter Sylvia. Sadly, I believe many of their children met sorry ends. The old boy died in 1989, leaving Isobel alone. Some years after that, Jock's sister Anne came to live with her; I think she had been living in Stirling. The two old ladies ran the place right up to when they died, first your grandmother Isobel in 2000 and then Anne in 2003. They used to rent out the two fields, but also kept a few sheep and chickens around the house. They seemed to cope all right, by all accounts. You'll hear more about them in the village, no doubt. Anne was close to a hundred when she finally passed on.'

Edie had left Perth and continued her journey up the east coast towards Aberdeen. She was grateful to Mr Sutherland for enlightening her of what she might find on her arrival at Formylie Farm, south of Stonehaven. The house had been unoccupied for three years, but he'd assured her that a neighbour had a key and had been keeping an eye on things. She had bought some meagre provisions in a Co-op along the way. Not knowing how long she would stay or what condition the house was in, she decided some cheese and biscuits, fruit and coffee might suffice until she decided what to do. It all felt so odd, being alone, without Kamal taking charge. Just being in Scotland. Thank goodness for Joy and her warm welcome two weeks ago after her plane had landed in Edinburgh. Thirty years, and the two friends held each other as though they had parted yesterday.

Enough of this, she thought, I must get back to this new house of mine. It has been quite invigorating, even though the wind has done battle with my hair and my poor face has been smattered with ice. Edie put the car into gear, and with a spray of gravel, she sped out from the viewpoint and made towards the old farm. Turning off the main road, she gritted her teeth as she bumped her way over the ruts in the farm track. Ahead, the property stood guarded by a sprawling and majestic sycamore. Behind the farm sheds stood a copse of Scots Pine, huddled together, grown huge with memories of boys and ropes and of childhoods of long ago. Melancholy trees, Edie thought, imagining the sough of the wind through the misshapen branches, and of histories that only the stones, trees and parklands could share.

The farmhouse was modest, built of local stone about a century or more ago. The woodwork was weathered with only a faint stain of bottle-green giving the illusion of how it might once have looked. Edie parked the car and walked round to the kitchen door. The house was very cold and she shivered. Inside was a scullery with a walk-in pantry to the side. The stone floors were in need of a good mopping and everything was covered in dust. The Belfast sink was stained brown from the constant drip of a tap. Above the sink was a sash window, the cords worn and broken and hanging uselessly at each side. A curtain of faded orange cotton seemed to have been an attempt to brighten the dark interior. Edie looked around at the open shelving and saw signs of life from another era. Lambing bottles, shears, balls of twine, empty jam jars by the dozen, a pipe, a fat book. Curiosity made her reach up and take the book down. What did these farming folk read? Of course, she thought, the Holy Bible. Why wasn't she surprised? Its navy-blue cover was faded, and as she opened the book to sniff the tissue-like leaves, the musty odour seemed to infiltrate the room. *'In the beginning God created the heavens and the earth'*. Still holding the Bible, she walked into the sitting room and placed the book on the table beside an armchair. This room was all brown. Brown lino on the floor, brown-stained wallpaper, and the soot from the fire had stained the ceiling, giving the feeling of being in a box. Edie looked at the fireplace with its blackened range, over which hung a hook for the griddle and a toasting fork. Beside the range stood a coal scuttle and between the two armchairs lay a faded rust-coloured rug.

This was where her widowed grandmother had lived alone before being joined by her husband's spinster sister Anne. Edie imagined the two old women in their worn clothes and white hair, sitting across from one other. She could picture their legs, swathed in black woollen stockings and stretched out on a stool in front of the fire. She could almost smell the scones and pancakes as their yeasty aroma filled the room.

Edie went through to the scullery and ran the tap for a good while before filling the kettle. She found a cup and saucer in the sideboard, thick with dust, and from her bag of provisions she made herself a cup of instant coffee. Now sitting by the ancient two-bar electric fire, she ran her hand over the cover of the old Bible. Inside on the frontispiece were written the names of Isobel and Jock Farquharson and their eight children, seven boys and one girl, just as Mr Sutherland had told her. Each were listed by their dates of birth and their names. And then after their birthdates, written with a shaky hand, were the dates of their deaths. Old Isobel had been predeceased by her husband and all eight of her children. Oh, how awful, she thought, that is just too much pain for anyone to bear. Edie looked down the list for her father. She saw him, second from the top: Francis Findlay Farquharson, born 8th February 1924.

Chapter 2

Edie never knew her father. He had been murdered in Glasgow. Slashed with a razor, her mother's sister Phamie had said, left to bleed in the stairwell. 'He had it coming, always fighting. I knew he was a bad lot and I warned your mother but she wouldn't listen.' Edie could hear her aunt's voice, bitter and unforgiving: 'No thought for anyone but himself. Razored across the face and throat.' Phamie had screwed up her mean little eyes, 'Probably just as well.'

Edie shook away the memory and walked over to peer at two tarnished silver-framed photographs on the sideboard. The sharp features of her grandfather Jock were stamped on each of his children, like a brand or an identity badge. Their children were standing in a descending line according to age, all recipients of the brutal barber style of the time, their faces expressionless. The eldest boy looked no more than fourteen. She flipped the frame over and prised open the rusty clips at the back. Sure enough, the names were written in pencil on the back, corresponding with each child: John, Francis Findlay, William, Sylvia, Alasdair, Ian and Neil. She counted them. Seven. She thought there were eight children. She carried the photographs back to the chair and reopened the Bible at the family history. She looked again at the dates of death. Edie sighed, of course, Peter had died at birth. She was about to close the Bible when she saw an envelope tucked between two pages at the back. She pulled it out and looked inside. Scraps of paper. Gently pulling each one out, she found she was holding a collection of newspaper cuttings. Poor Granny, Edie thought, she had carefully saved these mementoes of her lost children, a papery memorial. She squinted at the small print but the words eluded her. 'I need my specs; now where did I leave my handbag?' When she was comfortable once more, Edie read the brief obituaries. John the first born was commemorated by an article in the local paper, he had been crushed by a tractor, leaving his child bride a widow. Baby Peter had died at birth, he had been Granny's fourth son.

Alasdair had died aged only nineteen in a fatal motorcycle crash. Ian had died of tuberculosis aged twenty-six, and Neil had drowned; he'd been on a fishing boat off Fraserburgh. The only daughter, Sylvia, had died aged 39 in Aberdeen Infirmary, the notice said, of an illness, bravely borne.

Flicking through the sad little pile of obituaries, she came to the death notice for her father. It was very brief: *Francis Findlay Farquharson. Second son of Jock and Isobel Farquharson, Formylie Farm, near Stonehaven. Tragically killed in Glasgow aged 30. Sadly missed by his wife Violet and daughter Edna. 7th April 1955.* Edie looked out of the window. She knew this, her Aunty Phamie had kept nothing from her, but somehow reading the word 'April' brought immediacy to the fact. April didn't seem to be the right month for a life to end. It was the month associated with growth, renewal, birth and light. Not of a body lying cut and bleeding on the cold cement floor of a Glasgow tenement.

And what of William? she mused. There was the date of his death but no newspaper record. I wonder how he met his end? He was born the year after my father but didn't die until 1984. He would have been about sixty.

Edie took off her glasses, her head resting on the leather back of the chair, and for a moment she closed her eyes, feeling the quiet of the room, the suspension of time, the silence of the lost years. Adjacent to the fireplace was a small alcove, presumably a press or shallow cupboard at one time. She picked up the other framed photograph depicting a wedding scene; her grandparents. Jock, as a groom, was raw and angular. His gaunt face, hooded eyes, and chiselled cheekbones reminded her of an ancient Greek statue. Edie squinted her eyes to study the face of her grandmother. She looked at the rounded cheeks, the wide-spaced eyes, the serious mouth, and noticed the gloved hand resting on her husband's arm. 'And you lived here in this house until you were in your nineties.' Edie said. 'How I wish I could have met you.' She smiled at the stark contrast with her own nuptial scene. She thought of the kampong on the other side of the world, where black-toothed hags had sat snickering whilst chewing betel nut, and pigs and chickens skittered about in front of the stilted house. Seven thousand miles might have divided them, culture and oceans might have kept them apart, but here she was looking at dates and obituaries, and wondering. She wasn't sure what she wondered, whether things might have been different if she had stayed within a ten-mile radius of her gene pool, whether her life might have had a different outcome if she had married Bones, her hippy boyfriend from the Edinburgh days. Then she remembered - Bones had had an unhappy ending.

Oh well, she sighed, what might have been I'll never know, but I wonder if knowing how my grandmother coped with so much sorrow might have helped when things went so dark for me.

Chapter 3

Edie's reverie was disturbed by a sharp knock at the back door and an immediate shout, 'Hello! Are you there?'

Edie jumped up, spirited by the disturbance, glad of the distraction. 'I'm here!'

'And you've settled in well, have you? Found everything?'

'I have, things seem to be in working order.' She looked at her visitor, bemused by the woman's familiarity about the house.

'I'm Aggie Smart, a neighbour. I live in the old railway cottage about half a mile up the road. I used to come by every day to see Anne and get her shopping, you know, when she wasn't able.' The woman stood framed in the doorway, looking comfortable and familiar in her surroundings. 'Mind you,' she ran on, 'she was fit and able almost right up to the end; she was such an independent soul. It was so sad when she fell and broke her hip. She was that skinny, like a matchstick she was; the bone just broke and the poor thing had to have it splinted. Then they took her away to Aberdeen.' Aggie's face turned sour.

'The poor soul.' Edie nodded.

'She was like a broken flower. Like a snowdrop that had lost its place in the wild.' The woman paused theatrically; she was a natural orator, fully aware that she had her audience enthralled. She lowered her voice and her eyes grew large with meaning. 'Poor thing just crumpled; the life force seemed to seep out of her. It was a tragedy.'

'But she was ninety-eight,' Edie reminded her. 'It was a good age.'

'Maybe it was, but she lost the will to live when they took her in there. She loved living here, loved living with her sister-in-law, poor thing, Isobel died only three years before her. The two old women were as hospitable as you could wish, full of the stories and they gave you the best cup of tea in the district.' Aggie looked pointedly at Edie's cup and saucer.

'I have Nescafé if you would care to have a cup with me?' she looked enquiringly at the older woman. 'These cups are small, and I could do with a refill.'

Aggie immediately bustled through to the scullery and set about refilling the kettle. Edie took in the red jacket and the wide-cut brown trousers, the brown brogues and the hands roughened by life in the country. She guessed her neighbour to be in her late sixties.

'It's nice to have some company,' Edie smiled as she set out another cup beside her own. 'I only arrived yesterday afternoon and it's all very strange for me. I'm glad to see you and hear stories about my relatives.'

'Oh well,' Aggie spooned in the coffee. 'There isn't much to say. The old ladies made their scones and knitted and were usually glued to the television. I was always afraid to come in, they had it so loud. They were very fond of their "soaps" and had a thing about wrestling. Didn't seem natural somehow, the way they would be glued to those big chaps throwing each other about. Now, me, I prefer Casualty. I never miss it. I just love a hospital drama. What about you? Do you watch much television?'

'Not really, though I do like films. Living here I can imagine becoming absorbed in all the programmes; there's just so much variety.' Edie picked up her cup and turned back towards the warmth of the fire. She looked out at the windswept fields, the daffodils bent double in the exposed parts of the garden. 'It does seem colder than I remember. Isn't April supposed to be a warm month?'

'I've seen snow up to my armpits with the lambs struggling for life,' Aggie nodded sagely, 'but that can be one year. The next we're out with the barbecue, and the smell of sausages smoking on the coals would bring tears to your eyes. It's all very whimsical. But where is home for you? Edna, isn't it?'

'Edie,' Edie smiled. 'I haven't been called Edna for many years.'

'Right, Edie it is. That Mr Sutherland, the lawyer from Perth, telephoned Millicent in the shop and told her that you would be coming up. Will you be staying here long, in the house? Or will you be going home to where you're from?' Aggie's eyes glimmered with interest.

'I'm from Sabah, in East Malaysia. The town is called Kota Kinabalu. It's on the island of Borneo.'

'Now, I did hear that,' Aggie said slyly. 'Someone said you were from foreign parts, right enough.' She primly sipped her drink, not in any hurry to rush away. 'I remember Anne saying that you and Will were the last of the family. He died too of course, though goodness knows where. His poor mother never did know the facts. And we don't know if he had any family. He was another dark horse.'

Edie smiled. She thought it would be better to be upfront with this neighbour and put an end to any speculation as to why she might be here. 'I came back to Scotland for personal reasons.' She looked down at her half empty coffee cup. 'I did keep in touch with my old schoolfriend over the years. Her name is Joy; she lives in Edinburgh. I can't believe that it's been thirty years since I have been back in this country. To be honest, I feel as though I'm in a time warp. I left when I was just twenty-two, and I'm slowly coming to terms with all the changes that have taken place since I left.'

'So, it was through your Edinburgh friend that Mr Sutherland was able to get in touch with you?' Aggie's eyes were like two hard beads, alert to any snippets of information.

'Yes, Joy was my link, and thank goodness for that, or I might never have heard about this house, or my father's family.'

Edie looked out at the field beyond the crumbling wall of the garden. Two Canada geese had settled on a rise and were waddling into the wind. 'I'll just take these cups through,' she said. She needed to escape the gentle but persistent inquisition. The journey back to Scotland and the first two weeks with Joy had been a culture shock. Not only was she still deeply distressed by the events of the last few months, her return to the Scottish capital had brought her face to face with other people's problems and social issues. She had been appalled by the dirt and the beggars huddling beneath the ancient stone of the castle dominating Princes Street. Had it always been like this? She and Joy had wandered around the streets of Edinburgh, just as they had as students long ago, reliving their youth, then Edie winced as she recalled the days with Bones on the Royal Mile. Now as two middle-aged women they had walked in the showers of spring rain, pulling up their collars, and diving into shops and cafes. 'Do you remember, Joy, all the arguments I had with my mother? How she hated my white coat and long boots? Funny really as it was not so different from my own reaction to Tara's sequins on the silver dress that she had insisted on wearing for the school dance. I remember shrieking, "You can't go out like that! What will people think?" It was all so old, yet so familiar. But

Violet, her mother, was gone. Edie remembered writing to her after the birth of Adam and receiving by return mail a woollen matinee jacket, in buttercup yellow, complete with hat and mittens. The heat of the tropics soon reduced the garment to moth holes, and the child's prickly heat went into riot when it encountered the clammy softness of the wool. She kept it in tissue until it disintegrated, unable to discard the gift that had crossed so many miles. Aunty Phamie had written to her giving her an account of her mother's death. 'Cancer', she had written, 'and very quick'. Poor Violet, she would be dust now, part of the Scottish landscape around Loch Lomond. Edie stared down at the dripping tap in the sink, and her new reality, far from her marital home and far from her childhood home.

'Ah, there you are, I could have helped you with the kettle, were you just having a wee daydream?'

'I was, Aggie, sorry, thoughts just swirl about, and there is such a lot to think about at the moment. Come back, finish your coffee.'

'I was just wondering about your Uncle Will, he must have died over there,' and Aggie rolled her eyes to the ceiling, 'somewhere abroad,' she almost whispered.

Edie blinked. 'Well, I'm not the person to enlighten you, I didn't know anything about my father or his family at all.'

'Yes, well, it's sad, but there we are. Poor Isobel blessed with eight children and lost them all, while Anne never even had one, and neither did I. I just lived my life hoping and waiting. You just wonder what it's all for.'

Edie said nothing.

'And you, Edie? Have you got any children?'

'I do, but grown up now, I even have a granddaughter.' She smiled. 'Tara is married to Joe and they have little Clementine. She is two and a half already.'

'That's nice.' Aggie realised there was no other information to be had on that subject at present so she changed tack. 'So, what brings you here now, dear? If you don't mind me asking?'

'No, I don't mind,' It was pleasant to chat, even if it was to an inquisitive though well-meaning neighbour. 'I got a letter a while ago from my friend Joy. I had made her my power of attorney whilst I was away. When my mother's sister Phamie passed on, in 2002, Joy went to the house to sort out any letters that might need my attention. She found a letter, already two years old; it was addressed to my mother, informing her of my grandmother's death. That would be Isobel, here at the farm. Joy recounted the contents of the letter, but it meant very little to me, being so far away, and I couldn't see me coming back to Scotland in the immediate future. I was busy, my daughter got married that year.' She looked out of the window, registering the unfamiliar stone dyke. 'But life has a funny way of turning everything around.'

Aggie nodded her head encouragingly, leaning forward as though ready to catch the words and store them close for further examination at her leisure. But Edie put her glasses down decisively. She did not want to rake over those particular memories. Instead, she smoothed her hand over her trousers, playing with the crease below her knee. 'I phoned Mr Sutherland two weeks ago,' she glanced at the wedding photograph of her grandparents, 'and here I am. Better late than never.'

'Oh, quite so, quite so.' Aggie inhaled and let out a deep heartfelt sigh.

'I thought I might stay for a few days and look around. It might be nice to see the place that my father's family once called home.'

'Well, I can always help in any way, Edie dear. Me and my man, Bob, we've been neighbours to your grandmother for the whole of our lives. If there's anything you need to know, you just ask me.' The older woman smiled sweetly, and patted Edie's hand. 'But look, the sun is coming out now, I think I'll go into the town and see if I can get a new handle for my broom. I'll come around tomorrow about the same time and we can have another wee chat!'

Edie watched her go, a skip in her step. 'A broomstick,' she laughed, 'just the thing for a gossipy old witch!'

Chapter 4

Edie enjoyed her second morning in the house. She had spent yesterday afternoon in Stonehaven, visiting the harbour and walking down the High Street filling her bag with provisions. Steak, vegetables, cereal, bread and enough tins to stock the larder for the remainder of her stay. Now the house had the smell of toast and coffee. She prised open the sitting room window and let a sweet breeze stir the dust and blow away the musty smell from the unused room. Edie was not a good housewife; she had overseen her home in Malaysia but had relied on her local amah to do the real cleaning. Now, in this brown room, she meticulously polished the wooden furniture with the relish of a novice. Slowly she wiped the mantelpiece and then replaced the worn ornaments with a sense of childish delight. She wondered if her neighbour would visit again and made her way through to the sink to fill the kettle in case.

By eleven she was still alone so decided to inspect the garden and outhouses. The day was dry and patches of blue framed the branches of the still-naked sycamore. Edie tramped across rough turf towards an old stone well nestling below a timber and slate roof. She saw the bucket lying abandoned on the grass and hooked it back onto the rope before turning the handle to lower it down to the water. When she heard the pleasing sound of water and the gloppy sounds it made as the bucket submerged, she laughed in delight, and felt a sense of achievement as she rewound the bucket up to the lip of the well. 'Well, fancy that! I wonder if it's drinkable!'

'I see you have a taste for country living,' Aggie's voice called out.

'So, it would seem! Look at this well, I can't believe how efficient it is. Can I drink the water, do you think?'

'You certainly can. Your grandmother used it all her life. Even after they got the mains connected, she still said there was nothing like the water from the hills. Made the sweetest drink she knew.'

'What about frogs?' Edie looked down into the dark depths.

'There's nothing down there that will hurt you. Come on, we'll use your water and have a cup of your nice coffee. I brought you some seed cake which I got from Mrs Smythe; there's far too much for me and Bob. What do you say?'

'I'd like that very much.' Edie turned back towards the house, carrying her pail of water. 'I've been dusting and was going to look in the sheds at the back, but got waylaid by the well.'

'It's a lovely day, right enough,' agreed Aggie. 'I could give you a hand to take out the rug and give it a good beating. It's been lying there for years.'

The two women spent the next hour washing down the floor and gathering wood for the fire from the stack by the door. Edie scrambled over the uneven grass to pick a bunch of windswept daffodils which she placed in a vase by the window. The house smelt fresh, the coffee was made and the two women sat down to resume their conversation. It was so easy listening to Aggie, Edie thought, they just chattered away and somehow stories unravelled about her relatives.

'They were wild, those boys, ran all over the countryside full of their pranks. Bob and I were constantly at our wits end trying to keep track of them for your granny. I remember once when Frank, that's what they called your father, Frank and Will made a raft. It took them days to get it altogether, and then they persuaded wee Sylvia to come and join their games. They had her up on the raft, filling her head with nonsense, and then let go of the rope and off she went, sailing down the river with them whooping with delight, shouting to her that she was a Red Indian prisoner. Hooligans they were.'

'Was that not dangerous, with the sea so close?' Edie asked, remembering the cruel rocks she had seen the previous day.

'Terribly dangerous.' Aggie leant over. 'Young Cameron Stewart was swept away by the current. He was only three and his poor mother never got over it. No, you should never play with fire or water, but boys will not be told. Fortunately, Sylvia was rescued by some men down at the bend in the river. As a result, her two brothers felt the leather of their father's belt. Not for the first time, either...'

'What became of Jock, my grandfather? You don't talk of him much.'

'He died dear, terrible it was.' Aggie, her eyes intense, whispered meaningfully, 'Prostate.' The lines gathered like storm clouds over her brows. 'Poor man, he was whisked off to Aberdeen and his last days were spent looking at tubes and shop flowers in vases. He hankered for the land and the wild coastline, right up to the last.' Aggie bit into her cake and chewed slowly, taking care of the caraway seeds that had a habit of getting beneath her plate.

Edie sipped her coffee, all the time storing up the flow of tales that Aggie recounted, saving the precious fragments of her father's past like lost pieces of a jigsaw. She would join them all together one day, and maybe learn something of the man he had been. Francis Findlay Farquharson. She had read his name on the electoral role when she had looked up the records in East Register House in Edinburgh. Double trouble, she thought.

Chapter 5

Edie strolled around the perimeter of the garden, trying to make out what once might have been a flower bed, and gazing into the distance at the white glare that was the North Sea. She was bemused that anything could grow in such an exposed and windswept part of the world. For a moment, she thought of the lushness of her hibiscus plants and the wetness and greenness of the jungles of Malaysia. Another world, another lifetime, and she felt the searing pain of loss. She screwed up her eyes; she mustn't think of that, she didn't want to think of her garden, the colours, the lime bushes, or of her house with its deep veranda. Instead, she focussed hard on the stone dyke surrounding this garden. She touched the boulders, each one heavy and snug in its allotted slot, and thought of how rocks are moved from place to place, how they tumble from mountains and end up in heather-clad hills, and then are moved again to form cairns and monuments, while some make it to the rivers and are washed down to the sea, and others are shunted by tractors and men. Edie rubbed her hand over the coarse grain of the granite. I would have followed him to the ends of the earth, she thought, and I did really, well it felt like it at the time.

'Hellooo!' Edie turned at the sound of Aggie opening the garden gate.

'Having a little drink?' Aggie noted the glass in Edie's hand.

'I am, can I offer you one, or would you prefer a coffee?'

'No, I don't mind a wee tipple, but I prefer to do it inside, if you know what I mean,' and she winked slyly. 'Don't want the neighbours seeing it all through their binoculars. They'll have notions and the word will be spread far and wide by tea time.'

'But it is 4.30!'

'Maybe so, but this house has seen grief, my dear. Your ancestors didn't hide their problems in the bottle the way folk do nowadays. Oh, for goodness' sake, the two old ladies were so down on those fillim stars, as they called them, who would knock back the gin at the slightest provocation. I remember your poor Aunty Anne had to pinch her nose while the doctor forced a spoonful of brandy down her throat when she broke her hip. They didn't go in for recreational tippling,' Aggie sniffed.

Edie drained the rest of her glass, and looked about. She didn't see any glints of binoculars but you never could tell. She followed Aggie into the scullery and noted the woman heading for the pantry and helping herself to a glass. Dutifully Edie poured a good measure of the red wine into the proffered glass before refilling her own. They moved as one to the sitting room and took up their seats.

Aggie began to speak, slowly at first. Her eyes took on a faraway stare as she absentmindedly ran her hand over the Bible that Edie had left on the side table. 'The minister used to spend a lot of time here. He called in every week and the three of them would sit and talk and talk. He could tell a joke that one; the three of them would be laughing like hyenas when I came in with their groceries. He would tell stories, oh, such wonderful stories.' Aggie paused, as though seeing again the quaint trio sitting around the roaring fire.

'Where is he now, this minister?'

'He's retired. He lives in a wee house up in the hills. He's in his eighties now, lost his wife just last year. Poor woman.'

'Why? Why do you say that?'

'Well, she was married to a man that can't stay still. He was always off gallivanting here and there. He was like a flea, zipping about the countryside on his bike, or in his car, visiting hospitals, jails, schools, and old folk. You name it. He didn't seem to spend much time with her.'

'He would have known everything that went on,' mused Edie. 'Did he know my father do you think?'

'I doubt it, but he would have known others in the family. Your father left here a long time ago and he never came back. He only came back as a clipping of news in the paper. He broke his poor mother's heart. You would have only been a wee baby yourself. Did your mother not say anything?'

'Nothing. She behaved as though he had never been. She and her sister Phamie brought me up. I was only told that he had died and it was sad. No explanations were given to me.' Edie poured the remaining wine into their two glasses. 'It wasn't until I was thirteen that I learnt that he had been killed in Glasgow.'

'Well, who told you that?' Aggie's eyes lit up.

'My mother. I came across some stuff in an old suitcase one day when I was rummaging about in the store cupboard. I found a man's jacket and shoes, and a crumpled silver horseshoe, the kind brides carry with their bouquets. There was a card from my Aunty Phamie, wishing them a happy marriage. So, I asked my mum about it, but she got all secretive and defensive and accused me of looking at things I shouldn't have been.'

'And…?'

'And then she said she was sorry she had hung on to all that rubbish. I was upset, for this was the first time I had seen any evidence of having a father, and so I accused her of being selfish and of having no feelings.'

Edie looked down at the shabby rug. She saw the scene of her mother standing with the suitcase, her hands shaking, her eyes like slits as she turned to her daughter. *Don't you talk to me about being selfish, young lady, and don't you dare stand on your moral high horse and accuse me. I spit on the memory of that man. He was nothing; he was murdered in a tenement and his body left by the bins. He is better off dead. Just you give thanks, Edie my girl, that you have a home with me and your aunt. Forget the Farquharsons. Forget you ever saw that moth-eaten rubbish.*

The cold detached look that had come into Edie's eyes dissolved as she looked at Aggie. 'I don't know what happened between them, but he was never mentioned again. Later on, I did glean some gory bits of information from my aunt when she went on a tirade. He was razored by thugs. I looked up old newspapers, but the murder was never solved. Probably gang violence. There was a lot of it about in those days.'

'Your grandmother heard nothing, not even from your mother. She used to tell us that she had a granddaughter, but she never met you and I think that gave her a lot of pain. But look at the time, Edie. I'll have to be off. Bob will be waiting for his tea. I'll see you tomorrow; maybe I can come over and give you a hand in the kitchen. Have you decided to stay for a bit?'

'I'm still not sure. I have a lot of things to think about.' She stood up and walked with Aggie to the back door. 'Thank you for coming round, it was good to talk.'

Chapter 6

It was only a fortnight since she'd arrived and yet Edie felt quite at home in the old house. She had dusted, aired and cleaned the rooms. The kitchen had been scrubbed and the windows gleamed, letting in the May sunshine. Edie made coffee and went outside to sit on the edge of the well. The sky was blue, only a few wisps of cloud hung carelessly, like a flimsy lace shawl in the sky. Around her the signs of early summer were in the air. A green fuzz of leaves had appeared on the sycamore, and from its branches she heard the early morning caw of a crow. The smells of the countryside rose around her and she could hear a tractor on a neighbour's land. From across the fields came the sound of new lambs bleating and crying. It was all so different to where she'd grown up, like a scene from a story book. Her mother and aunt used to take her to Portobello where she played on the sand, and sometimes they had picnics up on the wild lands around Arthur's Seat, but those visits stopped as Edie grew older and she and her mother became more and more estranged. She never did find out anything more about her father, except that he had been murdered in Glasgow. Now suddenly by chance, here she was in his family home where he'd been born and had grown up, where there were pictures of his siblings and parents.

For thirty years, Edie thought, I've listened to the sounds of different birds, seen a different cycle of seasons and had my own family. She looked down into the black water of the well. Her eyes grew hot and she swallowed hard, trying to stop the rush of tears. Her poor, poor family, torn and scattered. And Adam. The tears which had threatened now ran uncontrolled down her cheeks. It was like a vice on her heart, this pain, this constant pain. How she missed him. She tried not to see the face of her husband, Kamal, as he had looked that night on the veranda. Instead, she tried to focus on Tara and Joe and little Clementine. Just at that moment a car she did not recognise drew up at the gate. A dog barked and the crows rose from the tree and flew, cawing, into the sky.

'Hello there! You're up early,' the elderly stranger greeted Edie as he got out of his car and slowly made his way towards her.

'So are you,' she replied, patting the dog that had come scampering alongside him. It nuzzled her hands. 'A cocker spaniel! He's a friendly chap. And does he have a name?'

'His name is Kipper,' the man replied, 'and mine is Robert Hunter. I used to be the minister of this parish but have been retired a while now. I heard you were in residence so I called by to say hello and welcome. I was just down at the shop to get my milk and paper. You must be Edie.'

'I am, and I'm very pleased to meet you, Robert. My neighbour Aggie has been telling me about you, of how you were a very good friend to my grandmother and great aunt.'

'I was, Isobel and Anne. I knew them for many years but, like so many of my friends, they have all passed on. Not long before I go too, I suppose. I shall be eighty-five this July, but still fighting fit, though I keep all my troubles at bay with half the chemist shop on my kitchen shelf. The doctor seems to think there is a pill for everything, so I just go along with him. I have blue ones and white ones and goodness knows what they all do, but if they keep me ticking that suits me just fine. Ah! What a wonderful morning. How are you liking being in this part of the world?'

'I love it. I was just thinking how different it all is, and yet somehow so familiar, as though scenes like those around us have been here forever. Illustrations in books and snippets from poetry, the land and the farmlands and the patchwork of greens and browns seem to have been in our psyche forever.'

The two stood for a moment, taking in the iridescent line of the North Sea on the horizon ahead of them, and behind the house, the pine trees appearing to march over the hills. They could see sheep, stark against the new green grass, huddles of farm buildings and the ever-crisscrossing maze of stone dykes.

They gazed in a silence that Edie was the first to break. 'I've just boiled the kettle. Please, will you join me for a cup of tea or coffee?'

'That would be grand, Edie, thank you. Now, come here, Kipper, I'll tie you up out here, away from the temptation of rabbits that you might be savouring. He spends all his sleeping moments dreaming of the great chase, but at this time of year, with the lambs about, I wouldn't like to see him shot. The farmers are not keen on dogs racing through their fields.'

Edie took the opportunity to wipe her eyes and discreetly blow her nose. The tears that she had spilled into the old well were still wet on her eyelashes and she didn't want to have to answer any awkward questions. She smoothed her cheeks with her hands as Robert secured Kipper with a bit of rope he took from his car. The dog seemed happy to lie panting on the grass beneath the tree.

Robert followed her into the kitchen and gasped at the change he encountered.

'Goodness me,' he exclaimed, 'what a difference! You certainly have been busy in here; I wouldn't have recognised the old place. And the smell! Oh, what a wonderful smell, is that a lemon cake I see on the worktop?'

'It is, but not made by me. That was Aggie; she is so kind and has helped me to scrub this place and get rid of so much of the old junk. She brings me cake and scones nearly every day. Please, come through to the sitting room.'

Robert looked around before settling himself into an armchair. 'You haven't changed much in here; I see the same order of things, much as they always were. The old girls loved their TV - have you got it working?'

'Yes, I look at the news. It's company in the evening but I'm not as addicted as my old relatives might have been.'

'No, they liked their entertainment. I have fond memories of my times visiting here.' Robert looked at the chairs placed as they always had been, and for a moment he saw the two old women, like a frame in his mind, a reel of film unfolding as Isobel dimpled sweetly: 'Is that you, Mr Hunter? Come away in and see what Aggie has brought us today, a fine bit of Battenburg cake. Just cut a good slice for the minister, Aggie, he needs a bit of fattening up with all that bicycle riding and walking the hills the way he does.' Anne was straining to read the paper: 'I know there's a good match on this afternoon, Minister. It's the Haystack man that's wrestling. Maybe you'll stay and watch with us? Come and sit down and we can listen to one of your stories before Big Daddy comes on.'

Robert blinked and returned to the present. He glanced around him. 'You've certainly freshened the place up. I never really noticed how brown it was in here, so dark with just the little lamp and the fire. I suppose they liked it that way.'

'I've enjoyed tidying it up, but I didn't realise how long I was going to stay here. I actually thought I would just put it on the market and leave, but you see, I don't really have anywhere else to go. I've lost touch with everyone in Edinburgh, well, except for my old schoolfriend, Joy.' She sat down opposite her visitor and they bit into their slices of cake and sipped their coffee. Edie studied the man opposite her, once the minister of this parish. At eighty-four his bald head was shiny and as brown as a hazelnut. Rimless glasses accentuated his hazel-coloured eyes and his cheeks were reddened from the outdoors. His body was frail now but she could see he had once been fit and strong. He wore corduroy trousers and under his jacket she could make out a sky-blue jumper over a checked shirt. Sturdy brown brogues marked him as a walker, then she remembered Aggie telling her about how active the minister had always been.

'Well, my dear, this is very pleasant. I'm glad you've decided to stay for a while. The weather looks settled and perhaps you can visit some of our beauty spots around the area. Further up the coast, there is the old church where Lewis Grassic Gibbon got his inspiration for his great novel, and you can walk and see the Mearns just as he described it. Are you familiar with *Sunset Song*?'

'I am, and I've loved it for years. It was the only book I took away with me. I thought it would remind me of Scotland.'

Robert, alert to changes in the mood of a parishioner, perceived in Edie's manner symptoms of distress. He had noticed the tears adhering to her eyelashes on his arrival but he'd made no indication of his awareness. 'Perhaps you will let me be your guide. I would be happy to take you to Arbuthnott and show you around the Grassic Gibbon Centre one day this week if you like.'

'Oh, I would like to do that,' Edie replied, full of sudden enthusiasm. 'I keep finding things to do here; I still need to sort out the garden and cut the grass which is so long. It's as though I don't want to leave, yet I should. I just don't know what to do.' She felt the scratchy feeling start behind her eyes again. She must not cry. Not now.

'Well, Edie, whatever you decide to do, this place seems to be what you need at the moment, so enjoy it while you can. Perhaps you could paint this room while you have the energy. A good coat of something light and bright wouldn't go amiss. That is, after you have done the garden and been out and about with me. I must be on my way now but I shall come by next Wednesday and you can drive me to Arbuthnott in your car. I'm afraid of my abilities on the big roads now so I would be happier to guide you, if you don't mind?'

'That would be wonderful. Thank you, Robert.'

'Goodbye, Edie. It was a pleasure to meet you and a pleasure to be back in this house. Walk down by the cliffs today, and think about the good things in your life. You will know when the time is right to go home.'

Chapter 7

In the weeks that followed, Edie saw a lot of Robert Hunter. She often visited him at his home and became accustomed to sitting by his table overlooking the fields that sloped in a gentle myriad of colours down to the North Sea. Their afternoons spent together were calm, probing, and Edie relished the sympathy and support that the minister offered.

'How did you get to the other side of the world, Edie, if you don't mind my asking? Were you always keen on travelling?' His eyes lit up ready for a good yarn. 'Did you meet your husband overseas?'

'No, I met him here in Scotland, but I should explain.' Edie took in a deep breath and let it out slowly. She fiddled with a button on her cardigan, before finally looking up. 'When I met him first, I was on the rebound and I'd decided that I wanted to change my way of life, totally. I was still living at home in Edinburgh with my mother but we weren't close, in fact I don't remember ever connecting with her at all. She and my aunt worked in a photographers' shop; their world revolved around that and their work colleagues. I just didn't want to be part of it all. I was studying at Moray House, the teacher's training college,' she smiled, 'and I met an artist.'

Robert sat back and grinned, 'Aye, the artists were the romantic ones, even in my day. But go on, Edie, tell me about the artist. I take it he didn't become your husband?'

'No, as I said, I met Kamal on the rebound. I remember a very cold January day in Edinburgh, back in 1974. I was twenty and I imagined myself to be in love. The man in question was not a student, but an artist. I never told my mother of the liaison because I knew she wouldn't have approved of his lifestyle. He was a hippy, I suppose, living in a passion of paint and music. For me, his aesthetic lifestyle appealed to my own narrow, conventional tastes. His name was Bones and he lived in a top floor tenement flat in St Mary's Street off the Royal Mile.'

'Bones?' Robert interjected. 'An odd sort of name?'

'I know, but he was very thin, skeletal you might say. His real name was Seamus but everybody called him Bones so I did too. We had a pretty wild affair, but it was not meant to last and eventually we broke up. You probably think that I'm digressing because you asked me how I met my husband, but the reason I told you about Bones is because if we hadn't broken up, I would never have met the man who I did marry.'

'I see, please go on.' Robert leant back in his chair.

'Well, a week or so after Bones and I broke up, I walked into the Student Union. I was so cold and wanted a cup of hot chocolate to warm me up. I fumbled in my purse for change for the vending machine, but my fingers were almost rigid with cold and I managed to drop my handbag, spilling coins, lipstick, lighter and cigarettes all over the floor. I felt such an idiot. Anyway, to cut a long story short, an Asian man who happened to be passing bent down and retrieved my items for me. He gave me the most beautiful smile and asked me what I was studying, then told me his name was Kamal Shariff. He had qualified in London as a lawyer and was working as a junior in a law firm in Bristol, whilst studying for the Bar exam. He was up in Edinburgh visiting a student friend. It was by pure chance that we met.'

'That's an intriguing story, so I guess that he suggested joining you for a hot chocolate and you both decided that you were attracted to each other?'

'I suppose in a nutshell that is what happened. Yes, I did like him, he was very attractive, calm and self-possessed with lovely manners and I think he liked me. He was from Malaysia, which sounded so exotic to me at the time.

'Did you ever see Bones again?'

'I did, but not until the end of February. I was at home with my mother one Saturday morning and she was drying up the breakfast dishes. The phone rang, and she answered. "What did you say your name was?" I knew at once that it had to be Bones. Apparently, he had to see me, right away. My mother was all concerned, asking who this person was and what was so urgent. I hadn't told her anything about my private life, so goodness knows what she would have thought if I suddenly produced Bones then Kamal all on the same day. Well, if I was secretive, I'd had a very good teacher.'

'What do you mean?'

'My mother always kept her own private life so secret it was though she had it covered in a black shroud. She did eventually tell me that my father had been murdered but then she clammed up about it for the rest of my life.'

'Maybe she didn't know the truth of what happened to him,' Robert interposed gently. 'Perhaps you shouldn't be too hard on her.'

'Anyway, I thought I had better go and see Bones, considering that he'd phoned me at home. That was definitely not like him.' Edie paused and looked out of the window. 'I'm so sorry, Robert, I really don't want to talk about him anymore, not now – maybe another time.'

Robert could see the tears swimming in her eyes, threatening to spill over. He handed her the box of tissues he kept by his armchair. They stayed quiet. Only the sound of the clock broke the silence, its ticking soothing and rhythmic. Finally, Edie spoke again. 'Kamal Shariff never knew about Bones or the wild girl who had been his girlfriend. He didn't need to know about that. To me Kamal was a handsome Asian prince who transformed the ordinary into a world with untold adventures. I wanted those adventures; I wanted a world where the ordinary would be extraordinary. From our very first meeting, I knew that I would have followed him to the ends of the earth.'

Robert smiled, his head nodding. 'And your mother? What did she think of you going off with a foreigner to lands unknown?'

'Mum cried. We actually got on better when she knew that I had made up my mind. I think she understood why I wanted to distance myself from Scotland and the life we had led there. My father had been murdered - goodness knows how or why, and Bones…'

Edie took a breath. 'I wanted a fresh start. Kamal was a gentleman. He promised me that he would give me a life that I could never even have dreamed about. And he did. But when the time came for me to go away with him to Malaysia, I was suddenly heartbroken to leave my mother. Just before I left, she gave me her pearl earrings. They were so precious and I have worn them all through the years.' Edie pushed back her hair. 'Look, I have them on now. But I remember the day I left, poor Violet, she looked so sad, and we cried and made promises that we knew we would never keep. I never saw her again.'

Chapter 8

Edie parked her car beside the sycamore tree and stood for a moment under the fuzzy green growth of new leaves. The sky was streaked with crimson, a dark ridge of ominous black cloud hovering on the horizon. She listened to the raucous noise of the sparrows, no doubt fussing around the purple hebe bush at the corner of the garden. She knew they were nesting and squabbling there.

Talking to Robert Hunter had brought back unbidden memories of a time before Kamal, before her life in Malaysia. Of another Edie, just a girl who had loved a boy. *I was so young*, she thought, *so impressionable. Poor Bones.* She let herself into the house and straight away poured herself a large gin and tonic. She walked through to the sitting room and sat down by the window, then gazing out at the stone dyke, she held up her glass and said, 'To you, Bones, this one is for you.' She stared out at the dusk and the darkening fields but she saw nothing for her thoughts were in another place, in another time...

Oh, Bones, I can see you now, just as though it were yesterday, me marching down the Royal Mile and into St Mary's Street, just as I had done so many times before, my black cape billowing around me. Full of anticipation to see you. I remember pressing the top buzzer of the black door on the right. The crackling sound of the entry speaker, signalling for me to push open the main door. I stepped into the stone stairwell. It was dark, the walls painted a strange ochre colour, only a glimmer of light filtering from a window high up in the stairwell. Graffiti was scrawled on the walls and the stairs smelt of bleach. On the third floor, I stopped, gasping for breath as I tried to smooth my hair and compose myself. You answered the door only after the fourth ring. You were stoned, you always were.

'What took you so long?'

'I had lectures. I came as fast as I could.' I took in your unwashed hair, the black growth around your cheeks and chin. The smell of the flat was stale and thick with weed. 'Have you eaten?' I said and I kissed you.

'Thought I'd wait for you, babe,' you drawled before the inevitable question, 'Do you want a joint?'

'OK.' I slipped off my cape and went to lie on the bed which was rumpled with tangled sheets and discarded clothes. You lay down beside me and I took the joint, sucking the fiery smoke into my lungs. I closed my eyes and it felt as though the swirls of smoke were twisting around my brain. I loved looking at your face in profile, your features softened by the smoke screen. Of course, you were no oil painting, but you were arresting, with dark eyebrows like George Harrison. I used to love walking with you in the autumn, your gangly body conjuring up the image of an artist, a non-conformist, so different from the schoolboys I had previously dated. I loved your long hair tied back in an elastic band. Your blue eyes were clear then, so full of hope and fun. But that afternoon you grew distracted. I passed the joint back to you, but you shook your head, your hands already busy rolling another. I sucked in again, holding the smoke as long as I could, while watching you spread the Rizla paper and artistically arrange the tobacco into a line. You then produced a green Golden Virginia tin in which you kept the cannabis. I loved the whole process, the crumbling of the chocolate-coloured resin along the frills of tobacco, the placing of the filter into the end and then finally rolling it up and licking the edges of the paper.

'I missed you, babe,' you said, lighting the joint, the end burning into a tiny flame before catching.

'I brought us some gin.'

'You always know what to bring, sweet girl. What day is it?'

'It's Tuesday; it's bloody freezing out there. You're lucky you don't have to go to college anymore.'

'My life is over, Edie baby, I'm all washed up. No one wants my paintings; no one wants to hear my poems, nor my songs of love. I'm no one with no aim left in life.'

'Oh, come on.' I cuddled into the angular hollow of your arm and chest. 'It's January, everyone feels like that. Put on some music while I pour the drinks; we can have a Tuesday party.' I waltzed around the bed, swaying to the sounds of Donovan emanating from the tape deck beside the bed. I poured the gin into wine glasses and filled them up with orange squash and water from the tap. I was feeling really mellow; the flat felt warm and messy and Donovan was singing of soldiers and seagulls and freedom. Outside the sleet pelted the glass panes.

'Give me the drink, sweet Edie, and let me look at you.' You lay back, your head leaning against the ripped wallpaper above the bed.

Later I remember tiptoeing over the cold lino towards the bathroom. You were snoring, deep in a drunken sleep, the gin bottle empty and the ashtray full. I splashed water onto my face and the sight of myself in the mirror made me shudder. I was such a bedraggled mess; that freaked me out as I still had an essay to finish for the next day. My eyes were like black holes, mascara imbedded into the hollows making me look as ancient as thirty or something. Oh God, what was I going to do? I noticed that the door to the cupboard under the sink was open. I nudged it with my knee but it wouldn't shut so I bent down and saw that a pudding bowl was preventing the door from closing. Reaching in to move it, I suddenly yanked back my hand. It was as though a cobra was curled up in the bowl. But this was no snake. I knew what syringes meant. I knew what heroin did. There was no way back for you, my darling Bones. I knew that as well.

I let myself out of the flat and wrapped my cloak about me, the wool was comforting and the wind was sharp but the sights of the Royal Mile were lost to me. The summer days of wandering around these closes and licking lollies with my hippy boyfriend were over. The nights of making plans for a life in Paris after I graduated were gone. We were going there for you to paint, to sing your songs of life and death, and for me to be your muse, to love you and cook the lentils. I used to fill my days with dreams laced with hope.

Returning to the present, Edie padded back to the kitchen to refill her glass. She had not thought about Bones for years. That minister had a way of stirring up memories she would have preferred to keep buried. She had omitted to tell him how it had all ended. Edie settled herself into an armchair and took another sip of the gin before resuming her memories of that time. After breaking up with Bones, she had stayed well away from St Mary's Street. She had thrown out her black cape, and full of resolve to get rid of her arty persona, had persuaded Joy to come with her to buy a new coat. She had liked the old cape but it was time for something different, something light and fresh. She'd wanted a new start.

'But it's January, shouldn't you wait until Spring?' was Joy's response.

'You can have a fresh start whenever you like.'

Joy helped her choose a new white coat which showed off her legs to their best advantage. A couple of weeks after she had broken up with Bones, Edie was wearing the new coat when she met Kamal. He had qualified as a lawyer and he seemed so self-assured. He was Malay, with soft brown skin and sculptured features. His hair was blue-black, growing back from his forehead and falling onto his collar. His eyes were dark and sparkly; his smile seemed to split his face with the most beautiful teeth.

'It's all very well having a new coat, but what about your head and your hands? I think I want to lavish you with lambswool from the Hebridean Islands that are home to rare intrepid sheep. You shall model hats, mittens and scarves for me and I shall sit here in this palatial Jenners department store and you can try on every woollen hat they have.'

'You can't do that, that's so extravagant, we can go to Marks and Spencer; and I can get something there instead.'

'I insist. We must do this properly, then we shall visit the Tea Room afterwards.' She felt his strong hand on her elbow as he manoeuvred her through the throng of Saturday shoppers. He frowned at counters displaying cosmetics. 'Where would the hats be? Maybe we should try Ladies Fashions. Come, we'll look for something warm to go with your very short coat.' His eyes creased and took her in his arms. 'What would you like, a beret? I believe they are very fashionable.'

'Certainly not,' she kissed his cheek. 'I just want a ski hat, if we can find one.' An assistant came forward, she was young, with strangely protruding teeth and a wild permed hair-style. 'Can I help you?'

'Yes please,' said Edie. 'I'm looking for a hat and scarf and maybe some woollen gloves.'

Kamal studied Edie's face as she picked up one hat then tried to match it with a scarf, then repeated the whole procedure with a different colour combination. A smile played around his lips as she finally came over with a cornflower-blue hat and matching scarf and gloves.

'Good choice! You look as fresh as a spring day; you will rival the bluebells when they come. And look at your eyes, never have I seen such a beautiful girl.' He led her to the cash desk and duly paid with a flourish. After tea overlooking Princes Street, the two sauntered out of the elegant shop as though they had just invested in Christian Dior. Warm at last in the face of the cruel north wind whipping across the Forth, the two ventured to the Royal Botanic Garden, exploring the arboretum and feeding the squirrels before finally taking refuge in the tropical glasshouses.

'You see these ferns and trees, they grow wild in my village in Malaysia, and we have these big red flowers and those yellow ones. You would love visiting my homeland.' It felt good, even in the cold Scottish winter, to be with this man who brought warmth to every outing. Days and weeks went by and Edie and Kamal were inseparable exploring the different areas of Edinburgh, their arms linked together. She felt treasured and safe. It was a good feeling.

It wasn't until the end of February that Edie saw Bones again. There were snowdrops coming through in the public gardens, and slushy piles of snow piled up on the pavements. She was at home with her mother when Bones had telephoned saying that he wanted to see her. That was definitely not like Bones. She avoided her mother's questions, put on the new white coat, and left the house. She could still hear her mother's voice squawking: 'Some coat, barely covers your backside – I don't know why you don't just wear a long jumper and a pair of tights!' Edie smiled at the memory; her glass was nearly empty again. She might need another refill.

She had got the bus to North Bridge and walked down the Royal Mile to St Mary's Street. Her fingers trembled as she pressed the buzzer with Bones's name on. The intercom crackled, releasing the lock. She ran up the stairs, and banged on his door.

He greeted her with his usual drawl, 'Hey there, little lady, why haven't you been back?' When she stepped inside and leant up to kiss his cheek, he stood swaying in front of her. New purple circles around his eyes made him look like a comic figure, accentuating his corpse-like demeanour. She could smell the dope. She actually relished the familiar rush it gave her. Since meeting Kamal, she had led a fairly chaste life, drinking only white wine spritzers when he drove up from Bristol each weekend to see her. Now she almost craved getting high.

'Do you want to roll up, sweet Edie?' Bones took her hand and led her to the bed but she pulled back.

'I don't want to do that anymore. I imagined you were sick, after all, you'd told Mum it was important. I was worried!'

'It is important. I want to say goodbye, babe, that's all.'

'Goodbye? Why?' and then she noticed the sink, filled with dirty plates. Bits of pizza lay half eaten by the kettle, as though forgotten.

'I guess Paris is not going to happen, is it?' He stood looking down at his naked feet.

'No.'

'And now you wear a new virginal coat. A change of image, but you still flaunt your lovely legs, my darling.'

'I outgrew the cloak image.'

'You were wild, babe, under that cloak, and you only flaunted yourself for me.'

'Stop it, Bones. We had fun, we had last summer and the autumn, but I can't be with you anymore. I can't handle…'

'Mr H. Is that it? I guessed you found my pudding bowl. Well,' and he stopped and looked out of the window. Rain was falling. 'I don't want to live, little Edie, I can't live with rejection, for my art, my poetry, my songs. I'm glad I had you, even if it was just for a season. Will you get high with me, just one more time?'

'I'm here,' and she reached for the green tin.

She had woken later from the drugged sleep of alcohol and dope. It was seven o'clock in the evening. Her clothes were tangled on the floor and she felt across the bed for Bones. He was gone. Her mouth was dry from the cigarettes and she needed to use the toilet. She fumbled for the light, and gathering up her clothes, she quickly ran across the hallway to the bathroom. The pudding bowl was on the rim of the bath. The syringe was not there. She tidied herself up, dressing quickly, and then went to explore the other rooms. She found him in the sitting room. He was only wearing jeans and his knees were hunched up, the tourniquet still hanging from his arm and his head thrown back. He looked green in the light of the street lamps. She arranged a tartan throw over his body and squeezed herself down beside him, cradling his head in her arms. His breathing was shallow, his eyes were open but the eyeballs were flung back into his head.

'Bones, wake up,' she whispered, 'please, wake up.' He felt cold. She tried to rub his shoulders, chafing the skin and patting his cheek. 'Please, Bones, wake up.'

She didn't know how long he would stay unconscious. She knew nothing of the effects of heroin, nor of how long it lasted. She imagined it was like opium, where the addict would sleep and dream, preferring the life of a subterranean trance to the harsh reality of the waking world. But this didn't feel right. And he had been so matter-of-fact earlier. His brain seemed to have been on another level.

'Wake up, Bones, come on, please, I need you to wake up.' She persevered, until finally she left him and went through to the kitchen and picked up the phone. She felt so afraid, at a complete loss. She should have called the ambulance, she knew that, but she also knew that it was too late. He didn't want to be saved. She decided to call her mother, who asked after Mr Bones. After explaining that she was with Joy and would probably stay over with her, Edie just told her that he was depressed and that they'd had some tea and a chat. She went back to the sitting room and stood for a minute. The body had changed position. The head had fallen forward. That was when she started to cry. He had died alone. She should have stayed with him just another minute, he would have felt the warmth of her body, her breath on his skin, a human voice urging him to wake up, to live, but instead it was as he predicted.

He had died alone. Finally, she rang 999.

Chapter 9

It was a week before Robert Hunter visited Edie again. He arrived just as she was ladling soup into two bowls, one for herself and one for Aggie. 'Hello, am I just in time for some of that soup? It smells so good.' He rubbed his hands in expectation. 'How are you today, Aggie, and how is Bob keeping?'

'Well, you know, Reverend Hunter, he hasn't been so well this year, what with his bronchitis and so on. We've to go back to the surgery to get some tests done.' Aggie seemed to swell with importance as she relayed this sombre news. 'But how are you? It must be lonely up there on your own, so far from the village.'

'Not at all, Aggie, I am just fine. Come, let us go through and give thanks for this fine soup.'

Edie settled them around the table by the window. 'Are you really not lonely?' she asked, her eyes warm with sympathy.

'In my job,' Robert began, 'I have met some wonderful people from all walks of life who have taught me a lot about the human condition. I remember visiting one of my parishioners, an old woman with failing eyesight. Her room was dark, full of furniture but there was no television, although she said she enjoyed her radio. I asked her if she had family. She replied that they were scattered and didn't visit, so I asked her if she was lonely. "How can I be lonely when I can shut my eyes and they are all here?" she told me. "I see faces, hear voices and I see pictures." I asked her what pictures she could see. Well, do you know? She had been everywhere! She and her husband were seasoned travellers and had swum in the South China Sea and seen condors over South America; they had travelled by canoe down the Amazon and seen crocodiles and anacondas. I would sit and listen to her travel tales, and when I left her and stepped out to the rainy Scottish street, I felt uplifted from the visit. She had given me the richness of her company. I have never forgotten her. So, in my small way, I have learnt from her, and I too can conjure up my own pictures and there is a wealth of wonders that I can relive.'

'That is such a nice story, Robert, you really do know how to draw us in.' Edie made a play of gathering the plates and carried them through to the kitchen, needing to be alone to gather her own thoughts, just for a moment. The story had moved her and she felt a longing for her other life, for the house with the veranda and the garden with hibiscus, for her children and her friends. She filled the teapot and arranged the tea things on a tray before re-joining the others. 'When did you come here, Robert? Did you not tell me that you were once a minister in Glasgow?'

Robert looked at her and smiled. 'Yes, Edie, I did know your father. I know that is what you are really asking.' He took off his glasses and polished them on his handkerchief. 'We were about the same age, and after he died, I carried on working in Glasgow for a while, and then I decided to study divinity in Edinburgh. It may have all been a coincidence, but I did feel drawn to this part of the world so I was lucky to get a calling to this parish. God works in mysterious ways, so they tell me! Inevitably I became very close to his family.'

'Did Jock and Isobel know you knew Francis Findlay?' Aggie's eyebrows had shot up to her hairline.

'Yes, eventually. I was able to shed some light on his time there.'

'And me? Did you know me?' Edie asked.

'No, my dear, I never met you, nor your mother or aunt. Your father was secretive about his life in Edinburgh and it wasn't till after he died that I learnt about his family. I tried to see your mother but she refused any hand of friendship from anyone at the time. I think it was his murder that led to my road to Damascus.'

'You mean you weren't a minister back then?' Edie asked again.

'No, I was a journalist. I had come down from the Isle of Skye, and am sorry to say I was a wild young man. I wanted to drink the distilleries dry, one by one. That was my aim in life, my goal. I could think of nothing else but drink. I drank till I dropped and often I dropped on the street, so I spent many a night in the lock-up, sobering up. My poor parents were elders of the kirk; they came down to Glasgow to see me and were appalled at the state I was in. It was around that time that I met your father, Edie.'

'Do you want me to go?' asked Aggie. 'I don't want to feel I'm interposing or anything.'

'No, please stay, Aggie, you were a good friend to the family.' Edie turned to Robert and braced herself for the truth. 'So, you met him? Were you friends? Was he really a bad man?'

'Some might say he was bad, but I think he had issues that troubled him. He couldn't take authority and resented being told what to do. Belligerent he was, stroppy, quick to take offence. The drink didn't do him any favours either. He grew mean, his eyes would glaze and he would look through someone with such hate. I remember once in a pub we were having a laugh then suddenly he turned on me. It was like looking at two bits of steel in his eyes. The warmth had gone.'

'You said you were a journalist, so what was he?'

'He told me he was a freelance insurance broker and I had no reason to doubt him; he never veered from that story. His behaviour had me totally convinced. It was only after his death that I found out the truth that he was working as an undercover reporter investigating the gangs.'

'So did he meet his end by getting too close to a source?'

'I'd say so. The night he was killed I had advised him to go home, but he'd missed his train, again. Those brutes from the Gorbals were waiting for him.'

'How did you know he had been killed?'

'I had to cover the story, but had to keep it fairly quiet as the investigation was ongoing. That's why you wouldn't have learnt much in the newspapers that you looked at. I honestly didn't know about you or your mother before he died.'

'So, apart from being mean and drunk and resentful, do you think he was once OK?'

'His mother said he was the best scholar the school had ever seen, but he had issues with his father, old Jock. The two did not get on, and the old man tended to beat him. I think as a result of that, Frank carried hatred and resentment towards any kind of authority for the rest of his life. He came across wild, yet passionate about his beliefs, and his mother also said he was a boy that walked alone.'

Edie started to cry. The tears that had been threatening finally slipped down her cheeks and she pulled the box of tissues towards her. 'I am so sorry, I don't want to get emotional, but it's just so sad.'

Aggie put her arm around her and said, 'Of course it is, pet, now you just blow your nose, and I'll make some more tea.'

'I think I'll go now,' said Robert. 'I have wanted to tell you this for some time, Edie, but this is the first real opportunity. Chance has brought us together, and it is better to know. Now you can let the facts settle themselves and if there is anything more you need to know, I'll be happy to help.'

'It was just so unexpected,' sniffed Edie. 'I've been thinking about him and the family so much since I arrived, now suddenly I am learning about a real person. It explains a lot in my own life too. Can I call you soon - I think I need to talk about other things?'

Chapter 10

Kamal sighed deeply as the plane landed at Singapore's Changi airport. Beside him Edie was peering out of the window to see this new land he had brought her to. He smoothed his hand over the bottle-green suede of her miniskirt and his eyes took in the matching waistcoat. She had been so proud of her outfit, her 'going away' gear as she called it, even though they weren't married. She had bought it with her last month's salary from the school where she had taught in Edinburgh. Kamal was glad that Edie had been able to finish her teaching qualification, for he knew it would give her some degree of independence, even if their relationship faltered. He was aware that the cultural differences awaiting her would test her resilience, but he didn't have the heart to tell her that the leather boots would soon be covered in green mould and the suede suit would never be worn again.

'Kamal, I'm so excited, we're actually here in Singapore!'

'We are only here for a couple of days, remember. After that we'll take the train across the causeway to Johor in Malaysia, and then by taxi to my kampong. I thought you'd like to adjust to the climate a little before you meet my family.' Kamal reflected that it was really for himself that he was procrastinating, for he knew there would be fireworks awaiting him when he brought this tall fair-haired foreigner into his close-knit Malay community.

'I know, but we're together and we shall celebrate tonight; shall we have champagne?' Edie was ecstatic and still a little drunk from all the Bacardi she had consumed from the drinks trolley.

'Yes, we certainly shall. I know of quite a tasteful hotel on Orchard Road where we shall stay. We can freshen up and I shall take you out for satay and fried rice. But remember when we go to the kampong we cannot drink. My parents are very strict Muslims, and while we are there, we must respect their ways and customs. After all they were my ways once, and I must also observe the holy month of Ramadan.'

'I know, Kamal, I understand, but tonight we can be ourselves. And then after a few days we can move away from your parents and find our own place, can't we?'

Kamal looked away. He knew he could not do that. He had obligations to his family; he had to return the investment they had entrusted in him. He hoped to find work nearby and that meant they might have to stay for a while. He smiled evasively and pulled the stray blonde tresses from her face and squeezed her thigh. Gesturing at the overhead locker he said, 'Shall we go? Are you ready?'

Edie disembarked from the aeroplane and was immediately engulfed in a steamy wall of heat. 'Oh goodness, Kamal, it's so hot! I don't know if I can stand this!' Inside the terminal, she caught sight of herself in the mirrored columns and winced at her bedraggled hair and black shadows under her eyes. Is that me? she thought, I looked so smart and sophisticated when I left Edinburgh. She shuddered at her unsuitable choice of clothes, then dutifully followed Kamal as he pushed their luggage trolley towards the exit. She gulped as the doors opened and the dark night enveloped her. 'I can't, I can't go out in that, Kamal, I need some tissues, my face is melting.'

'Oh, come on, you'll be fine, the taxis are air conditioned and soon we can both shower and change into something more suitable for the tropics. The longer you stand here dithering the hotter you will get. Come on, there's a taxi.'

The first thing Edie did on arriving at the Mimosa Hotel was to strip. Almost before the door was closed or the suitcases opened, she was clawing at her waistcoat and pulling at her skirt. The stockings seemed to have glued themselves to her thighs, and once removed she immediately binned them. She made for the shower and let the cool water wash away her irritations. As she dried off and put on fresh clothes, her good humour returned and she took in the splendour of their room.

'This is so luxurious, isn't it? Thank you, Kamal, for bringing me here. When can we eat? I want to try everything!'

Kamal smiled. So far so good, he thought, she has a positive disposition; I just hope she has the strength for all that is to come. 'Come on, my love, let's go and explore. I have plenty of tissues here in my pocket, they will help a little when we go outside.'

Edie loved Singapore; she bought batik wrap-around skirts with matching T-shirts, sandals and loose dresses. Kamal let her enjoy being a western woman in the Far East, and followed her around Robinsons department store. They ate curry puffs in Holland Village and noodles in the hawker markets. She relished the local drinks made from fresh limes and didn't seem to crave gin or wine. The Mimosa Hotel, hidden from the rush of the main tourist sector, was a converted colonial mansion with high ceilings, mosquito-netted beds, and a beautiful modernised tiled bathroom with a powerful shower as well as the traditional dragon pot and dipper. There would be plenty of time for native conveniences when they reached Kamal's village, but for now, the Mimosa was the perfect refuge to escape the suffocating heat and smells and to ease the jet lag after their long flight.

Two days later the couple left Singapore by taking the train across the narrow causeway linking the island to the Malaysian Peninsula. The journey was not long, but Edie absorbed the sights from the local train while the sounds of the clackety wheels on the iron rails and the excited chattering of a bevy of schoolchildren clad in pristine white uniforms seemed to match her own enthusiasm. When they arrived at the station in Johor Bahru, she was struck anew with the onslaught of colour and movement and people rushing about.

'Look Kamal, look at those poor people.' Beggars and hawkers sat with their hands outstretched, beseeching her to give them money or to buy something. She dropped some coins into half a coconut shell, a little disturbed by the blind man's milky eyes staring up at the sky.

'Come on,' urged Kamal, pulling her along as her fingers dipped again into her purse at the sight of an Indian woman in a filthy sari and with two tiny children at her side. 'You can't give to all. Come, let's get into this taxi before someone else grabs it.'

They both sat back in the car, savouring the journey along lonely roads which curved through the shady canopy of rubber trees. His head was full of thoughts about his family and of uncertainty about the welcome that awaited them. Her thoughts were of the strangeness of it all and of how much she had to learn about this man beside her, of his family and of this exciting country that she had travelled to.

'So, Kamal, this is West Malaysia where we are we now, is that right?'

'Yes,' he explained, 'the Malaysian Peninsula is West Malaysia and there are eleven states here. We have just left Johor Bahru which is the capital of the state of Johor. Kuala Lumpur, in the state of Selangor, is the national capital of the whole of Malaysia, both west and east. There are two more states in East Malaysia which is on the island of Borneo. You'll soon learn the names of all the states, but one day I do want to take you to Pahang, the largest state in the west, because that's where the indigenous tribes still live and also where you are likely to see tigers.'

'Well, I can't wait to see it all,' replied Edie as she gazed out of the window. 'How much further is it? Will I be able to get a teaching job here? Where are the nearest shops? Will they be like Robinsons? I loved Singapore; can we not live there?'

Kamal grinned at her incessant stream of questions and answered them as best he could. The road was long and winding; the never-ending plantations of rubber and oil palm trees mesmerised them until the peace was shattered when their driver decided to do several terrifying overtaking manoeuvres to pass a line of logging lorries.

Edie patted her eyes and cheeks with the ever-ready tissue. 'Good grief, is he insane?' she whispered, looking at the bristly short-back-and-sides of the Malay Jackie Stewart impressionist.

The car abruptly turned off the tarmac road and as it continued for several miles along a red laterite track, the enclave of rubber grew darker, the sun totally obliterated, until finally the neatly planted trees gave way to virgin jungle.

Edie turned to Kamal, her lips bravely trying to smile. 'Where are we going? I thought you said it was a village?'

'It is, my love, a kampong is a native village. Our people grow vegetables and bananas,' he added vaguely. 'You'll see, there's a river and some fields and animals.' He looked out of the window, avoiding her staring eyes.

Eventually the car laboured up a steep hill. Vegetation and grasses grew lush and wild. Trees with polished bark rose like monoliths out of the dark interior. Sprawling bushes, broken branches, yellow flowers passed in a jungle of confusion. On either side of the track, grey macaque monkeys screeched at them from hanging vines.

In spite of her trepidation, Edie laughed. 'Look, Kamal, their eyes are so bright and just look at that baby!' She was so enthralled with the sudden brush with animals that she had only ever seen in a zoo that she completely forgot about the dress shops of Singapore. 'Oh look! Look at that bird, did you see the colours?'

The car finally turned a bend and there below them, Edie got her first view of the kampong. The jungle trees had been cleared and she saw a great serpent of a river curling, muddy brown, in the morning sun. Along its banks were stilted wooden houses, decorated with flashy curtains and pot plants of bougainvillea. Coconut palms grew randomly, while beneath them, chickens scratched and children and dogs wandered about.

'It's so pretty, I had no idea!' Edie smiled, 'So this is home?'

Kamal nodded and squeezed her hand. He was scanning the village with a familiar eye. Men were looking up from their vegetable patches and women were coming out of doors. He focussed on a modern blockwork house at the end nearest the forest. His mother would be preparing food; he knew there would be a feast in the making. He felt a growing sense of excitement as the car finally drove down the dusty track by the football field, coming to a stop by his boyhood home. Faces appeared from neighbouring houses, men sauntered along from the river's edge, and there was a murmuring as they viewed the return of Kamal Shariff and this white woman at his side. Sniggers could be heard from some elderly crones who viewed the scene from the comfort of their rattan mats in the shade of the stilted house next door.

Edie stood blinking into the sun. No one approached her. She watched Kamal being embraced by a skinny man with no shirt, just a colourful sarong wrapped around him, then a buxom woman appeared and shrieked with joy and threw herself into his arms. Children screeched and it was as though the villagers were all related. Perhaps they were, she thought. She shrugged and paid the taxi driver and he helped her unload the cases before nodding to her sagely, 'Welcome to Malaysia, Missie.'

Chapter 11

Edie stood alone, watching as Kamal was surrounded by his relatives and ushered inside the house. For a moment she waited, uncertain and feeling very awkward, conscious of her white cotton trousers, pale blue shirt and her long hair hanging loose. Her Marianne Faithfull persona and the fun hippy culture that she had left behind felt very far removed from where she now found herself.

'Hey, come on, come inside, come and meet everybody,' one of the sisters called as she grabbed hold of Edie's hand.

Edie stepped into the sitting room and was met with a sea of happy faces and a wave of excited chattering. Kamal caught sight of her and stepped forward, closely followed by the skinny man and the buxom woman who he then formally introduced to her as his parents.

His father shook her hand and his eyes twinkled as he gazed at this intriguing foreign woman in front of him. 'We are delighted to welcome you to our kampong and into our home, Edie. Kamal has told us much about you in his letters to us and we are very honoured to meet you at last. I am Hassan and this is my wife, Minna. We are both very proud of our only son; Kamal is a good man and a good Muslim. We hope you will be very happy here.'

Kamal's mother then took her hand and gave her a lovely smile. 'It is such a pleasure to meet you, Edie. I hope that you will take good care of our son. Now, I know that we shall have many things to talk about, but right now, I also know that you must both be very hungry after your long journey, so after you meet his sisters, we shall all sit down to eat.'

Edie looked around the room and Kamal's sisters came forward in turn to introduce themselves, all so friendly and welcoming. I have to remember so many names, she thought anxiously. Two sisters were called Fatima (Why? No one told her why), but they were addressed as Ma and La. OK, that was quite simple, but the others were called Amira or Ooty, and Jasmine or Long.

Kamal was addressed by his family name, Tam. Edie's eyes were round and questioning. 'Why Tam?' she said.

Kamal's father came to her rescue, 'Kamal's name is derived from his place in the order of births. Long, for example, is given to the first born. Kamal was third born and given the name Hitam, which means black in Malay, and is subsequently shortened to Tam.'

'Oh, I see,' said Edie, not really understanding at all, but she smiled at the sisters anyway.

'When his nieces and nephews were born, he became Pak Hitam to them, which means Father Black.'

Kamal's mother laughed and winked at Edie suggestively. 'When you marry my son, you big white woman, you will be Mother Black!' This seemed to be a hilarious suggestion, but Edie was not offended at the thought; in fact, she felt flattered at seemingly being accepted into this family.

They all fussed about before finally sitting down on the rattan furniture; a throw depicting a large mosque had been spread over the back of the settee. Edie found herself squashed between Ma and La, her elbows glued to her sides, her cup of tea balanced precariously on her knee. She was offered small coconut macaroons and bright pink cakes which were all delicious. All the time, Kamal's mother kept a watchful eye over her plate and her cup. Edie noticed that the father was deep in conversation with Kamal. Looking around the room, she saw that it was full of bookcases decorated with framed photographs of various children and relatives. In the far corner of the room was a dining table, covered in what looked like a carpet, but Edie realised that it was another picture of a mosque.

'My husband made the pilgrimage to Mecca, three years ago,' the mother informed her, noting Edie's interest in her decorative style. He is retired now. For a time, we all lived in Johor Bahru where he was a telephone engineer. Now we have moved back here to the family kampong. We like the simple life and give thanks every day to Allah and his prophet Mohammed, peace be upon him. We are blessed in our family. Do you see what Hassan wears on his head?'

'Yes, it's...'.

'That is the white cap to say that he has indeed made the pilgrimage to Mecca.'

'I can see that you are all very proud of his great achievement, Mrs Shariff; it must be a great honour for him and your family.' As Edie sipped her tea, she could feel the mother's strong will and devotion to her faith, even as she chattered on about her family.

Now that the initial introductions were over, the women went out to prepare the evening meal. Edie heard the clatter of tin plates, the hiss of frying meat and vegetables; her nose tingled with the intoxicating smells of garlic, ginger and spices. When she eventually sat with the family around the table, Kamal loaded her plate with fried rice, pieces of chicken and various vegetables all swimming in fragrant sauces.

'You like?' one of the Fatima sisters asked, spooning onto Edie's plate some strange paste roasted in a banana leaf.

Edie nibbled a forkful and let the flavour permeate her tongue. 'That is delicious; what is it called?' She took another mouthful.

'We call it *otak-otak*,' Kamal informed her.

'Brains, is what the translation is,' his father volunteered helpfully.

'What?' Edie grabbed the napkin, and started to gag. She felt her stomach heave. Desperately she tried to rise from the table, but Kamal held her down. Edie looked at him, her blue eyes like saucers, tears threatening.

'Stay,' he gently ordered. 'It is only called that because it describes the appearance of the delicacy. It is a jellied prawn paste. It is delicious, enjoy!'

The father laughed loudly. 'You should see what they eat in Saudi Arabia, they really do eat brains there, I was there you know? I made the Hajj.'

'Yes, Kamal's mother told me; that must have been a wonderful journey for you.' Edie played with the food on her plate and hid the offending paste beneath a spoonful of rice.

'I am a blessed man,' he continued as he looked around his table, clearly pleased with his family. 'I never want to forget my journey to Mecca.'

Edie nodded along with the others, but, she thought, I have such a lot to learn about Kamal, his family and how to fit in with this new way of life.

By half past ten, the party had dispersed. Outside the darkness was absolute. Pinpricks of light came from neighbouring houses, and Edie savoured a moment alone on the outside step. All she could hear were the static noise of crickets and the bellowing noise of bullfrogs by the banks of the river.

'You come now,' Ma broke into her reverie, 'you must take a bath.'

Edie, quite bemused, looked towards her suitcase. She thought of all her new clothes, bought especially in Holland Village and Orchard Road in Singapore. Thank goodness Kamal had the foresight to book them into the hotel and not come direct from the airport to the kampong. She would have died for sure in her suede suit and boots. What had she been thinking? Her long hair had been freshly shampooed that morning, so she just pinned it up and headed for the bathroom, a small concrete room with a huge Ali Baba type earthenware water container in one corner. A red plastic dipper floated on the surface, apparently for the purpose of tipping the cold water over herself in order to 'take her bath'. Thank goodness, she thought, I don't have to get my hair wet at such a late hour with no hairdryer to hand. Gingerly she filled the dipper and poured the water on to her legs and knees, then, gaining courage, she poured the next scoop over her shoulders and shivered as it ran over her breasts and belly. She soaped herself with the Lifebuoy bar provided, and then briskly rinsed herself off. It was then she realised, standing shivering, that she had forgotten to bring in a towel.

'Hello,' she called, opening the door a fraction, 'can I have a towel please?' It was La that brought the towel, and Long that offered her a small stool. Edie looked at it.

'Please sit.' Long instructed, then went out and returned carrying a basin of water with two short wooden paddles in it. Edie noticed Arabic writing on them, and wondered what on earth was going on now. She dutifully sat down, careful not to give offence to her hosts. Next thing, to her abject and total shock, the basin of cold, and later she learnt, holy water, was poured over her head.

'This is custom,' Long said, 'to purify you for marriage.'

'What?' spluttered Edie, her hair like rat tails stuck to her back. 'Whose marriage?' She and Kamal had talked about it, but only as a vague idea, they hadn't wanted to rush. Now it seemed the family were worried about the possibility of them living in sin. 'Whose idea was this?' she asked her future sister-in-law.

'You cannot live in sin, it would bring shame to our parents, so it is all arranged. You are to be married tonight as a matter of convenience. Now, you come, we find a dress for you.'

Edie stumbled through to the bedroom, clutching the small towel to her private areas, her hair still sopping wet, dripping from her anointing. Oh Lord, this isn't what I expected, she thought as she sat down on the bed, but she had to admit it was quite interesting. Her natural curiosity took over and she started to enjoy the proceedings. Her hair was towelled dry, combed sleek and shiny, and finally half was pinned up with a diamanté clasp and the other half fell over her shoulders.

'Come,' said Ma, 'put this nice Malay outfit on. We borrowed it from a friend, she's quite tall for a Malay girl so it should be good for you. Nice colour, you like?'

Edie did like the knee-length tunic, sugary pink with silver-thread embroidery, over a long white satin skirt. Then the jewels were brought out and she was adorned with golden bangles, rings and earrings. Looking into the small glass, she was quite taken with her appearance. My goodness, she thought, I look quite the exotic Asian princess.

However, as Edie gingerly stood up there was a gasp of horror. 'Ai Ya!' screamed the sisters in unison. 'You cannot be seen like that!'

Edie squinted into the dressing table mirror and saw her upper body looking shimmery pink and bejewelled. What was the fuss? Then she looked down, and understood at once. The forbidden ankles were on show, a full justification for a flap and panic in the ranks. Kamal had warned her about how naked knees and shoulders might offend the less worldly in the village. 'What can be done?' she asked. 'Shall I just wear my white trousers under the tunic?'

The sisters shook their heads in unison. 'Of course not,' quipped Long. 'We shall fix this. How could we know that you would have legs like bamboo poles?'

Just then Kamal's mother bustled in, full of importance, her lips pursed. 'You must hurry now, the kadi, that is the Muslim officiate, will be returning before midnight tonight. He will do the wedding then. No question about it, it must be done.' She looked down at the exposed legs, a frown appearing to slice her forehead in two. 'Don't worry, I have a sheet that will be suitable. We'll get the Singer sewing machine from Ooty, down the street, she can sew it up for us.'

'Are people coming to the ceremony?' Edie asked the matriarch. 'Will there be a service?'

'Just the official, that is all, and family, but everyone in the village saw you arrive so they will want to see that you are properly married. We don't want shame in this family.'

Edie sat back down on the bed, removed the inadequate skirt for the sisters to lengthen, then retrieved her shirt from the morning and pulled it over her exposed white thighs. Listening to the sisters' chatter, she had no idea what they were saying but their panic was evident. It was now eleven thirty and she and Kamal had to be at the official's residence in just over twenty minutes. She wondered how he was getting on. Would he be all dressed up in something exotic? She hoped he had no misgivings about getting married so quickly. It was all happening so fast, yet she felt quite exhilarated. Suddenly she heard the arrival of the sewing machine and of material being ripped. The hum and the paddle of the treadle was in action and then Long and Ma burst into her room to show her the altered garment. They had sewn an extension to the waistband to make it appear long enough to cover the offending ankles.

Edie, complete in bridal finery, tottered out of the room to meet her groom. Kamal, attired in traditional Malay ceremonial dress and with a black velvet *songkok* on his head, took her hand. 'You OK, Edie?' He smiled at her, his eyes twinkling. 'I honestly didn't see that coming. Should I ask you now? Will you marry me?'

Edie giggled and squeezed his hand as she led him out to the front of the house. 'It's lucky they never saw my white winter coat!' She looked up at the starry sky and breathed deeply to calm herself. The screeching of monkeys, the barking of neighbourhood dogs and the chattering of her new family in a language as yet unknown to her washed over her and she was overcome with a burst of optimism. 'It is our life, Kamal, no one else's. We shall be happy in our own unique way.'

And just before midnight they were married by the kadi in his residence, witnessed by Kamal's male relatives. As they walked home after the ceremony, old crones sat under bare electric lights, spitting the bloody juice of the betel nut into the dust, flashing their black teeth at the newlyweds. Edie adjusted the sheet on her waistband and smiled. So long as it all looks good on the outside...

She would think that same thought again later as they were ushered into the hurriedly prepared wedding bedroom. Kamal's mother had placed a large bolster down the centre of the bed; Edie assumed that meant there was some significance in the crossing over to the other side. Kamal told her that she must wet the front part of her hair in the morning to signify that she was no longer a virgin.

'That ship sailed a long time ago, but I suppose we should respect their culture.' She grinned cheekily, running her hand gently across her new husband's chest before passing out cold through sheer exhaustion.

Edie woke the next morning, bright and happy, and was shocked to hear roosters crowing, squawking children outside, and sunshine like a pot of hot honey baking them in their tangled sheet. Edie took a minute to focus on the light motes dancing in the shaft of gold, then remembered the night before and the frantic rush to get to her wedding. 'Oh Lord, get up, Kamal, its late, where are my clothes? I'd better wear this long kaftan; I don't want to offend anyone this morning.'

The two made their way through to the breakfast table where the relatives were already seated. Edie looked at her plate of rice and peanuts and chicken curry, and after a tentative spoonful, soon ate with relish her soon-to-be favourite, *nasi lemak*. This is my first breakfast as a married woman, she thought. What a pleasant thought, but then she realised to her horror - her hair was dry! Oh, the shame. Suddenly she felt self-conscious, she had totally forgotten about splashing some water on her head. Brazenly she ate on, smiling at the seated group, hoping that they would assume that Kamal had forgotten to appraise her of this particular custom.

Chapter 12

A week later, Kamal's mother ushered Edie to sit outside with her; she clearly had something she needed to say. Wild grasses grew thick around the monsoon drain and a black, orange and white cat strutted importantly past, no doubt on a meaningful mission. Edie studied her mother-in-law as she spoke. Her dark hair with just a mere suggestion of grey was pulled back into a bun. Her face was smooth, with flat features and a dominant lower lip. The almond shaped eyes were deep brown and seemed to Edie to be constantly trying to fathom out her new daughter-in-law.

'You like it here?'

'I like it here very much, you've all been so kind to me, Mrs Shariff. It's very different from my life in Scotland and it's certainly a lot warmer. I couldn't believe the heat when I arrived in Singapore, I thought I'd stepped into an oven. But here I am now, getting to know you all, eating your delicious food as well as learning to cook. I just wish I could speak Malay.'

'You call me, Minna, that is my name, no more Mrs Shariff. You have a mother in Scotland?'

'Yes, her name is Violet.' For a moment she saw the face of her mother at their tearful parting. 'I've written a letter to her, telling her of our marriage. I think she might get a surprise.'

At once, Minna's frown deepened and her face changed. 'She will be happy to learn that you are now a respectable woman. It is not decent for a single woman to travel with a man who is not her husband.'

'No, I suppose not,' Edie agreed, 'but I must do something useful. I am a teacher. I need to get a job while I am here'.

'Better you learn to speak Malay. I asked Tam to get some books for you; as you know, he has gone to Johor today with his father. Also, it's good you learn to cook. You like cooking?'

'I do, especially here, it's more interesting than anything I've attempted before'. An image of heating up baked beans for Kamal in his lodgings in Bristol came unbidden, but at the thought of the Malay dishes she had tasted, she absent-mindedly patted her stomach.

Minna followed her hand with her eyes, immediately suspicious. 'You got baby in there?'

'Oh, heavens no!' Edie laughed. 'I just love the food here. Well, I did get a shock with the talk of brains, but I am intrigued with the variety of food available in your country.'

Minna relaxed and pursed her lips. 'Good, that is good. But today you help chop vegetables; later we shall go to the market and I will show you what to buy.'

As Edie was being interrogated by Minna, Kamal was sitting with his father in a coffee shop in Johor Bahru.

'Why are you reading that Straits Times, my son?'

'Looking for jobs, Dad. You know I have to find a job.'

'There are jobs for lawyers here in Johor. Why not just ask about?'

'I have, but I'm really interested in a more diverse practice.'

'You're not talking about Kuala Lumpur, are you?'

'Actually, I was. It would be excellent for me, and for Edie. She could get a job at the Alice Smith School and we could find somewhere nice to stay. I don't think we want to stay too long in the kampong, Dad. We both need to work, but I will send money home, you know that. I have a big debt to repay to you.' Kamal squeezed his father's hand and looked into his eyes, 'I'm so very grateful for everything you have done for me, you know that too.'

Hassan sighed deeply. He gazed into his cup, contemplating what he was going to say next. 'You will respect our religion, my son? I know you have chosen a western woman to share your life, but she does not know our ways.'

'Relax, Dad, Edie is happy to be here and she will be a good wife. I would have got around to marrying her eventually, but thanks anyway for hurrying the process. I think she was quite bemused.'

Both men laughed and Kamal returned to his newspaper. Staring right back at him was an advert for a lawyer. It was perfect but it was not in Kuala Lumpur, it was in Kota Kinabalu. He read it avidly, noted the terms and salary, and the contact numbers. Casually he folded the paper and rolled it into a fly swat and swiped an insect on the table. 'Come on, Dad, let's see about some Teach Yourself Malay books for Edie. She will certainly need some basic vocabulary.

Over the next few days, Edie washed their clothes in a large blue *dhobi* bucket, then watched the suds disappear down the monsoon drain. It was therapeutic and she had a feeling of satisfaction as she pegged their kaftans and shirts to the line. The cat rubbed against her legs while the insects hummed and the sun burned down on her delicate skin. Afterwards she was relieved to lie on the bed in their cool, shady room. She turned on the transistor radio every morning at half past nine, and with her cup of tea and a biscuit, she listened avidly to *Learn a Word a Day*. Today's word was *terima kasi* which meant thank you. Well, that was useful, she could start immediately with that one. She had built up a smattering of words to help her say good morning, good night and I'm sorry. The books were good, but didn't really help with pronunciation. Kamal was enthusiastic and taught her words on their pillow that made her laugh but had no bearing with any of the books or the sober voice on the radio. This must mean I am being immersed, she thought proudly as she nibbled the biscuit: '*Terima kasi, ada baik!*'

Suddenly her concentration was disturbed. A small tap at the door announced Minna and first daughter Long. Edie put down her cup and sat up expectantly. What could be the matter now?

Minna looked her in the eye and said, 'You need to prepare for a very important occasion, Edie, the holy woman is coming to our kampong on Thursday.'

'Oh, do we have to do more marriage blessings or something?'

'No. but now that you are married, it is important you are true only to your husband.'

'Well, yes, I know that, Minna,' agreed Edie, 'but we have already promised to love and cherish each other.'

'In Muslim countries, it is necessary for all women to have a special operation. It is done at a younger age normally but you will be fine; you can have some medicine and you will recover quickly. Only a little pain.'

'What kind of operation? I intend having children, I don't want anyone touching my ovaries or anything,' said Edie uncertainly. What on earth did they mean? She started to feel nervous and looked about. Where was Kamal? He would explain, surely.

'The holy woman will make a small cut in your private area, it is good. Helps with hygiene and all Muslim girls get this. Even boys get this. We have a special celebration and good things to eat. Boy becomes man and girl becomes woman. It is written.'

Suddenly Edie understood what they were talking about, slowly the realization was sinking in. Of course, she had heard of male circumcision. She had even heard of tribal customs. She had watched a documentary with the famous anthropologist Margaret Mead, highlighting the rituals of manhood and the cutting of the foreskin, sometimes with the sharpened ridge of a coconut shell, or sometimes with a rather dirty-looking knife. But female circumcision was a hazy idea. Something that she had never come across or given much thought to. Now, here were her new relatives announcing that she was going to be 'done' next Thursday. Good grief, she felt sick. This was barbaric. She was a Christian; she was not a Muslim. She had not signed up for this.

'I want to talk to Kamal,' Edie said.

Long took her hand and tried to calm her. 'He will tell you it is the custom. It is normal for all girls to be cut when they are small. For boys, it is around the age of eleven.'

'And you?' Edie asked, 'When were you done?'

'My sisters and I were done at the age of seven. We got cakes and good things to eat. My mother gave us medicine so we had no infection. Don't worry, it is not too bad. This holy woman is good, she has been cutting girls like this for many, many years.'

Minna nodded sagely. 'She is coming to do six girls in our kampong, she will do you at the same time. It will be a good thing.'

'I want to talk to Kamal,' repeated Edie. Her manner was cold and she crossed her legs and folded her arms.

'If you want to be a good Muslim wife, you must do this,' Minna looked at her pointedly before turning towards the door.

'Is it written in the Koran? I do not believe that the prophet would demand this.'

'It is our way.' Minna said and went out.

Long followed her but glanced back at Edie. 'It is not like Africa, this woman only cuts the top part, what do you call it, the clitoris?'

'Good heavens, how can you say that? I don't want any cutting at all.'

*

When Kamal came home, Edie was still in their bedroom, tight-lipped and pale. Her eyes were red rimmed from a flood of tears. Kamal came and sat with her, his arm around her as she started to weep again.

'I can't believe this, it is 1976, we are modern people. What right have they to force me to do some strange tribal ritual? I bet it is not in the Koran. Is it, Kamal? I am only twenty-two, I will die of blood poisoning, and what would some crazy woman use? A knife? A razor? What?'

'Scissors, I think.' Kamal smoothed her hair and felt her shudder in fear. It was barbaric torture and he was totally on her side. 'Let me talk to the imam, you may have a point. If it is not written in the Koran, we will not allow this to happen.'

'I won't let it happen anyway,' stormed Edie, getting up, and reaching for her suitcase. 'I'm not staying here to be mutilated against my will. What will they do, hold me down, sit on my legs? I'm sorry, Kamal, but I'm leaving.'

'You are leaving me, after just two weeks?' Kamal smiled. 'Come, my sweet girl, I won't let anything happen to you. You are Scottish, you are brave and you are right. We will leave, and we will leave soon, but say nothing just yet. Trust me. We will talk to my parents and try to appease them so that they will not lose face. That is so important in families in Asia. My father will talk to the imam for us. Now, put away your suitcase and come for a walk with me.'

Thursday came, and with it, the imam. He was a tall thin man of about fifty years, clothed all in white and with the white taqiyah skullcap on his head. Hassan treated him like royalty and the two sat together on the rattan chairs with the mosque picture facing them.

'There is nothing in the Koran, my son, to say that the procedure should be done for religious reasons. Your daughter-in-law is right. For ourselves the procedure follows a custom that has been ours for centuries, but she is a foreigner, and for her she may be excused.' The imam nodded sagely. 'Mixed marriages bring their problems and their joys, but I hope when there is a child, she will bring him up in our ways.'

'Oh definitely,' Hassan agreed, 'there are no doubts there; she is a westerner but she has embraced our culture. Their children will be Muslim, praise be to Allah.'

Edie heard the news of her reprieve in the kitchen and let out a sigh of relief. She would not have gone through with it anyway, but at least now she had the blessing of her husband's family if not the total approval of Minna. It was with much trepidation that she accompanied Kamal's female relatives to the house of his sister Ooty, whose young daughter was getting cut that morning along with five other girls. Their ages ranged from five to nine and the poor little victims were standing crying, terrified of the ordeal to come. Edie watched as the mothers shook their girls, 'Stop crying, stand up straight, it will be quick.'

The bedroom shutters were closed and five village women crowded the room, muttering, their eyes darting towards the bed then the door, waiting for the first girl to enter. Edie was appalled at the sight of a pair of nail scissors, some rags and a wad of cotton wool next to a kidney bowl and a basin of water; a bottle of Dettol seemingly the only indication of any sort of First Aid. Edie shuddered and watched in horror as the first child was led in. One of the women put a rag between the girl's teeth, then another forced her thin legs to open. The girl struggled, ashamed of her nakedness and her exposure. Two other women held her arms and shoulders and forced her to stay still. The holy woman picked up the scissors and pulled at the flesh covering the small ridge of the clitoris. She tugged it taut and with a fast snip she sliced off the delicate membrane; blood spurted and the mutilated child screamed in spite of the gag and her small body writhed in excruciating pain. The cotton wool turned scarlet. The tiny piece of skin was wrapped in a cloth to be presented to the child's mother. Edie felt her head spin; she lurched out of the house and was violently sick in the open drain. As she returned to Minna and Long, she wiped her mouth. 'I can't stay, I'm sorry. I think I'm going to faint.' She staggered back to the house, tears streaming down her face, and fell on to her bed. 'I want to go home, I want to go home,' she sobbed. 'What on earth have I done coming here?'

Minna returned later, her lips turned down in disapproval, and immediately retreated to the kitchen where she set about chopping onions. Long came over and sat beside Edie on the settee. She tentatively took her hand.

'I've made a scene, haven't I? I certainly didn't help the young girls waiting.'

'You're a foreigner; they know you don't understand. They think you are impure anyway so I wouldn't worry too much.'

'Was it like that for you?'

'Oh yes, but as I said I was seven. Eventually you forget the actual pain and we are made to believe the procedure makes us clean and ready to be a good wife.'

'Is it painful when you have intercourse with your husband?'

'No, not at all, but there are no feelings on my side. I love my son and I love my husband. I am a good wife. I have heard that some cultures cut away much more leaving the girls very scarred; sometimes they even sew up the openings. That is far worse, but here, only the small cut is required.'

Edie shuddered, remembering the small child, her legs being forcibly pulled apart and held down, those awful nail scissors and the sudden blossoming of blood.

'Those scissors were not even clean. What about infection?'

'We have Panadol for pain and my mother has a supply of antibiotics. In the old days many died of septicaemia, but now if there is a bad infection, we can go to the hospital. It is OK. They know what to do.'

Long was matter of fact, showing little emotion. She patted Edie's hand. 'Don't worry, I know you will be a good wife to my brother. You are brave to come to our country, you don't even know how to speak our language. You must love him very much.'

'I do.' Edie stood up. Smoothing her dress and turning towards her sister-in-law, she said, 'Thank you, Long.' She went to the bathroom and splashed cold water over her face and eyes. She glanced at a chichak on the ceiling, its sucker-like pads holding it safely to the surface. A spider had made its web in the corner, tiny flies still struggling in the intricacies of silk. A cockroach was poised by the sluice drain, its long antennae waving like tiny batons of an orchestra conductor. Edie took it all in; she was determined to succeed in her new country. I'll just have to hide my emotions, she thought, it's not for me to stand on a moral high ground and assume everyone is the same as us in the west. I have to accept things as I find them. A few days ago, she might have screamed at the sight of the cockroach, or had a fit at the sight of the large brown spider that now appeared from a hole in the plaster, just the way she had on her second day when she saw weevils running around the breakfast cereal or burrowing in the flour. Edie left the bathroom and went to look for her husband.

Kamal was drinking a Coca Cola with his mother in the kitchen. Immediately he saw Edie, he put down his glass and came towards her. 'Are you OK, sweetheart? I heard you had a rough initiation this morning?'

Edie leant into his chest and smelt the familiar tang of his soap and shampoo. Again, her eyes filled up at the thought of the little girls, but she bit her cheek and smiled weakly. 'It was pretty grim; there is no way I could have been a nurse. I'm afraid the first sight of blood made me faint away, but I'm OK now.' She hugged him close and over his shoulder she smiled at Minna who then made a tutting noise with her tongue and shrugged her shoulders.

'Come,' said Kamal, 'let's walk down to the river and watch the boys fishing. It's cooler now but cover your arms as there are mosquitos, they bite at this time of day.'

Edie slipped on a long-sleeved blouse and pulled on her socks and canvas shoes. She had no wish to get malaria or dengue and remembered feeling very relieved at the sight of the mosquito nets over their bed when they had arrived. She had felt like a queen in an elegant four-poster, without the grand awnings, but the nets did give an extra sense of intimacy. She took his hand and together they made their way down the sandy path towards the river. Palm trees lined the way, their fronds huge and feathery, and coconuts lay randomly in the rough grass beneath. Edie cast a surreptitious glance towards the house where the butchery of the girls had taken place that morning. The shutters were closed and she thought she could hear a faint wailing coming from inside. Chickens scurried about, busy with their business; a caged bird warbled and screeched, obviously upset by the noises of distress from within the house. Edie averted her eyes and looked towards where the sun was about to set. The river glimmered black and oily, the kampong houses resembled cut-outs from a stage set and all around, the sky was peppered with peach and violet swirling clouds.

'I used to fish here as a boy.' Kamal pointed towards the river bank where three young lads with fishing poles sat gazing intently at the dark water. 'It's good for cat fish mostly.' He let out a stream of Malay to the boys who just shook their heads. '*Tidak apa!*' he grinned and he gave them a thumbs up.

'Are there crocodiles?' Edie asked, scanning the floating logs suspiciously.

'No, not here, they are found further north, mostly in the tidal estuaries. But listen, I need to talk to you, I have some very good news.'

'My goodness, what?' Edie turned to look at him, her eyes wide.

'I have an interview for a job. I didn't want to say anything, just in case they didn't want to see me, but I have to go next week.'

'Can I come?' was Edie's first response, and then she laughed. 'Listen to me, I feel like your shadow. Do you want me to come or do I have to stay here?'

'No, I thought we could go back to Singapore together and you could stay in the Mimosa for a couple of days while I go for my interview. If I get the job, I'll ring you then you could fly over and join me.'

'Fly over where? Exactly where is this job? I thought you were looking around this area.'

Kamal's face lit up into a wide smile, his eyes shining with obvious excitement. He took both her hands, and whispered, 'Borneo!'

Chapter 13

Edie felt as though she was being catapulted through the sky. She was on her way to Kota Kinabalu in Sabah, one of the two states in East Malaysia on the island of Borneo. The small plane was tossing about amidst huge mushroom clouds and she threw up in the bag provided, shuddering at the memory of the breakfast of greasy noodles served on the flight. The plane continued to buck and roll through the turbulence, and she clutched the armrests and stared fixedly ahead, willing herself to keep calm. Kamal would be waiting for her, she just hoped she would still be alive to meet him.

At last, the captain's voice came over the speaker system, his tone warm and cheerful. 'Good morning, ladies and gentlemen, apologies for this bumpy ride, but we have passed through the storm now and the view is very clear. If you can, take a look out of the right-hand side of the aircraft; there you will get an excellent view of Mount Kinabalu which is 4095 metres high. We shall soon reach our destination and fine weather is expected on the ground. Sorry again for any discomfort you may have experienced.'

Edie, sitting by the window, looked out and saw the most beautiful mountain shimmering in the sunshine. A low cloud was nestling along its serrated top, but she could make out the ridge and the unexpected sweep of the peak. For as long as she could she gazed at the mountain. I wonder if we'll climb it one day, she thought, but her reverie was interrupted as the plane seemed to nosedive down towards the runway. After the zigzagging landing, Edie was convinced that the pilot had just completed his maiden voyage. She sat shaking as the aircraft finally came to a standstill, then quickly wiped her mouth. As the passengers started to embark, she smoothed her hair and stepped out of the plane where she gasped in surprise, for there, almost next to the runway was the ocean, the South China Sea, and rising from the sapphire blue expanse were tropical islands, just a motor boat ride away. She walked towards the terminal building and felt bubbles of excitement replace the knot of nausea.

'How was your flight, darling?' Kamal grinned at her. Edie melted when she saw his bewitching smile light up his face. 'Were you all right, you look a bit pale?'

'I threw up, it was awful and the pilot was just so jolly I could have killed him. Still, he got us here in one piece. I am so pleased to see you; being with you somehow always makes things right and then I feel better.' She hugged him close.

'I have so many things to tell you, Edie, I hardly know where to start, but let's get on our way.' They climbed into the taxi and Kamal chattered on as they drove away from the coast along a road lined with market stalls, all piled high with pyramids of fresh fruit and vegetables. The car weaved around bicycles and stray dogs until eventually it approached a more urban area. 'There's the State Mosque with its golden onion-shaped dome; it's quite something. This whole road is cleared if the Sultan of Brunei or the Chief Minister passes by. I was nearly driven into the ditch by the police outriders when I first arrived.' As they continued through the town, Kamal peppered the conversation with place names that Edie hoped would soon become familiar: the Jesselton Hotel, the night market, the Post Office, Kampong Ayer. 'That's Signal Hill and Jalan Istana where the diplomats and bankers live,' he said, pointing to the turn-off. 'But we are going out towards Likas and we'll take a turning up to Tuaran Hill where I cannot wait to show you our new house. I think you will like it very much; there's a lovely cooling breeze especially in the mornings and evenings.' Indeed, it was a large white wooden house on a hill above the Tuaran road with the jungle encroaching all around and an emerald lawn of rough jungle grass, seething with red ants, giving the illusion of a beautiful colonial residence. What he omitted to say, Edie was soon to find out.

Once inside she soon discovered that the cupboards were graveyards of sawdust, courtesy of the white ants, the shutters didn't close properly and yet there was a metal grille across the front door to keep out intruders. Edie would soon learn to accommodate the other insect residents of her new home, who all seemed to share the same intent of returning it to nature. Beautiful hardwood floors ran throughout the bungalow, gleaming and smelling of fresh polish. Yellow curtains framed the windows and a soporific fan turned lazily as it pushed the torpid air around. Edie inspected the bathrooms, fortunately ensuite. Two steps led down to a tiled bathroom with all the necessary fixtures.

That was a relief, at least. No big water container and dippers here. The kitchen was small, dominated by a large white fridge humming happily. A window framed with blue and white checked curtains overlooked a steep slope where a giant mango tree grew close to the garden boundary. Beyond that was jungle. But raising her eyes she saw the red roofs of the town clustered beyond the tree line, and there in the distance was the sea, glorious and perfect, its surface shimmering in the sunlight.

'I am Moy Moy,' a fat Chinese woman announced. 'I am here.'

Kamal suddenly remembered his manners and introduced the amah. 'Moy Moy will do the cleaning and the laundry. She worked for my predecessor and knows all about European ways. She has been looking after me for the past week and she can also cook if you want her to.'

Moy Moy pointed to a shack beside a track leading from the back door. 'I am there.'

'Oh, I see,' said Edie, suddenly a little lost for words. She had not expected to have a servant and was not sure how she should treat her. 'Do we need to get you anything?'

'I have bed and ironing board. I make rice here, OK?'

'Of course,' Edie smiled.

'Will you be all right, sweetheart, I have to get back to the office but I'll be back around five thirty. You have Moy Moy if you need anything.'

'I make you mango juice, Mem. Plenty of mangos on tree now.'

'Thank you, Moy Moy, that sounds very good. Yes, I'll be fine, my darling, don't worry, but come here and give me a hug before you go. I'm going to freshen up and unpack now.' The two swayed together under the fan, and Moy Moy discreetly retreated to the kitchen.

As soon as Kamal left, Edie headed to their bedroom and immediately opened her suitcase and found her sponge bag. I so need a shower, she thought, that plane journey was just awful, I smell disgusting. I do hope there's hot water. The shower was blissful and she felt herself relax as the warm water washed away the memory of the turbulence and horrors of the flight. She scrubbed her hair and brushed her teeth and changed into a yellow cotton sundress. It was wonderful to unpack her clothes and put everything away properly for the first time since leaving Scotland. At last, she thought, maybe now I have a home of my own.

Suitably transformed and with her glass of fresh mango juice in her hand, she settled herself in the lounge. It's quite sparse, she thought as she looked about her, I'll need to put up some pictures and maybe arrange some books on a shelf. Thinking about books, she remembered the one she had bought at the airport, an account of Borneo by a traveller who had spent time in South East Asia. Edie flicked through the pages until she came to the chapter about Sabah and Sarawak, the two Borneo states which formed East Malaysia. She read that the massive island of Borneo was dissected into different countries. The independent country of Brunei sat between the two states of East Malaysia, Sabah and Sarawak. The rest of the island's landmass was Kalimantan which formed part of Indonesia. On the facing page of the book was a glossy picture of the island of Borneo itself, the third biggest island in the world and so very green. Oh my, she thought, it's like a fabulous jewel, a fairytale place of fantasy and adventure. Her eyes followed the threads of impossibly long rivers; the darker tones on the photograph were of jade green, depicting dense rainforest contrasting with the yellow and golden mountain ranges which speckled the island like the lights within an opal. Borneo was described as being 'north of Java, west of Sulawesi, and east of Sumatra.' She sighed and took a sip from her juice. Those are names that conjure up romance and images of adventure stories. She looked at the turquoise seas surrounding this spectacular landmass, so different from the cold North Sea and chilly Atlantic Ocean that she had once known. She picked out the South China Sea to the north and north west, the Sulu Sea to the north east and the Java Sea to the south. She closed the book and examined the back cover, which described Sabah as being a land below the wind. She frowned as she read about the 'typhoon belt' to the north, which seemed to bypass Sabah, making it a safe haven for seafarers. 'Pity the pilot on the plane this morning hadn't read this book,' she muttered, 'he was certainly flying too close to the wind.'

She wandered outside, down the steps of the veranda, and viewed the long driveway curving up to the house. She strolled across the grass, dotted with colourful shrubs whose names she would learn, and turned round to look at the wooden house built on top of blockwork pillars. The roof was covered with red clay pantiles. The windows were open, and mosquito-netted shutters opened inwards, to be closed in the evening. On the right-hand side of the veranda a large bougainvillea bush, luxuriant in deep magenta blossom, clashed violently with clumps of orange canna lilies. To the left, and just outside the master bedroom, Edie saw a mature frangipani tree, its branches long and twisted, its profuse blossoms delicate and waxy. She walked over and plucked one of the flowers and held the silky yellow centre to her nose. The perfume was intense.

Feeling an unfamiliar tickle on her foot, she gulped and was about to swat the offending insect but instead managed to remain calm, having already suffered from this particular bite in Johor. A cavalier red ant was nosing its way over her sandal and had stopped to pause, no doubt for orientation, on her big toenail. Edie bent down and flicked it off with her finger. She noticed a column of red invaders around her and also from this view she could see right underneath the house. There was the usual detritus of planks, broken chairs and rotting leaves. Edie shuddered at the thought of what might be curled up under there. 'I think we should get a dog,' she muttered, 'and maybe some cats. I quite like the idea of some hunters that might be on my side.'

Glancing beyond a dilapidated wooden storage shed that might once have been a garage, she saw a small hill on which grew two magnificent rain trees. They were majestic and imposing and close enough for her to see the creepers that wound themselves around the long branches, rather like a hairy scarf.

Above her, the sky was thick with cloud, and although the temperature was hot, in the high eighties, Edie could feel the storm that had plagued her incoming journey that morning. It was imminent.

Moy Moy sauntered to the front door and stood with her hand on her hips, surveying her new mistress out in the heat. 'You want lunch, Mem? I made you poached eggs, also beef stroganoff for tonight's dinner. Tuan said just to cook, like I did for the MacKenzies. You like, OK?'

'Oh yes, that would be wonderful, thank you, Moy Moy. I was just looking under the house and was wondering about snakes. Do you get any here?'

'Sometimes. Also, black biters you call scorpions, they come here. We very close to jungle; on the other side men are building houses, so snakes have to run away.'

'I see.' Edie was now adamant that she would have a dog. She remembered hearing about Malays and their feelings about canines, that they were unclean, but she had asked Kamal's father and he had assured her that in the Koran it was decreed that Muslims were to love all creatures. It was said that a dog had guarded a cave of some hero. She liked the idea of her own personal bodyguard up here on the hill surrounded by the last vestiges of jungle.

That night, Kamal studied Edie's profile as she sat on the step of the veranda. The deluge of rain was pounding the roof of the house. Lightning lit up the rain trees, making them look stark against the night sky. He couldn't believe his luck. He had got a job with an eminent law firm and at last he was practising law in his native land. He knew that his job would involve a lot of travel around Sabah, Sarawak and even sometimes to Peninsula Malaysia, but seeing Edie now in her new surroundings, he had no fear of her settling in. Her innate curiosity, her pragmatism and her realistic take on life would stand her in good stead. He got on well with his Chinese colleague, Michael Low, and Amelia, his Australian wife, had assured him that she would introduce Edie to the International School at Likas.

Kamal stretched back in his chair, replete after dinner. The fan barely turned and outside the thunder seemed to have receded to a distant rumble. The storm was passing. 'Amelia is coming around to see you tomorrow, she said she wants to show you around.'

'That's kind of her, how long has she been living out here?' Edie left her perch on the veranda step and came in to sit opposite him on the settee.

'A couple of years I believe. She knows everyone so she might know if there are any teaching vacancies. Now do you want to finish this bottle of wine or shall I?'

Edie passed her glass over to Kamal. 'Definitely! A little slosh for you and a big slosh for me please. Cheers!'

The following evening, Edie was alone in the house. Kamal's chair was empty and she had eaten a solitary meal of rice and chicken. The fan turned; the night sounds seemed louder without his comforting presence. Moy Moy had retired to her shack and Edie was aware of the darkness and every strange creak within the house. I never thought I would miss Minna and all her family, she thought, but it is lonely up here on my hill. A chichak darted down the wall. Suddenly she heard a sound. It was quite faint and it sounded like an animal. 'This is all I need,' she muttered, 'a predator ready to break in'. The sound seemed to be coming from the old shack in the garden. Edie gingerly stepped out to the dark veranda. There was a moon above and a faint light lit up the broken-down shed. There was the sound again, a persistent mewing cry. Edie gingerly walked towards the sound, and outlined by the moonlight, a small creature was quivering by the shed door. 'A kitten,' she breathed, 'a little tabby kitten! You poor little thing, are you abandoned? Come, let me carry you, I hope you won't scratch me.' Edie managed to lift the small animal and carry it back to the house. 'You are a sweet little thing, and obviously lost and hungry, let's see what Moy Moy has left over in the fridge.' Edie fed the little cat rice and bits of chicken and it ate till its belly resembled a barrel on spindly legs. 'You arrived just when I needed you,' she told him, cuddling him on her lap. 'We shall be friends. I am going to call you Tiger Tim, because you came from the jungle.' Tiger Tim purred.

The following weeks passed in a blur. Amelia Low was a formidable friend to have. She had already learnt to speak a passable Malay; she was a keen golfer and was inured to the expatriate way of life. Thinking of her new friend, Edie decided to write to her old friend in Edinburgh:

Dear Joy,

It rains every day at 3 p.m., and the lightning nearly cracks my eardrums. The thunder is terrifying; I feel as though the timbers of this house will just crumble with the reverberations. The white ants or termites come out in their millions just before a storm and crawl about the floor, casting off their wings like dying swans. It is all so gruesome, and Moy Moy is just so lackadaisical with her broom. She swishes about, moving the poor creatures on to a shovel and tossing them into the monsoon drain. Later the rain just washes them all away. What freaks me out is: where do they come from? They must have been breeding like frenzied creatures in the woodwork and cupboards, only to come out and die just before it rains. Anyway, it's the thunder that scares me half to death. I feel like 'Ma Broon', and just want to hide under the bed.

I have met Amelia, a very friendly twenty-five-year-old Australian and she has become a good friend. She and my little kitten, Timmy who appeared the night Kamal went away to Sandakan on a case, have become my constant companions. Amelia has the body of a tennis player, long, curly blonde hair like one of Charlie's Angels. When she bakes cakes, she just sieves out the weevils, saying that their eggs are destroyed by the heat of the oven. I follow her about like the new girl that I am. I long to just sit and put my feet up at the yacht club and read a book but instead I have been introduced to tennis and golf. All this while I am nearly expiring with heat. Amelia has her amah guard her twin two-year-old daughters, just little tots, all morning while she golfs, then she collects them and we sit at the yacht club and she teaches me to knit. I really need to get a teaching job so she took me round to the school, a big sprawling building with bamboo tats over the windows, and open plan classrooms with French doors facing the sea. The headmaster promised to let me know if he has a vacancy, so that is encouraging. The children were sweet, all in little yellow gingham uniforms, and as far as I could make out, represent nearly every nation on earth - I exaggerate, but you can imagine!

I miss you, my dear friend. Till next time, and write to me soon,
Edie

Kamal found Edie sitting for once alone at the yacht club; the second-hand car he had bought for her was parked beside the array of speedboats nestled under the casuarina trees. He signalled to a waiter to bring two beers and he went to join his wife.

'This is a nice surprise.' She squinted at him through her sunglasses and put down her book. 'Why aren't you slaving away in the courts or the office?'

'The thing is, I have to go away again. There is a problem with the logging rights on the Kalimantan border, I might be away for three weeks or a month. And no,' he grinned, 'you can't come with me.'

Edie laughed. 'Don't worry about me, I have Timmy at home, and elsewhere I'll be bossed about every day. It's amazing that I'm alone today; goodness knows where Amelia is. She was supposed to meet me here at eleven.'

'She is visiting Annika Sewel from the Chartered Bank on Jalan Istana. Michael has just heard that they are leaving and Amelia was going to help with ringing round for packers. She told me to pass on her regrets and she would meet up with you tomorrow. What are you doing tomorrow?'

'Tennis,' Edie pulled a face. 'I hate playing her, she is so competitive. I know, she is kind and so on but I just feel like her little doll that she bosses about. Anyway, when are you going away?'

'Tonight, on the seven o'clock to Kuching. I have a meeting there in the morning so let's go home now; I need to pack, then you can drive me to the airport.'

Dear Joy,
Kamal has been gone for six weeks. He was supposed to go for just three and I am so forlorn. The worst thing though was the other afternoon. I am so embarrassed - I had been having a nap after being beaten at golf again by bossy boots Amelia, when I heard a croaky voice calling at the veranda door. I knew that Moy Moy was also having a rest in

her shack. Fortunately, I had closed and locked the metal grille doors. Outside, I saw an old, blind man who had staggered up the hill to sell silk paintings. I didn't have any money on me and he didn't speak English, so I gripped the bars of the grille and said loudly, as one is wont to do when speaking to blind people, even though they are not deaf: 'Tolong, Tolong!' thinking that it meant: 'I'm sorry, I'm sorry!'.

Well, yesterday I met a new woman friend called Maggie, who is married to an engineer at the airport. She is English and her husband is Malay, like mine, and she has been here for about four years. We bonded over Guinness. Her husband is away in Miri for a month, so we consoled each other by knocking back a few bottles. She is quite a colourful character and her Malay is quite good. She was cackling away as on the label of the bottles we were drinking from was the Malay slogan: 'Guinness baik untuk anda' which unbelievably means: 'Guinness is good for you'! And by golly it was, and after a few she nearly cracked up when I told her about my visit from the blind man and I had cried: 'Tolong, tolong!' Apparently, I had been shouting 'Help! Help!' No wonder the poor man looked so confused as he tapped his way back down the driveway. Come to think of it, he didn't offer to help me, I could have been being held prisoner or anything! Anyway, so much for my Malay lessons.

I feel this indolent way of life is wearing a little thin, I really need a job. Perhaps I should go and offer my services to the school for free.

More later,
Your friend, Edie.

When Kamal finally returned home, he found a triumphant Edie, exuding confidence after securing a job at the International School. 'I just went down and suggested I do voluntary work. Mr Mann said that was not an option as he did have a Primary 2 class and would I be interested in the job? Oh, Kamal, I nearly bit his hand off, so I have been working non-stop for the last week!'

Kamal hugged her and shook her hand formally. 'Congratulations, my darling! You are a great teacher; it suits you to be happy. I'm so pleased to be home again.' He looked around the room, 'I see you've been decorating; I like the bookcase and where you've hung the pictures, and by the way, how are you getting on with that cat?'

'Timmy splits his time between me and Moy Moy. I think he enjoys her company more. You should see him chasing her broom around when she sweeps the floor. He has certainly made himself at home with us all. Oh, I must tell you, I met a new friend called Maggie Rajah and she runs a kindergarten and we have had such fun, she ...'

'She has introduced you to Guinness, I see,' interjected her husband. 'I did notice the bottles in the crate at the back door when I came in. You be careful in that car.'

'I will, don't worry. And did you miss me? You've been gone so long.'

'I did miss you terribly and I brought you back some local batik sarongs, special designs from the native people who live in the heart of Sarawak. Come, come to bed and show me how much you missed me.'

Chapter 14

Edie spent the next few months immersed in her school duties and class preparation. She and her class of six-year-olds were on a joint mission of discovery. Weighed down with books featuring the trees and flowers of Malaysia, and armed with their notebooks and clipboards, she took the children for walks in the surrounding countryside and forests. The children painted traveller palm trees and exotic wild orchids. They searched for the Borneo swallowtail butterfly, never seen in Peninsular Malaysia, and were rewarded during a jungle outing when they found one drinking at the edge of a muddy river. Its body and wings were dusted with green except for a patch of smooth scales on the hind wings which were a brilliant shiny blue.

Kamal had got used to their dinner conversations being peppered with descriptions of the five-bar swordtail butterfly or the life cycle of the termite. This evening, however, as they sat across the dining room table, a bowl of rose hibiscus between them, Kamal thought about his own work and how some of it was beginning to mirror, or more truthfully conflict with, his wife's passions. He had expected to cover criminal law in the new practice, but on starting the job, he'd discovered that he was required to represent corporate clients instead. He had needed to familiarise himself with the impact that the lucrative logging and mining contracts were having on the country, on its economy and on the indigenous people living within the forest. Deforestation was accelerating as the valuable timber was being rapidly cut down and sold, then further intensifying as the oil palm industry placed further demands on the land. Meanwhile the country's economy was booming and the logging companies grew richer. Rumours of corruption were rife. People living within the forests gained little of the wealth and in many instances were being forced to give up their way of life by having to relocate to urban areas where often they were not equipped to earn a living. Inevitably, law firms were in high demand to deal with the legal disputes that inevitably arose as the various parties fought for their own interests. And of course, all the plants and animals being wiped out could not seek legal redress. Kamal sighed deeply. He was not comfortable with the role he was playing in defending the interests of the logging companies. Warily he answered Edie's questions about what he did. He was fully aware that she would be indignant if she realised exactly how he was involved.

He looked down at the hibiscus blooms, a miracle, and seeing him focussing on the beautiful flowers, Edie interrupted his thoughts. 'Do you know, Kamal, well, I read this in my book, that early in the morning, the petals and sepals are ivory white with just traces of pink at the bases. Then as the sun rises, light pink colour appears on the more exposed petals and gradually increases in intensity as the morning progresses. By noon all the petals are rose-pink. The colour reaches its peak around two o'clock, then by five the flower loses its brilliance and withers completely! So now, I place some of the blooms in water to preserve them for a while so that we can savour them in the evening by candlelight.'

'They really are beautiful, Edie, and I love hearing about your walks with your children in the countryside.'

She pushed her glass away, the wine untouched, and changed the subject to one that was worrying her. 'Do you really take the corporate side, Kamal? Don't you want to preserve the natural heritage? All of this deforestation, with the logging and mining and so on, is destroying the natural habitats of the animal and plant life. Everybody knows this. Will my lessons be history lessons in a few years' time?'

'The client pays, you know that. They need legal advice and they come to us. That is all I do.' But of course, he did feel some pangs of guilt. He knew that the logging was also causing perennial and recurring flooding as well as drought in the country.

'I thought the government were setting aside land for national parks?'

'Yes, they are; they'll not only be part of our national heritage but also part of world heritage.'

'Well, I just hope that any wildlife that survives the destruction of their habitat will be happy to stay within their reduced boundaries.'

'What I am hoping to do is to get involved with representing conservationists or some of the indigenous people who are losing their land. I have spoken to the partners about it, Edie. And try to remember that I'm not responsible for causing the deforestation. I have to work at my profession and after all I am only trying to make a living. I don't want to fall out with you about this.' Kamal finished his wine and made to stand up. If only she knew, he thought, how difficult it was to change office policy and forsake the generous fees from some very rich clients.

'Well, let's hope the partners agree with your proposal. Anyway, I'm really tired, Kamal, I'm going for a shower.' Edie pushed her chair back and kissed his forehead before going through to their bedroom. She needed to calm down after the talk with Kamal and she felt an overwhelming desire to sleep. In the softly lit room, the bed with its ivory lace bedcover looked so inviting. She slipped off her clothes, showered and brushed her teeth. When Kamal entered the room, she was lying on her side, already fast asleep. He withdrew and padded back to the lounge where he picked up her abandoned glass of wine. He sipped it thoughtfully. One of these days he should take his religion seriously and forego the joys of alcohol, but for the moment, he was content. His family were all well in Johor and his wife was asleep, no doubt dreaming of more flora and fauna. His own conscience was appeased for the moment by voicing his plans to make changes. He was earning decent money and their bank account was healthy. He tried not to think of that pretty girl he had met in Kuching. It was nothing, he reassured himself. Just a casual fling, but, and he breathed out sharply, she was quite a sexy piece.

Chapter 15

Adam was born in the New Year. A splendid child with a thatch of black hair which all seemed to be growing skywards. His coffee-coloured skin and dark eyes bore no resemblance to his pale, wan, worn-out mother. Edie held him to her breast and watched the hungry gums latch on to her nervous nipple. 'Well, you've come into the world knowing what to do to survive, that's for sure,' she laughed, grimacing faintly as the pain of the new sensation took hold.

Kamal was puffed up and proud, surrounded by his mother and father and the two Fatima sisters, Ma and La. Ooty and Long had not made the journey as they were busy at home with their own families. Edie looked about her, at the sunny room, her proud relatives and the baskets of orchids that had been delivered by her friends at school and the yacht club. Soon, she thought, I'll have to tell them that Adam has already had his circumcision. There will be no brutal rituals performed on my son when he is ten or eleven years old!

She sensed that Minna was dying to get her grandson to herself and sling him into one of the sarongs that she'd brought with her, not to mention taking over the cleaning of the house and cooking of the meals. 'Your amah is very lazy you know, I think she will leave you now, too much work, nappies to wash, baby to carry. She not good amah. Maybe I will stay for a while to help look after everything?' Edie looked down at her little son's head and heard the machine of persuasion being put in action. This was the plan. She might have guessed. 'No trouble,' Minna continued, 'Hassan and my girls will go back to Johor and I will care for you. You rest for one month and I will do everything. This is our way.'

Edie said nothing. There was little point. She looked at the array of cards clustered on her bedside table, hiding the book that Amelia had given her yesterday: *Baby and Child Care* by Doctor Benjamin Spock. She smiled, knowing that she was surrounded by love and well-meant intentions. She had briefly looked through the book, daunted at how much there was to soothing, feeding and caring for an infant, but one paragraph came to mind now as she looked at her mother-in-law: 'Perhaps a child who is fussed over gets a feeling of destiny; he thinks he is in the world for something important, and it gives him drive and confidence'. She hugged her baby close to her, remembering the instinct that drove her body to deliver him. Again, she thought of Dr Spock's words: 'Trust yourself, you know more than you think you do'.

'Of course, Minna, please stay, I would like that. You know so much about babies and I know so little. It would be such a comfort, especially since Kamal will be travelling away again soon. But let's try and keep Moy Moy on our side.'

Minna's face split into the widest smile, her teeth glinting with gold fillings, 'Praise be to Allah!'

After the first week of brutal sleeplessness, the next two weeks took on a relative spell of quiet and peace, when Adam slept and ate and stared with mystified eyes at the frills on his bassinette. Minna attended to his every whimper and smiled fondly while she studied his scowls and twisting mouth as he dreamt away the quiet afternoons. This left Edie time to gossip with her friends and eat banana fritters prepared by the amazingly attentive Moy Moy. 'Motherhood seems much more civilized than I had envisaged,' she announced to Amelia whilst drinking tea from a china cup and saucer. Her friend nibbled a biscuit whilst declining to comment. From across the room Timmy the cat surveyed the new arrival with disdain.

'Poor Timmy has his nose out of joint; he waits until Adam is asleep, then he jumps up on my lap to reclaim his territory, don't you, puss?' The cat immediately took that as an invitation and jumped from the chair he was preening on and leapt up beside her. 'You are still my best cat in the whole world.' Timmy stretched out contentedly before turning onto his back. She obligingly stroked his tummy.

Minna, who had also taken charge of the cooking, was convinced that she could find better bargains than Edie, who loved to buy from the Tong Hing Supermarket in Kota Kinabalu. Clad in her pretty sarong kebaya and coolie hat, she decided to make it her mission to discover the various bus routes into town. After snooping around the various shophouses and fancy hotels, she soon made her way to her favourite destination, the Central Market. Here she eyed the sellers with suspicion and spat at their prices for snapper and crab. She bargained for papaya and bread fruit, determined to build up the young mother's strength and milk production. Unknown to her, Amelia had been providing bottles of Guiness and Sweetheart Stout to Edie for the very same reasons. Now proficient and knowledgeable with the layout of the market, Minna slopped through the wet corridors of the fish section and bought an array of silvery specimens which she could already see grilled and crispy on a platter. Pleased with her purchases she decided to go for a cup of milky *long chai* at the eating stalls adjacent to the market. It was while she was passing the caged chickens and was sniffing the cumin and coriander spices that she espied on a shelf an array of blue and white dishes. Most were a common Chinese design depicting a large blue carp painted across a white background. But one pot was different. It was a square shape with two handles sticking out like rigid ears. Deep blue in colour, the piece seemed to call to her. 'How much you want for that stupid pot?' she shouted at the Chinese boy in charge of the stall which was also selling fresh eggs and chicken feet.

He glanced at her without much interest. 'My Ma said all pots twenty dollar, you want to buy?'

Minna picked up the pot and studied it. It was well made, quite unique. She had never seen one like it before. There was a Chinese mark on the base. 'I give you ten dollar, OK?' She looked at him. Her normally soft brown eyes had turned to black onyx.

'My Ma said twenty dollar; she said all pots twenty dollar.'

'But this pot is no good, can't hold anything. Just good for my grandson's teeth. What about twelve dollar, OK?'

The boy recognised the uselessness of the pot. 'OK, I'll wrap it quick before Ma gets back'.

Minna walked out into the hot midday sun, adjusted her coolie hat and arranged her bags over her arms. She decided to add some lime green glutinous cakes to her shopping. 'Lucky pot, I think.' Her life was good.

Minna left to return to her own home, and when she did, the peace left with her. Adam sensed that his adoring grandmother was gone; there were no more sing-song lullabies, he was expected to sleep when he wanted to play, he was ignored when he needed a snack and the warmth of her sarong cocoon was replaced by his mother's spindly arms. Edie divided her time breastfeeding her seemingly starving child whilst balancing the tome of Benjamin Spock in her free hand. She tried to feel reassured that what she was doing in the way of mothering skills was correct. Amelia persuaded her to bring Adam to the yacht club. With Minna gone, Edie felt ready to bring Adam out to meet the community. He lay in his bassinette staring up at the casuarina trees and squinting at the sunlight. His sleep-deprived mother gazed at the glittering sea, hoping the fresh air would help him to sleep through the night.

'You're not the first and everyone with kids will tell you the first year is hell. Just hope that your marriage survives. Mine is still teetering and I've had two, thank God for the playgroup.' Amelia sucked noisily at her fresh lime juice. Edie was silent, she often wondered about her friend, so bossy and self-assured and always so busy. Was everything as it should be in the Low household? The two couples didn't socialise as such, Michael preferring the company of his Chinese colleagues, and Kamal was hardly home at all these days. Edie looked over at the other family groups around adjacent tables, many of them parents of the children she had taught.

A pretty Eurasian lady waved and called out to her. 'How are you? We heard you had your baby; you must come and play mah-jong with us now that you're on maternity leave.'

Edie waved back, 'Thank you, I'd like that, but what about this little fellow?'

'Not a problem, we all have small kids, just bring him along.'

Amelia groaned, 'You'll get sucked in and before you know it, you'll be doing Scottish dancing and going for pleasure jaunts to the islands.'

'But that's good, Amelia, I can't really play golf and tennis at the moment and I don't trust Moy Moy one hundred percent, as you know. These ladies are like me and I need a distraction. Anyway, I thought I would have seen more of Kamal than I do.'

'These Asian guys are all the same, they just want to work, make loads of money and gamble. That's all Michael does. He goes off to Genting Highlands, gambles everything, and then comes back, all sheepish with a crocodile handbag for me or some other peace offering. You wait and see, Kamal will start with diamond earrings, always a sign that they have a guilty conscience. By the way, Michael has bought a new car, a yellow Porsche. Do you fancy a spin? He's away for a week and I know where the keys are.'

'No! I do not. I can just see you speeding along then getting stuck behind a herd of buffalo. I would never get back in time to feed Adam.'

'Your loss, my friend. I think I'll take it out tomorrow.'

*

Kamal returned from Kuching on Saturday. He came into the house with a skip but stopped abruptly. On the veranda under the table that was always laden with Edie's growing collection of plants lay the corpse of a banded flying snake. Its black and red colours were still bright, it had not been dead long. 'Edie, where are you?' He stormed in, his face a picture of fury.

'What is it? Are you all right?'

'When did Moy Moy sweep last?'

'I don't know,' Edie answered, wondering what this was all about.

'There is a dead snake out here and you have our child lying on the floor unattended.'

'But I'm here, Kamal, I just went to the bedroom to put on some lipstick, I heard your car on the driveway.'

'And he could have been bitten.'

'What kind of snake is it?' She stepped out to the veranda and looked to where her husband was glaring. 'Gosh, those colours are bright,' she said. 'Is it dangerous?'

'All snakes are dangerous to a three-month-old baby, that amah has got to go.'

'Oh please, Kamal, don't sack her, we get on so well. She may not be perfect, but she is very calm.'

'Calm? You think calmness is the main quality required of a servant?' He stepped past her and picked up his son. 'You are a brave boy, Adam. I am sure you will grow up strong in spite of these women who are supposed to protect you'.

Edie folded her arms and turned away. She walked through to the kitchen. Moy Moy was making a big deal of washing lentils. She was totally absorbed and looked startled when she saw her mistress suddenly appear. 'Tuan is back, did you not hear him?'

'No, Mem, the man is cutting the grass, big noise.'

'Well, leave those lentils, go and get the man. Now! Tuan found a snake!'

'A ya!' Moy Moy shrieked. 'Where?'

'It's dead. Hurry! Tuan very angry. Get the man to take it away.'

Edie watched Moy Moy as she walked through the laundry room and sauntered along the track to where the man was strimming the edges of the flower beds. She could at least run, she thought; nothing ever seems to faze her. Edie walked over to the window and looked into the branches of the mango tree then down to where the wild grasses grew beyond their garden.

The jungle was so close, it was a wonder they didn't get more unwanted visitors. Maybe Timmy had brought the snake into the house, he's always hunting in the bushes. Last week she had seen him pounce on a large toad and drag it off somewhere. She had hoped that he would have hunted to protect her, but at least this time the snake was dead. Turning round, she saw Timmy leap up to the laundry room window. He meowed his greeting to her, and already purring, ran over to rub himself affectionately against her legs. She picked him up, 'Oh Timmy, you must be more careful, that snake could have killed you. Next time, stick to grasshoppers or beetles.' She buried her face into the cat's soft fur. Well, I am seeing a new side of my husband, she thought, and she tried to forget Amelia's words.

Chapter 16

What a blissful Sunday, Edie sighed. She was sunburnt and tired. She played with the remote control of the TV, setting up the new video machine that Kamal had brought back from a trip to Labuan. There was a Clint Eastwood film on later, but her eyes were stinging from the saltwater and she craved sleep. I could watch it tomorrow, she thought.

'You look relaxed,' Kamal smiled, coming to sit on the rattan settee beside her. 'It was a good day; I enjoyed it very much.' He watched her playing with the remote, 'Clint Eastwood, which one?'

'*A Fistful of Dollars*. They seem to be doing his early ones which I actually never saw.'

'I was a big fan; I used to go to the cinema in Johor Bahru and see them as soon as they came out. I loved them and recording it is a good idea; we can watch it whenever we want.'

'Adam had such a happy time on the island, I couldn't believe the way he kept crawling into the sea. I'm so glad he is fearless with water; it will be easy to teach him to swim. Did he settle well?'

'Yes, he just drank his bottle and his eyes were closed before I could even put him into his cot. I think he got a little too much sun, we must watch him carefully.'

'Thank you for settling him.' Edie took his hand and squeezed it. She felt a warm rush of affection towards him and was thankful for their day together with their new friends. The Andersons and Davidsons both had boats and it was Patricia Anderson who'd invited them to come out with them this Sunday. 'Did you like Phil and Patsy?'

'Yes, they're fun. It was good to get away from the town and the island was shadier than I imagined. I thought we were going to be grilled like snappers when I saw where the boat was heading, but no, it was relaxing sitting under the casuarina trees. Drinking in the sun gives me a headache though; I saw you drinking white wine as though it was water.'

'I know, and yes, I've had some pills just now. But the barbecue was delicious, so were the fried prawns and curry puffs. Did you see Adam with the little Davidson child? She was good with him, little Felicity; she kept feeding him bits of mango and papaya. I hope they'll ask us to go with them again.'

'Yes, it was good to meet Kate and Alistair as well. It was a good day out.'

Kamal stretched out his legs and the couple closed their eyes, each content with their day and with each other. Outside the cicadas kept up their constant clamouring, while the fan seemed to beat out a syncopated rhythm. They were making friends and although he had to travel away a lot, Kamal was at peace back home with his Scottish wife with her long feathery hair and her sunburnt shoulders. This time it was he who squeezed her hand.

Chapter 17

A massive storm broke on the last day of school. The children ran around the classroom full of glee as they gathered up their tinsel and cards and rammed their carefully made tokens of Christmas into their satchels. Swathed in lightweight plastic macs, they lined the corridor waiting for their parents or drivers to collect them. Edie stood at the school steps, opening doors and ushering the children into the appropriate car. Her sandals were soaked as the puddles rose higher and there were rumours that the main road through Likas was blocked by flooding. Eventually she returned to her classroom and surveyed the empty room. The school cleaning staff were already armed with mops and cloths.

'Happy Christmas to you, Mem. Have a happy holiday!'

'Thank you, Ang, and I'll see you next term.' Edie walked back to the staffroom where she put on the kettle. There was no point going out just yet. The roads would be chaos.

'Great minds,' commented Sarah Campbell, the deputy head. 'We might as well have some of these biscuits the parents gave us.' She settled herself down and patted the chair next to her. 'How has it been, Edie? Have you enjoyed being back after having your baby?'

'Very much. Adam now goes to Maggie Rajah's playgroup in the mornings and I pick him up after school. He loves it as she has two boys of her own, so he enjoys their company.' She took a sip of her tea. 'You're from Scotland as well, aren't you?'

Sarah nodded enthusiastically, 'Yes, I'm from Arbroath, in Angus, and Derek is from Aberdeen. We usually go there at Christmas but this year we're postponing until the summer. He's with the World Health Organisation and has a conference in KL in early January.'

'Gosh, that must be interesting,' Edie was aware that there had been a surge of vaccinations throughout Sabah and Sarawak recently. Her friend, Alistair Davidson, was an ophthalmologist whose work took him into the jungles to treat people with cataracts. Another friend's husband was a kidney specialist, but Edie's own knowledge of the medical care in Kota Kinabalu was rudimentary. She gave thanks that so far Adam had only suffered from prickly heat and the odd cold with high fever, then recalled her mother-in-law's warning: Don't be proud, don't boast, don't let the spirits take him.

'What are your plans for the holiday, Edie?'

'Well, and I know this might be too short notice, but I wonder if you and your husband might like to come to a New Year's Eve party that we're hosting? I want it to be a Scottish occasion and there will be dancing and a piper. I think you would be my perfect ally!'

Sarah whooped with delight, 'Absolutely! We'd love to come. Can I help at all?'

'Yes, I was hoping you'd say that! I thought we could teach the guests an Eightsome Reel, and I am sure most of them will know how to do a Gay Gordons. My husband got me some Scottish music when he was in Singapore so we can select whichever tunes would be best. The piper is from the Gurkha regiment in town, so we'll have to pick him up and take him back afterwards.'

'How many people have you invited?'

'Maybe thirty to forty, and I have to think about the food. The yacht club will lend me plates, cutlery and glasses.'

'Then I'll help with the cooking.' Sarah was totally involved now, her organising skills to the fore. 'Have you a dress code?'

'I thought formal,' Edie laughed, 'just to make it an occasion, and we'll put little tables outside and lanterns in the trees.'

'And I could make some tablecloths.'

The few minutes allotted for a cup of tea turned into over an hour of frenzied planning. Edie eventually sailed home in a whirl of excitement, and roared up the hill to her bungalow to find that Kamal's car was already parked outside. She burst in, full of anticipation, only to see him sitting with Adam on his knee. The child was babbling, 'Da Da Da,' and pointing at Timmy perched on the window sill.

Edie blanched. In her exhilaration she had forgotten to pick him up.

Kamal glared at her. 'Where have you been?'

'At school; I stayed late to avoid the traffic.'

'School finished at one o'clock. It is now past three!'

'When did you get Adam? I was going to get him …'

'But you didn't! Maggie Rajah rang here. My flight was early, so fortunately I was here and was able to collect him myself.'

'I'm sorry, Kamal, I lost track of time. I was talking to Sarah Campbell. I have never forgotten before and no harm is done.' Edie stretched her arms towards Adam.

Kamal stood up and pointedly marched past her, taking the little boy through to Moy Moy. 'Give him some milk and a biscuit,' he instructed.

'Kamal, please,' Edie called to him. 'Let me explain. Please don't let's fight about this, please.'

'I think we shall go to Johor for the holiday. That way my family can look after Adam.'

'But what about our party? We're having a lot of people; we've sent out the invitations.' Edie could feel the sting of tears.

'Is that all you think about? Your expatriate friends, your yacht club cronies?'

'But you like them too, Kamal. You always say you enjoy their company. And the men are your business colleagues as well.'

'I am a Malay man and my son must not lose sight of his Malay heritage. We have a mixed marriage and we must both compromise. My mother would not have forgotten to pick up any of her children. It is unforgivable.'

Edie drew herself up and walked out to the veranda. The bushes were still heavy with water, the rivulets of the deluge still trickling down the driveway. Above her the rain trees stood stark against the yellow streaked sky. She could hear the scream of monkeys from the nearby jungle. No peace on earth here, she thought. The recent Christmas preparations at school seemed so far away.

Chapter 18

Edie stepped off the veranda and defiantly walked to her car, jumped in and swiftly put it in reverse. With stones spraying she turned down the driveway, not looking to see or even caring if Kamal had come out to prevent her leaving. She was not sure where she was heading, she just drove the familiar road past the State Mosque and along towards the airport. She veered to the right and found herself en route to the yacht club. She parked under the dripping trees and walked away from the sea towards the clubhouse. There she ordered a fresh lime and soda, and clutching the ice-cold glass, she climbed the stairs to the veranda, pulled a chair to the edge and sat back with her feet up on the railings. The sea was grey, smooth as a sheet of satin, and the sky was dotted with ominous puffs of navy-blue cloud. The storm was in abeyance. Images of her life with Kamal floated in front of her eyes and she fought the sting of tears as she imagined her hand touching the smoothness of his shoulder, hot from the afternoon sun. She saw him cradling little Adam and holding his hands as he learnt first to totter and then to walk. She did wonder if he was being faithful to her. He would be gone for weeks at a time, but she trusted him, she had to. And he still loved her, she knew that. His laugh, his soft voice when he whispered her name, the tentative touch of his fingers as they laced them with hers at parties where they felt alone and unsure. He had never given her diamond earrings or crocodile handbags. Surely that was a good sign?

'Well, hello there, stranger!' Amelia stood framed against the sky, bringing her vibrancy and purpose to a much-dejected Edie.

'Hello to you too! It's so good to see you; you are probably the best person to have appeared just at this moment. I have the blues, the end-of-term blues as well as the Christmas blues and,' she finished lamely, 'just about everything is wrong.'

'Hold on, I'll be back.' Amelia disappeared as quickly as she had arrived. She returned with a waiter who was carrying a tray of four gin and tonics.

'Four?' asked Edie, looking around her. 'Who else is here?'

'No one, but we'll drink the first one quickly and it'll save us going for refills.'

'Fine! Well, cheers, bottoms up and season's greetings!' Edie relished the first gulp, closely followed by a second.

'So, you have the blues, can I help?' Amelia asked, sipping her drink and scrutinizing her friend from over her glass.

'It's Kamal.'

'Ah, serious, or a tiff?'

'I don't know. Just cultural, I think. I forgot to pick up Adam and it's as though I have failed every test that would give me the "Mother of the Year Award". We have to go to Johor for Christmas now and spend time with his family or I shall look like the arch-enemy of the Malay race. Oh dear, why is he such a tyrant?'

'He will calm down, but he'll hold a grudge for ages, I can guarantee that. I suggest you do go, play nice, lick the mother-in-law's toenails and then come back and be totally indispensable to him. Show him you are the perfect ideal of a wife, the trophy wife that will make him the envy of all. What about your New Year party? Is that still on?'

'Too right,' Edie took another reckless gulp, enjoying the fiery feeling radiating through her bones. 'I have a new Scottish friend, a fellow teacher who I didn't really bond with until today and we've made lots of plans.'

'Well, that's settled,' grinned Amelia. 'I'm delighted about that. I'm getting a dress made especially. It's yellow silk.'

'The colour of the Porsche!' giggled Edie, 'You are incorrigible, Amelia Low!

'I know, Michael is still seething about that. He nearly had a massive coronary when he found out I had bust the whole right wing of his precious car after crashing into the buffalo. Who knew they were built like tanks?'

'I'm surprised you didn't kill it.'

'Poor thing just staggered on to its side and lay there, dazed, then got up and wandered off into the rice paddy. It did look at me with those big limpid brown eyes and I felt a moment of real fear. I didn't want it to die.'

'Lucky for you, or the farmer would have been demanding a huge sum as compensation.'

'I know, Michael was just about ready to kill me for damaging his pride and joy. I was shunned and ignored for ages after the accident.' Amelia's lips twitched, obviously seeing a picture in her mind that amused her.

'What is it, what are you grinning about now?'

'Well, talking about grievances and forgiveness, Michael is the King of Grudges. Although we made up and the car is repaired and we seem to have retained our relationship, it has been touch-and-go. Sometimes, when he's had a skinful of whisky and he thinks I don't know what he's doing, he'll go into the safe and take out the pictures of the crash that the police gave him and he lays them all out on the table, then he has another drink and starts raving about women and all the evils and wrongs in this world that originated from Eve. It is so funny. Hopefully he'll get over it in time, though I do wish I could get rid of the car and the photographs and put an end to the endless self-flagellation'.

Edie and Amelia had another tray of drinks brought through. After the fourth gin and tonic, on a very empty stomach, Edie was unsure of how to get down the stairs, how to drive, or even how to get home. She actually wasn't sure of anything anymore. She could only focus on Amelia if she stayed very still, otherwise her image blurred and became two. It was very confusing. The last time she felt like this was in a flat off the Royal Mile in Edinburgh. 'Have I told you about Bones?' she slurred to Amelia, who seemed to be hovering ghost-like, just out of range.

'We all have bones, Edie, I broke both my clavicles when I fell off the wall bars at school.'

'Poor Bones,' Edie sniffed, 'poor, poor Bones,' and at last the tears came; they had threatened all day but now they fell at the memory of another time, another Edie and an Edie now caught up in a world that was not her own. 'Amelia, could you just hold still so I can at least see one of your faces, I know what I am going to do,' and Edie opened her eyes wide, raising her brows to the sky and presenting Amelia with a view of the entire whites of her eyes, she raised her chin and her whole head fell backwards, a dizzy sick feeling came over her as the night sky with its dazzling stars whizzed around.

'Edie! Wake up! What are you going to do?'

'I need to go to the market, need to buy a papaya,' and she slumped forward face down on the table.

Amelia heard the squeal of brakes from the car park below and she peered over the edge of the balcony. A car door slammed and an agitated Kamal stood looking around till he finally noticed the blonde Australian leaning over the balcony. He bounded up the stairs and soon took in the sorry scene.

'Right, Amelia, let's get her down. Are you able to help or shall I call a bar boy?'

'I can help, she's just a little upset, that's all.'

Kamal looked from one woman to the other and shook his wife's shoulder. 'Wake up, Edie. Can you walk?'

'Sure,' she slurred and shut her eyes again.

Kamal looked at the empty glasses on the table. Could they really have consumed so much gin? Didn't they know the bar boy poured doubles during happy hour?

Somehow the trio got down the stairs and into Kamal's car before he went to sign the chit for the drinks. Frowning, he checked on the two women who were now starting to giggle. He started the engine and drove Amelia home before taking Edie back to their bungalow on Tuaran Hill.

The next morning, he had left for the office before Edie woke up. When she did surface, she came out to the domestic scene of Moy Moy and Adam outside on the veranda. In true Asian fashion she was chasing him around with a bowl, spooning mashed up boiled egg into his mouth as he turned to her, mouth open like a little bird, but only when he was ready.

'Tuan gone?' Edie asked.

'Gone, long time, you want coffee, Mem?'

'Definitely. Do we have any papayas ready just now?'

'Four, you want to eat now?'

'I am going to cook something.'

Moy Moy looked startled. Edie lifted Adam back into his high chair and tried to make him eat his breakfast. Moy Moy sauntered back to the kitchen to make the coffee, nodding her head knowingly as the little boy started to howl and threw his spoon on the floor.

Later, much later, after a day of swallowing painkillers and sleeping during the hottest hours of the day while Adam took his nap and Moy Moy sat in her shack manicuring her toenails, Edie finally emerged and wandered into her kitchen. She leant on her elbows looking down over the town, taking in the view of the sea with its distant ships on the horizon. She shook herself; this would not do. She went to her bedroom and rustled through her things to find the *Australian Women's Weekly* magazine. She flicked through the pages until she found the recipe that might do the trick. It was coq au vin. Not too hard, just tip all the chicken into a frying pan, give it a good sizzle then add mushrooms and onions that had been fried in butter first, then pour in a bottle of red wine and some cornflour and *voila*, into the oven with it. A perfect complement to her *piece de la resistance*, papaya crumble.

Edie's preparations were well underway when Moy Moy appeared with Adam on her hip, closely followed by Timmy the cat. They had been out talking to the gardener who was taking a break from sweeping up dead leaves. 'Perfect!' said Edie, wiping her clean hands on the kitchen towel. 'We'll play with the wooden puzzles now, Moy Moy. Will you make tea for us please, then peel the potatoes. Tuan should be home by five, then I'll finish getting dinner ready. But first cut some potatoes into chips for Adam; he can have a treat tonight to go with his meat balls.'

Mother and son sat on the floor in Adam's room, the puzzle pieces scattered all around them: trains, cars, trees, tractors, fish and aeroplane parts all mixed up. Much to Adam's delight, Edie was diligently doing the puzzle. 'Find me a red car, Adam,' his mother would demand and the little boy would search through the chaos until he came up with the correct piece, 'Now put it in, or shall I?'

'Mummy, do it, I busy.'

'Yes, Mummy likes doing puzzles, now find me a yellow scooter, good boy, you are good at finding things, do you want to put it in?'

'Mummy do it.'

Slowly the floor regained its calm order, until suddenly Adam stood up and ran on his sturdy legs to the sitting room. 'Dada! Dada! Dada!'

Kamal lifted him high, narrowly avoiding the spinning fan above them, and came to stand over Edie who was putting the last pieces into the train puzzle.

'You missed a bit,' and he smiled.

'Mummy did it all!' Adam said proudly.

Edie looked up at the pair and met her husband's eyes. 'Sorry.'

'Me too.'

'I've made dinner, for later, after Adam is in bed.'

'You have? Oh my, I can't believe it. You really must be sorry.'

Edie watched Kamal take Adam down the winding path to the *padang* to look for grasshoppers, Timmy nimbly leaping behind them, pouncing on grasses at the slightest rustle. She turned away and heated up the oil in the pan ready for the chips which Moy Moy had put on a tea towel ready to be cooked.

The kitchen was already filling with the odour of the casserole in the oven and the papaya crumble was cooling on top of the counter. It too emitted the most satisfying smell. Edie tipped some chips into the seething oil, but the resultant sizzling fizzed up in a myriad of angry foam. Tiny drops of the oil rose up and over and splashed on to the open flame. At once the yellow flames flicked up as though alive and in seconds the pan was engulfed.

'Get Tuan! Quick, hurry!'

'OK, Mem.' Moy Moy took in the situation and set off down towards where Kamal and Adam were playing.

Edie stood still. What should she do? No air, cover the flames, keep calm. Turn off the cooker. Vital. She took the tea towel and rung it out under the tap. The flames were still licking up the side of the pan. Slowly, with no sudden draught, she lowered the damp towel over the flames and smothered them. Careful, she thought, the oil is boiling. She removed the singed and burnt cloth and immersed it in water again. She repeated the process. Her eyes were wild and she looked for other means to stop the fire. She took the oven gloves, opened the oven and removed the lid from the casserole and placed it over the burning oil. It worked. The flames died down. Not until then did she pause to breathe. It was out. She opened the windows and let the acrid, smoky fumes disperse.

Meanwhile Kamal, down on the *padang*, saw the unusual sight of Moy Moy strolling towards them. She was taking her time; she seemed to be humming and looking around at the evening sky which was already suffused in pink and apricot light. 'Moy Moy! Is everything all right?' Kamal shouted.

'Fire, Tuan, fire in kitchen. Mem said get Tuan, quick, hurry!'

'What!' He gestured to the amah to look after little Adam before running back up the hill towards the house. Puffing from the exertion, he found Edie sitting on the back step of the kitchen, her head resting on her arms. Kamal took in the burnt material in the sink, the black sticks floating on the oil, and deduced what had happened. He was overcome with admiration; he knew she was brave and he knew she was capable of emerging herself in a new country and culture but now he knew she had an inner strength, she was self-reliant. How many local girls could have coped as she did? They would have panicked, run away, called for someone else to help. But not Edie. He felt choked with gratitude. 'Well done, my precious girl, you did well,' was all he could say, but his heart was overflowing. From the oven there came a different smell, wonderfully rich, of chicken and wine and gravy. 'You did all this too?' he gestured to the casserole still in the oven.

'I did, I wanted to say sorry properly.'

Later that evening, as the candles flickered on the table and the wine glowed blood-like in their glasses, the couple pushed aside their empty plates and held hands.

'Papaya crumble, now there's a first,' smiled Kamal. 'Who knew it would taste so good?'

'The East meets the West.' She was thrilled with her attempts this evening, and was now actually looking forward to spending Christmas in Johor, in a Malay, Muslim village where there would be no tree or stockings or anything for little Adam. Perhaps next year? He would be older then, but for now, she was happy to be close to Kamal again. It had been a turbulent twenty-four hours, but there had been some sort of compromise between the two. After all, the New Year party was still going ahead. She smiled triumphantly into the darkness.

As Edie lay in her husband's arms that night, replete from the 'making up' love making, she nestled down and listened to a chichak on the walls, the bull frogs croaking down by the mango tree, and just as sleep overtook her, she wondered what she would wear to the party.

Chapter 19

Edie was exhausted. The short flight back to Kota Kinabalu from Johor seemed interminable as Adam struggled to be free from the seatbelts that held them together. She had sung and read and counted his toes but he remained fractious until the descent and then had screamed throughout the whole landing procedure. Now, safely at home, the two sat cuddled together under the fan reading a *Thomas the Tank Engine* story. She dropped a kiss on her child's floppy black hair, 'Nenek will be missing you, my darling.'

'Nenek,' confirmed Adam. He turned a page of his book and pointed at an engine. Edie smiled as she conjured up an image of Minna visiting her friends in the kampong, her little grandson tottering along beside her. Such visits took hours as there were ducks to see on the river, tame birds in cages, orange cats and kittens to stroke and a hen with fluffy yellow chicks that swarmed about pecking at the grain that Adam was allowed to toss from an old biscuit tin. It had been an idyllic time; Edie had enjoyed visiting her sisters-in-law and sitting in the familiar room with the holy cover on the sofa and the mat from Mecca on the table. Surprisingly she hadn't really given Christmas a thought, but she had enjoyed the Malay curries every day and *ikan bilis* and freshly grated coconut and the whole rigmarole of the cooking process.

Standing framing the doorway, Kamal interrupted her reverie. 'Sarah Campbell is on the telephone for you. Who is she again?'

'She is the deputy head from school, she's Scottish, and she is helping me organise our New Year's Eve party.'

'Hmmm.' Kamal sat with Adam to resume the story while Edie took the call in their bedroom, Timmy immediately making himself comfortable on her lap.

'Hello, Sarah, I'm so glad to be back!'

'At last! We have so much to do, Edie, but I've finished the tablecloths and now we need to go to the market and buy lanterns for the tables. The people you sent invitations to have all replied; we're expecting thirty-five including the British High Commissioner and his wife. You said you have the music?'

'Yes, of course. Are we still planning to mix everyone up, giving each person a new partner for dinner?'

'Amelia has done that. She's made a basket of girls' names, like Juliet, and a basket of matching boys' names, like Romeo. I do hope I'm not paired up with that Italian sea captain's son who is here for the holidays. He doesn't speak a word of English.'

'The Gurkha regiment has confirmed lending us a piper for the New Year but one of us has to collect him and take him back afterwards. It can't be me as Adam is awful at the moment with teething troubles, and I don't really trust Amelia since she is planning to enjoy herself, if you know what I mean.'

'Yes, so it's me then, that's fine. I won't drink too much anyway as I shall be busy organising the food. The golf club has agreed to do three curries but I thought we can manage the rice and puddings ourselves.'

'OK, Sarah, let's meet this afternoon at the yacht club and we can talk again. I'll get hold of Amelia and we can all go to the market tomorrow for the lanterns and some orchids for the tables.' Edie put down the telephone. She was back. Moy Moy and the gardener had better get the house and garden ship-shape for the best New Year's Eve party ever. She looked out of the window at the area designated for the tables and chairs. Fallen frangipani blossoms dotted the rough grass where they would dance the Eightsome Reel and see in the New Year under the stars, but she was afraid of the red ants. Maybe she should see if there was any ant killer in the market; there was just so much to think about.

Finally, the big night arrived. Kamal had spent the afternoon with Derek Campbell and the gardener setting out the tables on loan from the sports club. Sarah lovingly placed her home-made batik cloths over each one, transforming the plywood tops into a dining experience worthy of a High Commissioner. As night fell, Adam splashed in his bath then demanded a final reading of *Thomas the Tank Engine* before falling into a fitful sleep with the help of a large spoonful of Rose Hip Syrup. Moy Moy boiled rice while the gardener sliced bananas into small bowls. Edie and Kamal laid out their clothes and showered and preened and emerged as strangers to themselves in their elegant evening attire.

Appraising his wife in her sheath of white satin, Kamal grinned suggestively, 'I wonder if we have time?' Her long hair grazed her shoulders and the red lipstick transformed her usual pale pallor. She was radiant.

No, darling, even though you look as suave as any mannequin in the Globe Silk Store in Kuala Lumpur!' she laughed. 'Try to loosen up a bit, I think the trousers are meant to lose their creases!' She giggled at him, but inwardly her stomach was going through some violent backward flips at the sight of her very sexy husband. She hadn't really looked at him like that for a long time.

First to arrive were Amelia in yellow silk, her home-made Pavlova dessert held aloft like a floating offering, and Michael, bearing two rattan baskets which he handed to Kamal. 'The guests' name tags,' he announced, raising his eyebrows as he did so.

Amelia grinned at the look on both men's face and disappeared into the kitchen before promptly returning to Edie's side. 'What IS she wearing?' she gasped.

'Who?'

'Moy Moy.'

'I don't know, she's been sulking in her hut, perhaps because the waiters have taken over her domain.'

'Well, I suggest you come and look,' Amelia took her friend's arm and propelled her towards the kitchen.

'Why, Moy Moy,' Edie's eyes widened in surprise. 'You look very nice.'

'Moy Moy wearing good apron, got from Mem McKenzie, lot of years ago. You like?'

'I do,' spluttered Edie, eyes agog. 'And you have a new dress?' Edie squinted at the black crepe dress that had been adjusted to fit her amah's ample frame. The apron, embroidered with purple and orange pansies, was held in place by thin straps which strained to meet at the back in a meagre bow. Moy Moy had curled her normally straight hair. She was practically unrecognisable. Edie hugged her, 'You look so pretty, thank you for wearing your special clothes tonight.'

'Moy Moy knows lot about parties. I go now and hand out drinks?'

'Maybe you should just arrange the food on the big table for now? The waiters have the drinks all under control.' Edie was at a loss as to what else to say. She just hoped that Adam wouldn't wake up; he'd be terrified at this apparition that had once been his beloved Moy Moy. She returned to the lounge to see that Sarah and Derek had just arrived, each carrying two bowls of trifle full of mangoes and decorated with passion fruit.

Sarah was wearing a lacy blue empire-style gown. 'I brought my ballet shoes,' she said, somewhat smugly. 'I didn't really fancy dancing in bare feet out on the grass.'

'More to the point,' said Kamal, 'have you parked next to ours, as you'll have to get away to fetch the piper later?'

'Aye, we drove straight up,' interjected Derek, 'but the others are parking down in the *padang*. Shall I put on some music to set the tone?'

Kamal stepped forward, rather stiffly, his bow tie holding his neck straight. 'Let me show you where I've set the music up. I finally managed to get the speakers wired up this afternoon after you left.'

Amelia rushed up, 'Quick! Where are the name tags? Some people are coming now.' She spotted the baskets and rushed to the veranda steps to make sure that each guest selected their party persona. 'Hello, lovely to see you, please choose a name!' She laughed as she pinned Robin Hood onto Alistair's jacket. 'Welcome, Robin, now you must search for your maid Marion!'

The lounge soon filled up and the waiters they'd employed from the golf club circulated with white and red wine, beer and juices. The spirits were lined up on the sideboard, with large ice boxes full of sodas for mixing. Crystal glasses stood in regimented lines. People were laughing, meeting other guests not usually from their own social circles, enjoying the novelty of such a gathering.

Edie came forward as she saw Amelia with the ambassador and his wife. 'Hello, welcome,' she said, wondering whether she should curtsy. She noticed that Sir Anthony was impeccably dressed, smooth silver hair, such presence, but his wife... Now, she was not what Edie expected at all. Lady Agnes was in a green and black batik caftan. A little crumpled. Had she ironed it? Edie imagined her ladyship would be totally camouflaged once they went outside to the garden. She looked down at Agnes's sandals and noticed that the lady's toenails were like blunt squares. Edie contrasted them to Moy Moy's scarlet toenails which were filed to dangerous points. She shook herself, what was she doing, thinking of this now?

Sir Anthony chose Henry VIII and Lady Agnes immediately laughed uproariously, 'How appropriate, dear, I am actually Anthony's third wife! Let's hope I last a while longer and am not destined for the chop just yet.'

Enthusiastically she pushed her hand into the basket and pulled out Olive Oyl. 'Perfect, I was hoping for a bit of fun,' and she strode forward into the throng to look for Popeye.

Edie smiled at the High Commissioner, 'I think you will only get the choice of one of your wives tonight, Sir, and I'm not sure who she will be.'

'Oh, what a pity, I'd have liked to share my evening with all six, now that would have been some party!' and he sailed off, his eyes darting around the ladies' bosoms for a sign of their identification.

'Definitely not what I expected,' giggled Edie. 'Are we nearly all here?'

'Only four more names to go,' Amelia jiggled the baskets, and took a large gulp of her red wine. 'So far so good.'

The party moved out to the garden. The night was warm, the crickets sang in time with the music and the newly paired couples sat under a crescent moon. Kamal as Popeye sat with his Olive Oyl, and Edie as Cleopatra sat with Mark Anthony, alias Tony Peterson from the Chartered Bank. The curries were good, conversation and wine flowed. Eventually the plates were cleared and people sat by the lantern light, a little apprehensive about the next item on the agenda: the Scottish dancing, out here in the garden. Kamal changed the music and suddenly the pounding beat of the drums and bagpipes transformed the sedentary guests to take to the grass. Edie and Sarah marshalled them into their places. 'Let's just do a walk through first,' commanded the women, falling into their roles as schoolteachers. 'Hold hands and we shall walk round for eight, then back for eight, come along Popeye, hold your partner's hand and mind her toes,' Edie called out the instructions and somehow the dance got completed. Red faced and very hot they lined up again for more; it was all intoxicating and the music lifted them up and before they knew it, it was eleven o'clock.

'Sarah!' Edie shouted. 'Get going, you have to fetch the piper, he's expecting you at eleven-thirty.'

'Yes, I know, I'm on my way. Only had a few wines so I should be fine.' Sarah got into her car and headed off to the barracks where the handsome Gurkha soldier stood ready, complete in full uniform, very excited about this new experience. He held his bagpipes in their case. 'Hello! I hope you haven't been waiting too long? What is your name?'

'No, Ma'am, only a few minutes, and my name is Gurung. Happy to be of service.'

When they arrived back at the party, Gurung was not quite so relaxed. The lady's driving was more appropriate for the race track, he thought. When Sarah offered him a drink, he shunned the cold water on the tray and selected a generous measure of Johnny Walker instead.

'Very good choice, have another when you are ready as we still have time until the witching hour!' Sarah laughed happily and left Gurung by the detritus of the dining room table. Sipping his drink, he looked at the empty plates and the half-full bowls of creamy desserts.

'Have some,' Amelia offered. 'Do you like pudding?'

'Yes ma'am, I do, and I don't mind if I do, thank you very much.'

Edie checked her wrist watch; it was a quarter to twelve. 'Amelia, where is Sarah, we need her to get her piper in position.'

'Look, they're over there, she's helping him down the veranda steps. What on earth is wrong with him? He was fine when I saw him gobbling up the pavlova.'

Gurung fumbled with his bagpipe case while attempting to follow Sarah to his position beside the hibiscus bush. It was very dark; the lanterns did not exude a lot of light and no one had told him about the monsoon drain that surrounded the bungalow. He found it by himself.

'Oh my God! Get out!' shrieked Sarah. 'What on earth are you doing down there, get up. You need to get piping! Don't you know what time it is?'

'Time to get going, I say,' said the poor Gurkha. 'I feel a bit sick.'

'Hurry up, get up, are these your bagpipes? Try and sober up, this is not what I had in mind. Can you walk straight?'

'Yes, yes, of course. I am a soldier; I can parade when I want. Let's go.' As he blew into the bag, a stray screech escaped.

'Well, that sounds about right,' said Sarah, her Scottish ancestry rising to the fore. 'Away and play.'

Gurung took in the scene before him; his cheeks puffed out and he blew, his fingers dancing over the chanter as the howling melancholy of the music filled the last few minutes of the year. Edie listened to a medley of tunes she had heard so many times on Edinburgh's Royal Mile. She looked around at her guests who all seemed enthralled with the novelty of the occasion.

It was Sir Anthony, the High Commissioner who broke the spell. He ran forward into the circle and gestured to the piper, 'Stop! Stop! Desist! *Berhenti*!'

Gurung stopped piping, nodding at the man who was standing with his wrist watch held in his hand.

'Get ready, everyone, 10,9,8,7,6,5,4,3,2,1. Happy New Year!'

Immediately there were greetings and kissing and shaking of hands, and, to everyone's surprise, the Italian teenager fired a party popper. Edie and Kamal held hands, Derek put his arm around Sarah, and Michael Low looked over at his dazzling Amelia who was smiling happily at the High Commissioner. He walked over to them, and took his wife by the hand, and whispered, 'You are incorrigible, and you are mine. Don't forget it.'

Gurung waited until all the couples had kissed and shaken hands and kissed again. Someone gave him another drink. It was very nice. Edie elbowed her way over to the drunken piper to remind him of his duty. 'Auld Lang Syne,' she hissed.

'Yes ma'am, coming up,' and the sounds of the familiar tune prompted the gathering to form a circle and hold hands.

Should auld acquaintance be forgot,
And never brought to mind?
Should auld acquaintance be forgot,
For auld land syne?

Lady Agnes was quite overcome by it all and hugged Edie tenderly. 'What a wonderful party, my dear. Much better than last year in Shanghai.'

Before people started to leave, Sarah had one more task to perform, and that was to return Gurung back to his barracks. 'Come on,' she ordered. 'Home, for you; here is a little tip on top of your wages, you did us proud,' and she stuffed a twenty ringgit note into his uniform pocket.

Gurung nervously got back inside the lady's car. Immediately she stepped on the accelerator and the car shot off down the drive, round the corner and on to the main road. Gurung shut his eyes, but that made it worse as the whisky was making his head spin. Somehow, they arrived at the barracks and she went round to his side of the car to help him out. She got back behind the wheel and flew off, leaving him standing on the pavement. Gurung was in shock. Where were his precious bagpipes? He ran out on the road and waved frantically until Sarah made a U-turn. She slowed down and leant out. 'What now?'

'You have hijacked my bagpipes, Ma'am.'

'Oh, for goodness' sake, why didn't you say?'

Gurung opened the passenger door and grabbed his case.

'Right, I'm off now, Cheerio!' The car screeched into reverse and for a few seconds the piper was pinned against the wall with some force. Again, Sarah drove off at high speed, totally oblivious to the poor man's suffering.

'That was close,' Gurung muttered, 'a proud Gurkha soldier being crushed like a mosquito by a woman. Lucky no one to witness.' He limped into his compound, looking forward to a quieter life. Meanwhile Sarah headed back to the party, singing loudly as she drove. It did occur to her she might be going a little fast, so slowed the car down to a walking pace. Best not to draw attention to myself, she thought.

Much later, when all the guests had left, Kamal and Edie sat on their veranda, looking up at the stark black outlines of the rain trees, dramatic against the breaking dawn. The sky was painted in golden streaks, whimsically changing colour as the night receded. They heard the scream of monkeys and the high-pitched squawking of birds, and they acknowledged that they were home in the world that they had chosen.

Edie was happy. She had no yearnings for the cold Scottish hillsides, nor the bleak grey tenements of her childhood home. She was here, with her husband and son. What would the New Year bring?

Chapter 20

Adam Shariff stood for a moment, drinking in the vast sandy beach. In the distance he saw the shimmering haze of the blue horizon. The sea met the shore in gentle waves and he surveyed the seemingly endless sand, thinking that it would be excellent for running and running, free from his parents and his five-year-old sister. At seven he had grown tall. His face with large brown eyes and compressed lips gave the impression of a boy that gave life a lot of consideration. He had welcomed his little sister Tara with suspicion and distaste at first, but as she had grown and her sense of humour developed, he found that he had a life-long ally. Now the two were bonded as though two parts of a broken rock had miraculously been put back together. 'Can I run?' he asked.

Kamal nodded. 'Go, boy, but wait for us before you go in the sea; there might be fierce currents.'

Adam took off as though released from a bow and he didn't stop until he came to where the waves frothed and bubbled on the hard sand, making lines like the contours on a map. All around him little crabs burrowed to safety as he tried to step on them. It was a stimulating game.

Adam was excited to be in Kuantan, the biggest city in the state of Pahang. He was thrilled to be away from school for the two-week break and he really liked the car his father had borrowed from Grandpa Hassan. It was an old Alpha Romeo in a bright red colour. The two-hundred-and-forty-mile drive from Johor seemed to go on forever and he had never seen his father drive in such an exciting way before. With the windows down, he and Tara had stared, mesmerised, at the never-ending rubber and oil plantations, when suddenly his father accelerated at top speed to pass some logging lorries. His mother screamed, of course, but Adam loved it.

The family had rented a house from some rich man in Kuala Lumpur, a colleague of his father's, and it had jungle all around it. A turning off the main road took them along an old laterite track and his mother seemed quite anxious by the loneliness of it all. When they eventually arrived, Adam and Tara had raced through the house, exploring the rooms and the garden outside. A veranda encircled the house and all the rooms had doors that could open on to it. Chairs and pot plants were placed outside and the family had eaten breakfast at a little table, enjoying the antics of the monkeys that were leaping about in the trees.

'We'd better keep everything locked up,' Kamal had advised, 'those monkeys will be down here as fast as lightning to eat anything we leave unattended.'

'They can have my sandwich,' said Tara. 'I hate tuna, I just want nasi goreng, or rice with soy sauce.'

'Me too,' agreed Adam. 'Why can't we have nasi goreng, Mummy?'

'Because I haven't brought all the things we need to make it. Besides we can go to the restaurant after we go to the beach tomorrow, that will be nice.' Edie looked questioningly to her husband.

'Sounds like a good plan, I saw lots of eating places as we drove by.'

The children then ran off to continue exploring and had gingerly opened a large outside store cupboard at the back. It was quite dark, spider webs were thick and sticky, but Adam ventured inside.

'What's in there?' asked Tara, safely keeping her distance, 'I hope nothing with black legs and big teeth?'

'No! Come and see, it's OK, just some cobwebs, but look - lots of bicycles! This one might be just right for you, and I like this one. I think it's a Chopper. I've always wanted one of these. Let's get them out and try them!'

They wheeled them onto the track and Tara immediately fell off hers. At five she was still learning, but Adam was proud of his cycling ability and sped off into the trees. He was pedalling well, concentrating on avoiding the potholes and rocks, when he gradually realised that the heavy tree canopy was blocking the sunlight. It seemed to have got dark very quickly and Adam sensed that he was not alone. He noted the ferns and thick vines and the carpet of fallen brown leaves. What might be lurking in there? The jungle seemed quieter all of a sudden. With a mild sense of panic, he turned around and pedalled back to the house as fast as he could, only to find that Tara had abandoned her bike and gone back inside where she felt safe.

*

After a good night's rest, Kamal suggested that they leave the confines of the jungle for the day and explore the vast beaches along Kuantan's coastline where they could go swimming. So, there they were; Edie was busy laying out a coconut mat and putting out the flasks of tea and juice for their picnic. They had found a shady spot amongst some casuarina trees which seemed like a good place to escape from the full glare of the morning sun. The tide was nearly out and Kamal was standing like a sentinel watching his son who had already run down to the water, but Tara was still struggling into her swimsuit. Adam soon grew tired of being on his own and ran back towards his family.

'Come on, Tara, hurry up, I'm going to dig up those crabs and there are lots of cuttlefish bones. Those are squid, aren't they, Mummy? We can make boats. Can I have a drink?' He finally drew breath.

Edie handed him a beaker of juice. 'Daddy has just gone to that stall over there to buy some rambutans. We can have a nice snack later.'

'Yes, but come on, Tara, let's go, you can bring the bucket.'

Tara finished adjusting her swimsuit and gingerly placed her bare feet on the debris of blackened seaweed and shells that had collected by the grass line. She picked her way over the crunchy surface before finally running after her fleet-footed brother.

'Look, Adam, what's that over there near the water's edge? Let's go and see what it is.'

The children immediately altered their course and came to an abandoned clay pot, sitting proudly on the sand. It was round, flat at the bottom and tapered to a wide lipped opening at the top. There were no markings that they could see.

'What is it? What's it doing here?'

Adam peered inside. 'I don't know. It's full of seawater and it looks like there are sticks in there.'

'Do you think it's a cooking pot?' Tara suggested. 'It's a nice pot, maybe Mummy would like it, she could plant a flower in it.'

'I'll tip out the water and all this rubbish,' said Adam, with a sense of importance. He found it quite heavy but managed to roll the pot over and tip the contents onto the beach. He imagined the sticks inside were probably from someone's idea of a fire or barbecue.

'You left some in,' said Tara, helpfully. 'This one looks like a flat stick.'

'We don't need the sticks. Let's wash the pot in the sea.' Adam heaved it up in his thin arms; it was not so heavy anymore but it was still awkward to carry into the water.

From the picnic spot, Kamal watched the children fussing with some kind of container at the water's edge. 'I think I'll go and see what they've found, it looks interesting.' He strolled over the sand and stopped short when he saw the object that the children were washing. 'Hi kids, I see you've found a nice pot. What was in it?'

'Just sticks, Daddy, that's all.' Tara said as she tried to dig for a burrowing crab with her hands, to no avail.

'Where did you put them?' Kamal asked Adam.

'Over there on the sand,' the boy pointed. 'We just tipped them out. Mummy could plant a papaya seed in it, or a pineapple, like we did in school.'

Kamal sighed. He looked around, there was no one about, only the lady selling rambutans. Perhaps it would be all right. He knew that the bones, for that is what they were, would have been put in that pot after a cremation. Probably a long time ago, or they might have fallen off a boat; the bones had obviously been destined for the sea, one way or another. Now however, the pot seemed fated to come with them. 'Yes, we'll take it back with us. It will be our special garden pot.' Although his tone was optimistic, Kamal did feel a wave of apprehension; he could almost hear his mother and her old Malay cronies whispering about the curses and the *hantu* that travelled from the spirit world. Had the children disturbed something from the other world? He shook his head, what am I thinking? I'm getting as bad as she is.

That evening, when the sun had set, Edie sat with the children on the veranda of the holiday house. They were all showered and clean, their beds were ready, and Kamal had sprayed the rooms. Around them, the jungle was waking up and Edie knew that here in Pahang it was still dense and full of creatures and people she had no knowledge of.

'I didn't like riding my bike in the trees, I thought there were eyes everywhere,' said Adam.

'You were right to turn back,' his mother reassured him. 'Best to go altogether, I think. You know that Daddy will be staying on in Pahang for a while after we go home, don't you? He has work to do with the logging company.'

'Will he cut down trees?' asked Tara. 'Will they put them on those big lorries?'

'No, dear, he will be representing a client who has the right to some land. They want to clear all the forest to plant other things.'

'Like what?' persisted Tara.

'Well, like rubber trees and oil palms. They want to cut down the trees because lots of people want to buy the wood.'

'Wood makes paper,' said Adam.

'And you do know that when we go home, Daddy will be working for a while in another country, not very far away, but he will have a new house and we can go and visit. The country is called Sarawak, right next door to our country which is called Sabah. The town he will be living in is called Kuching.'

'Kuching means cat in Malay,' said Tara. 'Moy Moy told me.'

The three of us will go back to school,' continued Edie, 'but the next holiday we'll all go to Kuching and maybe go on an adventure. There is a river there that takes you right into the jungle. We are so lucky as Daddy knows the man that can arrange it.'

'We are having an adventure now,' said Adam. 'Listen to all those noises; we have never been this close to the jungle before. I hope no snakes get into the house. They can swallow you whole, you know,' and he stared at Tara.

'Mummy, make him stop,' whimpered the little girl.

'Ssssh, time for bed. Come, let's get you settled and under the mosquito nets.' She looked at them fondly, 'You have had so much sun and exercise today and I don't want you to worry about anything, we are all safe in this big strong house. Sleep well.' Edie kissed their dark heads and let herself out of the room.

Morning broke with the warbling of wood pigeons and the cackle of some bird, high in the tree tops. Adam freed himself from the mosquito net and ran through to the lounge. All was quiet, his parents were still asleep. He gingerly opened the door and stepped out of the house. The clay pot was lying by their discarded sandals at the bottom of the veranda. Beside it in the sandy soil he saw a footprint of an animal. It was huge. Adam looked about. A previous feeling of not being alone caused a shiver of fear to run through him. His eyes darting about, he slowly climbed back up the steps to the veranda and ran into his parents' bedroom.

'Daddy, quick, come and see! A huge cat has been looking at our pot! It was so close, quick! Come and look.'

His mother clutched her dressing gown around her and went very pale. His father bent down to examine the giant paw print, definitely bigger than the normal pussy cats that they knew.

Tara emerged sleepily from their bedroom. 'What's going on? I was dreaming, a really scary dream. I dreamt a tiger was looking at me through the window.'

Edie let out a gasp and gathered the little girl in her arms. 'Time to go?' she pleaded with her husband. 'We could find somewhere in the Cameron Highlands for the next week; maybe there will be more people about up there!'

Chapter 21

Dear Joy,

Here we are, back in KK, but my heart is heavy. It's Saturday morning and I'm sitting here at the yacht club and the children are playing on the sand with their friends. Gaya Island is bobbing on the horizon, beckoning me to skim over to its salty white beaches and palm-fringed shorelines. It is just too romantic, but Kamal has been posted down to Kuching in Sarawak (land of the head-hunters and home of the famous Rajah Brooke), coming home for the odd weekend only.

I miss him, but I must tell you about the incident on our holiday in Kuantan, up in Pahang State in West Malaysia. It was just too scary. We were on the beach and the children found an old pot full of sticks which Adam then tipped out on to the sand. Anyway, we brought the pot home with us, but Kamal told me later that the sticks were actually cremated bones, and of how his mother used to warn about curses if people interfered with the afterlife. I thought nothing about it, until the next morning that is, when we found tiger prints all around the house we were staying in. The creature had even been on the veranda. Poor Tara must have awoken in the night and actually seen it watching her through her window. I tried to reassure her that it was only a dream.

Well, we left quite hastily after that. Kamal mentioned it to the owner of the house, who confirmed that there'd been sightings of an adult male along a river bank further upcountry. Adam told us that he felt he was being watched when he was riding his bicycle through the trees, so perhaps it had picked up his scent. Well, we brought that pot (presumably a cremation pot) back home, and Timmy the cat stalked around it, sniffed it, then suddenly hissed at it. It was so unlike him. I've now filled the pot with a tree fern and hidden it behind the bougainvillaea shrubs out of harm's way!

Anyway, the children and I are back at school. Adam is doing well with Sarah Campbell. He absolutely adores her. I don't have Tara in my class now as I have a Primary 2 this year, but her teacher told me that Tara is not academic as she just wants to draw all the time and has little interest in letters or numbers. I quietly refrained from comment. The child is a natural scientist; she has everything classified and arranged in her bedroom, and has a wealth of knowledge about local trees and butterflies. At five, I am not too worried about her.

Adam misses his father so much. Kamal suggested we fly to Kuching for the summer holidays, instead of him coming home.

Edie put down her pen and took a sip of her lime juice that was forming puddles of condensation on the table. She saw that Kate and Alistair Davidson had just arrived at the club and waved them over, while their daughter Felicity headed straight down to the beach and started playing with Adam and Tara.

'Hello, Edie, how are you, what's new?' Alistair pulled up a chair. 'We're not disturbing you, are we?'

'I'm fine, Alistair, I'm just feeling a bit sorry for myself with Kamal away so much, but I'm very pleased to see you two. And no, you are not disturbing me, I was just writing to my friend Joy in Edinburgh - I was trying to think how to explain to her what Kamal is actually doing in Sarawak. How do I condense into a few sentences the legal battles arising from the destruction of the rainforest and the impact on the indigenous people who depend on it for their way of life?'

'Being seven thousand miles away, I doubt if she could even begin to comprehend what's going on here anyway. By the way, how is Kamal getting on?'

'Well,' Edie frowned, 'it's early days. He's made a few journeys by longboat to remote regions upriver and he's even stayed in a Dayak longhouse. He's met many people who have been displaced by the dam being built at Batang Ai.'

'Yes, and another dam is being planned at Bakun. Meanwhile, logging companies are buying up land leases as fast as they can, no doubt assisted by corrupt officials. The government keeps reducing the length of the logging licences, but the shorter they make them, the greater the pressure to maximise profit and further devastate the rainforest.'

'It's not only people that are being displaced either, is it? What about the flora and fauna that will be lost forever? It's all so depressing.'

'It is very depressing. As you know, my work as an ophthalmologist involves quite a bit of travelling upriver. It's shocking how the forests of Borneo are rapidly disappearing before our eyes; trees are being felled at a rate unprecedented in human history, logged, burned and the land cleared ready for replanting with oil palm.'

'Kamal says it's the same in Pahang. He's visited some of the indigenous people there, helping develop a legal strategy for the consequences of logging.'

'Let's just hope something positive comes out of all the destruction, but as we all know, officials have a tendency to let power take over their better judgment, especially when the great god of money is involved.'

Kate walked over the grass and placed a tray with two beers and a fresh lime juice on the table. 'Hi, Edie, my goodness, you two look very serious, what are you talking about?'

'Hi Kate, we're just discussing the devastation of the rainforest here in Borneo.'

'Yes, well, I doubt if you have a solution to that.'

'None of us do, except the obvious of course – stop destroying this magnificent rainforest!' Alistair wiped his brow and picked up his beer. 'It's a double-edged sword, really, as it always is with development. Obviously better roads and transport routes and a better electricity supply for everyone is important, but as for the long-term effects of such so-called progress after centuries of a way of life are destroyed, only time will tell. What about the Dayaks, what about the environment, what about the wild life etc. etc, etc…? So good luck to Kamal in trying to salvage something good from this mess.'

'What does he say about it all, Edie?' Kate asked.

'Well, he's really only just started his cases in Kuching, but I understand that several thousand or so Dayaks who have been settled in Sarawak for hundreds of years have had to be rehoused after their longhouses were destroyed. Thousands of hectares of land were flooded to make room for the dam construction. It seems that each family gets a house and some land to farm or grow fruit etc., but…' Edie screwed up her eyes against the sun and tried to remember what Kamal had said on the telephone last night. 'This new way of life that's being forced upon them is against the tradition of the longhouse which has always been a communal way of life where people shared the work and the rewards. They have been fairly self-sufficient, making a living from farming, fishing, raising livestock, collecting jungle produce and hunting, but now all that is changing as they are made to adapt to a new way of life.'

'And in time, surely the young people will move away, won't they?' said Kate. 'The attraction of the towns and cities will be only hours away by motorbike or car, and only old folk will be left.'

'Oh dear,' replied Edie. 'We are being gloomy, but you are right; although the road to the dam's reservoir has been improved, it still takes four to five hours to drive from Kuching to the dam site. Not exactly a speedy trip.'

'Enough!' Kate put her hands up, 'Let's talk about something else; for now, let's just enjoy our drinks. Edie, do you and the children want to come out to the islands with us tomorrow?'

The sea hardly seemed to move as the morning drifted on. Only soft frothy ripples marked the incoming tide. The ocean glittered and far away a small boat cut across the horizon. The children got up from where they were scooping out a maze of channels in the sand and as one they ran down to the water with their buckets to test their great feat of engineering. Edie looked at her abandoned letter. How to connect Joy with all of this? Far away, on a cold morning in Edinburgh, her friend would be going to school, head down against the icy sleet, and cars would be throwing up slush as they sped past, unaware of the splattered legs they left behind them.

Chapter 22

Kamal was satisfied with his meeting with Datuk Jason Wong at the newly opened Hilton Hotel in Kuching, the capital city of Sarawak. The two men had discussed the legal disputes arising from the new dam construction at Batang Ai. After being ensconced in the airconditioned lounge of the hotel he decided to stretch his legs by taking a stroll to a barbers' shop at Padungan. Settled in the worn black chair, he closed his eyes and relaxed, all the while trying not to think about the not-so-clean comb, nor the barber's fat belly hovering around him. Still, the neck-and-shoulders massage was very welcome and he felt good. After paying the meagre price of a few ringgits, he wandered along the river.

With the sun burning his head and back, he was relieved to come across an empty bench beneath the towering flame trees and sat down to absorb the scene around him. It was mesmerising watching foliage being swept down towards the sea. The current was strong. Sampans powered only by a small motor, their passengers tightly clutching their possessions, criss-crossed the wide brown river. Kamal ran his fingers through his newly-cut hair and it occurred to him that he was beginning to look like his father, his hairline receding like the tide and those silver strands multiplying by the day. He was enjoying his relocation to the Kuching branch of his law firm, and the satisfaction of being able to liaise first hand with the local personnel. The work was challenging but he found that he was good at negotiating between the different factions in the dam project. Edie was content to stay on in Kota Kinabalu for she loved her job and the children were settled. She didn't want them moved until the inevitable separation that would occur when Adam and Tara needed to go to boarding school in Singapore, there being no high school in Kota Kinabalu.

Kamal considered having a curry in India Street and the deeply satisfying smell of spices enticed him over to the covered walkways of the Old Bazaar and Gambier Street where traders were selling batik clothes, knick-knacks and ancient relics of the indigenous people. He wandered along and sat down in a simple restaurant with only six plastic tables. An array of dishes was arranged in large aluminium containers; curries, vegetables, boiled eggs. A large covered pot presumably contained rice. Today it was the roti paratha he yearned for, the springy dough freshly made and fried on a hotplate out on the pavement, and a dish of hot curried chicken on the side. He placed his order and waited under the frenetic rotations of a single fan.

Kamal's law firm had initially rented him a small serviced apartment in Kuching; it was quite modest and set back off a busy road. He relished the freedom of spending the evening away from the office and his colleagues. Hotels were all right for short visits, but the apartment was more convenient, especially since he was enjoying his bachelor status away from the family. It had also been ideal for entertaining a lively bar hostess now and again, very discreetly of course and surely it did no harm. A man needed to relax, have a bit of fun. His train of thought led to his current passion, but this time the girl in question was becoming an obsession. She was fiery hot, insatiable; he could not stop thinking about her and he knew he was playing a dangerous game. Their liaison had begun a few months ago, after she joined the law office as a junior secretary. Kamal had found that he was helping her more than strictly necessary to familiarise herself with office procedures and so on. 'Don't worry about that, why don't we do that together? I need to refresh my letter to the minister. Why don't we go and have dinner after work?' Her name was Rose. She was very demure, reminding him of a doe, so shy and delicate with long tapering fingers that tapped on her keyboard. Her lashes framed black pools of onyx, but he swallowed as he remembered the night he had told her that he was letting his serviced apartment go. He could visualise her looking at him over the candlelight, her eyes wet with unshed tears. 'It'll be fine, Rose, we'll still be able to meet at the Aurora or the Holiday Inn, but you know I had to take the offer of the new house as my family are coming over soon. They need a bigger place for the holidays and I was lucky to get the chance to rent this house as the owners work away and will be gone for a year. It won't be for the two of us, Rose, we can't meet there, but we could arrange trips away, maybe to Sibu or Brunei.' This was no small indiscretion, he knew that. This beautiful Malay girl touched bass chords deep within his soul, and when he was away from her every girl with long black hair swinging down to her waist made his heart beat erratically. I am besotted, he thought, I am going to get a heart attack with this one. Kamal hoped that Taj, his Kuching counterpart on Jalan Chan Chin Ann, was none the wiser and if he did suspect he hoped that he would keep silent. No need for Edie to find out.

Kamal finished and paid for his simple meal then headed out to the bustling street. He sighed and looked over to the northern side of the Sarawak River to Fort Margherita, built by Charles Brooke in 1879 and named after his wife. He remembered visiting there with Edie and the children back in 1985. They had taken a sampan across the river and scrambled up the hill to the fort. Edie had read every piece of history framed on the wall, calling out for them all to listen and learn about the first white Rajah, James Brooke. He smiled as he recollected his wife on that day, her face flushed and perspiring as she fanned herself with a tourist guide book. 'My goodness,' she'd exclaimed, 'he was an Englishman and arrived here on a schooner and teamed up with the local Rajah Mudah. He was promised the whole kingdom if he helped suppress the local revolts. And he did. With his mighty weapons and guns, he quashed the local rebellion and so became the Rajah of Sarawak. His family ruled for the next one hundred years. My goodness, that is quite something. And look here, Tara, here is Margaret, the wife of the second Rajah, Charles Brooke. She was the Ranee of Sarawak, yet she gave up her crinolines and wore local Malay clothes, just like me! Well, I gave up my jeans, so not quite the same.'

Kamal watched a huge log float past on the swirling river. Gazing at the white fort he remembered climbing up the spiral staircase and looking over the crenellated battlements at the modern town that had since sprung up. Once British soldiers would have surveyed the river for pirates from this spot, and later Japanese soldiers had held the fort during their time of occupation in the second world war. He could see Edie, always the effervescent Edie, painting a vivid picture of the history of the fort to the children. Images of their unique wedding when she wore the sarong kebaya with the extra piece of sheeting sewn in to disguise her offending ankles flashed in front of his eyes. So why was he being unfaithful to her? He loved her, there was no doubt about that, and he loved his children. So why? And could he manage to keep his two loves apart? He shook himself; he didn't care for too much introspection. He looked at his watch and knew it was time to go to the airport. His family was arriving in just over an hour. They were his number one priority; Rose would have to wait.

*

Adam and Tara were so excited to be in Kuching again. Daddy had his own house now, and they didn't have to squash into that small serviced apartment he had last time. After landing at Kuching airport, Kamal had driven them to the house a short way out of the city. The flooring downstairs was made from ironwood and polished to a high gloss. Upstairs, the floors were of rich dark parquet. Their own home on Tuaran Hill also had wooden floors, but not hard like this, and Moy Moy was always having to polish and treat them for burrowing creatures like termites. The children chose their rooms and hurled their suitcases onto the beds before taking off to explore the koi carp pool and the small garden at the rear of the property. Papaya trees and pineapple plants were intermingled with *bunga raya*, vibrant and scarlet in the morning sun.

Tara found a fat cat, black with bright yellow eyes, lazing by the storm drain. 'I think it's a relative of the black panther,' she announced, tentatively putting out her hand, and caressing the silky fur. She was rewarded with a deep throbbing purr. 'Feel her, Adam, she is so soft.'

Adam put out his hand and immediately the cat's paw whipped up, its claws striking like a cobra's fangs. The boy pulled back, stunned at the attack and the blood dripping down his fingers. 'What did I do?' he grimaced, trying not to cry, and ran back into the house.

'What happened?' Edie immediately took his hand and led him to her bathroom. She bathed the scratch with disinfectant, and put on a plaster. 'Did you tease her?'

'No, I didn't. She was purring for Tara and I just wanted to pat her. Why did she do that?'

'I don't know, Adam. The Malays have a strong connection with cats and many of the *bomohs* use the cat, tiger or panther as their spiritual guide.'

'What are *bomohs*? I've heard that name before.'

'Witch doctors, or *shaman*.'

'You don't believe in witch doctors do you, Mum?'

'Well, I keep an open mind. They form a huge part of the beliefs of the forest people here in Borneo. Many believe they can help with healing and that they will protect you from bad things.' Edie let her mind wander to Amelia and the story she had related of the latest developments in the ongoing adultery scandal. Apparently, Vincent Wong, the anaesthetist at the hospital, was having an affair with Marianne, the wife of the Australian architect Geoff. Edie and Amelia had suspected that there was something going on but it was not until they had attended a dinner party at Maggie and Joseph Rajah's house that Edie was able to confirm it. She stooped down under the table to retrieve her napkin and seen Vincent Wong's hand disappearing up Marianne's thigh. It was awkward but none of her business and she had averted her eyes. She did feel for his wife Ling who was innocently laughing with Geoff. Later she had relayed the revelation to Kamal who had shown no interest at all and dismissed it. It was not until a month later that Marianne started to get ill. It started with a pain in her shoulder and her arm and she had no appetite. Geoff was not too concerned, thinking she had contracted some small infection, until he came home from work one afternoon and found his wife weeping on the front steps. Amelia had recounted to Edie in horrific detail how the couple had seen a ring of white powder strewn all around their house. Marianne feared that some voodoo curse had been placed upon her and imagined that a doll had been made in her likeness and she would be made to suffer for her involvement with the wronged woman's husband. But how could she explain all this to Geoff? Innocent Geoff who had no idea of the illicit affair that had been going on whilst he was working away, visiting remote sites where buildings he had designed were now under construction. Edie shuddered. It was horribly real. Poor Marianne had discovered a lump in her breast and had flown back to Australia. Geoff had returned with her. No one knew as yet if he would return, or if Marianne would survive. Edie shook herself; there were so many things she could not explain to herself, let alone to her ten-year-old son. Her imagination was running wild but she did have respect for the Dayak's beliefs, and the communion they shared with the animal and spirit kingdom.

'I heard that a *shaman* can act as a go-between between the human world and the supernatural world, and they beat their drums and go into a trance and they believe they can speak to spirits to detect a person's illness.'

'And if they do?' Adam seemed to have forgotten the scratch on his hand. 'What do they do then?'

'Well, I know some tribes, like the Melanau, make a small carved likeness of the person then mark the body where the sickness is, like the head or the stomach, and then they take the effigy and put it into a little carved canoe and sail it off down the river. I suppose they believe in the holy man and have faith that the illness goes away when the boat travels out of sight.'

'So, they are good guys?' asked Adam.

'I believe so. They have the capability to fight against evil forces using the power of the mind.'

'Like Luke Skywalker fighting Darth Vadar?'

'Yes, but many tribes still worship animals that have long been feared by man such as the python, the crocodile, the tiger and the panther.'

'So,' replied Adam, suddenly remembering his sore hand, 'people could believe that bad spirits can live in these dangerous animals?'

'Maybe, if you offended the spirits in any way, but let's not get away with ourselves, a pussy cat scratched you. That is all. She may have a memory of another boy who might not be as kind as you and thought she would take revenge for some past cruelty - who knows? Perhaps you could feed her some tuna tonight and see if she is prepared to forgive you!' Edie put away the thought of that clay pot full of bones they had found on the beach in Kuantan, but she shuddered as she returned the disinfectant and cotton wool to the bathroom.

The summer holiday passed with adventures in the forests and jungle trails. Tara especially liked the visit to see the biggest flower in the world, the rafflesia, and relished its stinky odour that attracted the carrion flies it needed to pollinate it. She cut out pictures from the guide book and pasted them carefully into her scrap book, and drew clever portraits of orangutans and proboscis monkeys they saw whilst visiting the different parks.

'You are clever at drawing, my darling,' Edie was admiring her young naturalist's attempts to capture the muscular bodies of the hairy apes. 'That proboscis monkey looks as though he is wearing tights. It has a fashionable hairy jerkin on the top, pity about his nose but I suppose he might be thought of as quite a dandy in the jungle world.'

Edie kept herself busy and tried not to worry when Kamal was late returning from the office. He seemed distracted. 'I hope they are not working you too hard?' she commented after he had failed to turn up for the evening meal for the second time in a row.

'No, no, it's the new girl, she is a bit slow that's all. I had to show her where to find the correct letters that were needed for references. She hasn't worked in a law office before.'

'That seems odd, don't they need special training - a bit like medical secretaries?' Edie dished out a plate of macaroni cheese that she had reheated.

'Yes, usually, but she is very good at dealing with clients and ministers and so on. Quite a good asset to the office.'

Edie looked suspiciously at her husband as he pulled his chair into the table and made a play at shifting the food around his plate. She said nothing.

*

Towards the end of their stay in Kuching, while the children were reading in their rooms in the heat of the day and Kamal was still not home from the office, Edie finally took the chance to write to her friend in Edinburgh.

Dear Joy,

We have had such a busy week starting yesterday with a whirlwind tour of the Sarawak Natural History Museum. The building's facade is graced with a huge plaster black-and-green Rajah Brooke butterfly. We visited all the anthropology, ethnology, zoology and geology collections and the children were especially enthralled with a giant fur ball that had been removed from a 15-foot man-eating crocodile. It had a dental plate still attached to it. Imagine! There was also a watch that had been removed from its stomach! There were even real human skulls (taken by head-hunters) hanging over an open fire. The history here is quite gruesome.

Then on Tuesday we endured a five-hour car journey to the jetty of the Batang Ai River (where the hydroelectric dam has been built) then a further two-hour journey on a longboat upriver to the middle of nowhere, where the LONG house is situated at Nanga Sumpa. The boat trip was magical, with so many monkeys in the trees screeching at us as we passed. We even saw a python being devoured by a monitor lizard on the banks of the river. The python had got trapped in a fisherman's net, and so of course it was easy pickings for the lizard. It looked horrible! When we finally arrived, we were shown to our rooms (which were very basic but comfortable). Our funny-man guide, Paul, had such a brilliant command of English and later took us over to meet the chief, a gentle soul who offered us rice wine, and we sat and conversed with the many indigenous people who inhabit this longhouse. If a son is away, a chair is suspended on the wall opposite the door to his family's room until he returns. Some of these men have been working in Glasgow, Norway, Germany, often as riggers or roughnecks working on oil rigs. They have all returned to their jungle homes, head-hunters no more, but still wanting to preserve their way of life. How sustainable that is, with TV and temptation, who knows? The younger generation hold the future in their hands. As for us, we slept under our mosquito net, listened to the cicadas and the bullfrogs and in the morning the warbling birds. We woke at dawn to the roosters crowing, and later Tara discovered a scorpion lurking under her travelling bag. She gave a little yelp, but was surprisingly self-contained. To the naked eye, the jungle looks like a myriad of greenness, with no obvious signs of life, just the constant orchestra of cicadas, BUT... at night! Oh, dear Lord.

After some Dutch courage which consisted of two cold beers, we put on our head torches and ventured out along the pathway into the forest. The forest suddenly became alive with a thousand eyes. The torch glare made spiders freeze in their tracks and the stick insects were so ghostly and grotesque. We stayed for a while, mesmerised by the sounds and the fear, and I think we were all glad to retreat back to the relative safety of our wooden longhouse.

And now we must pack up and return to school and Kamal will come back with us for a while. This will be Adam's last year at the International School in KK, before going on to the United World College in Singapore next year.

Edie finished her letter. She had written a positive account of their holiday but she had omitted one small detail. After a trip to Labuan, a small island off the coast of Sabah and an offshore hub for deep-water oil and gas activities in the region, Kamal presented her with a small blue box. She had been unable to meet his eyes. 'So, you found time to shop,' she said as she fingered the soft velvet material. 'I thought you were so busy trying to get a meeting with the agricultural minister at the regional development conference that you didn't have time to ring us.'

'That's right, I was, so I brought you something very special. Why don't you open the box?'

Edie did as he instructed but she didn't really need to look. She knew exactly what she would find. And there they were, nestled in the soft velvet was a pair of exquisite diamond earrings.

She wore them the following day, feeling a trifle self-conscious as their elegance clashed with her white cotton trousers and insipid blue cheesecloth top. It was the day of their departure and the cases were packed up and taken out to the waiting car. 'Come on, Adam, where are you? And where is your sister? I hope she doesn't think she is bringing that cat with her. Tara, hurry up! We have to go, now!'

At the airport, they waited as Kamal checked their luggage through. After taking Tara to the rest room, Edie found her husband talking intensely to a Malay woman. She walked over towards them, squaring her shoulders as she went. 'Hello,' she looked pointedly at the woman, 'I'm Mrs Shariff, how are you?'

The flustered woman looked to Kamal to explain her presence, but he had decided to make a small drama of looking over to check where Adam who was browsing in a store selling local crafts. 'Sorry, Edie, this is Rose from the office; she brought me a contract to sign before I left. There was no time yesterday.'

Not convinced, Edie's voice was terse. 'I'm pleased to meet you, Rose. I've heard a lot about you.'

Rose averted her face and made to leave. 'I hope you all have a good flight home. Sorry, I must go now. Goodbye.'

Edie's eyes narrowed as she watched the trim figure disappear through the crowds, another dark-haired beauty amongst so many.

Later that evening, back in their bungalow in Kota Kinabalu, Kamal sat back in his chair, his silver-framed glasses perched on his nose as he read the newspaper. Edie was tidying up the toys the children had left scattered about, before preparing to go to bed. Holding a plastic glider plane in her hand she asked, 'What do you really think of Rose?'

'I don't know, I haven't really known her long enough to form an opinion.'

'Do you think she is attractive?'

'I haven't thought much about it.' He looked startled at the way the conversation was going and decided he needed to adjust his spectacles.

'Well, what were you talking about so seriously at the airport? It didn't look to me as though you were discussing work or signing any documents.'

'I've no idea, I don't remember. What is this, Edie? This questioning? She works in our office, it's no big deal.' He turned a page of his paper and tried to look engrossed.

'OK, if it's no big deal, I'm going to bed. Thank you again.'

'For what?' He looked up, a frown darkening his brow.

'For the earrings, of course. Goodnight.'

Chapter 23

It was the Christmas holidays and the family were reunited again in Kuching. Today they were driving to Damai Beach to stay and maybe even climb up to the forbidding peak of Mount Santubong, its height dominating the horizon from Kuching and all the way along the swirling bends of the Sarawak River to the peninsula of land that juts out into the South China Sea. Huge salt water crocodiles guard the murky mangrove-lined estuary and emerald pit vipers laze innocently on low leafy branches along the river bank.

'Come on, Tara, hurry up, you can finish that drawing later.'

'I'm coming, Mummy. I'm drawing a picture of the fish pond with the koi carp in it. There are so many of them, red and silver and some have black marks. There are two turtles as well and I love them so much.'

'Fine, but you can finish it later. Daddy is in the car, let's go.'

Tara reluctantly put down her picture. She wanted to give it to her father's friends when they got back from overseas. Tara loved this house with the carp swimming in the pool outside the sitting room window. She liked watching the fish and listening to the conversation between her mother and Veronica, the lady who lived down the road, talking about the first white Rajah James Brooke and then the second Rajah called Charles Brooke and his wife Margaret. She remembered visiting Fort Margherita when they had first come to Kuching. Veronica had given them a book called *My Life in Sarawak* written by the Ranee Margaret. Tara had never seen her mother so absorbed. Since that afternoon, Edie had been constantly asking everyone to listen as she read out pieces from the Ranee's descriptive writing.

But now, the family were celebrating Christmas on Damai beach. Adam was delighted to have the freedom to explore; he was almost twelve and had grown tall in the last year. Although he had the Asian features and colouring of his father, sometimes Edie saw the sharp cheek bones of her own Scottish ancestors. He was a good-looking boy and she hoped that he would do well in this new phase in his life. His first term in Singapore had come to an end, and although he liked the school and the new subjects that were being introduced, he resented the restrictions and rules. He was drawn to a group of boys that liked to stray to the local *kedai* after school or sneak out of bed at night and raid the matron's pantry. They were small crimes but already he had been on the receiving end of one lash of the cane from the headmaster. He took it bravely, proud to be accepted into the bad-boy gang.

Having settled into their rented house by the beach, Edie watched her children run to the sea's edge, shrieking and leaping over the white surf. The clouds were gathering and she could see another storm was brewing. It was the monsoon season and she had a feeling of foreboding about tomorrow's climb to the summit of Mount Santubong. Of course, Kamal and Adam were gung-ho, saying that the mountain was nowhere near as high as Mount Kinabalu which was 4095 metres high. This one was only 810 metres high and they should be able to climb it with ease.

That evening the family sat around a large table. The maid, Massiah, had prepared their dinner of *nasi goreng*, the fried rice dish containing prawns, chicken and green leafy vegetables all minutely chopped and intermingled with boiled rice then fried before finally being topped with a fried egg. Tara insisted in covering the whole thing with tomato ketchup, whilst Kamal smothered his with bright red chili sauce. Edie dripped soy sauce onto hers and Adam just spooned his into his mouth at a furious pace with no sauce at all.

'Honestly, Adam, do they starve you at that school? Slow down, you can't swim anymore today, the tide is coming in and crashing onto those rocks. It's not safe.'

'Listen to your mother, boy. We need to make an early start tomorrow so we'll turn in early and get a good night's sleep. That wind is getting up and the rain is bouncing on the roof already. Maybe we can have a good family evening; how about a game of whist, like we used to?'

Edie nodded. 'Yes, I brought the cards with me. I'll get Massiah to clear up for us.' The holiday season was getting off to a good start, she thought. Kamal seemed content to be spending time with her and the children, for although as a Muslim he did not believe in Christmas, he did acknowledge that it was a holiday worth celebrating. Coming away to the beach was a good idea.

That night in bed, he turned to her and took her in his arms. It seemed months since he wanted to hold her and she returned his embrace with a longing that came from deep hurt and loneliness. Outside the surf crashed into foam on the shoreline, the thunder cracked and the thin walls of the house juddered. The night sky was lit with jagged lightning before more rumblings shattered the peace. The drumbeat of rain continued on the roof and the storm drains overflowed with the deluge of the rain. Edie clung to Kamal as though her life depended on him.

In the morning the storm was over. The sea was calm and inviting, the cicadas filled the air with their constant static, a yellow butterfly dipped into a drenched purple flower. Edie looked at a large rock protruding from the water. She stretched herself, feeling a luxurious sense of satisfaction. The sea washed over the rocks as gently as her husband had washed her back that morning. They had shared a shower but Kamal had taken the dipper from the large dragon pot in the bathroom and poured streams of warm water over her soapy body. She shivered as she remembered his hands caressing her, and as her hands lathered his shoulders in turn.

'Good morning!' shouted a voice from out on the porch.

'He's here already,' shouted Edie. 'It's just gone eight o'clock, come on Adam, have you packed your rucksack?'

'Yes,' the boy muttered.

'Hello, it's Omar, isn't it? You're to be the guide for today?'

'Yes, Madam; we are lucky the storm passed over in the night but we must take extra care on the roots of the trees. The ground will be very slippery.' His white-toothed smile was infectious and Edie drew comfort from the guide's confidence.

Kamal shook Omar's hand enthusiastically and ushered his family out to the porch where they donned their climbing boots. Omar loaded their rucksacks into his Jeep and they all squashed in for the short drive to Santubong National Park and the start of their trek to the summit.

'What a good day for the climb, I think we may get up to the top by lunchtime. No problem, sun is out now, no more rain till this afternoon. Better you keep close to me as the tracks will be tricky after the storm. You all have plenty of water and snacks? Good, and good eyes for looking?'

Edie and Tara had decided not to climb to the summit but to follow a lower track, not so long or steep, to a pretty waterfall. They would not require the help of Omar, but they too had plenty of water and biscuits.

'Have fun and please take care,' Edie said as she hugged Adam and then kissed Kamal. As the two groups separated for their different routes, two Chinese women overtook Adam and his father. 'Look Tara, those two ladies must be climbing to the summit too. They are going at a smart pace; they must be in their late forties by the look of them.'

The day was steamy and moisture dripped from huge leaves, the size of which Adam had never seen before. Tree roots snaked at his feet and long ropes of vines snagged his boots, threatening to pitch him over the side of the narrow pathway between eighty-metre-high trees soaring up to the heavens.

'Some of these trees are over eight hundred years old,' informed Omar.

'Look up there,' pointed Adam. 'Aren't they proboscis monkeys?' He was lost in a world of excitement and adventure, but also of primeval fear. Ahead of him the footsteps of Omar crunched through twigs and he constantly pulled at strands of spider webs that clung to his face as he marched forward. Adam stopped to wipe his dripping face with the towel his father had draped around his neck. He took a sip from his water bottle, and looking up, he could see tiny patches of sky through the dense canopy. Each treetop formed a complicated mosaic pattern in its struggle to ensure that each leaf would achieve maximum sunlight. So absorbed was he with the height of these giants, he didn't see the huge red ant with its bulging abdomen climb over his shoe and on to his sock. Just a tickling feeling alerted him and with a switch of his hand he got the monster off, but only just in time. The powerful mandibles of this species would have caused severe pain.

The trio climbed higher, the path was almost vertical, and being so absorbed as to where to place their feet, they hardly noticed anything else around them. It was Omar who pointed out the skinny green viper dangling like a piece of string from a branch, waiting for any prey to come to its waiting jaws. It was quite different from the fatter pit viper, which loitered on more substantial surfaces and tended to be camouflaged in leafier surroundings. Earlier Kamal had pointed at a thin snake, the colour of the shadows, disappearing under a rotting log. Every shrub had needle-like thorns and some of the larger fronds were lethal with their serrated spikes. Every piece of bark had mosses and leathery mushrooms growing on them. Parasites fed on the living and the dying.

The trio continued their climb with only the jungle noises to keep them company. The loud tap-tap of the woodpecker and the screech of some bird high in the canopy disturbed the buzz of the cicadas. There was no sign of the two women who had passed them at the beginning of their hike. The trio stopped for a snack before the serious ascent to the summit of Santubong. Kamal commented on the sturdy ropes attached to trees in order to help climbers with the last scramble that was almost vertical.

'Well, Adam, we've been going for three hours already. We must be almost at the summit. I hope your mother and Tara are down from the waterfall by now.

'They probably had a swim in the waterfall, lucky things. I'm boiling hot. Look at my towel, it's soaked with sweat. Can I have another biscuit?' Adam was getting fed up and his legs were aching from the tough climb. He sat down, but leapt up almost immediately as he saw the tail of a brown lizard whip past his thigh. 'Ugh, this place is scary, it's full of creepy crawlies.'

'You're doing really well, Adam.' Omar tried to encourage the boy. 'You are only eleven-years-old, after all, and the steep parts are hard. Clambering over fallen trees is not easy, even for me, but we are nearly there. And you might see the ghosts of the princesses at the top.'

'I heard that the mountain was supposed to look like a woman lying on her back,' said Kamal.

'Yes, according to the legend, two beautiful princesses who were sisters, Sejinjang and Santubong, both fell in love with the same prince and both wanted to marry him. Always a tragedy,' said Omar with a knowing look as he continued. 'But after a terrible fight between the princesses, the King of Heaven turned both princesses, and the prince as well, into mountains as punishment for acting on their feelings of jealousy. So, we won't dally when we get to the top, just have a good look around and then we'll start our descent which will be quite gruelling. We don't want any accidents and I hope you still have plenty of water. Pay attention to where I am putting my feet. The Fire Department has been out several times this year rescuing people off this mountain. Many people take a wrong turning. It is not a good place to get lost.' He urged them forward.

Adam grumbled as he dragged his feet up to the final climb, 'We could have just bought a postcard, it would have been so much easier.'

*

Much later in the afternoon, Edie scanned the road for a sign of the vehicle bringing back her husband and son. She was not really worried, just a little anxious. After all she and Tara had returned from their walk to the waterfall three hours ago, and had already been for a swim in the sea and had a shower. Their whole experience had been magical, and apart from a small graze on her knee Tara had done well with the climb through the forest.

'Stop fussing, Mummy, they'll be back soon, well I hope they are because the storm clouds are starting to make the sky very dark. I wouldn't like to be sliding down through that mud.' She returned to her comic, lying on her bed, legs akimbo.

Sure enough, just as Tara predicted, the first drops of rain splashed on the driveway, making spots the size of golf balls. Edie and Massiah rushed to close the windows against the oncoming deluge.

'It's four o'clock, they should be here by now. Should we get in touch with the Fire Station?' Edie wrung her hands and paced up and down. 'I know we were told to alert them in case,' and she ran out to open the door again, 'well, in case they are needed to form a rescue party.' The noise was deafening and the rain unforgiving. It fell in torrents and the small garden disappeared beneath a mini lake.

Finally, they saw headlights and the vehicle pulled into the driveway. Sodden and exhausted, Adam and Kamal alighted from the jeep and with a grinning Omar beside them, plodded up the steps into the house.

'We made it!' cried Adam, quite forgetting his bad temper of earlier. 'It was so hard and so steep and if we hadn't had Omar, I don't think we would have survived as the paths all looked the same after a while. I felt like a real live explorer and I saw a snake and a centipede and a huge ant tried to bite me!'

'Oh, thank God, you are safe. I knew you would be!' Edie gave Adam and Kamal a huge hug before doing the same to Omar who grinned back at her, once again flashing his white teeth. 'Thank you, Omar, for taking such good care of them.'

'No problem, Madam, but I think there is a problem this night. The two ladies we saw this morning have not signed in. We always have to sign when we leave and again when we return. Their names are still there but they have not returned yet. My heart is beating for them. I fear for their survival.'

Kamal nodded in agreement. 'The Fire Department has been notified by the rangers and they will put together a rescue operation. This rain is not helping and it will be almost impossible to get up there in all the slime. The paths are awash. It was very difficult doing the last bit coming down, I can tell you.'

'It is always very difficult to follow the paths on the descent and very easy to take the wrong one. I hope they are able to take shelter and stay in one place until the storm eases.' Omar frowned as he spoke, for he had grave misgivings about the fate of the two missing ladies.

'They looked so confident this morning,' said Edie. 'They had good sturdy boots on and seemed to know what they were doing.'

'They did but I wonder how fit they really were? How much stamina? Maybe they like to play mah-jong and sit about then suddenly decide to do exercise? They could get a snake bite or fall or anything?'

'Two ladies, just like the two princesses.' Adam thought of the earlier legend. 'Maybe they've been cursed?'

'Oh Adam! Please don't say that. You know I have a fear of all that sort of thing.' Edie scowled and tried to rid herself of the constant fear of the parallel spirit world that was so prevalent in the local tribes. She thought of the curses that could be inflicted, the wooden effigies that were made, the worship of animals. She shivered. She suddenly remembered that clay pot of cremated bones from their long-ago holiday in Kuantan. Oh! I am getting silly, she thought. 'Anyway, thank goodness you are all down safely. Was it amazing at the top after the climb?'

'Everything looked blurred,' said Adam. 'The sea was as grey as a battleship and all the rivers were muddy brown and the jungle was just a mix-match of green. It looked like one of those paintings people do with watercolour when all the colours run into each other. This painting looked like the artist's water after he's washed his brush in it. It was just a smear of sludgy colours.'

'Well, that actually sounds quite nice,' smiled his mother, 'easy on the eye, but I know you were expecting a clearer bird's eye view. Maybe you could go again when the weather clears? But now it's time to wash up and eat. Massiah has made some very good Malay curry and you must be starving.'

Omar took his leave, happy that his charges were returned safely and with no incident. The boy was impetuous, he thought, he tended to rush without thinking. Not so good at listening. Omar had seen a lot of different characters climb this mountain, each with their different personalities and approach to the jungle. The father was calm, solid, but the boy? He shook his head. The lad was sturdy and strong, with natural ability but not a good mental attitude, but he was still very young. This time, though, it was a good outcome.

Two days later the local newspaper headlined the news that two Malaysian Chinese women were missing on Mount Santubong. They were tourists from Kuala Lumpur, perhaps in their late forties. Relatives had confirmed that they had no experience of mountain climbing, but enjoyed walking. Their names were being withheld until they were found. It was sobering for Edie's family at how close the end could be. One slip, one wrong turn, it could end so tragically.

On Christmas morning, Edie was surprised to hear a knock on the door. Who did they know up here on Damai Beach? She wiped her hands on the kitchen towel and went to answer it.

'Omar! How nice to see you again. Happy Christmas to you!'

'Yes, Madam, it is nice to see you too. I have news for you. The missing ladies have been found. They are very sick and were taken to hospital in Kuching. They are suffering from severe exposure and lack of food and water. One lady has broken her leg. She fell on some rocks, I think, but they are alive. I wanted to tell you and Mr Kamal and Adam and your small girl. Good news for Christmas time, yes?'

'Oh yes,' agreed Edie. 'Come inside and share your news with us all. This will help us to have a really happy Christmas. Thank you for coming to tell us. Massiah! Please get some coffee and cake for Omar, we must celebrate.'

Chapter 24

Edie stared into the mirror. She was forty-one now. Fine lines traced her eyes and lips, and a thread-like line ran across her high forehead. She rubbed some cream into the offending creases. Still, not too bad, she thought. Her hair was still fair, and due to the heat, she tended to wear it in a ponytail these days, but it did seem wispier than before. She was aware of how thin it was compared to the lush black tresses of the local women. She pursed her lips and turned away from the mirror. She would not think of these things now. Jealousy was eating her up and she felt so alone. She wished Kamal would come home more often and reassure her of his love, without the need for diamond earrings to prove his commitment to her. It was hard being alone. Even looking back to her upbringing, she had felt loss, like she was a child of no one, with a distant mother and a dead father. There had been no idealised parent on whom to model her identity. Everything she had done over the last twenty years seemed episodic; her role models were fictional characters taken as parent surrogates. She often wondered what it was that had guided her through her marriage, her role as a mother and her place in Malaysian society. Sometimes she felt like a broken entity, reassembled by the need to be the support for others.

Her own father, Francis Findlay Farquharson, had left her mother and herself when she was just a baby, and she knew nothing about him. Sometimes she reflected what might have been. Would she have seen traits of him in Adam? In Tara? There was a wilfulness in Adam that often perplexed her. It was more than the complexity of adolescence, there was a dark side to the boy that she found distressing. Throughout his time at the United World College in Singapore he had studied hard, been keen on sports and flown with a worldly set of youngsters whose parents were rich jetsetters. It had been challenging for Kamal. He could not compete with the likes of the Chinese business men who flew their children to Zermatt to ski, or to Perth Australia for diving holidays. Adam's contemporaries were rewarded with BMW sports cars for passing their leaving certificates. Adam was rewarded with a family dinner at a nice revolving restaurant in Singapore's Orchard Road. At eighteen, Adam refused to talk to them when he was at home. Edie knew Kamal was deeply hurt by the boy's obvious feelings of superiority and resentment towards his parents. Maybe when he goes to university, Edie thought, he will meet a different group of people.

By contrast, Tara hated the United World College, hated the set of girls that held none of her interests. 'Please get me out of here,' she pleaded in every letter home.

'There must be somewhere else she could go?' Edie had beseeched Amelia, her stalwart friend, always the person who knew exactly what to say or what to do in any situation.

'Michael's family are well connected in Singapore,' Amelia had said. 'We sent the twins to the Methodist Girls' School. It has a good reputation and a good work ethic. The girls are doing well and I think Tara would like it there. Then maybe she could share the lodgings with Lucy and Claire at Michael's aunt's house?'

Edie was so grateful for the offer and had been successful in transferring her daughter to the new school. At sixteen Tara was studying sciences and had her heart set on getting into university and studying zoology. Edie had no doubts about her beautiful daughter. Tara had grown up into a long-legged girl, with a short bob haircut and wore round John Lennon glasses to emphasise her studious phase. She was passionate about music, all sorts of music, from Beethoven to Sting to Eric Clapton. 'How can you possibly concentrate with this row going on,' Kamal would say to her, totally bemused by the cacophony of sounds emitting from his daughter's room.

Edie turned back to the mirror and frowned. Was that a grey hair? She stood up to change into a fresh green dress with thin straps. The soft material fell down to her ankles. She was happy that her skin was still smooth, the fine wrinkles on her face not too bad in spite of the sun-soaked weekends spent on the islands. She was still thin, and still working as a teacher at the International School at Likas. Her colleagues came and went due to work contracts, and she enjoyed the animated interchange with so many nationalities who came to work in beautiful North Borneo. So why was she feeling so glum today, so introspective? She hadn't given her father a thought for years. And Kamal? Always travelling, new cases taking him to Miri and Sandakan and often to

Kuching. He was respected, he worked hard and their marriage seemed to be a success. Edie smiled as she recalled their dinner party the other night with Sarah and Derek Anderson and their old friends Kate and Alistair Davidson. I'm so lucky, she thought. I am just worrying over nothing. But she hoped she would hear from Adam soon. He was in Singapore staying with Victoria, some Chinese girl and her family. He had been accepted to do a degree course in electrical engineering in Kuala Lumpur. Not so far away, she reflected, he can come home easily. Edie looked out to the frangipani tree that framed the bedroom window. The waxy blooms were dotted like stars amongst the emerald leaves. It was then that the phone rang, jarring her reveries.

'Hello! Adam! I was just thinking about you, are you coming home?'

'I've been refused the place,' he said, his voice curt and unemotional. 'We all had to do a test and they found out I'm colour blind. That's it, my dream is over. You can't have a colour-blind electrical engineer.'

'Oh no, I am so sorry, Adam.' Edie could feel his pain through the words he didn't say. She could imagine him standing by the telephone, quite forlorn, the way he used to look when he was a boy. 'Please talk to your father, he will know what to advise.'

'Victoria's dad said I should do mechanical engineering as I have all the right qualifications. He said that Sydney in Australia has a good reputation and Victoria's brother is there. What do you think? Would Dad be able to fund me?' The words tumbled out, as though rehearsed.

'We can ask him if that is what you would like to do. Oh Adam, this is so unexpected, I can imagine how you must be feeling.'

'Maybe he might stretch to a car if I got in?'

'When are you coming home? We could book you a flight this weekend?' Edie asked hopefully.

'No, I said I'd go with Victoria and her family up to Genting Highlands. Her dad likes to do a bit of gambling, then we're going to watch the motor racing at Batu Tiga Speedway Circuit. It should be a great week. Anyway, can you talk to Dad for me? And please can you send over some money as I am a bit low on my allowance. Just transfer it to my bank account. I'll get it on Tuesday when I get back from Genting. Thanks, Mum. By the way how are you?'

'Fine,' said Edie. 'Thanks for asking.' And she put the receiver down.

Chapter 25

Tara woke up in her old bed at home. She was disorientated after the long flight from Sydney yesterday. She stretched and for a few moments allowed herself the feeling of being a child again in her old bedroom with its yellow walls and dark brown curtains covered in the shapes of lions, giraffes and other African animals. How many mornings had she lain like this, listening to the dogs barking from somewhere down the hill, or the sound of Moy Moy's soft swish of the broom as she brushed dried up leaves into the monsoon drains around the house. Outside the hot purple shades of bougainvillea would be attracting tiny white butterflies. She remembered collecting the caterpillars and putting them into jam jars with leaves in order to watch the whole process of their metamorphosis. She jumped out of bed, pulled back the curtains, and sure enough there was the scene just as she remembered it. The towering rain tree, the frangipani, the canna lilies and the course grass. Grabbing a sarong, she stepped into it and knotted it at her chest and went out to see who else was up.

Edie was sitting on the rattan chair on the veranda, marking essays that her class had written. 'Hello, Mum, I thought I might find you here.'

Edie looked up and smiled at her. 'Good morning, darling. Tea? I was just going to get myself one.'

'Tea would be lovely, Mum.' Timmy the Second jumped off Edie's lap and up on to Tara's and snuggled down. 'You are a funny old thing, puss, you seem to spend your life asleep. Not one bit like your predecessor who wouldn't leave the gardener or Moy Moy alone. How old is he now, Mum?' She carefully removed the cat from her lap and was rewarded with a lazy meow of indignation.

'He's nearly two. But poor Timmy the First,' sighed Edie, 'I miss his naughtiness and the way he used to hide behind the curtains or furniture and leap out to attack my legs when I least expected it. But this one is a better hunter. Moy Moy is always complementing him on his kills. So, I suppose he does need to sleep during the day.' Edie leant over to pick up the cat again and nursed him as though he was a baby. His paws went around her neck. 'You are such a warm cuddly thing, aren't you, but you must take care, there are nasty reptiles lurking out there in the bushes.'

'I can't believe Tiger Tim got bitten by a snake; I suppose his eyesight wasn't very good for he hardly ever ventured outside on his own towards the end. After all, he was nearly eighteen which is old for a cat.'

'Yes, but Moy Moy has always complained about that part of the garden down by the old mango tree. She is constantly berating the gardener as he hardly ever cuts back the long grass. And of course, that is where she found poor Timmy. He'd obviously disturbed a cobra. It would have been very quick. Their venom is lethal.'

'I am so sad about that,' said Tara. 'Poor Timmy, he seemed to have been with us forever.'

'He had; he was my first friend here. He did enjoy catching grasshoppers and the odd frog, and many years ago when he was just a kitten, he brought a dead snake into the house. Your father was livid as Adam was just a baby at the time. It could have been catastrophic but fortunately it was all right. It's ironic that my poor little cat who never hurt a fly was killed so tragically.'

'And now this new puss seems to have stolen your heart.'

'I know, Amelia found him for me; some people had some new kittens and they all had the same markings as our Timmy, so I couldn't resist him.'

'And now we have the fearless one, Timmy the Second, who will probably live for ever! By the way, where's Dad?' Tara looked about, for it was Saturday and she knew her father didn't usually go to the office at the weekends.

'He's sorry, he had to go to Sandakan, but he'll be back tomorrow. It means we can have some time together, just you and me. What would you like to do?'

'Let's go to the yacht club, I'd love to just relax. I'm so tired after the flight, and also from the end of term parties. Have Lucy and Claire been home, do you know?'

'Yes, they have, but they've gone again. They are growing up so fast, just as you are, and look at you with your tattooed lips. Why on earth did you do that?'

'I look so sallow all the time and I don't like lipstick so one of my friends suggested it. Although after I had them done, I got such cold sores, they were grotesque.'

'Did it not hurt?' Edie compressed her own lips in sympathy.

'Not at all. They send you to the dentist first, you get all numbed up with Novocaine and then they do it. Simple. I quite like the dark brown outline, it's quite subtle, isn't it? You didn't pick up on it yesterday when I arrived.'

'True, it is very natural. I have seen it in magazines. Amelia was talking about getting her eyes done. But, tell me, how are you getting on at uni? Are you settling in all right, and what about the residence you're in? Do you still think zoology is the right choice for you? I want to know everything, but first let me get the tea.'

When they were settled again, Tara held her mug in two hands and put her feet up on the coffee table, shifting one of the children's school books to the side. 'It's great, Mum, really, just as I told you in my letters and on the phone. Sydney is amazing, and there are so many students from all over. I share a room with an Australian girl called Marie who is studying music and English literature. She drags me out to see concerts and I take her for visits to nature reserves. We both like contemporary music so it's good.'

'And Adam?' Edie looked up over her mug of tea. 'Do you see much of him?'

'I did when I first arrived. He was really helpful getting me settled in after you and Dad had gone back, but I don't really see him now. He seems to have his own friends, a bit like when he was in Singapore. I don't really get on with them, you know, he's still seeing Victoria Chan. Her dad is a billionaire, I think. Not sure Adam is going to be able to afford such an expensive girlfriend, the way he is going.'

Edie breathed in and refrained from interrogating her daughter any further, even though she sensed there was more to tell. The last phone call from Adam was more than upsetting. He was so drunk he could barely speak. He'd failed his second-year exams and was doing resits. Edie looked out at the bright colours of her garden. Minna and Hassan had been on the telephone from Johor that morning, always anxious to hear updates on their precious grandchildren. So proud they had been that Adam and Tara were studying in Australia, and their kampong jungle drums were constantly being updated by Kamal. It was easy to talk of Tara, a good student, level headed, but Adam? How to talk about her boy? What had gone wrong? What would he do if he failed again? Kamal had become withdrawn, refusing to discuss his son without losing his temper. His trips away had become more frequent and he had only returned yesterday in order to meet Tara off the plane.

She stood up and walked down the steps and picked a few sprigs of bougainvillea to put in a vase. The vibrancy of their colours and the blazing yellow of the sun brought her back to her own reality, and she promised herself a quiet time in the afternoon to re-read *My Life in Sarawak*, the book she had been given by her friend Veronica in Kuching. The words of the Ranee Margaret Brooke soothed her and she felt drawn to the woman whose own life could not have been easy. She too had looked to nature and seen beauty and calmness and purpose when things had been challenging. Often Edie sat at the yacht club, the turquoise sea fringed by a straggly row of casuarina trees, the islands in the distance bobbing on the horizon like mushrooms, and she thought of how the lady from long ago described them: 'The natives call them talking trees from the sound they make when the breeze stirs their lace-like branches looking as though the slightest puff might blow them away in clouds of dark green smoke'. How exquisite, Edie thought, but I wonder if she had problems with a social-climbing drunkard for a son, or a husband that removed himself from any scenes of confrontation after spitting out his pent-up venom on herself. She shuddered at the thought of Kamal and his anger when he had got the news that Adam had failed. 'Fancy rich boy, is that what he thinks he is? Daddy can buy the car, put money in his account and buy him the latest fashions! And now the drinking? He conveniently forgets about his Muslim heritage and the money that we have both worked hard for to keep his great lifestyle. Well, if he fails, good luck to him. Maybe his dolly bird's rich father can pick up his costs instead of me. But I've heard of Steven Chan, he didn't get as rich as he is by supporting deadbeats.'

'Come on, Mum,' Tara brought her back to the present, 'let's get ready for our day out, I can just feel myself floating on that warm green sea. Oh, how exotic, and maybe we can have some *nasi lemak* for lunch. I have missed all this so much.'

Later at the yacht club Edie sat at the table near the beach while her daughter ran off to immerse herself in the warm South China Sea, so much calmer and warmer than the bracing Pacific that washed Sydney's beaches.

Amelia found her friend still sitting there, idly flicking through an Australian magazine that Tara had brought back. 'Well look at you! So relaxed and happy to have a chick back at home. You are so lucky, mine are still away.'

Amelia settled herself down and called over to the passing waiter, 'A fresh lime and soda please.' She looked questioningly to Edie, who declined. 'Who would have thought I would have such caring girls, a student nurse and a trainee hospitality manager. And by the way, Tara is looking fabulous.'

Squinting her eyes into the bright sunlight Edie adjusted her sunglasses and watched her daughter duck diving like a slippery seal and disappearing below the waves. 'She's tattooed her lips, I couldn't believe it, but do you know, it looks good, just the outline, so she looks permanently made up. I'm quite tempted to do it myself.'

'Kamal away?'

'Yes, he went early this morning.'

'Kuching?'

No, Sandakan, said he'd be back tomorrow. Where's Michael?'

'In KL, you know what he's like with the motor racing, you just can't keep him away. I thought your boy was keen as well?'

'Oh, he was keen when he was in Singapore, but how can we afford to keep up such a lifestyle. I am at my wit's end, Amelia. What is going to become of him?'

'Still drinking? Has he sat his exams again?'

'Yes, to both questions,' sighed Edie. 'He's awaiting his results. If he fails, Kamal wants him to find a job or do something else, but what? He never did get over the disappointment of not getting to do electrical engineering. Maybe he should try something completely different; he has always been keen on the outdoors so maybe he should try coaching or something.'

'Coaching!' Amelia laughed, 'That pays peanuts, that wouldn't suit him at all. I think he sees himself as being a bit more glamorous than that. And besides, what would he coach?' She glanced at the magazine that Edie had discarded. 'Why doesn't he try something like journalism? He can write and he has a wealth of knowledge about this part of the world. Could he not retrain at that?'

Edie's eyes lit up. 'You always seem to come up with a good solution. I could suggest it to him.' She looked up at the soft feathery needles on the trees above her, some had fallen on to the table, spindly miniature wishbones. Picking one up she said, 'This is the second time today I have thought of Margaret Brooke, the second Rajah's wife.' She looked out at her daughter still floating on the sea, 'Some years ago we spent Christmas at Santubong in Sarawak, you may remember? Kamal and Adam managed to climb to the top of the mountain. The weather had been appalling and a couple of ladies nearly lost their lives that day, but fortunately they survived. I remember how proud Adam was of his achievement. At the time I was reading Margaret's autobiography for the first time. Ever since he was little Adam has always been fascinated with native stories and legends and curses, just as I am. We were talking about the legend of the two princesses who lost their lives and were turned into mountains, and later that evening I read to both Adam and Tara the story of the moon goddess.'

'Right,' said Amelia, bemused at how the conversation had abruptly turned. 'So, we've gone from Adam in Australia, to Adam as a potential journalist, and now we are going back to the last century to a lady who retold local myths. How does this all connect?'

'This lady, with her collection of stories and ancient beliefs has stretched her hands to me across the void of time. Did you know she once lived in this part of the world? I read about how lonely her life was, she suffered unbearable loss, but she saw beauty in people and their lives. I somehow feel a connection with her, and every time I'm worried, I delve back into her story. I know some of the fables are just folklore but the children used to like them. I remember that particular night in Santubong, telling Adam and Tara about a classic tale of unrequited love. I still think of it; I know it's a silly tale really.' Edie sipped her drink and looked away from her friend. 'In a nutshell, the daughter of the moon allows her earthly husband to visit his earthly family for two weeks on the understanding that he will return to her. Of course, he doesn't make the deadline and it's far too late. The moon goddess waits for him and waits for him until she finally gives up. She turns her back on him. Of course, as soon as the man realises what he has lost, he is distraught and he spends the rest of his life climbing mountains in search of moonbeams, but she always eludes him, and so he dies of a broken heart.'

'Sounds like a familiar tale,' Amelia laughed.

'True,' agreed Edie, 'but it was the ending that touched me.' She rifled in her beach bag and brought out the worn copy of the Ranee's story.

'Listen, tell me if you don't think this is beautiful. Margaret is about to go to bed, thinking of the story of the moon goddess, and she looks out of her window and views the silhouette of the dark shapes in her garden. It was almost midnight. She heard the wind through the casuarinas and saw the moonshine trickling into the garden; it was as though the trees were talking, telling their secrets to the stars.'

'Hmm, and here we are under the talking trees, and you are getting comfort from a lady from long ago. You are always the romantic, my friend.' Amelia leant forward and took the book from Edie.

'Adam is breaking my heart, Amelia. He doesn't know what he wants, he seems to think he is so much better than all of us, no longer interested in anything except living the high life with his rich friends at our expense and I am so afraid for his future. Maybe he should go back to his roots, back to the Malay jungle and the mountains and the wildness that so enthralled him as a child. Maybe the trees are sending a message. People do take breaks, maybe I could persuade Kamal to get him employed in one of the National Parks.'

Amelia continued flicking through the battered book that seemed so important to Edie. Privately she thought the talking trees story was a lot of nonsense and she felt Adam needed a good slap around the ear, but she doubted if that would do any good. Instead, she said, 'The boy is nearly twenty-one. You have given him every opportunity but now it's up to him to sort himself out and make a success of his life by his own means. If he fails his exams this time, tell him you can't support him anymore. He needs to face up to reality. When I mentioned to Michael how things were with Adam in Australia, he suggested that Adam would be great as a tour guide, driving a van around, a free spirit and his own boss. It might give him a breathing space away from the academic expectations that you and Kamal are placing on him, away from comparison with the high achievements that Tara is capable of at university. He might like something like that, a lot of kids take off, travel, find themselves, then who knows? He may then want to come back and climb mountains and wrestle with tree roots and listen to the talking trees.'

Edie reached over and took her friend's hand, tears spilling down her face.

'Thank you. I know you're right. I'll talk to Kamal about it, he can lay down the law to Adam.' She sniffed and wiped her eyes and replaced her sunglasses.

Overhead the casuarinas continued their silent conversation with the afternoon sun.

Chapter 26

Edie was restless. Pulling on a long grey cardigan, she strolled out to the stone dyke and stood gazing at the brown fields, ridged from the plough and already sprouting with the fuzz of new green shoots. Above her the harsh chattering of a magpie broke the silence. From afar she could hear a barking dog, reminding her of Kipper and Robert Hunter. Would he call round today? She hoped he would. Their last meeting had unsettled her, much more than she could have imagined. She squeezed her eyes shut, blocking out the view of the fields and the rolling hills of this Scottish panorama, feeling yet again the rush of pain and raw emotion that still enveloped her. For a few precious moments she allowed herself to think of her home in East Malaysia but then she shook her head, blocking out the memory and the reasons why she had left. The dog continued to bark as Edie looked towards the sycamore tree and down the driveway, but there was no one approaching the house. She thought again of Robert, and admitted to herself that the minister's words were haunting her. It was as though shadowy figures from the past were taking on a reality and she was intrigued by that thought. She walked back over the rough grass and noticed that stacked against the gable end of the house were planks of wood and rolls of tangled wire, slowly rusting beside the mossy pieces of timber. Maybe a chicken shed, she wondered, and for a fleeting moment she imagined a washing line strung with boys' socks and shirts flapping in the wind from the North Sea, and chickens cackling beside the line and a woman pushing the hair out of her eyes as she stooped to a retrieve a pillow case from the washing basket. I'm getting fanciful, she thought, and went inside to fill the kettle. Coffee first, then I'll telephone Robert and ask him if he feels like company.

Later that morning, Edie drove to the local Co-op in Stonehaven to pick up some caramel doughnuts. She hesitated before adding eggs, cheese and healthy-looking leaves to her basket. She turned her car back down the road, branched off to the right and up through the fields until she arrived at the minister's house. 'Good morning, Robert, I hope you have the coffee cups out,' she shouted, at the same time trying to appease Kipper who was overwhelmed with joy at the sight of her. 'Down boy, these are my good jeans, I just washed these yesterday; now look what you've done, you've left two big muddy paw prints on me. Oh, you are a nuisance.' She patted the dog's sleek coat and fondled his ears, feeling his breath panting on her cheek. 'A nuisance, but a loveable one.'

'Good morning to you, Edie, I see you are enjoying country living! Come in, and get back here, you daft dog, go and lie down in your basket. I have the best instant coffee there is, no need for fancy Italian names here, it's just black or black with milk, which do you prefer?'

'I like mine white with sugar, please, Robert, and I've brought some cakes with me. I just can't get enough of all these treats.'

The pair took their coffee mugs and the plate of doughnuts over to the window niche where Robert liked to sit. It was a comfortable room with books lining the walls and a red oriental rug giving the room warmth. Outside the garden was struggling to survive. Bluebells were growing in clumps under a vibrant yellow gorse bush and everywhere there were signs of life. Edie stared at the bird feeder which seemed to be overwhelmed with all the tits and chaffinches that were diligently pecking the nuts and grains he had provided.

'I get finches here too,' Robert said proudly. 'Green ones and gold ones, they are a delight.'

'Well, there are only crows and magpies down at my ancestors' house, and sparrows, but I did see a robin which was lovely. I haven't seen British birds for so long.'

'You wanted to talk, my dear?' Robert looked at her questioningly over his spectacles.

'I do, yes, but not today if you don't mind.' She put her plate down and wiped her fingers on a tissue from her handbag. 'I haven't been able to stop thinking about what you told me about my father last time we spoke, mostly about his time in Glasgow. Then later you said you had got to know his mother as well when you began your ministry here in this parish. I wondered if there is more you could tell me about him?'

'Aah, yes. Well, I can try, but your grandmother only told me snippets although some of them were quite illuminating. I'll see what I can remember.'

Edie sipped her coffee and waited expectantly.

Chapter 27

Francis Finlay, or Frank as he was known, scraped the stick of chalk on the blackboard. He etched the numbers of the long division sum in front of his classmates and quickly worked out in his head the mental arithmetic required to complete the correct answer.

Clad in the academic gown of his profession and clutching his cane in gnarled old hands, the dominie stood like a scrawny raven. 'Correct,' he barked. 'Now class, you will write the twenty-third psalm and I will be looking for light strokes to ascend and dark strokes to descend. What did I say, Jimmy MacDonald?'

'Light to ascend, Sir, dark to descend.'

'Correct, boy.' The schoolmaster looked around at the thirty children whose ages ranged from nine to fourteen, and scowled. 'If I see a blotch of ink on the page, or the wrong pressure of the pen, you will feel the birch on your soft pink hands, do I make myself clear?'

'Yes, Sir,' the class answered in unison as they dipped their pens into the inkpots on their desks and began the tedious task of writing in beautiful script: 'The Lord is my shepherd...'.

Frank had a natural knack at penmanship, his book was filled with perfect cursive handwriting, but just as he was dipping his pen into the ink, his brother Will nudged him, 'I could do with my piece of bread and jam now, my belly is making a right din.'

Frank glowered, 'Look what you made me do, you and your bony elbow. I'm in for it now.'

And what is going on here?' the dominie's shadow fell over the blotted page.

'I didn't mean to, Sir, it just sort of fell off the nib.'

'Stand! Don't you give me anymore impertinence, boy. Spell the word 'impertinence' on the blackboard.'

Frank stood up and once again took the stick of chalk to write but his hand shook in trepidation: I M P E R T N A N C E was the word that appeared on the board.

'Enough! Come here and stand before the class. Hold out your hand. Two grave misdemeanours you have committed in the space of as many minutes, so as God is my witness, I will correct this at once and you will learn how to spell and to write without mistakes. It is a great gift to be able to communicate, boy. I will make sure you know that by the end of this chastisement. Four strokes of the birch rod for you, two on each hand.'

Frank didn't go straight home after school. Instead, he skirted the track and made towards the wood above the farm. He could see his father at the plough, urging Maisie the Shire horse to walk on steady. Frank's fists were shut tight; he could still feel the sting of the cane and when he opened his hands he saw the four bloody welts across his palms. It was not unusual to be beaten at school, there was not a day that went by when the dominie did not dish out punishment to his scholars. Frank had nursed bleeding hands since he had started in the senior class. By contrast, Mrs MacLean, his early years teacher, had cherished her charges and sat them round a hot stove on winter afternoons, teaching the girls to knit and do cross-stitch and the boys to make baskets out of raffia. Everything changed as he made the transition up through the classes.

Finally, after scuffing stones under the trees, his stomach got the better of him and he picked up his satchel and made his way home. Normally he would have walked with John or Will, but today he nursed his own sense of anger and frustration and he was not in the mood for his brothers or their wild pranks. Last week they had felt the leather of their father's belt. Frank remembered how John had squandered his penny on a toffee from the shop, and after making a good soft mess of the sweet he took it out and rammed it into the post box. Mrs Wiseman, the postmistress, was not fooled by the boy's plea of innocence when she accused him, knowing fine well who had bought the offending toffee. She had taken the matter home to their father. Old Jock felt belittled by the shame of his son's sin and had decided to give each of the older boys a fierce beating. It was always the same, the old man would fly into a rage and the belt would come off or his huge spade-like hand would smack them around the back of the head. Frank scowled at the image of his father, a tall, wiry man with a long gait, striding through the fields, or his jacket pulled up at the back as he bent over the spade or weeded the ground. His eyes were ice blue as he focussed on the punishment before lashing out like a fierce beast. Only baby Silvia was spared the harshness and unpredictability of his temper.

When Frank did get home, thanks to his brothers, his mother already knew that he'd been given the cane. When she saw him, she stopped stirring the broth and put her hand out to him. 'Show me, son, you'll need some salve on that. I can do it now before your father gets in. What did you do this time?'

'Splattered ink on my jotter.'

'That's not like you, you're good at the writing stuff. Well, come here and I'll wipe the blood with a warm cloth. Only another year at the school, but dinnae let your father see it or there will be more trouble.'

Frank looked at his mother, so soft and round in contrast to her lean and lanky husband. Her body was cushiony, and her children often leant on her in order to feel a connection with the woman who had nursed them as babies and infants. But now they were older they found that she radiated a warmth which did not extend to any physical expression of affection. Frank was relieved that old Jock never hurt her.

The door opened and his father came in, wiping his feet and making towards the sink to wash the dirt off his hands. The boys ran to sit on the benches alongside the wooden table. His father approached the table and cast his eyes over the family.

'Francis Finlay, go and fill up the bucket from the well for your mother, I see there is none in the kitchen.'

'Aye, Father, if I must. Can I just eat my broth first?'

'You dare to answer me back? You'll get the water now or you'll feel the weight of my belt across your backside, now get out and do it when I tell you.'

Frank's face was dark with anger, his bleeding hands were bunched into defiant fists as he passed his father who swung out and smacked him hard around the head.

'I said, do it now, boy, or else.'

'I can do it, Father,' ventured Will, coming to his brother's aid. He felt a certain amount of guilt for the morning encounter with the birch.

'And why is that?'

'Frank's hands are sore from the cane this morning,' piped up seven-year-old Ian. 'Frank got four of the best.'

'I knew he was a good-for-nothing. Come outside with me, boy, and I'll watch you lift the pail of water with your poor little hands which have never done a day's work in their lives. Then you can see what happens to boys who show disrespect to the head of the house.' Jock unbuckled his belt as he pushed Frank towards the door.

The family sat with their heads bent, terrified in their own ways about the turn of events but relieved that it was Frank and not them.

Later when the house was still and only the sound of the autumn rain battering on the windows disturbed the night, Frank lay on his side, his night shirt sticky with blood seeping from the wounds inflicted by his father. He was conscious of the sleeping forms of his brothers, Will softly snoring beside him and the restlessness of his older brother, John in the bed next to them. A branch tapped at the ill-fitting pane of glass and Frank eased himself out of bed.

'What are you doing?' John whispered.

'Just away to the wee room down the path, get away back to sleep.'

'Dinnae let the cat in or the old boy really will skin you alive,' and with that, John rolled over and went back to sleep.

Frank picked up his school satchel from the back door where he had dropped it and crept quietly through to the living room and sat down at the table by the window. Lightning lit up the fields outside. He pulled paper out from the centre of his jotter and took his pencil from his bag. He held it with care, his palms were still stinging from the cane. He wrote:

Dear Sir,

I am thirteen years old but I have only five months to go before I turn fourteen and I will be at liberty to leave the school. I am looking for a position on your newspaper. I have a good eye, I have been told, and have a good hand at the writing. Perhaps you would be kind enough to offer me a position on your paper, and I just want to add, I am very keen to learn. I will try my hand at anything.

Respectfully,

Francis Findlay Farquharson

He read it through and was proud of his endeavour. Carefully he folded his letter into four and slipped it back into his satchel, away from any prying eyes in the family. He would need an envelope and a stamp, but Mrs Wiseman would be able to furnish him with that. He still had a few pennies saved from his days at the berry picking in the summer. Outside the rain was getting heavier, a rumble of thunder shook the house and more lightning lit up the stone dyke around the house. He and Will were supposed to fix some of the loose stones tomorrow, it being Saturday, but the rain might prevent that with a bit of luck. That would give his back and hands a chance to heal. Frank flinched, remembering the agonising thrashing he had endured earlier. Never mind, he thought, I can play the old man's game for a few more months and then I'm out of here for good. After that I never want to see him again.

A wet autumn turned to a wet winter and the family struggled to make ends meet. Frank kept away from the house as much as possible. The smell of drying clothes draped in front of the smoky fire caused damp and little Silvia and five-year-old Ian were the worst affected as they struggled with bronchitis for weeks on end. His mother begged extra oatmeal on credit from the shop and made skirlie from onions and oatmeal fried in lard in a large skillet. It was a satisfying meal and filled their bellies, and with jam sandwiches and boiled eggs the family got through the dreich days. Occasionally when she got a pound of mince from the butcher, she stretched it with a handful of oatmeal, the boys would wolf it down with a heap of tatties, those were good nights. Old Jock glowered from his seat at the fire, his pipe sending up puffs of blue smoke into the already suffocating atmosphere. His presence put the family on edge and one by one they would slip out, making any excuse to hide from his simmering, unpredictable temper.

One warm day, the three older boys lay in the woods up on the hills overlooking the North Sea. John, just turned fifteen years old, was back from his bothy in Perth for the weekend. He had left school in December and was now earning his own keep, proud of his new-found independence. Frank and Will lay on their back sucking gobstoppers, content with the day. John was regaling them with stories of his bothy life, of the songs and of smoking real cigarettes.

'And what about the work?' Will asked.

'Och, it's fine, you just have to do what the farmer tells you, and he's a good bloke. I had to weed the turnips, which just about killed me, a' that trouble just to feed the beasts. But it's a'right really and there's nobody worrying about fancy writing or anything.'

John bit into an apple and threw the core over at a crow which was standing on one leg and eyeing the lads up from his perch on a broken branch. 'Hey, look at that bonny pig over there,' John pointed. 'What's it doing there? Hey, Porkie!' he shouted, 'Are you no a bit far from home?'

Frank sat up eyeing the pig. 'Let's catch him and rustle him back to the house, I could fair go a pork chop.'

'We can't kill it,' Will said. 'We could just take it home and see who it belongs to.'

'Aye, and maybe no one will know and then we can keep him. We can fatten him up and have him for Christmas,' added Frank, already standing and walking slowly towards the festive feast.

The boys managed to get a hold of the animal and assess its size and strength. John picked up a sharp stick. 'I don't think we can carry it so we'll just have to push the beast along.' He jabbed it with the stick and the pig snorted. 'Aye, it's moving, we just have to give him a fright to encourage him. That's it, Piggy lad, just walk this way, it's not that far. We'll get him back and put him in the shed; maybe we'll get a reward for our troubles. That would be grand, we might even get a tenner!'

Meanwhile, as the boys were rescuing the errant pig, their father was at the receiving end of a tirade of abuse from the farmer on whose adjacent land he worked. 'This is your final warning, Farquharson, if you answer me back one more time, or ask for anymore money for your vagrant-like bairns that you can't control, or show your temper on my animals, you are out, I've had enough of the likes of you. One more chance, now get on and fix those fences before you knock off.'

It was close to five when Jock secured the last straining post. He wiped his forehead and replaced his cloth hat on his head, collected his piece box from the barn and headed down the long track that ran adjacent to his own field. The farmer owned all the land as far as the eye could see, all except the Farquharson strip that had been in his family for decades. It was fine land but hardly adequate to support a family of nine. The sycamore at the gate was thick with foliage and he noted the chickens that Isobel had got were thriving in their wire enclosure next to the shed. Maybe he could wring one of their necks at Christmas, but he spat into the grassy verge with contempt as he remembered the farmer's words and wondered if he might wring the fat bastard's neck instead. Aye, he thought, it would give me great satisfaction, the puffed-up wee tweedy toad, threatening me like that.

It was the pig he heard first as he rounded the gable end of his house. He eyed his two youngest children who were loitering by the hens. 'What's that racket coming from the shed?'

'Frank is going to kill the pig for dinner,' Ian announced.

Silvia lisped, 'He's nice, a nice pig. I dinnae want to eat him.'

Jock inhaled deeply and looked across the fields towards the farm he had just left. His face blanched in anger. 'I'll see about that.' He strode round the house in great strides to find his wife. 'Where are they?' he demanded.

'Oh! You heard?' Isobel smiled, then realised that something was very wrong. 'The boys found a pig...they...'

Jock strode through the house to where the lads were collecting their fishing poles from the hall cupboard. 'So, it's thieving now, is it? Am I to wait for the police to come from Aberdeen to get you in their black van? You think you can help yourself to livestock and rustle them back here and hide them in my house? And you?' He stuck his face at John who stepped back in shock. 'You with your manly sense of importance and all your bothy tales? Is this what they teach you there?' Jock's eyes were now red-rimmed and mad-looking. 'Get out. I'll teach you not to steal and bring more disgrace to my name.'

Frank looked at his father with contempt. He straightened his back and led the way outside, his two brothers following. He glanced at his mother, her eyes wide with fear, but saying nothing, as was her way. They waited in turn for the punishment. First came the sound of the belt buckle and the familiar swish of the strap. Will got two across his back, and John got a hard crack across the head by the calloused hand.

Frank stood defiantly. 'We found it, you old fool, it had strayed and we brought it back to see if we could get it back to its owner. There was no stealing.'

'Old fool, am I? Well, a pig in the shed that doesn't belong to you is thieving in my book. You can argue until you are black and blue in the face to any policeman in the land and they will still not believe you. But you can save your words for the law, laddie, because you don't get to speak to your father like that. The feel of my belt is too easy for you, boy!' Jock looked about him for a better weapon, and grabbing a heavy stick, he shoved Frank over to the well. His greater strength overwhelmed the boy and he tipped him over the edge until his head was lowered towards the water. He raised the weapon and struck him hard on the shoulders, backside and legs. Again and again, he beat him, blinded with a primeval sense of anger and frustration.

'Get off, you mad bully.' John lunged at his father.

'Stop him!' shouted Isobel. 'Please stop him before he kills him.'

'Aye, I've stopped,' Jock grunted, sweat beading on his brow, 'but I've a mind to kill the pig and destroy the evidence. No one around here will believe in your fairy stories.' He stepped back from the well and ominously retreated to the kitchen. He returned with a knife and made towards the shed where the pig was squealing in indignation.

Frank lay dazed on the ground, his body broken and bleeding. 'Are you all right, son, can you get up? Let me put some salve on those cuts.'

John shook his head, deeply disturbed by the way the incident had got out of hand. This was far worse than the usual thrashings they'd had to endure throughout their childhoods. He helped his mother lift Frank up whilst Will ran ahead to get his brother a drink.

'I'm leaving, Mother,' Frank groaned. 'I won't be coming back.'

'No, Son, you can't go, not yet. I know your father is not good with the words, not like you, the dominie says you have real talent, he doesn't want you to leave the school. Can you not stay for a wee while longer. Maybe till you're fifteen?'

'I'll kill him, Mother, if he doesn't kill me first.' Frank grimaced as she dabbed the cloth on his battered body, her touch so gentle. 'I'm sorry, but it's time.'

Chapter 28

'And who are you, marching in here looking like a patient that's just rolled off an operating table?' The prim receptionist eyed the gangly youth with suspicion.

'I sent you a letter,' came the gruff reply.

'Oh, did you now? And what did you say in the letter? That you were qualified in street fighting and had run away from the school?'

'I need a job; I need to get away from the farm. The dominie says I've got a good hand at the writing and I was his top scholar. I had a wee bit of bother at home, if you get my meaning?'

'Aye, I can see the wee bit of bother might have given you a reason to run. I won't ask questions but you look a bit young for a job on the newspaper. Have you had anything to eat?' The receptionist opened her drawer and retrieved a packet of Rich Tea biscuits. 'I'll make us a cup of tea then you can tell me what you can do.' She looked at him with concern and a frown creased her perfectly smooth brow. 'I don't know, there's something about you. Maybe there's a look of my wee brother in you that's making me soft, but I know he would never seek work if he was in trouble, he's a right lazy little toe rag, but I can see you might be different. A woman's instinct, maybe that's what it is. Now you sit over there, I won't be long.'

Frank sat down and slumped against the wall; he was bone weary. After two nights staying with John at his Bothy, trying to avoid the farmer's beady eye, he had felt strong enough to flag down the bus to Perth and search for the newspaper's address to which he had so recently sent his optimistic application. His body was wracked in pain, it was a wonder his back or arms weren't broken. His head was still matted with blood and he still had dizzy spells from the concussion he'd suffered after the beating. His belly growled for food; he needed some sustenance to get through the next few days.

The receptionist returned with the tea, only to find 'the poor lad' as she had described the unexpected visitor to Mr MacBride, her boss, fast asleep with his head fallen on to his chest. She returned to her desk and drank her own tea and nibbled her biscuit. I wonder, she thought, and went over to the tray of pending letters, not yet dealt with. Sure enough, there was the letter, in the boy's beautiful writing, conveying his naïve hope of betterment.

'Mr MacBride, can you just read this and come and have a look at the lad.'

'I'm due at the court in half an hour, Miss Mackay, you know I have to cover that case,' but he registered her expression and relented, 'All right, let me see it.' The newspaperman read through the lad's letter and his mouth twitched. 'Very well, let me look at this great writer.'

The two returned to the reception area and just as they stepped into the room the phone rang, loud and shrill. Frank jumped, suddenly alert, then groaned at the sudden pain shooting down from his shoulders.

'Perth Dispatch, good morning, Miss Mackay speaking, can I help you?'

Mr MacBride walked around the desk and stood in front of the boy. He saw a tough-looking lad with an intense and alert expression on his face, a lad who had clearly suffered more than a few knocks in life but was still ready to take on the world, a lad who seemed determined to make something of himself. Macbride himself cut an imposing, no-nonsense figure and yet there was a twinkle in his eyes. 'So, young man, you are looking to learn the newspaper business, are you? I hope you are better at writing than you are at fighting. Have you had these injuries seen to?'

'No, Sir, I just had to get away, but there's nothing serious, I don't think, just my head is pounding. But I would be very grateful for a start. I'm quick at learning, Sir, I just need a chance to prove myself.'

'Aye, you do. Presumably you are homeless now?'

Frank looked away, not ready to betray his father's ruthless behaviour.

'I've worked on this newspaper for over forty years, son, and I've seen a lot of things that still manage to upset me, but I never lose faith in humanity and I think I see strength of character in you. My wife is a nurse at the infirmary. I am going to stick my neck out and give you a start. You can learn from the bottom up and if you do well, I'll start you in night school to help you train as a cub reporter. You'll get a few shillings a week and I know a fine boarding house at the South Inch who will take you in for bed and board. Jessie is a good woman and has housed quite a few of our staff over the years. In the meantime,

Miss Mackay will take you over to the hospital in her lunch break, and you can get yourself checked over. She will also see you settled at Jessie's. Take care, young man,' and he looked down at the letter. 'Francis Findlay Farquharson?' Do we call you all of that, quite a mouthful, don't you think?'

'Most people call me Frank, Sir.'

'And I'm Mr MacBride to you, son. I'm putting a lot of faith in you, boy. I don't know why but I think you have the gumption to get on in life. It only needs to start with a small step,' and he smiled, folding the letter carefully and turning round to brief Miss Mackay of his intentions.

The receptionist winked at Frank and went off to make him a fresh cup of tea.

Chapter 29

Violet Watson was a shorthand typist at The Scotsman newspaper's offices on the North Bridge in Edinburgh. Every day she would step into the grand building, clipping up the stairs in her black court shoes and gabardine coat, her blonde curls bouncing on her shoulders, quite unaware of how attractive she was. At twenty-four she was totally focussed on the day ahead and she still could not believe her luck at achieving such a job. Violet had excelled at night school where she had added shorthand and book keeping to her basic typing training. She had a natural flare for shorthand and was constantly practising, converting shop names and such like into the Pitman squiggles as she travelled to work on the trams. She had a good grounding in her secretarial life, as employers were keen to engage such an efficient typist and she had already worked in a law office and a bank, but she particularly liked it here at The Scotsman. The news articles and editorials she typed up, following breakneck speeds of dictation from frenetic reporters, were far more interesting than the staid letters in the law office. There were flower shows, weddings, court cases, horse racing at Musselburgh and all the domestic dramas that suddenly made the front pages. Her sister Phamie had chosen a steadier career working as a shop assistant in the Co-operative store on Leith Walk and could not understand Violet's desire for studying beyond the school leaving age.

This morning, Violet breezed into the typing pool and immediately her heart sank, for there was Betty Jones with a clipboard and envelope in her hand. Another blooming wedding, thought Violet, and I'll have to part with some of my meagre earnings for someone I hardly know, just so that my name goes on the office card. She smiled sweetly however and said, 'Ah, Betty, it's you again. Who is the lucky girl this time?' and she rummaged in her purse for a couple of shillings. 'Pat from accounting? That's nice.' She moved over to her desk, a little crestfallen as that money would have been a help towards the nice cardigan she had seen.

'Violet Watson?' A voice shouted above the noise of the typewriters.

Violet looked up expectantly. 'Yes, that's me.'

'You've been assigned to a senior reporter; Mr Farquharson needs a full-time typist for a while on the piece he's working on.'

'Shall I come now?' Violet reached over for her shorthand pad and headed to her new assignment.

Frank Farquharson turned away from the window where he had been lost in thought. He had been gazing down at the rooftops and streets that ran alongside Waverley Station. He'd come a long way since his apprenticeship in Perth and was now a senior reporter for this most prestigious newspaper. He liked the freedom to report on social injustice and many of his articles about tenement living and overcrowding had been published. There still lingered a deep hatred within him for certain types of men, and this hatred had manifested itself as a cold detachment and a fondness for the bottle. After a few beers or glasses of hard spirits, his colleagues knew to keep their distance from him, recognising a man who had his own demons to fight. Frank turned on hearing the door open and glanced at the pretty girl standing in front of him, taking in her fair hair and neat appearance. 'Thank you for coming so quickly.' He indicated the chair opposite his desk. 'Violet, isn't it? You come highly recommended; I believe your shorthand speeds are next to none. I hope you and I can work well together.'

'I love my work, Mr Farquharson. I always try to do a good job.'

Violet crossed her legs and sat alert, her pencil poised over her shorthand pad. Frank dictated his scribbled notes to his new typist and was pleased at how Violet transcribed his words into coherently typed paragraphs. The piece Frank was working on was an investigation into protection rackets and illegal gambling, and the more he investigated, the more he realised what a big thing it was. He had discussed with his editor the need for going undercover, and Sandy, his boss, had given him the go-ahead after warning him of the huge risks involved. They had decided that a suitable cover would be to give his profession, when asked, as being a freelance insurance broker since that would enable him to mix in all circles plus give him flexibility in his working hours. That cover gave Frank the freedom to travel to Glasgow and around Edinburgh where he could mingle with men at the factories, football matches and bars, always keen to have a drink and a bet with them, but leaving those around him unaware that the man in the pea coat and flat cap was taking in every word they said.

In the weeks that followed, his working relationship with Violet grew into a good partnership as she sat in the office, often bemused at the articles she was typing relaying facts that she had no previous awareness of. For even growing up in the tenement building she shared with her family in Leith there had been little contact with men at the pub or outside the factory gates or at the docks. The men she knew tended to drink like fish on their paydays and sometimes there would be a lot of wild shouting about money. Often wives could be seen surreptitiously scurrying to the pawnshops with their little bits of treasures that might put food on the table for another week. But what Frank was dictating was about vice and addiction on a grand scale. Gambling on the Football Pools was legal because it was conducted by post and involved an element of credit at a humble level, but it seemed that there were other ways to place bets illegally. Newsagents, tobacconists and hairdressers acted as covers for the bookies.

One rainy morning in October, Violet was poised as usual with her pad and pencil, but couldn't resist interrupting Frank's flow of dictation. 'Imagine that,' she said, 'I had no idea you could place money on a horse while you were buying your sweets at the local shop. What if the police were to come in?'

'Aye, they're quite fly with their transactions, but the need to gamble is a powerful force. Have you never had a flutter yourself, Violet?'

'Certainly not,' she quipped. 'I can just imagine my mother's voice berating the waste of good hard-earned money, literally tossed down the drain.'

'Well, you see,' explained Frank, himself not averse to "wasting" the odd shilling on a likely winner, 'the main excitement of betting is the state of hopeful suspense which occupies the mind for several hours at a stretch. You could get a big win, you could triple your money, but your mother is right, you could lose it all in an instant! I've noticed that some of the blokes I talked to are getting quite a bit of satisfaction from becoming experts in the pedigrees of horses and greyhounds. It's a grim world out there,' mused Frank, taking a break from trying to unravel his notes to the ever-diligent Violet. He couldn't help noticing her nicely turned knees and slim ankles. 'Life seems hopeless to so many, they are in mundane jobs, money is tight, there is no release from their drudgery. Only at the pictures and dance halls can they get a bit of escapism. Have you ever been dancing at the Eldorado in Leith on a Saturday night, Violet?'

'Of course I have, who hasn't?' she replied, tossing her head indignantly.

'People need a release from their lives, they need to meet up and have some fun, to forget they might be sharing fourteen to a room. Sometimes it feels like the whole city seems steeped and rolling about in sexual desire. For men anyway. It fills the streets and overflows all the dark little corners, and the only refuges are the pubs which ironically, convention forbids women to enter, but which, nevertheless, are always well attended. Men just wrap themselves in the familiar cloak of alcohol.'

Violet frowned. 'I can't help thinking about the prostitutes. They seem to be happy plying their trade right under the noses of the churches and even St Giles Cathedral itself. I suppose you have pity for them too?' Her face was tinged with pink as she probed this subject with her boss.

'Yes, I do, but the ladies of the night have always been with us; they are still part of the Edinburgh scene. They mostly live in the poorest districts but their main beat is Princes Street which I suppose they see as being the socially exclusive shopping precinct. The Royal Mile is little better than a slum.'

'Have you interviewed any prostitutes yourself?' Violet asked, her eyes wide with interest.

'I have; they all have their different stories and the poor women are just trying to make ends meet. Once upon a time they could scrape a living being milliners and seamstresses but those trades are dying, hence the increasing number of furtive prostitutes on the streets. I don't believe it's faulty morality. I put the blame at the employers' doors, those who pay starvation wages, and the bastards who get fat on sweated labour. I apologise for that language, but it makes me as mad as hell.'

'You do feel very passionate about it all. I think your article when you finish it will be quite a revelation to the general reader.' Violet was quite surprised at how much she herself was learning about her city. Within her own home she and her sister had been brought up with the strict codes of the church and Bible studies. Every minute not at work was spent cleaning or mending or helping their widowed mother. A polished fire fender, gleaming brass and mopped stairs were the highlight of their lives. She was finally beginning to see another Edinburgh through the eyes of this passionate young man.

Frank grinned at her, enjoying the blush spreading across her cheeks. 'Maybe you and I could have a bite to eat after work, would you like that?'

'Aye, I would,' she smiled, 'but I can't be late home as my mother is quite a dragon and keeps close tabs on me and my sister.'

'Right, we have a date. We'll have high tea on Princes Street and then I'll see you on to your tram, how's that?'

Violet flicked her hair back, her eyes shining. 'I'll meet you on the steps at five, but for now I'd better get on with this typing. I have about forty pages of shorthand to decipher; you're a hard boss to please, Mr Frank!'

Chapter 30

Married life for Violet was everything she had hoped for; she and Frank had a small flat in the close, one floor up from her mother and sister. Frank lavished her with love and affection and even helped her carry the heavy washing down to the wash house. Many men would have seen it as soft doing a woman's work, but he would come home and whirl her around and kiss her and tell her he loved her and hadn't he proved it, for now she had quite a belly on her and they had bought a second-hand sprung pram together. The coal fire was burning by the polished range and Violet smoothed the nice quilt on their bed, a patchwork that had taken her months to complete in tiny stitches, using up all the bits and pieces of fabric that she could glean from her family and neighbours. She was furious when the midwife had come and sat upon it, as proud as the Queen of Sheba she was, with no regard to Violet's hard work.

'You're a lucky lass, no mistake.' Violet's mother bustled around the room, searching for dust or a spot on the floor that she could point to. She inspected the embroidered bib that her daughter had completed and the small matinee jacket on the knitting needles. 'You've turned out all right, Violet, and I can see you hang out a good washing. Not like that lassie that just moved in on the ground floor, she has the effrontery to hang out grey brassieres. Imagine? It makes you wonder how she keeps her house if that's what she parades on the washing line for all to see!'

'She's not got much money, mam, and her husband has been laid off; I think she has a hard time of it. Maybe we should practise some Christian charity with our neighbours?'

'Aye, maybe you're right, I suppose I could ask her if she wants any help, though she might think I'm just being nosey. Where is your good man off to today?'

'I don't know, he said he's covering a big football match at Ibrox Stadium in Glasgow. No doubt there will be the usual broken-bottle violence, no matter who wins. Rangers or Celtic, they just use it as an excuse. And those Bridgeton Billy Boys are scary with their gangs and razors and their hatred for Catholics, always hanging out at the Orange Order marches.'

'Are you not worried when he's away there?'

'Of course I am, but he's been doing it ever since we met. He'll be fine, and I've made mince for the dinner, he likes his mince and tatties.'

Frank and Violet's courtship had been a natural continuation of their office relationship. She had been elated when he suggested they get engaged and even more elated with the fine presents she received from the office staff. She smirked at the thought of the money that had been donated, remembering how reluctant she had been in the past to part with her hard-earned shillings for other girls' weddings. She was proud of her pots and pans and shiny cutlery and the grand maroon rug that hid the tear in the linoleum just near the fireplace. Sometimes she looked at the framed wedding picture of them both, so smart on that snowy day. She looked so happy in the long dress and fluffy bolero that she'd got with her saved up coupons from the Co-op. Frank was handsome in his dark suit, but she had known better than to ask about his family or if any of them would have wanted to attend.

Early on, when they had begun to get close, she had asked him about his home and his parents, and it was as though he turned to stone, his eyes suddenly cold. A twitch on his jawline told her that he was suppressing some violent emotion. 'I was brought up on a farm close to Stonehaven,' he eventually explained. 'I had five brothers and one sister, that is all you need to know. By the kindness of two exceptional people in Perth I have been able to make a life for myself and for that I am grateful. That is why I do what I do, I try to delve into the underbelly of the city and report the wrongs I see. But the less you know the better. Now, enough of that, I'm sorry to be so abrupt but I don't want to talk about it again, it's best sometimes to leave the past behind. I just want to say one thing more and that is this, I'm the luckiest man in Scotland for I have the best shorthand typist in Edinburgh and the prettiest girl in the whole city.'

As Violet was sharing a cup of tea with her mother, Frank was just off the train in Glasgow and was moving amongst the heaving crowds making their way to the football grounds. But that was not his destination today for instead he had sidestepped the rush and was making for the south bank of the River Clyde where he was a regular at a pub which served as a front for illegal betting and where the local whores plied their trade. He stepped into the bar and made his way through the busy room. The air was thick with smoke, hanging like a fog over the men who were leaning against the bar.

'Are you here for long, mister?' A hag with one tooth snarled at him from a bench that ran along the edge of the room.

'Nah, just for a pint and maybe a wee chat with Annie. Is she aboot?'

'Annie should charge you for her time, always tongue-wagging with you when she could be up against a wa' for half a croon.'

'Well? Will she be in, she said she'd be here?'

'Might, or might not. Did you no ken that she's taken up with that lad in that gang, the Calton Tongs? A right bad lot they are, even for round here.'

Frowning, Frank turned away and sat down on a stool at the bar.

'Are you thinking of putting a wee wager on the game today, Micky?' the pub landlord leant over, touching his nose and giving him a knowing glint.

'Aye, Jim, I'll put the usual on, and I'll have a pint and a half.' Frank slipped the notes over the counter, looking over his shoulder at the assembled men, wheezing and lighting up their cigarettes and drinking their beer.

'Can you give me a light, mister?' A thin girl with a torn blouse and a black eye pressed against him.

'You haven't even got a fag.' Frank looked down at the scarecrow of a girl.

'Aye, but you have, what dae ye say?' She touched his arm and beamed at him, revealing a broken tooth.

'Annie, what's happened to you? Who have you been seeing? That old crone says you are getting tangled up with the Tongs, that's bad news. You know they're into the protection racket and they're handy with blades and have no scruples whatsoever.'

'Och, come on, Micky, I can take care of myself. Anyway, I'm here and have some news for you. That big fella was here again the other day. He's shifty, asking questions about who's been using Jim's services, if you know what I mean. I think he's into a big gambling racket in the city. He doesn't like these small boys having a go and making a few bob. You should be careful - you ask too many questions yourself.' She screwed her eyes up as she lit her cigarette and inhaled deeply as she looked about. 'Who's that bloke over there, the drunk, can you see him? Over there leaning on the bar? Oh God, he's seen me looking at him. He's coming over if he doesn't fall flat on his face first.'

A tall young man, about Frank's age, staggered over to join them, and made a show of pulling in a stool and trying to focus on them.

'Hello,' he grinned. 'You two seem to be having a nice wee party. What about letting me join in? I can buy you both a drink. I've just come down from the Isle of Skye and I'm lonely here in this big city.'

'Aye, you're welcome, but Annie here is just leaving, she needs to take this pound note and buy herself a couple of fish cakes and a hunk of bread from Wee Molly's stand at the corner there. Will you do that, Annie? I'll see you in a day or two; take care and look after yourself.'

'Thank you kindly, Micky, I could do with something to eat. Aye, I'll be seeing you.'

'Micky, is it? Well, I'm Robert and I'm very pleased to meet you. What line of work are you in? I'm in the newspaper business myself, supposed to be covering the match, but I woke up in a cell with my head pounding so I needed a hair of the dog, if you know what I mean?'

'Aye,' said Frank, 'it can get you like that. I'm Micky, Micky Allen. I'm in insurance, a freelance broker, so I do quite a bit of travelling around. Why did you leave Skye, Robert?'

'Och, there was nothing going on up there, so I thought I'd try my luck here, and what do I end up doing? More school prize-giving and the odd court case! But great pubs, we'll have to go on a good crawl round the centre, what do you say? Maybe even try out the dancing at Locarno's, I hear they have a great band there?'

'That sounds like a plan, Robert, now let's have a top up. Jim! Over here, the usual please, plus what he's having.'

Frank eyed up his new companion. He was well dressed, tweed jacket and good strong shoes, clearly quite an educated sort. But not smart enough to keep off the bottle. Mind you, he thought, my own undercover work and the drinking and betting are getting a hold of me. I'm not too worried though but it might be a problem getting back to Violet, reeking of drink and short of money. She's a good girl and we have a nice wee baby coming in a few weeks. Hopefully I'll have cracked this case before then. I just need to find out who is controlling Jim and all the other outlets.

'What a day,' said Robert, 'I had to cover a court case at two o'clock and it ran on till after three, then the wee toerag was just held in remand till the next hearing.'

'That sounds serious, what was he up for?' Frank blew froth from his glass before taking a gulp of his beer.

'He attacked a distillery worker, jumped him on his way home when he was crossing the Glasgow Green. He thought the man had a half bottle tucked in his overalls, and then when met with resistance, he stabbed the poor bastard with a flick knife.'

'Murder?'

'Aye, but he might get manslaughter. The lad is only nineteen.'

Frank shook his head, imagining the sorry scene. 'I had a somewhat quiet day,' he finally said, 'well, compared to what you had to report.

The two men chatted on for a good while before Frank remembered to check his watch. 'Look, Robert, I'll just drink this up as I have to get my train now. I hope I run into you again.' They both stood up and shook hands.

'Cheerio, Micky, till next time.' Robert staggered back to the bench along the wall and immediately slumped over to the side.

Instead of heading straight for the station, Frank made a detour as he needed to call his boss to make his progress report. It was a fine evening and his footsteps echoed as he ducked through into a narrow close and out to a backstreet where he entered a telephone box. He punched in the numbers and pushed in the coins when he heard the pips. His call was answered immediately. 'Hello Sandy. Just a quick update for you. One of my contacts tells me that big, shifty fellow was in the pub here again asking questions about who's been using Jim's services. It seems he's into a big gambling racket in the city.' Frank spoke quickly, looking around at the quiet street. 'I'll keep my head down while I try to find out what's going on, but it definitely feels as though something is brewing. It's pretty nerve-wracking but 'll keep you updated.'

'We're concerned about you, Frank. You seem to be drinking pretty heavily – I can hear it in your voice.'

'I'm OK, boss. This undercover role is no tea party but I have to fit in with the types I'm mixing with. Have no fear, I have it under control.'

'I hope you do, Frank, but if your life is in danger, get the hell out of there with whatever you've learnt so far.'

'Thanks, Sandy. I'll be careful but I want to get to the bottom of this story and I feel I'm getting close.' Frank hung up and headed for the station and the train home for what would no doubt be another drama with Violet at the state he was in.

*

Frank and Robert continued to meet regularly. The next time they met, the well-dressed man from Skye had sobered up considerably, enough to share his life story. His name was Robert Hunter, the son of church people on the island. Maintaining his undercover persona, Frank never revealed his real name or his real profession to him, but presented himself as a drunken gambler with a temper while his natural aloofness and flinty stare gave the impression of suppressed violence. Robert was always aware of a sense of menace lurking beneath his friend's facade.

Wee Annie sometimes sidled up to the man she knew as Micky for a furtive chat and anything she could get from him, but as the weeks went by, Frank felt uneasy as more unfamiliar faces appeared in the bar. There were whispers about a rival protection gang and Jim was apprehensive about accepting wagers from unknown customers.

Frank became a father in October of that year and life with Violet and baby Edie was a real life-changer. He doted on the baby and worked harder than ever to bring in a good wage to support his little family. The Glasgow investigation was still on-going but he felt in his gut that it was nearing a conclusion. One cold November morning, instead of going to Glasgow as planned, he took a train to Perth. He smoked a cigarette, and puffed, and put it out, and lit it again. He was restless, he couldn't sit still. He got out of his seat and walked up and down the corridor as the winter landscape with its ploughed fields, sparkling with silver frost, slipped by. What on earth had possessed him to make this journey after all these years? His stomach felt queasy and perspiration was running down his arms. Was he sickening, did he need a drink to settle his belly? He paced back to his seat and loosened his tie. For God's sake, what was the matter with him? Finally, the train drew into Perth station. He walked briskly towards the bridge over the platform and made for the exit. Sunshine was splintering through some grey streaks of cloud, and suddenly, as he screwed up his eyes, there she was, a wee woman, all in black, her hat squashed on her head and secured with the jet pin he remembered so well.

'Mother.' It was all he could say.

'Aye, laddie, it's me. Come here and give your poor mother a wee cuddle.'

Frank leant over and kissed the old woman's powdered cheek, feeling her bony shoulders through the worn tweed of her coat.

'I'm much the same,' she said, 'but look at you! A big strapping lad with a fancy suit. You could have blown me over with the breath of a canary when I heard you wanted to see me. It was clever that you got in touch with John, he still comes by, but you ken whit yer faither's like. He's aye "gathering his brows like a gathering storm, nursing his wrath to keep it warm…", as Rabbie Burns once aptly wrote. He disnae get ony better, but Oh! It does my heart good to see you, son. It's been sixteen years, far too long, but I'm looking forward to the nice cup of tea you are going to buy your old mother, and maybe a wee scone?'

Frank gave his mother another kiss on her cheek and she took his arm as they crossed the road to the Station Hotel.

When Frank finally left Perth later that night, he was drained, memories of the past that he had kept suppressed had suddenly risen up as his mother filled him in with news of his brothers and Silvia. He in turn had shared his news about Violet and baby Edie.

'Oh, my boy, that's wonderful news. I would love to see my granddaughter; will I not get to see them?'

But Frank shook his head, 'No, Mother, not yet. I'm not ready for that. I have a lot on my mind with work at the moment, but we'll see, maybe in the summer.'

He had watched her small figure board the bus to Stonehaven, and waved until the vehicle had driven out of the terminus and round the corner. He was bereft, but glad that he had finally made the effort to meet her. His anger had never been directed at her, and it was clear that old Jock hadn't changed so there was no chance of ever returning to his old home. He turned away and walked back to the Station Hotel and went straight to the bar. 'A pint and a half please, and make that a double.'

He settled on a stool and lit a cigarette. He didn't notice the time passing, but the barman counted up his empty glasses and kindly leant over, 'Are you getting a train by any chance, Sir, it's getting late and close to last orders.'

Frank lifted his head and stared fixedly at the concerned barman, 'I am. Thank you, you're right, I am getting a train, now maybe you could give me a clue, which way do I go to get that train?'

'Violet, come on, I'm not that late, I just got held up.' Frank tried to cuddle his wife as he staggered into the house, throwing his bonnet on to the hook at the door but missing.

'What time is this to come home? And you reek of pubs and drink, again. I don't want you coming anywhere near baby Edie like this. And you can unhand me right now.'

166

'Oh, come on, Violet, I missed you, come here and give me a cuddle. The time just went and I couldn't leave. I had to meet someone. You know how it is?'

'No, I don't know how it is and what about the money you promised me for the coal and the shopping?'

'I've not got anything; I'll get you some next week.'

'And what's that stink on you? Like stale clothes. Have you been with someone else? Those prostitutes you are so protective of?'

'Violet, stop it right now. You are my girl and I love only you and baby Edie. Now *haud yer wheesht,* I need to get some shut-eye if I'm to get into the office tomorrow all bright and breezy.' And he collapsed right across her pristine quilt.

Violet wept.

Chapter 31

The trips to Glasgow continued, but Frank had fallen into the need to gamble, his small wagers often becoming big wagers as his winnings spurred him to take greater risks. When he lost, which was often, the remaining coins in his pocket disappeared down his throat. The harsh whisky blotted out his fear of discovery and he now stood shoulder to shoulder with the other men, lost in a world of depression. Working undercover, he had permeated a seedy and potentially dangerous world, but in his drunken haze he was unaware that he had fallen into the trap of thinking he was invisible to any suspicious gangster on the look-out for nosey reporters or cops.

Convinced that she was being betrayed, Violet had hardened her heart to his endearments and his false promises. It had been four months since he had given her money and she was now dependent on her mother and sister to make ends meet. When he did get home, the drinking was getting worse and he was hardly recognisable as the Frank she had fallen in love with. There was no way she would let him near Edie.

He had missed his last train to Edinburgh again. It was becoming quite a habit and he often ended up on his landlord's couch at the back, sleeping off the drink. He leant against the bar, aware of Robert beside him and wee Annie cadging cigarettes and drinks off him, but his ears were burning with the information she was feeding him. 'The Tong lads are up to something, Micky. They know there's a snitch and they know he's from around here. The big bruiser who covers this pub is planning a surprise for whoever he is. He already has a big empire in the barber shops and dance halls so he knows how to get rid of any opposition. I'm getting a wee bit scared, I dinnae want any violence coming to us in this cosy wee pub.' Annie finished her drink and clutching the cigarettes he'd given her, she scurried away to talk to someone else.

'What is she whispering about, Micky?' Robert asked. 'Honestly, I don't know what you see in her, she's always hanging about and she's got an odd smell about her.'

'Don't you say a word against Annie,' Frank spat back. 'Girls like that are diamonds, and she's been a good friend to me.'

'Yes, well, sorry about that, to each their own.' Robert downed his drink while his eyes followed Annie making her way through the throng of men, laughing at their chat and swishing her skirts around her skinny body as though she was doing a turn at a variety theatre. She reached the door and scurried out of the pub.

Frank pushed past Robert and followed her outside. He only had ten shillings left after gambling over twenty pounds of his wages. He could barely stand; Glasgow was spinning and Annie was walking at a fast pace. 'Wait up, lass! Give me a hand, will you?' He staggered and fell off the kerb and lay face down in the gutter, waiting for the world to stop its infernal motion. His clothes were soaked and blood was dripping from a nasty gash on his cheek.

'Micky, what are you doing? Get up, you cannae lie there all night. You're making a habit of this, it's the fourth time I've had to get you up from the road.' Strong hands grabbed his arms and pulled him up on his knees and he retched the contents of his stomach on to the pavement. Frank recognised the voice but couldn't remember the name of the lad who was helping him.

'Come on, Micky, come with me, I know just the place where you can sleep it off and you'll be fine again tomorrow.'

The lad got him on to his feet but Frank was aware of two other men, rough-looking sorts, who had somehow materialised out of the darkness behind the streetlight.

'I'm all right, lads, good of you to help me, but I'm as right as rain now, just need to get on my way.'

One of the men guffawed. 'Aye, he's right as rain, fresh as a daisy. Just look at him, he could walk a tightrope for the polis, if they were to ask him!'

Frank heard them sneering and ridiculing him as he tried to focus on the direction that he thought Annie had gone. His unknown companions grabbed his arms and led him down the road and across a junction where cars were passing. Puddles sprayed up from their tyres and he felt rain. He'd lost his cap. Where was that? Did he leave it in the bar? He was conscious of tenement buildings around him, he hoped the men would put him to bed in some dry room where he could get a sleep. Sleep would help. He imagined what he would say to Violet on his return: *I just couldn't tell you, darling, I had to keep it quiet. I had to protect you and the bairn. I don't want these gang lads getting too close to me now, it's only a matter of time and then I can publish the whole story. After that we could have a wee holiday, you'd like that, wouldn't you, maybe take a jaunt up to the Highlands?* He was being led somewhere; this was not what he had in mind. He was confused. What was happening? He stumbled on a loose step, but the strangers kept marching him forwards, down a narrow close to where the common bins were stored. A bright moon pierced the darkness and a fine rain was falling. He was wet, cold and disorientated.

'Where are you taking me, I thought I was getting a bed for the night?'

From the shadows an older, dangerous-looking man appeared, smartly dressed in a white shirt and dark suit, polished shoes and his hair slicked back with Brylcreem. Frank froze, he felt intense fear like ants running down his neck. His mouth was dry, his legs shaking. He could make out the faint scar that started below the left eye and ran down the man's cheek, a reminder of the bad days of the 1930s razor gangs. He knew he was in trouble.

When the man spoke, it was with a slow drawl, deep and menacing, 'Well, Micky, or whatever your name is, I don't suppose you know me but I know a lot about you. Young Annie has told me all about you, about your questions and your gifts of money and cigarettes. She's a very clever girl, playing the game to infiltrate my enemies such as yourself. She knows where her bread is buttered and no sneaky cop or journalist or whatever you are will destroy my business. I rule Glasgow and now you, Micky boy, will have no one to report back to. It's goodnight and sweet dreams for you, my friend.' Mean lips drew back to reveal a cruel grimace.

Frank looked into the cold eyes and he knew it was useless to talk, and anyway, what could he say? From far away, from another time, he thought he heard his mother's voice, '*Sweet dreams, lad,*' she used to say, '*Try and forgive him.*' He wished he could see her one last time, just hear her voice one last time, but it was too late now.

Razor man was drawing closer, slowly, like a black snake. 'I've a wee present for you, Micky boy, just a wee Glasgow kiss to send you on your way.' The crashing blow to Frank's forehead left him partially unconscious, but it was the slash of the blade across his throat that ended his life. It was over and tomorrow's newspapers would report his death.

*

170

Robert Hunter only found out about the murder of his friend from wee Annie after she sidled up to him the following morning. The Skye man was in the pub for his usual hair of the dog.

'Yer pal won't be back, Mister. He met his end last night, round by the bins at the tenements down the road. Poor Micky, I quite liked him too.'

'What?' Robert shouted, 'What do you mean, met his end? What happened to him? What on earth did he ever do to anybody?'

'Och, you're a right innocent aren't you, Mr Robert. Micky wasn't Micky, that wasn't his real name! God knows we'll find out who he was eventually. The polis will do their job, but for now I just want to warn you off, you seem like a good sort, a bit fond of the drink, but you are not from round here and you don't understand our ways. Get out whilst you can, go back home. That's my advice to you and you'd be wise to take it!' With that she cuddled in closer and grinned, showing off her broken tooth, 'But whit aboot a wee fag afore ye go?'

Chapter 32

Edie found she had nothing to say. Her tissues were wet from the tears she had shed as Robert recounted his story. He kept emphasising how little he really knew, how he had pieced together what he knew of Frank and what he had heard from Isobel, his mother. Also, by being a newspaper man himself, he had easily found out what Frank had been involved in. The character Micky had been walking a dangerous path and he had learnt how his friend was close to finding out the identity of Glasgow's number one gangster. She looked up from her mangled tissues. 'But they did meet again, my father and his mother. That is something. I found the fragile newspaper cutting, his death notice that Isobel kept in her Bible. I thought that was all she knew about him. But when she met him, he told her about me and Violet, my mother. That explains how the letter came to me, giving the news of her own death. I often wondered how the solicitors were able to trace me. The poor lady, and only hearing of her son's murder by reading a newspaper account. She must have suffered so much.'

Robert nodded 'I was glad that our paths crossed when I became a minister in this parish and I was able to tell her what I knew of Frank's life in Glasgow. Of course, I knew nothing of his Edinburgh life, it was she who enlightened me on that.'

'Oh, my poor mother, and I was so unkind to her. She knew nothing, and she too must have had such a shock. And she brought me up alone, well, with the help of my gran and my Aunty Phamie. And my mother never even met my father's mother. That is so sad, they might have found comfort in each other. But poor Grandmother Isobel, here in Formylie farm, living with such a violent man and losing all of her children, how on earth did she cope?'

'She was always a cheery soul,' Robert smiled at the memory. 'I can see her yet, sitting all in black with her thick lisle-stockinged legs resting on the stool by the roaring fire. She had white hair, parted at the side and held neatly with a Kirby grip. Her cheeks were pink and she always had a twinkle in those blue eyes. Her knobbly fingers always held knitting in spite of the arthritis and she had a great talent for socks.' Robert turned back to his guest, aware of how pale she had become. He had been rambling, a little lost in his own reminiscences of those times. He stood up and reached for her hand. 'Come outside with me, Edie, come and sniff the wind from the North Sea. Can you feel the chill, even on this fine day? I want you to take your car and drive along the road to Dunnottar Castle and stand on the cliffs above that ancient old bastion and look at the pounding surf on the rocks below and think about the woman who lived here. Think about what her life was like. You have inherited her blood, you are from her line, and whatever is making you sad, or whatever you are running from, the spirit of Isobel is not far away. I think you are like her, and when you are ready maybe you will tell me of what it is that has brought you back here, so far from your home.'

'His name…'

'Ssssh,' the minister admonished her. 'It's not the time, but I shall be waiting for you.'

Chapter 33

Adam Shariff was downing a bottle of ginger ale at a hotel in Manly, the up-market seaside suburb of Sydney. Sitting out on the decking of an old colonial-style hotel, with its quaint wrought-iron arches, he was aware of the hubbub of noise coming from the bar inside. It was Happy Hour; the young clientele were bronzed and their raucous chatter could rival the racket the yellow-crested cockatoos in the nearby bottle brush and jacaranda trees made from dawn till dusk. Adam's body ached; he'd been hanging from the Centrepoint Tower in the heart of Sydney all day. He'd got a job as a window cleaner, making use of the rope access qualification that he'd undertaken a year ago. It was both challenging and exciting doing a mundane job whilst hanging from a rope hundreds of feet up. It suited him fine. He'd previously been up to Darwin and over in Perth, working in the mines, three weeks on and one week off, filthy work that was. He'd certainly made some money but the heat and sweat and grit up his nose all day was more than he could stand. He'd packed it in and returned to Sydney on the promise of a better job. His sister was long gone; she'd returned home glowing with her first-class honours degree in zoology and accompanied by some clever guy from Singapore that she'd met at uni. Adam suspected that he would be summoned home for a wedding fairly soon. Tara was like that, dependable, the apple of the old folks' eyes. He squinted out at the glittering ocean, looking for any dark shapes or ominous fins. There'd been a sighting of a great white shark here a few days ago. He liked the sea but he preferred the thrill of height more than the terrors of the deep, and the rope work had made him lean, strong and very sure of himself. A voice interrupted his solitary musings.

'Hey there, it's Adam, isn't it? I'm new here. Someone gave me your name, over there at the bar, he said you might know where I can get a ride to Brisbane?'

Adam eyed the stranger, taking in the bushy beard and red hair, probably mid-twenties like himself, about six feet tall. He looked wholesome and robust, almost like a biblical character. He could be a student, but Adam doubted it, and what's more, he recognised the British accent.

'Yes, I'm Adam, but I'm sorry, I don't do that anymore.' He looked into glassy green eyes. 'I used to have a Combi Van and take folk up the coast for a bit of an adventure; it was cool but I've packed it in now. I did a rope access course instead and have never looked back. How about you? Are you staying here long?'

'I'm here for a year; I write articles for a travel magazine. I stopped off in Hong Kong on the way over. By the way, I'm Brent, Brent Brown. Named after "he who lives on a hill",' he added with a grin. 'I come from Sussex in the south of England but I wanted to see what's down under before I get stuck in some office somewhere.'

'Pleased to meet you, Brent, but I'm afraid I'm not much use to you in my present line of work.'

'You aren't from here either, are you?' Brent noted that Adam's accent was not that dissimilar to his own clipped English vowels.

'You're right about that. I'm originally from Sabah in East Malaysia. You may have heard of the island of Borneo? Head-hunters and primitive tribes?'

'Yeah; I've read about the decimation of the rainforest that's been going on too.' Brent pulled up a stool and sat down beside Adam. 'So, you're from there?'

'I am. My mother is Scottish and my father is Malay, originally from Johor. I was supposed to be a great engineer but I flunked out of uni. Then my girlfriend dumped me so I took to the road. My father gave me money to buy a car, but I bought a VW Combi Van instead and started taking travellers up and down the coast, about two at a time so we weren't too cramped. They paid me decent money and I had great fun too.' Adam paused, taking a sip of his drink before continuing, 'It was exciting. We wild camped or stayed in camp sites, had barbecues, avoided snakes and spiders, just living the dream. But after doing Coffs Harbour, Coolangatta, Tweed Heads and the Gold Coast about a dozen times, the old van started breaking down and to be honest I was getting a bit tired of it all. The result is, I decided to sell the van and use my savings to do the rope course. I'm really enjoying it; the outside life suits me.'

'And now, apart from your job at the moment, do you have any long-term plans?'

'Well, the work is quite varied, I can be doing anything, anywhere, so I'm happy here for now. What about you, can you abseil?'

'I can, actually.' Brent fumbled in his wallet. 'Look, I passed my rope access course when I was at university. I was keen on climbing in Wales and up in the Peak district. I did a bit in France last year as well, in fact I wrote about it in a holiday journal. I'm making a living writing about my adventures and still having fun at the same time.'

'Sounds good, maybe you and I could do something together after all. You're even getting me keen to try my hand at the journalism stuff as well. My mother's mad friend had visions of me being a travel writer, but I doubt if anyone would want to hear about a day in the life of a window washer.'

'Maybe they would if they knew how high you were dangling in the sky!'

The two decided to get some fish and chips. The sun set over Manly beach and for the first time in a long time Adam was in no hurry to return to the single room he rented in the nearby hostel.

The next day Adam introduced Brent to his boss, and the new recruit with his thick beard and hard hat took to the ropes with ease, dropping off the sides of some of Sydney's highest buildings. Each evening after work Brent drank beer and the two would eat steak or fresh seafood. 'You don't drink?' Brent asked one night. 'Is there a story there or should I mind my own business?'

'Let's say I had issues, but we'll leave it there for now.'

'Fair enough, now where are we off to tomorrow? Are you sure we couldn't take a break and head up the coast?'

'You do wear a guy down, persistent, aren't you?'

'I am starting to get twitchy; I want to see more of this country while I have the chance.'

'I can understand that and I could do with a break myself, as it happens.' Adam ran his hands through his blue-black hair, grown long on to his collar. 'Might be good to get off the ropes for a while. OK, we'll hire a car and stay in campsites and motels and cruise up to the Gold Coast. What do you say?'

'You're on!' Brent sat back in his chair and took a large swallow of his beer. Adam watched the condensation drip from his friend's glass and looked away.

The following week, much to Adam's amusement, they quit the window washing job and rented a van. They drove north, taking turns at driving the vehicle up the familiar Pacific Highway to Brisbane. He watched Brent jotting down his observations, double checking on spellings for the many aboriginal names they encountered as well as any unfamiliar trees and birds.

'These trees are like wallpaper,' Brent commented one afternoon; the drive had been long and the eucalyptus trees on each side of the road were dense. 'How can travellers stand it, this never-ending parade of blue gums, red gums, ghost gums for miles and miles?'

'Guess they suit the environment, sure is different from Borneo.'

'Yea, and Sussex. I kind of miss sycamores and oak and beach.'

'You haven't seen the damage when a forest fire goes through these places. God, it's awful, gum from the eucalyptus just whips up the fire and decimates huge areas of land, wiping out homes and wildlife, leaving the area a smoking ash pit. Kangaroos, koalas, all the creatures have a hard time with burnt paws, smoke inhalation etc., that's if they actually survive. It's devastating.'

'Yet driving past them like we are now, the area looks tranquil, I hope I don't see anything like that. Can you stop for a minute? I'd like to just walk about for a bit.' Adam pulled off the road at the next lay-by and Brent got out of the car. He paused, feeling the heat engulf him. He tried to take in the vastness of this great continent, the life going on unseen around him. From far away he could hear the sound of a whipbird, its familiar whip crack song so common in these forests. Brent retrieved his notebook from the car and wrote a short paragraph then made a sketch of the eucalyptus trees around him. 'That's good, now how far till the next stop?'

Adam taught Brent to surf, and the Englishman, with his strong fit legs and muscular torso, found his balance easily, flying over the waves and persevering every time he came a cropper. It was a good trip and they made it to Byron Bay where they sat around the bar, watching the crazy hippy people dance, still lost in the days of the 1970s and rumoured to live in the bush all week then coming out to play at the weekends. Some said they were feral, maybe they were, but Brent spent an hour engaged in conversation with an old couple with long grey pony tails and cheesecloth gear.

Adam observed how his friend ended each night with his notepad and pen, scribbling his impressions of the day. He was bemused. Did anyone really want to read this stuff? He thought about his previous travel experiences and of how mad some of these tourists were, always pestering him to visit famous beaches or fancy monuments they'd read about. I've never been like that, he thought, I just like to let each place take me over. Immersion is the best way and boy have I had some experiences, not all of them too great though. Frowning, he pushed the hair out of his eyes, reflecting how he once was, back in his Singapore days with his high-flying pretensions, but what a blast it had all been, and Victoria Chan, she had been quite a catch. He was glad that he'd flown with the high-flyers for a bit, but his return to earth had been quite an implosion. After he failed his exams and dropped out of university, he had drunk his way to the gutter. Beer and vodka had blotted out days at a time, and he'd ended up squatting in a filthy house in the Sydney suburb of Surry Hills. He remembered those dark days when he had learnt a lot about humanity amongst those who had fallen from their own life's high ideals. A heroin addict once held his head and helped him to drink soup from a dirty mug. An ice addict tripping on Crystal Meth had called an ambulance and forced him to go to the hospital because he could no longer feel his feet or hands. Adam had been and still was ashamed to have been the recipient of their compassion. It was a nurse who had turned him around and offered him a way out. She had introduced him to her grandfather, an old Aussie gardener who took care of one of the biggest of Sydney's cemeteries. Gray his name was, the skin of his bulbous nose scarred by skin cancer, his head covered with a broad-brimmed hat just like the one Adam now wore with the passion of the newly converted.

'Gotta protect your skin, mate, don't want to end up looking like me. I was the king of the surfies back in the seventies and look at me now, every new mole or lump gives me the heebie jeebies! But you can bunk down with me and help me with the mower, there's a lot of graves need mowing. Stay as long as you like, son, Tanya filled me in on your story.' And Adam did and old Gray gave him a home of sorts, and a different philosophy to think about. Several times he'd fallen off the wagon and not made it back to Gray's shack. The pull of the drink was too strong. He screwed up his eyes remembering the shame of the days when he retched up bile into the gutter, of the policemen shoving him and calling him names. He'd lost count of the pavements he had fallen onto and of the strangers who had put him in taxis and sent him back to old Gray.

'You got a problem, mate.' The old man patted his arm after yet another drunken episode. He placed a bucket on the floor as Adam slumped down on the settee on the porch. Gray's yellow mongrel rested his head on Adam's knees and looked soulfully into his eyes. 'My granddaughter helped you at the hospital but your body won't take kindly to this abuse, Adam. You need real help. I'll come with you, if you like, to the AA place. I went there a few years ago with my old cobber, he was just as you are now. What do you say?'

Adam had promptly vomited into the bucket and lay back gasping. He wondered if he had broken his shoulder last time he'd fallen. Creepers were growing out of the drain pipe, a lizard darted out from beneath a leaf, the bloody dog was drooling on his leg, the old man was droning on and on, all he wanted was a drink and he'd be fine.

He was lucky. Somehow, over time with the indefatigable help of the old man, he'd come out the other side. Gray had supported him through the worst and somehow, he'd finally managed to remain sober, eventually able to leave Gray and make a new life. But each day since then, he lived with the knowledge that he was only one drink away from that other place. It was hard, especially in Australia, living in a pub culture where men rewarded themselves with a drink after a hard day's work. Since those dark days he'd done OK. He'd even made a sort of peace with his father. He knew that time apart is a great healer, but now he looked over at his new friend, enthralled with the hippies of Byron Bay, passionate about his reporting. He liked his enthusiasm; he liked his verve for life, both qualities were contagious, Brent was OK, a good guy.

'What about you taking me over to where you come from?' Brent asked Adam the following morning as they sped up the road towards Brisbane. 'I'm intrigued, I wouldn't mind visiting your part of the world and see all those jungles and orangutans and wouldn't you be the best guide?'

Adam said nothing, just kept his eyes on the road. What was going on? This guy is starting to really get to me, he thought. First, he wants to do the ropes, then he gets me to do the road trip, now he wants to go to KK. And the thing is, Mum just rang last night telling me about Tara's wedding next month. She wants me to go home. I could afford to if I do another spell in the mines, it's good money, and then I wouldn't need to ask Dad for my fare which might surprise him. I expect he's completely written me off financially after all the history we've had. Maybe taking this guy with me might be a good thing. Keep the heat off me, and Mr Charming here sure has the gift of the gab with his nice English manners.

Brent butted into his thoughts. 'Did you hear me? How about us going to Borneo? I'd like to see all those tribes and they have that big mountain there, don't they? Fancy having a go at that?'

Chapter 34

Moy Moy leant her elbows on the chest of drawers in the kitchen and stared off into the horizon. The sun was high and the day promised to be hot. For many days it had rained and the path along to her hut was slimy with mud; the banana palms were dripping with moisture, the colours almost purple like those of the big forest beetles. She must remind that lazy gardener to cut back the lalang grass, it was growing too high and sometimes she had seen that old cobra hiding behind her house. Not good, she thought, it was time to clear the bushes and grass. She could hear Mem running about, first to the bathroom and now out to the veranda, always rushing about, never taking time to just sit still. She needs to stop, that one, needs to have a relax. She never listens to me, but Moy Moy knows it's good to have a relax. She pulled herself away from the view of the glistening sea in the distance and sauntered out to the washroom and out through the back door to find that no-good gardener.

It was not the best day in the world for Edie, she was late, she needed to get to Tong Hing Supermarket and then drive to the hospital. She dashed around the house, throwing shirts and dresses into the laundry basket, bashed her toe against the coffee table and smothered a curse, knowing that she would lose a nail in the weeks to come. Why were such petty things so painful? She pushed her foot gingerly into her silver sandal and grabbed her car keys. Honestly, where was everyone? Even Moy Moy had disappeared. She looked out towards the shack she lived in, down by the papaya trees. There she was, leaning on her brush chatting with the gardener, the pair of them looking as unperturbed as ever. 'Moy Moy!' Edie cried. 'I'm going out, please make rice for Tuan's lunch, he will be back at one o'clock.'

'OK, no problem, Mem, and what about you, are you eating lunch too?'

'No, not today.' Edie rushed to her car; she would definitely be late. The hospital only allowed visitors at specific times, and she needed to buy grapes. Isn't that what people do? Tong Hing had good red grapes in their latest shipment. She was frantic with worry as she drove erratically through the crowded streets, stopping to pick up the grapes on the way. 'Why?' she muttered to herself, how could this have happened to my strong vibrant friend? It is just so awful.' Amelia was barely conscious and fighting for her life after contracting the worst type of dengue fever. Evidently the virus had caused inflammation and swelling in the brain. Her friend was heavily sedated in an attempt to avoid a fatal haemorrhage or possible stroke or encephalitis. Michael had been distraught on the phone. She was stable, still very ill, but they were hopeful. The couple had been on a jungle trekking holiday in Pahang to see the ancient indigenous tribal villages. It had been wonderful, Amelia was ecstatic on their return, that was, until the sickness, the tiredness and the rashes appeared.

Edie mused on all of these recent events as she pulled into the hospital car park. Her friends were not faring so well. Poor Amelia, and now poor Maggie Rajah, her other long-time friend. Edie felt great unease thinking about Maggie. She was going to visit her after seeing Amelia. She found a spot just next to the A&E department, grabbed the grapes and slammed her car door. The heat hit her after the ice-cold air conditioning of the car. Squinting into the sun and fumbling for her sunglasses, she didn't see the kerb. With a horrible crunch onto the gravel, she fell forward and she knew as she hit the ground that she had broken her ankle, the sickening snap sounded like a twig breaking. She was stunned, aware of the sharp gravel sticking into her cheek and hands and knees. Slowly Edie raised her head and looked about her. All she could see were the purple juicy grapes scattered all around her. Well, that was a waste of money, she thought. The next thing she was aware of, she was lying in the recovery room of the hospital, with nurses in theatre scrubs adjusting machinery and drips.

'What happened? I just broke my ankle, why am I in this state?'

'You certainly broke your ankle, as well as your fibula in several places, so you needed surgery to put in a titanium pin. The doctor will see you later after you have come round properly. Rest now, you need to sleep for a while.'

'What about my friend, Amelia Low? I was coming to see her; I had some grapes.'

'Yes, she is stable, they are sure she will recover, they got her early. Dengue is worse if it goes undiagnosed, but for now we have both of you here. Maybe soon you will convalesce together.' The nurse gave her an encouraging smile and briskly walked away to continue on her rounds.

Edie closed her eyes and before drifting off to sleep, she remembered her chaotic morning and the minor trauma of stubbing her toe. Oh well, I won't see my toenails for at least two months with this Plaster of Paris stookie on. Her leg was suspended by a sling in the air. What about Tara's wedding? And what about Maggie Rajah? And Kamal? Should I worry? And Adam, did he not say he was heading home soon? Edie felt oddly calm. There was nothing she could do about anything and she fell into a deep dream-filled sleep.

Chapter 35

Tara Shariff flew home to Kota Kinabalu as soon as she heard of her mother's accident. Her fiancé, Joe Bin Musa, stayed on in Singapore as he was working with the forestry department. The couple had got engaged at Christmas and were now saving hard to buy a flat in the Jurong area of the city. Joe was in charge of urban forest rehabilitation and was passionate about his job, looking to expand his interest further afield. Kamal had told him about the drive for reforestation that was going on in Sarawak and of course he'd learnt about the dipterocarp forest at university. 'It's amazing,' he said to Tara, 'now I'm hearing directly from men who are involved in stopping the extensive devastation caused by logging. It makes me more determined to help save some of the hundreds of species of these amazing rainforest trees. Did you know,' he continued with passion, 'that some of these giants grow to heights of eighty metres and some are eight hundred years old?'

As a zoologist, Tara had achieved her own lifelong dream and was now working in Singapore Zoo with large mammals, in particular the proboscis monkeys and orangutans, both endangered species. She was fascinated with monitoring their care and behaviour whilst in enclosures and was hoping to get an opportunity to work in the field. She too saw a future in Borneo, back where she had grown up and where her love for nature had begun. But now, returning to her home on Tuaran Hill, she found her father quite distracted and her mother oddly serene. It seemed strange to see Edie not flying about on her various missions but calmly holding court from her chair, her leg in its plaster cast propped up on a stool and a walking frame at hand.

'I have invited your grandparents to come and oversee things for the wedding,' Edie told her daughter. 'As you can imagine, Minna was ecstatic so you will be following tradition to the letter T. No make-do sarong kebaya for you with an altered sheet to cover your ankles. And we will have it all here in this house. Does Joe have a lot of family, aunties and so on?'

'He does and Azna, his mum, is quite a traditionalist as well, so Granny-Nenek will be in heaven. Are the aunties coming too? Ma and La, Ooty and Long?'

'Of course. Also, Adam and a friend should be arriving any day now.'

'A friend?' Tara squealed, 'a girlfriend?'

'No, no girlfriends that I know of. It's a lad he met in Sydney, a fellow called Brent Brown from England. They seem to like the same things and have been doing window cleaning in Sydney, suspended on ropes. It all sounds a little risky to me, I don't fancy his chances if he falls off any of those skyscrapers. Anyway, they are both coming here for a while and are planning to climb Mount Santubong in Kuching, then doing Mount Kinabalu from here in KK.'

'And how did he sound? I haven't spoken to Adam for ages.'

'Remarkably up-beat and happy. I hope his father is reconciled to his change of career and his new lifestyle. One good thing is that he has been independent from us for the last three years, so he must be doing well in the rope access business.'

'That is good news, I'm happy for him. And what about Amelia, is she any better?'

'She is, still very weak and very tired but she is getting better all the time. Her girls are arriving in the next day or so. I think they might even be on the same flight as your friend, Marie. Isn't she coming from Syndey via Singapore? Anyway, you'll see Amelia tomorrow. I've invited her and Maggie Rajah round for afternoon tea to see you. Moy Moy is going to make her sago pancakes. You remember how you used to love them?' Edie adjusted the position of her leg and tried to sit up straight in her chair. 'You'll notice a great difference in Maggie, the poor woman has been divorced by her husband.'

'No!' exclaimed Tara.

'Yes. Just out of the blue one day, he told her he wanted her to sign a paper. He has already married some other woman; presumably the two of them have a little love nest somewhere. Poor Maggie, she had no idea, she's in shock. He has left her practically destitute after over twenty years of devoted marriage, well certainly on her part. Oh dear, it's so sad, she has become so sickly and goes about wearing scruffy trousers and T-shirts. She used to be so beautiful; I remember comparing her with the Mona Lisa with her dark hair and pale face and always so smart and immaculate. I was always a little in awe of her.

Remember she had that playschool business where you and Adam went when you were little? Well, he forced her to give that up. A few years ago, he was going through some mid-life crisis and he decided that they should go abroad and travel, which in fact never transpired. Now that this has happened, I've tried to persuade her to restart her business, it will give her an independent income at least until she decides what to do. Fortunately, her boys have grown up and are back in England now.'

'Do you think it might just have been a fling, like another mid-life crisis?'

'No, from what I hear, when they make you sign the divorce paper, it means they are serious. But at least this way Maggie is entitled to some money from him. I am told that when a Malay man wants to sleep with another Malay woman, the girl will insist that he marries her first. Often, they just set up their new wives of convenience, keeping their first wife completely in the dark while they carry on with their affair. But if they make the first wife sign the paper, then of course she is fully aware and is therefore legally divorced.'

'Is it just with Malay women that this occurs?'

'Yes, I suppose if they sleep with women of another race, they would just use hotel rooms for anonymity. In Muslim communities there are always the pious religious do-gooders who are jubilant to report adulterers to the Sharia police.' Edie sighed. She looked down at her hands resting on her lap and at her own wedding ring.

'Well, enough of this.' She wriggled in her seat to get more comfortable and smiled at her daughter. 'It happens and I am so sad for Maggie but we mustn't let it spoil your engagement or your wedding preparations. Joe is an exceptional young man, handsome and totally devoted to you as well as to his high principles for environmental change. I couldn't have picked better myself. Right, let's get some paper and make a plan of whom to invite and what we need to do before Minna comes over from Johor and takes over completely.'

Chapter 36

Tara was fascinated by the attention lavished on her by Nenek Minna and the aunties. She had been elevated to the status of a princess, much to her amusement. In contrast to these wedding preparations, her engagement had been as simple and perfect as she could have hoped. In December, Joe had proposed to her in Singapore after a romantic dinner under the stars and he had placed the diamond solitaire on her finger with no ancient ritual or interference from the family. Her parents had been delighted and conceded that western culture does play a part in this modern world they all lived in. But that concession was not permitted to apply to the wedding itself. Edie assured her in no uncertain terms that there would be no simple registry office marriage or token church blessing, The rules of procedure had to be followed and there would be no escaping any of the Malay rituals. 'Just go with the flow, enjoy the occasion, that's what I did,' Edie told her. 'And to be honest, I wouldn't have missed any of it, although my wedding was a bit of a shotgun affair and it certainly took your dad's family by surprise.'

Tara tried to imagine what her mother must have been like, aged twenty-two and so new to such foreign rituals. 'You were so brave, Mum.'

'I know, I was brave but I trusted your dad so I saw it all as a wonderful adventure. I had to.' A wry smile played upon her lips.

It was Monday and the wedding was scheduled for Thursday. Minna, now quite grey-haired and stout, was getting ready to leave early in the morning to secure her purchases from the market in town. She was dressed in her usual batik sarong with a turquoise lacy top. 'I need to get rice flour for cake making, some fruit and snacks, maybe some fish for curry. You, Edie, you can order the drinks from the supermarket, lots of Fanta Orange and 7up. We are going to have a nice party at the kampong tonight, and Ooty and Long have the henna that we brought over from Johor.'

Tara understood that this particular ritual was usually a fun evening with just the women involved. They would paint lacy patterned stencils on to each other's hands and feet with the ochre-coloured dye. She had invited Amelia's two daughters, Lucy and Claire from Singapore, and Marie, her old roommate from Sydney, to be her attendants at the wedding. They would all be arriving this afternoon. She couldn't wait to see Marie's face when she told her that they'd be downing glasses of 7up at her hen night. She and her father would go to the airport later to pick them up, that is if he was free. Nenek Minna had had him running about like her personal slave and Tara found it hilarious to see her father reduced to this state, quite lacking his usual grumpy dignity.

Her orders given, and with her basket on her arm, Minna swept out of the room whilst summoning her son. 'Kamal! You come with me, you can drive and you can wait while I do the shopping. Have you organised everything for the mosque?'

'I have, Ma.' Kamal picked up his keys and raised his eyebrows at his giggling daughter. 'Dad came with me yesterday and the imam will preside over the official ceremony at the mosque, just as we planned. It is all arranged. We shall all go there early for that, then come back here for our family ceremony.'

'And have you ordered carpenters to construct the dais and the frame over it for the canopy?'

'Yes, Ma, I have. Edie and the sisters have arranged for the silk canopy to be sewn up in time. Let's go now before all the bananas and rambutans are sold out.'

Later that afternoon, Marie, Lucy and Claire sat on Tara's bed. It had been so long since they had last met up together during a vacation in Singapore. 'This will probably be the last time we'll be alone before the family take over,' Tara said. 'Everyone is out, Adam has taken Joe and Brent off to the yacht club, so let's get a bottle of Mum's wine and you can tell me all your news.'

Marie offered to get the wine and glasses and returned to Tara's bedroom, amused at the lion and giraffe motif curtains that still draped the windows. Outside the sky was deep blue and a massive tree seemed to fill the whole of the outside view. She was a slim girl with wavy long blonde hair and had what seemed like tiny rocks dangling from her ears. She wore a flimsy lime-green dress with lacy flounces. She was a girl brought up on Sydney's eastern beaches, and exuded confidence and vitality. Her blue eyes sparkled as she handed out the glasses and poured the white wine with the panache of the wine waitress that she had once been. 'Cheers, my friend, I know you guys are going to have the best life. You are utterly made for each other, and cheers to us girls who are still waiting for Mr Right to show up!' Her wide smile was infectious and they all sipped the cold dry Australian wine. 'Mmmm, your mum has good taste, by the way!'

'So, tell us, Marie, did you get that job in the Conservatoire?' Lucy asked.

'I did. I had to work in a bar at Botany Bay for nine months but finally they offered me a position. I play piano, violin and harp, and I teach so I'm where I want to be and doing what I've always wanted.' Marie smiled a smile of satisfaction.

'Look at her! She's like the cat who's got the cream.' Tara patted her friend's arm, happy to have her close again. 'And I hope someone is still taking you out to see the real world outside, like I used to do?'

'Nope, I'm afraid my days of bush trekking in the Blue Mountains ended when you left; my only foray out now is to the shopping mall. Never mind, I'm here and hope to see some real jungle on this holiday.'

'If that's what you want, my brother is here with a friend; they are planning on going to Kuching in Sarawak after the wedding to climb Mount Santubong, maybe you could tag along?'

'I hope you don't mind leaches and vines that are ready to strangle you,' chipped in Claire, whose adventurous mother Amelia had always organised jungle holidays for her twins, with or without Michael.

Lucy laughed, 'Come on, she's born in Oz, she knows all about spiders and snakes. You go for it, Marie, take the chance if the guys offer to take you. As for me, I have to get back after the wedding; I'm a dedicated nurse, as you know. Also, a certain consultant has taken my fancy and I'm sort of hoping it's mutual.'

'Oh, that is good news, sis, we'll drink to that! Does he have a name? Mum would be ecstatic; she needs a lift after the year she's had.'

'His name is Dennis, he's in gynaecology and obstetrics. He's Chinese and brilliant at his job. But I think we'll keep it to ourselves for the moment, let's see how it goes. I don't want him scared away just yet and we don't want to give Mum any false hopes. What about you, Claire? What is going on with you?'

'It's all good, I've finished my training in hotel management in Singapore and I have been selected to go to Switzerland to train with the general manager of an alpine resort. There is a world-famous chef there who I can't wait to meet. Living in Zermatt might be quite amazing, so no jungle treks for me.'

The afternoon drifted on. Marie studied the three Eurasian girls, lounging on the bed and laughing with the ease that familiarity brings. They could almost be sisters, with their lightly tanned skin and sparkling brown eyes with lashes so long they almost fanned their cheeks. Marie studied Tara, soon to be the blushing bride, and saw the sleek short haircut, always the bob, and the classic sharp fringe above the largest doe-eyes she had ever seen. So pretty, so intelligent and always so in control. And nurse Lucy with her straight black hair, inherited from her Chinese father, and long legs she had from Amelia; she was the serious one and smiled only when necessary. Nice teeth, Marie thought, those girls have perfect teeth. She was aware that her own seemed quite small compared to the film-star smiles she saw on these girls. Claire of course was similar to her twin but had permed her hair and put a red dye through it. Shorter and a little dumpier than her sister, she camouflaged her curves by wearing flamboyant colours. It was good being here as part of this special wedding celebration.

Marie emptied her glass. 'God, I feel a bit squiffy.' She smiled dreamily, lying back on the pillow and closing her eyes. 'Not complaining you understand, I just hope this feeling lasts until tonight when we just have the soft drinks to keep our spirits up.'

'Don't forget you have to totter down to the kampong later so don't even think of wearing heels.' Claire too lay back on the bed and let the room swim around her. 'God, I'm tired. It's been non-stop since we got back.' She closed her eyes. The fan turned lazily above them and the afternoon drifted away.

Minna oversaw the preparations for the evening meal, 'Ooty! You can chop the garlic and fry up the onions, and you, Moy Moy, you wash the rice.' Moy Moy rolled her eyes, and sauntered through to the storage cupboard to measure out the rice. She was in no hurry. She took some time to gaze at the afternoon sun beginning to set over Likas Bay then sauntered out with the pot to wash the rice at the outside tap. She squatted down and in a lackadaisical manner she contemplated the water as it ran through the rice until she was satisfied it ran clear.

Hassan, Kamal's father, came to sit near her. Brent and Adam appeared from the kitchen door. 'Come here, boys, I'll show you how to sharpen a parang.'

'What's up, Kakek?'

'You should learn how to look after knives, especially if you are going to walk in the jungle. Come and sit here with me and Moy Moy and you can oil the parangs you bought at the market yesterday.'

'OK, let me fetch them from the room, you wait here, Brent, I'll get them. They're still in the newspaper the storekeeper wrapped them in.'

Edie, from her chair in the lounge, followed Adam's movements with interest as he retrieved the parangs from his room and then disappeared quickly through the kitchen. What's he up to? she thought, and what has he got in that package? She could hear the chitter-chatter of her Johor family cooking up a banquet in the kitchen. Slowly she heaved herself up and made her way with her walking frame, the heavy cast making it difficult to walk. Looking out of the laundry room window she scowled. Her father-in-law, the two boys and Moy Moy were all perched beside the open drain. Timmy the Second was sitting close to the party. He too seemed bemused with the whole process of oiling and rubbing the razor-like blades. 'Well, so that's what you are up to,' she called out. 'I don't see why you should need those weapons; you're only going to be walking and climbing. You shouldn't need to stray off the paths, the guides will be with you.'

'I know, Mum, but it's always good to be prepared. When will dinner be ready, and when are you girls going to get your henna tattoos?

'When Moy Moy finishes washing that rice,' Edie looked pointedly at her amah who seemed more interested in oiling a parang. 'I noticed Minna chopping a chicken with a giant cleaver and the aunties are preparing the vegetables. The girls are closeted in Tara's room, they must be having a nap. Poor things, they must be so tired.'

Moy Moy looked up at Edie, and a crafty glimmer lit up her normally impassive face. 'OK, mem, rice ready for cooking; come on, Timmy, I give you some food, nobody else remembers you in this house.'

Edie sighed at the obvious inference. 'Fine. So, dinner should be ready in the next half hour or so. Afterwards, as you know, we girls are going down to the local kampong for drinks and a hen party. Tara is getting the full treatment! I'm just a bit worried how I'll get there with my broken leg. I told your father I need to hire a wheelchair but he just chose to ignore my plea. Look at me with the Zimmer that the hospital gave me, I can't hobble down that steep narrow path in the dark with that thing.'

'We can help, Mrs Shariff, we can carry you down, it won't be a problem.' Brent grinned at her, his teeth glinting through his beard.

'Certainly not, I'm not having anyone carrying me in the dead of night.'

'No, not carrying you in our arms. We could put you in one of those rattan chairs out on the veranda. We'll take a side each like they did with the Chinese emperors. What do you think?'

Edie groaned.

Much later, when darkness descended and fireflies flickered in the jungle at the rear of the house, Moy Moy stood watching the procession trouping down the hill. Her face was expressionless. Look at Mem, she thought, all dressed in purple, sitting like a Queen Woman wobbling about with her big leg straight out like a broomstick. Those boys are not too good at the carrying, first they take her one way then put her down, then try another way, now they have one boy on one side and one boy on another. The old Malay boss-woman and her daughters, already gone first and very fast, not waiting to see if the mem will arrive at all. And Tara and her girlfriends, all dressed up, just like coloured birds you see in the mango tree, screeching about, getting in the way. Moy Moy knew they had taken another bottle of Mem's secret wine. Moy Moy knew, but Moy Moy doesn't say. Moy Moy just looking.

Chapter 37

The big day dawned, the frangipani tree outside her bedroom window was covered in waxy white and yellow blooms, and red ants scurried through the emerald-green grass. Behind the garden scene the giant rain trees stretched their branches like jade silhouettes against the deep blue of the sky. It was the picture Edie saw every morning of life since she had come to Sabah twenty-five years ago. Today was her daughter's wedding; she had often wondered how it would be, and where it would be held, and who Tara would have chosen. But now that it was happening, she could never have foreseen how removed from it all she felt. The house had been transformed; furniture rearranged in order to accommodate the dais with its silk canopy over it. She had helped Minna, Ma, La and Ooty sew the raspberry-coloured silk cloth and attach the saffron tassels so that it could be draped on the frame over the dais. A Persian rug had been lifted from their bedroom and placed on the floor of the platform, and from somewhere, she thought the Hyatt Hotel, Kamal had borrowed two large ornate thrones both heavily carved and painted gold.

Minna had bought two crimson silken cushions for the chairs so the couple would be comfortable for they would be required to sit in splendour for a long time. Fans were at hand for the bride's handmaidens to cool them down, rather like Indian *punkah wallahs*. Minna and her daughters, assisted by the ever-helpful Moy Moy, had been slaving in the kitchen to produce the traditional food to be served to guests later. There was to be *mee goreng* and *nasi goreng* and chicken and fish curries. Snacks and cakes had all been laid out for the hungry guests.

Timmy the Second meowed plaintively all morning, prowling around the kitchen. 'Aiya!' Ooty exclaimed, 'someone take that cat away.' Poor Timmy was taken meowing and protesting to the gardener's shed where he was locked in with a plate of cold sardines. 'We cannot trust him around the tables,' Ooty glowered, 'he'll be jumping up for sure and bring such disgrace in front of guests.'

Hassan and the boys had been ordered to move the dining room table out to the veranda and had then covered it with Edie's white bed sheet, brand new and purchased especially for the bridal bed, but that was another story!

'Honestly, Amelia,' Edie had vented her frustration over the phone, 'my mother-in-law has taken over that department as well, decorating Tara's bed with garish yellow satin sheets with matching pillows and a bolster, can you imagine? You should have heard her laying down the law to Tara and Joe as to what was required in the bedroom department. "It is vital they follow ancient tradition," she told me for the hundredth time!'

'Ha Ha! Did they get the speech about performing the sacred duty?'

'Well, sort of, but they are to have holy water sprinkled on them before retiring for the night, and in the morning the bride must have wet hair as proof that the consummation of the marriage had been successful.'

'Did you and Kamal have all that rigmarole? I thought you two had already been cohabiting in Edinburgh before you came to Malaysia?'

'Yes, but we had to go through the motions just to please the parents and everyone else in the kampong! I was so exhausted I slept like a corpse and in the morning, I completely forgot to douse my hair.'

'Were you not banished from the kampong for your heinous behaviour?'

'No, I just hung my head in shame but cheered up instantly when they brought out the wedding breakfast. Nothing was ever said, not to me anyway, but no doubt there was tittle-tattle about it in the village.'

Edie looked at her pristine white sheet spread over the dining table. She knew it was inevitable that it would soon be slopped with curry sauces and turmeric, probably stained forever.

All of Kamal's family were at the mosque for the *akad nikah* ceremony. Edie, still nursing her broken leg, stayed behind with Moy Moy and was now ensconced in her favourite armchair, her foot resting on a leather stool. Without the hysteria of so many people in the house, she had managed to wash and dress at her leisure, choosing to wear a dusky-blue silken kaftan with a string of freshwater pearls. She'd looked into her red lacquer jewellery case and lifted the slippery gold and silver chains and idly let them slide like cold snakes through her fingers. A crease appeared on her forehead. Her lips pursed. Feeling the small pearls her mother had given her when she had left for Malaysia, she remembered her parting words: 'Pearls, Edie, can be for tears but they have more lustre and warmth than any diamond.' She selected them and kept her eyes averted from the hateful diamond studs, guilty gifts from her husband. She had tied her hair back into a French roll and slipped a frangipani blossom in at the side, attempting to look like the Burmese lady, Aung San Suu Kyi. Edie and Kamal had bought gold earrings in the shape of the Chinese wedding symbol of double happiness for their daughter. They would give them to her later. For today, Edie mused, Tara was adorned like a butterfly and hardly recognisable. She had watched her daughter leave for the ceremony at the mosque, tottering on unbelievably high heels, her face made up so thick, you would think it had been applied with a shovel. Ooty had assured her that this was expected of Malay brides. Tara and her girlfriends had just raised their eyebrows and shrugged. The aunties had plied them with dragon-red lipstick and purple and blue eyeshadow. Their eyelashes stuck on as thick as hairy caterpillars. Edie looked aghast. Gone were the four naturally pretty girls. They had been transformed into glamorous Hong Kong film stars. Tara's glossy hair was covered in an ivory-coloured lace veil and her matching sarong kebaya was of raw Thai silk; she had wanted to keep the western tradition of wearing white or cream, as a tribute to her mother. Edie had laughed, 'Well, my wedding outfit was silvery pink, but I had no choice in the matter.'

Now sitting in her chair, beneath the fan, looking around at her rearranged house, Edie itched to write it all down and send an account to Joy in Scotland. What would she think of Tara and Joe, sitting on the floor of the mosque, Tara with her tight skirt and high heels, and the three lads, Adam, Brent and Joe's cousin Ali flanking Joe like soldiers. The glamorous handmaidens would be sitting next to Tara. For this was the wedding proper, the official ceremony and the solemnisation of the oaths, the only truly necessary step to be married. It had to be witnessed only by family and very close friends. Edie knew that the imam or kadi would read out religious oaths straight from the Koran and these would then be recited. She remembered the seriousness of the ceremony with Kamal, so long ago, and tried to picture Joe being informed of his duties as a husband and then having to repeat the oath after the imam in one breath. She would have liked to have seen that bit and she hoped Joe would manage. Tara and Joe would then sign the marriage contract to solemnise the marriage. After all the legal oaths were completed, the groom would be required to gift some money to the bride's family indicating his commitment to provide and fulfil the needs of his bride. Edie was sad that she wasn't able to witness the exchange of rings, and remembered how Kamal had no ring for their own shotgun marriage. She remembered how at the crucial moment, there had been a general fluster. It was Minna who came to the rescue, pulling off her own wedding ring and giving it to her new daughter-in-law. Edie looked down at her wedding band, the golden ring that she and Kamal had bought together in Johor with their meagre funds. More precious than any glittery diamond. She shook herself out of her reverie. Enough, she thought, all these trips down memory lane. They'll be here soon for the *majlis bersanding*, the wedding reception.

Edie heard a car on the drive and craned her neck, surely they weren't back yet? But no, the car door slammed and Amelia called out, 'Hi there, mother-of-the-bride! My word! You look stunning and so regal; you are going to put your daughter to shame sitting there like a dowager duchess with your feet up!'

'You don't look so bad yourself, my friend. I love what pink does to your skin, you just glow. How are you feeling?' Edie looked concerned. 'Still tired? You don't have to stay here long you know, just take off when you feel like it. Amelia sat down on the chair beside Edie. In spite of the makeup, she was very pale with dark shadows under her eyes. The two held hands. Edie drew herself up, and laughing, recounted the morning's dramas. 'You should have seen the girls leave, they had faces clarted like Dusty Springfield in the sixties, but the sarong kebayas were beautiful and they all looked stunning. Who would have thought it, you and me sitting here watching the next generation getting married. Where have the years gone?'

'I know, I was thinking the same myself. And fancy us, not even in charge, instead we are both recovering from illness and accidents. Is Maggie Rajah coming for the *majlis bersanding*?'

'I hope so, I tried to persuade her for Tara and Joe and also Adam's sake because they are all fond of her. We are here to give Maggie our support but she needs to move on. At least she signed the form agreeing to his taking the new wife or else she really would be destitute. He must pay her something.'

'How is Kamal?' Amelia asked. She fidgeted with her handbag, which made Edie suspicious.

'The same, why, is there something I should know?'

'No, but Michael did say that the work in Kuching is nearly over and that Kamal volunteered to stay on to see it completed. I think Michael was a bit surprised. I just wondered if everything was OK with you two, forgive me for prying.'

'No, we are fine. He is his usual impatient self, I just put it down to his liking for travel and new challenges. He doesn't tend to like staying at home for too long. But you should see him with his parents, which you will this afternoon. My God! Amelia, he has to toe the line, that mother of his is the bossiest woman I have ever come across. At first you think she is such a quiet sweet Malay housewife, subservient to Hassan in every way, the great Mecca pilgrim who must be revered at all times, but when she takes control, everyone marches to her drum. Even poor Moy Moy, who doesn't know much about marching in time with anyone or anything!'

Chapter 38

Dear Joy, Edie wrote. She was distracted and her gaze kept following a windsurfer skimming across the waves. The islands on the horizon appeared surreal, just a haze of misty, bluey-grey shapes; a few children were racing backwards and forwards to the sea. Edie felt drowsy in the heat of the afternoon sun. Her leg was still in plaster and she was growing impatient with her disability, but the doctor had assured her that it would be removed in ten more days. Amelia had kindly driven her to the yacht club, with a promise to collect her later. Edie refocused on her letter and continued:

> *Dear Joy,*
> *Where do I start? Tara's wedding was everything you could hope for in an Asian wedding. There was colour, pageantry, food, music, people, family and my goodness, was there family! They had come over from Johor and totally took over, which I was grateful for, as I am still so incapacitated. My beautiful girl, looking so regal and so demure, sat on her throne next to Joe, I could hardly believe she would be able to sit still for the whole afternoon. Then later the pair walked about accepting gifts and good wishes from the guests. Kamal was quite the host, circulating and being most entertaining. I didn't even know half of the men. I haven't seen him like that for ages. But the most bizarre thing was that Minna insisted that Tara and Joe should go down to the roundabout by the National Mosque for their photographs, the reason being that it's always planted with a kaleidoscope of colourful flowers. So off they went and the photographer had them posing in front of this array of colour like a couple in a magazine, it was hilarious. I felt I couldn't miss out on that, and made Kamal drive*

197

me there to watch. We had to park to the side as all the normal traffic
was whizzing about on their daily business.

Edie put down her pen. She would continue writing in a minute, for she had so much to say about the wedding and also, she wanted to share the news of Amelia's dengue fever and Maggie's dreadful marital situation, Joy being familiar with these people and all their ups and downs. But she found it difficult to write about herself and Kamal. He was the perfect father, the perfect host, and most certainly the perfect son, but a husband? She wasn't so sure. It had been months since they had been close. He was either distracted or travelling, but always returning with a piece of silk or a sapphire pendant; the last offering had been a crocodile handbag. 'I want you to look smart when we go out,' he'd said, 'dress up a little. We have to be seen as representatives of the successful law firm that we are.' He'd made Edie feel self-conscious in the cotton dress she loved. 'Look at you in that faded old thing. I hope you'll make an effort for our daughter's wedding. Buy something new and wear those diamonds I gave you. A lot of my business colleagues are coming and I don't want them to see you looking like a poor relation.' In spite of the gifts, Edie felt diminished by his hurtful words. What had happened to them? Where was her friend, her gallant prince who had once so beguiled her? Was there someone else? She had often wondered but he seemed so keen to come home and he did appear to love her. And there had been no papers for her to sign, so if there was someone, he can't be serious about her, could he? Edie looked out to the sea and distractedly wiped away a tear that was trickling down her cheek.

Chapter 39

Three days after the wedding the family had dispersed, leaving Moy Moy and the gardener to return the house to some state of normality: furniture re-instated, the laundry room a sea of detergent bubbles as linen was scrubbed and sheets, towels and white linen napkins hung out to dry in the hot sun.

The bride and groom had left for their honeymoon in Bali, the grandparents and aunties had returned to Johor, and Claire and Lucy had gone back to Singapore.

Marie had persuaded Adam and Brent to take her with them to Kuching; the plan was that the three of them would climb Mount Santubong together. Brent had doubts about the petite blonde musician, she hardly looked the outdoor type with her floaty beach dresses and long dangling earrings, but Tara had reassured him that her friend was tougher than she looked. 'She always did well on the trails in the Blue Mountains, I'm sure she'll handle trekking in the jungle without any trouble!'

Kamal flew to Kuching with them to resume the final stages of a difficult contract he was involved in. For the last few years, he had rented a small house at Damai beach, about an hour's drive from the city. For the working week, he rented a serviced apartment in the city, just walking distance from the office. The beautiful house with the koi carp pool that had been home from home for so many years was no longer available as the owners had returned from working overseas.

'Here's the key to the house in Damai,' he told Adam after breakfast in the hotel the next morning. 'You'll find everything there, towels and so on, a few pots and pans, but there are local places where you can eat and I doubt you'll be spending much time in the house anyway. Good luck with the climb, make sure you get a good guide and don't do anything foolhardy!'

'Thanks, Dad, we really appreciate this, are you sure you don't want to come too?'

'Another time, I have a lot of legal stuff to do. I might need to travel up to Sibu but I'll be back in a couple of days. You just enjoy the trek, and take good care of Marie, make sure she drinks lots of water. Dehydration is a killer.'

'We'll do our best. We'll see you at the weekend before we all head back to Sydney.'

Kamal watched the group pile into a taxi. He sighed deeply and walked away from the waterfront and the shops selling ancient artefacts and decorative woven red cloths, once worked by Dayak tribeswomen for proudly receiving human heads severed by their warrior husbands. He left the sarongs and carvings, walked past sugarcane vendors and stalls selling fresh coconut and papaya and for a moment he hesitated in front of a spice stall, inhaling the odours of cumin, turmeric, chili and coriander, and detecting the pungent whiff of *ikan bilis*, the tiny dried anchovies so delicious with *nasi lemak*. The clashing colours of the spices; orange, red, yellow and ochre were as exciting as those on a painter's palette. He looked at his watch, he still had half an hour, so he took a short detour and arrived at a small shop selling *roti canai*. Pleased with his purchase, Kamal resumed his walk away from the office and the busy streets. The sun was hot and the perspiration was beginning to soak the back of his shirt. He carried his plastic carrier bag with a sense of purpose, he felt happy, a man who had everything, a family, children and a good job. He knew he was ageing well; his once raven hair was of course now threaded with silver but it still grew thick, brushed back from his forehead. He was proud of his physique; he had not let himself go to fat like so many of his middle-aged contemporaries. The silver-framed glasses gave him some dignity, he thought. He turned into a small road with a few shophouses specialising in gold and jade jewellery. This was a Chinese district, and only select customers made their way to this part of the city. Certainly not many Malay people were seen around here. He turned into a dark stairwell, adjacent to the Handsome Goldsmiths shop, and ran up the stairs to a small landing. He glanced at the feathery fronds of plants growing from chipped clay pots. An iron grille was pulled across a blue painted door. He knocked on the door. It was opened immediately.

'At last! You've come back.' Rose pulled him inside. He had only time to put down the carrier bag before he was wrapped in her arms. They kissed, they held each other, and kissed again. She was pressed so close to him he could feel her breasts soft against him, he could feel her desire, it was intoxicating. She pulled him away from the door and through to the bedroom. There he was lost in her hair, her skin, her mouth and it was as though years had passed since they had been together.

Much later, dressed only in a towel wrapped around his waist, Kamal retrieved the carrier bag. He took out the curry and roti paratha and placed the impromptu meal on plates.

Rose stared at him, her eyes wet, 'I've missed you; Farah has missed you too.'

'Come on, eat something,' Kamal indicated the food. 'We're both hungry so let's enjoy this.

Rose obediently bit into the chewy paratha dripping with curry sauce. 'It's so hard, never knowing when you are coming. Why can't you divorce her properly? What about me and your daughter?'

'You and I are married, Rose, it's what you wanted and we are happy.'

'Maybe you are,' she pouted.

'You know I can't be with you all the time.'

'I hardly ever see you; you just drop in when you want. I thought you would spend more time with me and our child.' Her beautiful face had developed an ugly scowl.

'How is Farah? Is she still doing her gymnastics?'

'Yes, she's a good child, and for nine years old she is very smart. I took her out to Damai as you asked me to. I cleaned the house and took away all our things, so no crayons or slippers or anything is left there. Your son won't know you stay there with anyone else.'

Kamal leant over the table and took her face in his hands and kissed her lips, still stained with curry. 'We shall go there again soon, and we'll walk along the beach at sunset with our daughter. Don't worry, I love you, my beautiful Rose.' He patted her cheek and sat back in his seat. 'By the way I brought you a flower, an orchid.' He picked up the plastic bag and pulled out a single stemmed pink orchid.

Rose laughed, 'So pretty, you know I love flowers, but I love this one especially as it comes from you.' She jumped up and went to the sink looking for an appropriate receptacle to place such a delicate bloom, 'There's nothing suitable, what about a beer bottle instead?'

'And I brought you something else as well.' Kamal went back to her bedroom and picked up his trousers from where they still lay in a state of disarray on the floor. He rummaged in his pocket and took out a small box.

'What is it?' Rose stretched her eager hands towards the tantalising gift. 'An orchid, all in gold!' she gasped, 'Kamal, that is so much, I love it. And a chain, please put it on for me. Now I see why you bought the real flower as well.'

'Wear the yellow dress tonight, the one I bought you from Kuala Lumpur, it will set off the orchid pendant perfectly. We shall go out to eat, the three of us, when Farah comes home from school, to celebrate my home-coming.'

Chapter 40

There was no stopping Brent as he continued his ascent to the summit of Mount Santubong. He grabbed the ropes placed to help climbers over the smooth rock faces, finding suitable fissures where his boots could get a good purchase. My dad would be amused by this, he thought, having called me Brent, supposedly for 'someone who lives on a hill'. This climbing lark is second nature to me, I just love the challenge of going ever upwards.

The humidity was stupefying and both Adam and Marie reached for their water bottles and cautiously drank a mouthful, very aware they still had the descent to contend with. Adam was full of admiration for the plucky girl who had been climbing steadily, easily keeping pace with her two much taller companions. She must have big lungs with all that music-making she does, Adam thought, completely ignorant of any form of musical instrument playing. He clambered onwards and upwards, wiping sweat from his eyes and clutching lianas whilst avoiding snake-like roots at his feet. He had a vision of himself as an eleven-year-old boy climbing this very mountain with his father and Omar, their guide. He remembered the sulky lad he had been then, and how hard he had found the climb. It had not been so much the physical strain on his legs and shoulders because he had been a strong boy, but it was the effect of being alone in the deep jungle, amongst huge ancient trees with barely a glimpse of the sky above. He had found it as disquieting then as he did now. Was it the essence of the leaves, or the rotting vegetation? He couldn't say. But as he reached for the pliant saplings which were at hand to haul him up the steep trail, he wondered about other men, small barefooted men from generations past who would have made their way along these tracks just as he was doing now. Their bones would have become part of the soil and their ashes would have blown like smoke trails amongst the canopy, pointing whichever way the departed soul was travelling. He remembered the cremation pot that he and his sister had found on the beach in Kuantan all those years ago. Edie would have understood his premonitions, this fear of the spirit world. He had felt that something was lurking, like a shadow in his mind, and he shook himself, forcing himself to get a hold of himself. It was only a mountain, only a track, and in front of him the lithe young woman in her pink Lycra trousers was taking it all in her stride. She was almost running up the track, trying to keep up with Brent, the fearless one.

'That was truly amazing,' Marie laughed as Brent took her hand and helped her up the last few steps. Their hands lingered for just a few extra seconds and Brent grinned, his green eyes alight with the knowledge that maybe his feelings were reciprocated.

Your face is as pink as your yoga pants,' he grinned. 'You sure are a colourful sight up here.'

'And what about you then? With all that wild curly red hair and beard, the orangutans would think you were one of their own!'

Salleh, their guide, motioned for them to help Adam who was about to make his final steps. He was almost naked, just wearing camouflage shorts and local rubber shoes made from old car tyres. His hair was cut into a fringe close to his hairline. Marie was transfixed with the intricate tattoos that adorned his arms and shoulders. 'Look, up there!' The small brown man pointed high above them.

'Where? What can you see?' Adam scanned the wisps of blue and white sky above him.

'A hornbill, flying over that way! Can you see it now? And over there, can you see that hawk, just hovering, searching for movement below. Maybe about to dive down on its prey.'

After three hours of staring downwards at the path and clambering over fallen trees left to rot, avoiding scurrying ants and lizards, ducking under vines harbouring oddly shaped spiders, and stepping through masses of ominously piled leaves, it was sheer heaven to stare skywards and watch the sweep of a bird's wing.

Brent put a hand on Adam's shoulder, 'Let's do this again, what do you say?'

Adam grunted. 'Sure, but I need to get back to Sydney and earn some money – it's just draining away and these flights are not cheap. We need to get back to work.'

'Would you want to climb Santubong again?' Marie asked Brent, her eyes like blue pools. She looked at the perspiration dripping through the sodden bandana he had around his forehead. She inadvertently wiped his cheek with her small towel.

'Well, actually I want to go higher. I want to try Mount Kinabalu, it's over four thousand metres high. Now that's a mountain worthy of my name.'

'Mount Kinabalu has much history, not too easy, but maybe good for you young people to climb that,' Salleh said. 'Let's go down now, it will be easier today, there has not been too much rain so not too slippery. Be careful though, I will go first. Adam, are you happy to stay at the back?'

'Yep, no problem. I'll also be happy to get back to Damai and have a swim in the sea before I devour a huge plate of chicken biryani!'

The three returned to the house at sundown and pulled chairs out to the decking, looking out to the sea. The cold bottles were piled in an ice bucket which they had brought back from the restaurant. Adam opened a coke. Brent opened a beer and poured it into two oddly shaped glasses. 'Cheers guys! What a great day! Nice place your dad has rented, must be great coming here after a stressful day at the office. Does your mum come down much?'

'Hardly ever. She did when we were younger; we used to come all the time for school holidays, but then we stayed in a really cool house. I remember that. Tara used to draw the fish in the pond, she was always drawing. Koi carp I think, orange, gold and black monsters they were. But no, these days Mum tends to stay at home or go for trips to KL or Singapore in her holidays. As you know, she's still working but I was talking to her at the wedding and she was considering giving it up. Too many changes, new teachers with new ideas bringing more stresses to the job. She has been thinking of doing tutoring instead. Seems to be a market for that. Who knows? She's pretty independent.'

'Yeah, well, it's nice here. What do you say, Marie, do you fancy a midnight stroll, maybe walk out to the tideline?'

Marie took Brent's hand and looked Adam. 'Would that be OK with you, mate?'

'Right!' Adam laughed, clicking his glass on to Brent's. 'Good for you! Why didn't I see that coming? But yeah, I get the picture. You guys go right ahead. I've got my coke here and I might turn in, I'm pretty whacked.' He watched the pair skip and run hand in hand towards the sea. At first, they were just dark shadows, but soon the darkness blotted them out completely.

A sliver of a moon was veiled behind purple clouds. In the distance he heard the rumble and growling of thunder. He went inside to shower and prepare for bed. The room was large, painted cream and with pale blue blinds. The floor was covered in a blue carpet which felt soft under his feet, an improvement on the hard wooden floors he had grown used to. He sank down on the double bed and let out a sigh. He was exhausted but he thought he might read a few pages of the book he had brought with him, a biography. He liked those. He stretched over the side of the bed to retrieve his back-pack and pulled his book out. Something glinted in the carpet. What's that? He leant over and picked up an earring caught in the pile of the carpet. It was silver with a tiny red droplet of garnet, or maybe ruby, he wasn't sure which, but he was sure that whoever had lost it must be mad. He lay back against his pillow and studied the pretty jewel. Probably nothing, he thought, I'll give it to Dad, maybe he lent the place out to someone else whilst he was in KK.

He awoke much later to a colossal crack of thunder. The storm had broken in the night and the rain was coming down in torrents. Lightning flashed and Adam could hear Marie's squeals coming from the other room. Brent's rumbling baritone soothed her and soon the only sound was the deluge of water gushing down the storm drains outside the house. When dawn finally broke, the three looked out at the dripping breadfruit trees and the sodden canna lilies. The sky and the sea were a uniform gunmetal grey and the rattan chairs they had sat on last night and had forgotten to bring in were soaked, the cushions sodden.

'Oh, I feel terrible,' exclaimed Marie. 'At least we should have brought in the cushions. If we put them on their sides, they might dry a bit?' She gingerly lifted one cushion and leant it against the wall, then went for the second one. 'Oh look! Someone has left this plastic file under this one – it looks like some kid's drawing book inside. At least the folder has kept it dry. Do you think your dad lets this place out to other people sometimes?'

Adam took the book from her and flicked through the pages. His face was ashen. He said nothing, just studied each drawing carefully. It could have been Tara who had drawn these monkeys and pitcher plants. The child who had made these sketches had the exact same style as his sister. And when he turned over to the last page he inhaled sharply, for there in black and white was the classic rendition of the family portrait, of mother, father and child, a girl. The father was Kamal. There was no doubt, the artist had captured an uncanny likeness. There were the glasses, the hair brushed back from the face, and there too was the briefcase. And the mother. Long hair it seemed. Now he knew who had lost the earring.

'Are you OK, Adam?' Marie was concerned. Adam had gone deathly pale and his hands were shaking. 'Did the biryani last night not agree with you?'

'I just need a moment, if you don't mind. I just had a funny turn.'

'Have some water,' Marie rushed to fill a glass for him. 'We should all head off soon. Don't forget we're catching our flights to Singapore this afternoon and we need to return the keys to your dad's office. It's been such an amazing trip; I've loved it all. I can't wait to tell Tara how we got on as soon as she gets back from Bali.'

'Are you OK, mate?' Brent was concerned for his friend. 'Seriously, you don't look great.'

'I'll be fine.' Adam compressed his lips into a forced smile. 'I might just go to the airport now, and you guys can return the key. I don't fancy walking about much.'

'Sure, that's quite understandable, I've had upset stomachs like that before.' Brent followed Marie into the bedroom they had shared to collect their bags.

Adam fingered the earring in his pocket. What should he do? Whilst on the mountain he'd had a premonition that something bad was going to happen but nothing could have prepared him for this. What should he do? What should he bloody well do? His father was a Grade A Shit.

Chapter 41

From everywhere noise seemed to jar her brain. Screeching monkeys at the back of the house, a rooster in competition with hysterical dogs down in the kampong, the incessant buzz of the cicadas and the constant whine of the strimmer as the gardener shaved the grass around the house. Even the normally sleepy cat seemed to be yowling about something. What was going on? Edie got up from her chair and walked out to the driveway, shielding her eyes from the midday sun. She saw nothing, just the magenta bougainvillaea and the pretty bush made up of tiny purple and white star-like flowers which seemed to be a haze of soft colour as so many butterflies were drawn to its particular beauty. Timmy the Third was the tortoiseshell cat who had replaced Timmy the Second after the poor creature had been run over by a van down on the main road last year. Edie had been bereft when the vet had finally put him down. She remembered his kind voice on the telephone, 'I wonder if you are interested, an abandoned kitten has just been brought in. He's the image of Timmy the Second, and I thought of you immediately. Do you want to take him?'

There was no question in Edie's mind. It was meant to be. Now she could hear him meowing at something on the driveway. 'What's bothering you, puss?'

He seemed to look at her with a sense of 'I've got this, don't worry, I can take care of this,' and he hunched himself down, growling at the intruder.

'Good grief, Timmy, leave that alone! That's a giant scorpion and its tail is raised ready to fight. It would kill you, no doubt about that. Come away, we'll get the gardener to stop his infernal strimming and he can put it back in the jungle where it belongs.' The phone started to ring inside the house. 'Keep away, Timmy!' she shouted at the cat. She didn't trust him; he was full of feline hunting instincts. Edie knew all about the trophies that her cats had brought into the house over the years: dead toads, the odd whip snake and countless dead mice. Scorpions, she knew, were not to be trusted especially one that is cornered like this one with no place to hide. That evil needle was poised ready for the kill. She picked up the struggling cat and took him with her inside. The phone stopped ringing. 'Damn, now who could that have been? She looked at the small screen of her mobile phone. There was no recognisable number displayed. She was on a knife edge, expecting so many calls that weren't materialising. For the last week her life seemed poised waiting in a state of expectation. The noises were aggravating her. 'Oh, for goodness' sake, I just want some peace.' She marched back outside after first shutting the irate cat in her bedroom. 'You can stay there till we get that black visitor off the driveway.' More meowing followed her outside.

By the time the small drama was taken care of, Edie was desperate for a cup of tea. She found the kitchen empty; Moy Moy was presumably ironing in her shack. The phone rang again. 'Oh please! Let it be Tara, or Adam,' she prayed aloud. 'Hello! Is that you Tara?' The phone clicked dead. Hmm, that's odd, she thought, I've had a few of those lately, someone must have got a number mixed up. She took her tea and returned to her desk that she had relocated to a corner of the lounge. Her tutoring work needed a lot of preparation and Kamal had been generous buying her a computer and printer to help with her lesson plans and worksheets. She picked up a workbook that would be required for her three o'clock class, and smiled at the pupil's attempt to write a composition. Edie loved teaching and since leaving her job at the Likas International School she had teamed up with Maggie Rajah who had reopened her own kindergarten. Maggie and some of Edie's old colleagues were referring children to her for tutoring English and Maths at primary level, mostly Malay but a few Chinese children who were struggling and needed extra help.

A year had passed since Maggie had been officially cut out of her husband's life. Somehow the dark-haired Mona Lisa had regained her serenity and confidence, thanks to her friends and recouping her independence. Her ex-husband had set up home with his new woman in a small house near the airport. It was hard to think he could just abandon Maggie like that. The phone rang again. 'Hello!' Again, silence and then it went dead. Edie put away the child's workbook and looked up at the fan moving the languid air around the room. She felt tired, a headache coming on. Perhaps she should have a rest. Kamal would not be back till evening. He was now reinstated in the KK office, and he and Michael were involved in another big case involving logging rights around the National Park at Renau. The park should be sacrosanct, a place of beauty and wonder, dominated always by the giant mountain with the stegosaurus ridges along its spine. But greed of gold and corruption throughout the system required lawyers on both sides. For once, Edie was happy that Kamal's firm was defending the Park's right to prevent illegal logging. He still spent a lot of time travelling, as did Michael, but according to Amelia they had quite a lot of business meetings in Labuan. Edie was secretly glad he didn't have to go to Kuching anymore and was able to spend more time with her and their friends. But he was always distracted, always short-tempered, always shouting at Moy Moy needlessly. I suppose that's what happens as we get older, she thought. Maybe he will be better when Adam and Brent arrive in the next two weeks. Their aim was to climb Mount Kinabalu. The last she heard was they were keen to stay on in Sabah and perhaps do some rope work on the mountain. Young men always need challenges, she thought fondly, it will be good to see them, it's been over a year since Tara and Joe's wedding, and now a little baby was due any day. Edie scowled at the phone. 'Why doesn't she ring, what is going on?'

And it did ring. 'Hello!'

'Mum? It's me, are you OK?'

'Of course, the phone has been playing up, but it's so good to hear from you, Adam. When are you both arriving? I can't wait to see you. The mountain is waiting for you, looking pristine with just a soft feathery quilt on its top this morning.'

'Great, we've booked our flights and we'll fly via Singapore to stay with Tara and Joe first, then head over to KK, should be there on the tenth of June. We're bringing all our rope equipment with us. We've been working really hard, did another stint up at the mines near Darwin and we've saved a heap of money, so we should be in good shape to stay up in the National Park for a few months. You can imagine Brent is really excited about it all and is going to write a blog or something for his travel magazine. Should be cool. I don't think there's ever been a successful rope drop off Low's Gully, just a dodgy one by some soldiers a few years back.'

'Adam, just climb the mountain first, before you start adding more complications.'

'OK, but I just want to give you a heads up. Is Dad around?'

'He'll be back home this evening; did you want a word?'

'Nah, it's fine. See you soon, Mum, love you.'

Thunder rumbled; a storm was getting closer. Edie pressed her fists into her eye sockets, massaging the pain that was threatening to engulf her. Clusters of red stars radiated behind her closed lids. She turned her phone off, praying that Tara wouldn't be suddenly whisked off to hospital early, or at least in the next couple of hours. Edie needed to rest. She found Timmy, the valiant cat, fast asleep on her side of the bed. Edie lay down on Kamal's pillow, smelling the familiar scent of his hair, and buried her face into the softness. She slept.

Chapter 42

Adam was home. It felt good waking up and stretching his long body in his boyhood bed, his feet sticking out over the end. If he closed his eyes, he could still be ten years old, waking to the sounds of the mynah birds squawking outside his window. Just for a few minutes he allowed himself the luxury of doing just that, letting the sounds of the house permeate through its thin walls. The old house was becoming quite dilapidated with wood rot and damp patches from the incessant rainstorms, yet still the fans rotated over floors that gleamed with polish, cushions and curtains made from expensive fabric depicting a Chinese emperor's robes were still bright. The house might collapse from the infernal white ants burrowing through the timbers, but his mother and Moy Moy intended to go down in style.

'Adam! Time to get up, Brent has already been up for hours and he's been out for a run. He's having a shower and I think you should get up too.'

'OK, Mum, I'm on my way, just give me ten minutes.'

Edie sat out on the veranda, the cat on her lap, with three mugs of coffee on the table in front of her. There was a plate of sliced papaya and pineapple ready for breakfast. This was going to be a good day she thought as she swallowed two paracetamol and shuddered as the pills went down on a wave of warm liquid. 'Come on, lads, the coffee is getting cold.' She pressed her temples. The infernal headache never seemed to go away. She did think it was the weather and the constant thunderstorms but even on a morning like this, when the sky was as blue as a harebell, she was aware of the persistent throb. She must go and see Doctor Kana, he might give her something stronger. She made a mental note and added it to the long list of things she had to attend to. Most important of all was the party.

'Morning, Mum, sorry for sleeping in,' Adam leant over and kissed her. 'Hey there, mate!' He grinned at Brent who was standing on the steps surveying the garden, 'You were up with the cockatoos, or more like the bloody roosters in the kampong down the road. Where did you run off to at the crack of dawn?'

'Just down to the main road and along a bit, then up some track. Got a bit freaked with the wild dogs though, I was afraid they might have gone for me. Ugly pack of mutts.'

'Come and sit down, both of you, but before you do, call Moy Moy. We need fresh coffee; this is not worth drinking now.'

'No more word from Tara or Joe?' Adam asked. 'We thought she was ready to pop when we saw her yesterday.'

'Nothing, and she is due any day now. I shan't go for a week or so after the baby is born, better to let her have some peace. Then I'll go down to Singapore and try and get used to being a granny!'

'What about Nenek Minna in Johor, will she not be making the trip?'

'No doubt she will be over with her rice and home-grown wisdom,' laughed Edie. 'But to be fair, looking back I don't know what I would have done without her when you came along.'

'And Dad?' asked Adam, forking a large piece of papaya into his mouth.

'He left early for the office - you'll see him later. Did I tell you that Kate and Alistair Davidson are having a party? Their daughter Felicity is here for a few of weeks, do you remember her? You used to play together on the islands when you were small. Well, she's finished her studies and is now a fully qualified psychiatrist, so medicine must run in their family. She's been offered a position in a practice in London, I think. She's a pretty girl and quite kindly, been helping with the local SPCA charity; they do good work rounding up stray cats and dogs and neutering them.' Timmy the Third stopped purring, let out a strangulated growl and jumped off her lap. 'Honestly, I swear that cat can understand every word I say. He takes offence at the slightest thing. You should have seen him when I criticised his latest conquest.'

'What was it this time?'

'A big lizard nearly half his size. I told him to search for rats and mice. A much more useful activity. He just sat there, his paw on the lizard's tail and stared me down with those big yellow eyes. Didn't you, puss? Edie leant over and stroked her offended pet. Timmy chose to ignore the whole conversation, instead concentrated on an awkward section of his chest fur that needed washing.

'Who else will be at the party?' asked Adam.

'Lots of interesting people, especially for you two. A couple of botanists from Denmark who have just spent a week up at the National Park and have climbed Mount Kinabalu. They are making studies of orchids I believe, what better place to do that? Have you ever seen the rafflesia flower, Brent?'

'No, and I'm looking forward to it, they say you don't need eyes, just a nose to locate it!'

'That's right, it does smell disgusting, like rotting meat and it attracts flies just as though it were dead and decomposing. But oh my, it is huge - more than seventy centimetres in diameter! So, we'll have lots to ask the Danish couple when we meet them.'

'Are you OK, Mum? You do look pale. Not your leg giving you pain or anything?'

'No, not at all. My leg has healed beautifully and I've made a good recovery. I'm fine, just a little headache, that's all. Tell me, Brent are you still with Marie?'

Brent reached for his phone and his thumbs twitched over the keyboard. 'Pictures speak louder than words, take a look at this.' He handed her the phone.

'Brent! You wily old fox! And when were you going to tell me!'

Brent blushed a deep scarlet, clashing with his unruly mop of red hair. By comparison his shaved chin and jaw look oddly naked, the wild beard now history. Bashfully he retrieved the phone and looked at the image of himself and Marie. The petite blonde girl with the flowing saffron dress and loopy golden earrings was very noticeably pregnant.

Edie was ecstatic, 'Congratulations!' she cried, 'That is such good news! And when are you expecting this little one to appear?'

'August. Marie was hoping to come over and join me here, assuming we can get suitable accommodation. We'll see.'

'What? Do you think you'll stay, what will you do?'

Adam interrupted. 'First, we climb the mountain, then we decide. We've given it a lot of thought, but first things first. Anyway, what about you, Mum? Are you still happy here? Not missing school?'

'Oh, I'm fine, I have my tutoring and my friends, and I'm just a quick plane trip away from Tara. And your father is home more often now so that is always a good thing.'

Brent excused himself, and Adam took his mother's hand.

'Really? Is everything all right with you and Dad? I don't mean to pry, it's just that you seem quiet. Have you thought about going away for a break or a holiday?'

'Well, I'll be going to Singapore soon, so that will be a nice change. The truth is Adam, I'm a bit like a shrub. She glanced out at her flowering garden, at the new banana trees which were growing taller by the day, and the vibrant colour of the hibiscus amidst its deep emerald foliage. 'Perhaps my shrub may not be getting enough light at the moment, but I do have a good strong tap root. I know from my little knowledge of gardening that shrubs with tap roots don't take kindly to being moved. So, my dear boy, my shrub will have to stay where it is. It may have a less than perfect life, but it is my life and believe me it does have its compensations - like you and your sister. I belong here with your father. Malaysia has been my home for so long now that I can't imagine being anywhere else.'

Chapter 43

The Davidsons lived in a modern house in Tanjong Aru, just along from the yacht club. Their windows opened directly to views of the South China Sea and they woke each morning to the mesmerising colours of aqua and green, capturing the essence of both sea and sky while the perpetual splashing sound of the rise and fall of the tides created a gentle cadence to their lives. Kate always felt herself drawn to the garden, a perfect place to relax under the shady trees. Being so close to the sea she was relieved that they had invested in such a solid construction when they built their house, for over the years it had easily withstood the monsoon winds and storms.

Tonight, the night of the party, the house was draped in fairy lights, and kerosene lanterns lined the pathway to the main entrance. The sea was lit by a yellow moon and the sand was wet with only the scurrying crabs racing about in the receding tide. Adam and Felicity were sitting side by side on a log, looking out at the moonlight across the dark water. It felt good being together, they had grown up here and been toddlers who once played on this very section of the beach. 'I taught you to walk here,' Felicity laughed, and took a sip of her white wine, 'I felt so important as I was older than you, and was supposed to be in charge.'

'Yeah, a right bossy boots, you were,' agreed Adam. 'I was scared of you most of the time! But you've turned out all right, and now you're a qualified shrink, how does that feel?'

'Pretty good actually, but it's been a hard slog and a lot of exams, so frankly I'm quite enjoying being here. It's not too stressful and I like hanging out with Mum. I've also been learning a lot about what Dad does, with his travelling doctor experiences. And now here we both are, all grown up, sitting together drinking white wine on a moonlit night by the South China sea. Well, I am, but you seem to be drinking lime soda,' she probed gently. 'I have a couple of friends, sporty types, who don't drink, or maybe it's a religious thing with you?'

'No, it's not a religious thing although my dad's family are strict Muslims, but I did go through a really bad patch back in Sydney. Got sucked into the drink big time and went down paths I don't care to dwell on, so I think we'll leave it there if you don't mind, Felicity?'

'Sure, I'm not prying, but hey, what happened to that gorgeous girlfriend, Victoria wasn't it? You were quite the dashing pair as I remember.'

'Yeah, she's long gone and I'm happy as I am. It was quite a blast at the time, but I think I came down to earth with a bump, quite a colossal bump to be truthful, but now I'm as close to happy as I've ever been, no big pressures of trying to keep up with the mega rich, just setting myself small targets and getting the satisfaction of achieving things I set out to do.'

Felicity leant over and gave him a soft kiss on the cheek. Adam turned to face her, his eyebrows drawn down into a frown. This was not the Felicity from his childhood. Where was that skinny long-legged urchin with the tufty short hair that he played with, the girl who was like a sister and who'd grown up beside him through all the stages of school? This girl's face was luminous, it was the moonlight playing tricks of course, he knew that. Felicity had been drinking wine, it always made people impetuous, but there was something else, something in her eyes, those deep dark wells, and the perfect outline of her mouth, and that hair, that long brown hair. Adam's eyes took in the whole picture, it was a tableau, she was a girl from a religious painting. He leant towards her, and this time it was he who kissed her lips.

Edie found Sarah and Derek Campbell in the lounge, talking to Brent and the Danish botanists. She blew her friend a kiss before making her way to the kitchen. Much hilarity was going on with Amelia and Kate, trying to artistically place lychees on top of the small coupe dishes of mango soufflé.

'Come here and give me a hug, Edie,' Amelia shouted, 'and maybe you could help our hostess here?'

'Fabulous party, Kate, and look at you two, what beautiful dresses, where did you get those?'

'From my dressmaker on Gaya Street, she's the best, she can copy anything. I gave her the Vogue magazine and the material and just look at us, she did such a great job!' Edie did look at them, Amelia in raspberry silk, with a clinched waist and long skirt tapering down to her ankles. Kate had chosen navy-blue chiffon, with spaghetti straps and the dress seemed to hug her body. Her short dark hair gleamed like a cap on her head, and large hooped earrings gave her a look of cover-girl glamour.

Edie looked down at her own kaftan, it was quite old. Still, she was pleased with the way the rainbow-coloured threads sparkled in the fluorescent light of the kitchen, but she was conscious of her hair hanging lank and limp on her shoulders.

'Who is that woman I saw Kamal talking to out on the veranda?' she asked her friends. On her way to the kitchen, she had taken a detour over to the French windows and had peeped out. She had seen her husband in resplendent dark trousers and black silk shirt preening in front of a woman who might have come off the set of the Addams Family sitcom. She was clearly Chinese with long straight hair, parted in the middle. Edie had spied the clinging black dress, the too-red lipstick, the fake eyelashes and the platform heels. Kamal was leaning back on his heels and rising up again on his toes, in a strange self-important rocking motion.

'Oh her! That's Cecilia,' Kate enlightened her. 'She's a really rich tycoon, fingers in every pie. Very nice actually, though a bit of a vamp. But I wouldn't worry, it's the less obvious ones you have to watch. Cecilia has inside knowledge of the Kadazan, the local indigenous people, and she knows all about the spirits and witch doctors.'

'The *bomohs*?' Edie turned her full attention to Kate. She put down the lychees she was holding.

'Yes, they are like the *shaman*, the men or women who believe in the power of the mind, and the spirits of the mountains and trees. Surely you know all this, Edie?'

'I do. And I also remember poor Marianne and Geoff. She had that affair with Vincent Wong a while ago, then later she went back to Australia.'

Amelia sipped her wine. 'Did you know she died? She had breast cancer, but I know what you are saying. Someone had put white powder in a circle around their house, like a spell. Was it a *bomoh*? Was it a warning?'

Edie smiled at Kate and took Amelia's hand. 'Excuse us a second, Kate, we'll be back in a minute to finish the job.' The two women walked over to a quiet corner with a Chinese marble-topped table and two bentwood chairs. Above the table an antique Dutch lamp illuminated the space. They sat down.

'What is it?' Amelia looked closely at her friend. 'You actually look pretty awful, are you OK? Is it Adam, or have you heard from Tara?'

'No, they're fine. It's just that I've been getting a lot of headaches, awful headaches. They come on suddenly, just out of the blue. And I've had phone calls that just go dead when I answer. I'm scared, Amelia. These spells work, look at Marianne and you've just told me that she's dead!'

'What are you scared of? Why should anyone do something bad to you?'

'It's Kamal.'

'Kamal? What has he done that's any different from all the rest? He's a man, Edie, we live in the East, they aren't perfect, we all know that. You and I have lived with this hypocrisy for a long time.'

'I know, but I think he might be married to someone else as well.'

'Married, are you kidding? You don't know that, do you?'

'I don't know for sure, but I've often wondered about it. He had someone in Kuching during all the time he was there, I'm pretty sure of that. Remember how he didn't want to leave the office in Sarawak and come back to Kota Kinabalu? And after Tara's wedding he went back to Kuching with Adam and Brent and Marie. Oh, and by the way she's pregnant!'

Amelia shrieked, 'Pregnant! Amazing!'

'What is and who is?' Alistair Davidson interrupted, a big grin lighting up his face. 'You women always have the best conversations; we men just have to talk about trees and weather conditions and if we'll be able to access the kampongs up river.'

'Brent and Marie are having a baby,' Edie clinked her glass with Al. 'It is happy news, and Brent was really hoping to talk to your visitors. You said that they'd just come back from a trip climbing Mount Kinabalu. Brent and Adam are hungry for first-hand accounts of what to expect when they have a go at it.'

'Brent is over there already,' Alistair waved his glass in the direction of the lounge, 'he seems deeply immersed with Lars and Grethe. He doesn't waste time, that boy. And where is my lovely daughter, have you seen her this evening?'

Amelia shrugged, 'I think she might be sharing childhood stories with Adam; I saw them going out towards the beach about half an hour ago. It's a beautiful night for looking at the sea.' She smiled enigmatically.

Al took a sip of his whisky. 'They always were a good pair those two, all those happy days going to the islands, remember, Edie? Oh dear, we're not getting any younger, now where is Derek? I was hoping to nail him down for a game of golf.' He sauntered back to talk to more of his guests.

Edie got up and went to retrieve her handbag she'd left by the front door, and took out more pills and a tissue.

'Are you in pain now?' Amelia asked.

'Yes,' Edie blew her nose. 'It just doesn't seem to go away. I've tried everything, pills and lying in a darkened room. Even soulful music. Nothing works.'

Amelia's brow creased in sympathy for her friend. 'Tomorrow, I'm going to drive you to Doctor Kana's clinic and we'll see what he suggests. Are you really concerned that someone is trying to hurt you, is that what's worrying you?'

'It would make sense. If there is another wife, and if she did want to get rid of me, wouldn't she try anything in her power to keep Kamal for herself?'

'Maybe, anything is possible, but unlikely.' Amelia caught sight of Kamal coming in from the veranda with Cecilia hanging on to his arm. 'If he has married someone else, it would be a marriage of convenience in his eyes, just to appease the woman. Usually, it's a way to get what they want, while keeping the Sharia police away, and giving the woman a feeling of respectability. But I can't see Kamal ever abandoning you. You're imagining things, my friend, the headaches and phone calls could just be a coincidence. Let's get you sorted out with the doctor first.' Amelia smiled and squeezed Edie's damp hand. 'You should get back to the kitchen and help Kate, she's struggling with that new maid of hers who insists on cooking everything from packets! Not Kate's style at all.'

'Don't mention my fears to anyone, Amelia. I confided in you.'

'Don't fret, Edie, I have your back. Always.'

Amelia watched her friend make her way through the throng of chattering people in the lounge. She was troubled, in spite of her reassuring words. Michael had divulged to her some time ago that Kamal had a woman in Kuching, but that was years and years ago. Could the affair have lasted more than ten years? Amelia emptied her glass and sidled up to Kamal who was standing alone. 'Great party,' she smiled patting his arm with her polished nails. 'I couldn't help noticing that the sultry dragon lady has been monopolising you out there on the veranda. I haven't seen Cecilia for months.' Amelia adjusted a loose strand of hair. 'Where has she been hiding herself? I hope she hasn't been off cavorting with her witch doctor friends, doesn't she have a group of old toothless grannies that she likes to visit up in the remote kampongs?'

Kamal laughed, 'You are outrageous, Amelia, as always, and you've a vivid imagination. I can see you are dying to know what Cecilia and I have been talking about. But in a way you're right. She does have her contacts with the Kadazan, and I'm sure there are some *bomohs* amongst them, but what I wanted from her was information for my own business. As you know, Michael and I have to deal with the local men from the forest villages and the potential illegal logging that is going on. We know it's poverty that drives some of these indigenous people to log according to their customary rights and for their local needs and survival.' He sighed deeply and looked around the room, assessing who was nearby. He took a drink from his glass and continued, 'But what started out as a few trees has escalated to meet orders from unscrupulous dealers and corporations who are prepared to pay quite sizeable sums to these natives. Sadly, the soil left behind after the deforestation is poor in nutrients and vulnerable to erosion.'

Amelia's face fell. 'Oh,' was all she could contribute.

'And,' went on Kamal, 'the dragon lady, as you called her, is an expert on many things to do with Mount Kinabalu. She has agreed to meet up with Adam and Brent to brief them on some of the legends and local beliefs. I see Brent is through there talking to Lars and Grethe, but where is my son? No doubt you know where he is?' He gave her a waspish smile, his silver glasses glinting.

'Stop teasing, Kamal. I just like parties and I like to see people mingling, you know that.' She laughed happily, but when she looked into his eyes, framed with their protective steel rims, she realised that they were not warm, in fact they were unreadable.

Chapter 44

True to her word, the following morning Amelia breezed up Tuaran Hill and whisked Edie off to see Doctor Kana. Now they were sitting together on orange plastic chairs in the waiting room and watching a TV screen which was tuned to the latest Korean soap opera. It seemed that Doctor Kana liked his patients to be calm and relaxed. Edie fidgeted and looked around the room. Everyone seemed intent on the drama unfolding before them, though for the life of her, she failed to see any action. They had been waiting for ten minutes already and still the two main characters were staring into each other's eyes. The man stirred his coffee and blinked. The woman looked bashfully down. The other patients sighed in unison.

'Riveting stuff,' Edie whispered to Amelia. 'Pity there aren't English subtitles, the Chinese subtitles aren't much use to us.'

'Indeed, but they wouldn't help much anyway since they haven't spoken for ages. Are you OK?'

'Yes, the nurse took my blood and urine samples, and my blood pressure, but suppose the doctor finds out something really is wrong, Amelia?'

'Mrs Shariff, the doctor will see you now.'

'Here goes, wish me luck.'

Amelia stood up and gave her friend a hug. 'You'll be fine.' As Edie was led away Amelia continued watching the mesmerising drama on the screen, finding herself drawn into the minutiae of detail that the director had included in his film. Very clever, she thought, day to day emotional drama that any of us can relate to, that's why all these people are so transfixed, staring at the screen with bated breath. The actress leant down for her handbag. Was she getting a tissue or was she getting up to leave? Amelia would never know for just then Edie came out of the doctor's office, sniffing into a tissue.

'Oh my God, are you all right, come here, let me give you another hug.'

Edie surprised her by laughing, and for the first time in weeks her eyes were shining with genuine happiness.

'You're not going to die? It's not a tumour?'

'I have the menopause, it seems! Nothing more normal than that! Also, I have to go and get my eyes tested, the headaches are probably caused by eyestrain, I probably just need glasses.'

'Oh, thank you, God. I was just sending up some prayers, He must have heard me. So, no more nonsense about *bomohs* or curses?'

'But my phone? What about all the strange calls I've been getting?'

'We can block the number. It's nothing, it happens all the time. I think you were just letting your imagination run away with you. Now let's get out of here before this soap opera gets even more exciting!'

Edie laughed and followed her friend outside.

Amelia drove them to Tanjong Aru and pulled into the yacht club where they had arranged to meet Adam, Brent and the two botanists. They found the four already ensconced around a wooden table, their cold drinks dripping with condensation. Papers and note books were spread about and the conversation seemed very animated.

'Hi everybody, can we join you?' The two ladies pulled up chairs. 'Two fresh lime and sodas please,' Amelia called to the waiter who was hovering.

'Wasn't the party good last night,' Edie exclaimed. 'I loved the food - Kate always puts on such a good show. I'm sorry I didn't get to spend much time with you all but you looked very engrossed.'

'Mum, take a look at the notes Grethe and Lars have made about their climb, they're amazing! I almost feel I could climb that monster mountain right now with my eyes closed!'

'Oh my, you have such a lot of material there.' Edie leant over to peek at a couple of drawings. 'Would you mind?' She looked enquiringly at Grethe who immediately handed her a sketch of an orchid.

Adam registered his mother's upbeat mood, definitely on the effervescent side and a marked improvement from last week. Edie studied the Danish pair as the others chatted on. Lars was maybe thirty, tall and soldier-like with the blue-eyed, fair-haired look of the Vikings. She could imagine him in a uniform marching in front of the royal palace in Copenhagen. His wife had the athletic build of a swimmer with strong shoulders and a lean frame topped with short and spikey hair dyed red and orange. Edie could see her in her own country wearing sturdy black hiking boots under a loose cotton dress, but here in Malaysia she wore shorts and a T-shirt. Looking at the pair of them Edie would never have guessed they were so dedicated to their particular science and were prepared to scale mountains to find rare and elusive orchids.

Laughing, Grethe pulled out more papers from a cardboard folder. There were drawings and sketches of various species they had found. 'We have photographs as well, obviously, but I do like to draw the really pretty ones. Would you like to see more of them?'

Edie took the folder from her. 'Oh my! Look at this one; it's so unusual, it could be camouflaged. I see you've called it the jewel orchid or *anoectochilus lowii*. And these, so delicate, like dancers with very long complicated names. I love the colours. I have orchids growing in pots lined with coconut husk in my garden and some are dangling from tree branches, but these are in a class of their own, they are truly unique and exquisite.'

Lars took a sip of his drink and turned to Edie, 'Did you know that the rainforests in the parklands surrounding Mount Kinabalu are home to half of the world's flowering plants, including around a thousand species of orchid? So, we were lucky to find the selection we did. There are also several species of insect-eating pitcher plants. We were fortunate to see the *nepenthes villosa*. The mountain is a paradise for botanists, there are so many species there.'

'Do you remember, we used to call them monkey cups, Adam?'

'I do, Mum, I remember some guide we had in Pahang told us they were called *periok kera*, or monkey's rice pot. Doesn't *nepenthes* come from the Greek word meaning "removing all sorrow"? He told us it referred to a potent Egyptian drug of a similar appearance to the liquid in the pitcher. The insects probably die quite relaxed!'

Lars continued, as though he was giving a formal talk. 'Yes, that is possibly true. But did you know that some of those pitcher plants are large enough to swallow a rat.'

'That is large!' exclaimed Edie. 'The ones we have seen tend to catch beetles and insects.'

'And there are over twenty-nine species of rhododendron and of course the rafflesia. And ferns, oh my goodness, so many ferns. But as I told Adam and Brent, most of the hike up the mountain is through dense rainforest. There are few views of anything other than trees and plants until you reach the top, and that is mostly barren rock. For us, reaching the top was a wonderful bonus for our expedition. As you know, to enjoy the views of Borneo and the South

China Sea from the summit, you have to arrive there before the clouds roll in not long after sunrise.'

Grethe nodded, 'We were lucky, we had the most amazing view of the sunrise. Not everyone is so lucky though. Sometimes the summit can be dark or covered in dense fog. It can be dangerous and people can slip. I remember thinking at the time how treacherous it could be.'

'There have been accidents,' Brent said, 'and I've read that some people suffer from altitude sickness on the climbs and have to turn back.'

'That is true,' agreed Lars. 'The actual climb is unrelenting, starting at the Timpohon Gate at 1,866 metres above sea level and rising to Low's Peak summit at 4,095 metres. Obviously, you will already have researched all that yourselves, and you'll know that it's recommended to climb it over two days with an overnight stopover. That will allow your bodies to acclimatize and hopefully avoid the sickness.' Lars touched Grethe's arm, 'Remember we took plenty of stops as we searched for different species and we were not in a rush. That would have helped us to get used to the altitude.'

Grethe nodded enthusiastically, 'We did see a lot of climbers looking at us with interest and when they saw what we were collecting they were very surprised.'

Lars went on, 'The first day's climb takes around four to six hours depending on your fitness but you two are young and strong so you should make good time. The trail winds steeply over gnarly tree roots before coming across a mossy and cloudy world of trees draped in orchids – an amazing sight and we were in heaven! It was at this point we were able collect the photographs and Grethe made her sketches. There are seven shelters along the way where you can catch your breath and relax, but as you climb higher to the Laban Rata Rest House at Panalaban, that's at 3,272 metres high, the trees get shorter and shorter and the air gets thinner and thinner. We were so glad to take a break for the night. You will find the accommodation is quite basic. After eating a simple meal, we went to sleep very early because we had to wake at two in the morning for the final hike by flashlight to the summit. The second day's climb to the summit takes around three to four hours and the trail includes some very steep and rocky sections with wooden staircases and fixed ropes. It gets very cold up there. Then as I told you we were finally rewarded with a spectacular sunrise over the rocky granite plateau.'

'And did you see the Donkey's Ears Peak and Alexandra's Peak?' enquired Brent, looking up from the notes that Lars had given him.

'We did, we saw all five false peaks, as they call them. We were very fortunate, we had perfect weather and the visibility was good. The descent is quicker but pretty tough on the knees. That will take you maybe three to six hours, and you'll call into Panalaban again on the way for breakfast before heading back down to Timpohon Gate. It really was a wonderful adventure and very rewarding for us as botanists. So, good luck to you both and we hope you enjoy it as much as we did.'

'Thanks, we really appreciate all this information,' said Brent. 'I think we feel quite prepared now, but Kamal suggested we have a talk with Cecilia, the lady we met briefly last night. I think she wants to give us some inside knowledge of what the spirits of the mountain might have in store for us.'

'Why not?' grinned Lars. 'We should all have great respect for the beliefs of the local people, but frankly, white chickens and sacrifices, hmmm, maybe we take with a pinch of salt ...'

Chapter 45

The following week Kamal drove down Jalan Gaya and parked his car behind the Jesselton Hotel. He walked into the dark interior of the old colonial building and noted the precious Ming vases and beautifully arranged flowers set upon inlaid mother-of-pearl lacquer furniture. The hotel reflected the glory of times past, of Chinese culture and opulence. He selected a chair by the heavily draped window and ordered coffee. Taking out his phone, he saw that he had a message. Rose. Of course. She was very persistent. He knew that he should answer it but what was there to say? He turned the phone to silent, snapped it shut and put it back into his breast pocket. Their relationship was what it was and he gave her as much time as possible, but he found that her nagging was getting tedious. Her bouts of temper and demands for money were starting to weigh him down. He frowned as he remembered their last conversation when she had accused him of wanting to abandon her and Farah. She had threatened to enlighten his 'number one wife', as she spitefully called Edie, his secrets about his second family.

'Really, would you do that?' Kamal had asked, a little apprehensive that this spitfire might actually carry out her threats. 'I am not leaving you, Rose, but I have my job, my career, and you know I have always had my family. I have honoured our marriage, and have taken care of you and Farah, you know I have, but you cannot ask me to come to you every time you snap your fingers.'

'Yes, but you go to her, snap snap and off you go.'

'Rose, I am going to be a grandfather in the next few weeks, and yes, I will go when Edie calls because I want to visit my daughter in Singapore. Also, my son, he is home from Australia. Things have been bad between him and me for a long time, I don't know why, but I want to make things right. He hardly talks to me; it's as though he suspects something. You haven't contacted him, have you?'

'Me! Why should you say that? I am nothing, just a spare broom in your cupboard. Did I not clean-up for him and his friends when they stayed in our beach house? Maybe he has heard something on the jungle drums?'

Kamal shuddered at the thought that everything was going wrong. His coffee arrived and he tried to calm down, but his heart was racing. Could Adam somehow have found out about Rose and Farah? It would explain how his son always left the room whenever he came home. They had barely talked, even any communication about the forthcoming climb had been made through Brent. But today, Cecilia, Adam and Brent were all due to meet him in this hotel, so hopefully they would be able to pass an agreeable hour together. Cecilia had promised to explain to them about the respect that was required when approaching this sacred mountain.

Meanwhile, Adam was in a taxi heading back to town from the airport. He hoped he wouldn't be late for the appointment with his father, Brent and that scary looking Chinese woman, but the traffic was snarling and red brake lights were flashing on and off, so progress was down to a slow walking pace. Outside the temperature was soaring. He could see the heat haze hovering over the bonnets of the almost-stationary cars. He pulled out his phone and sent a text message to Brent: 'On my way, traffic bad, start without me'. There was no point in stressing and worrying about time so he forced himself to lean back and relax whilst he reran his farewell scene with the gorgeous Felicity. Their romance, though short and unexpected, had escalated into something good. She was a smart girl, very focussed on her future and amazingly seemed quite keen on him. It had been a long time since a girl had affected him in this way. This one might have been way out of his league had it not been for their childhood connection. He smiled as he conjured up her image. Felicity with her wide grin, sunburnt legs and long bouncy hair. They had enjoyed an amazing week, seven perfect days to swim and walk and talk. Not long enough, he thought, with everything else that was going on, but wow, what a distraction. Felicity had had to leave for London where she was starting her new job, but they had promised to write and meet up again at Christmas. And Adam had still the mountain to climb; hopefully he would be able to develop the experience into something else, maybe writing a journal, maybe even private tours, who knew? But watching Felicity as she walked through to the departure gate and out of sight, he knew this was no fling, in fact he believed he might be falling in love. He certainly could not have foreseen that, especially with a girl he'd known forever, and on a moonlit night on a deserted beach - it seemed too much of a cliché, but it really had happened. There was no doubt he'd come a long way since he'd hit rock bottom in Sydney. Images of the dark days of his addiction slipped into his mind and he screwed up his eyes at the recollection. He thought of Gray, that kindly old fellow who had given him work cutting grass in the cemetery. He and his granddaughter had helped him turn his life around. Then the meeting with Brent. That had been the best thing, that guy had rekindled his sense of adventure, and now that he had Felicity, she had given him hope for the future. Since meeting her his life had taken on colour, maybe his aura had changed. He remembered his mother always being fascinated by auras. If he did have one now, he felt it must be gold, for everything in his world seemed to have taken on a golden tint. He noticed the traffic start to move forward. Thinking about his mother reminded him of the oppressive atmosphere in the house when he had returned home. He'd been so concerned about his mother's depressive state even though she had reassured him she was happy with her lot. But lately her mood had lifted and she was back to being her upbeat self. He hoped that things had been resolved between her and Dad, but then he scowled. He still had the earring and the sketch book in his rucksack.

At last, the taxi dropped Adam off at the Jesselton Hotel. Stepping into the airconditioned foyer he walked through to a seating area where he found the three deep in conversation. Cecilia was gesticulating with her long red nails flashing like blood-tipped swords. He noted her garish red mouth and the false eyelashes and he shivered. She certainly looked like a woman you might associate with witch doctors. When she spoke, her eyes penetrated with an intense sincerity. It was as though she was casting a spell on them all, it was quite mesmerising.

'At last, mate, you made it!' Brent grinned; his eyes lit up with pleasure. 'I've taken some notes, but Cecilia is just giving us some really good advice. Coffee? The pot is still hot, just pull up your chair. Cool room this, love the old-fashioned décor.'

'Thanks Brent. Sorry I'm late. Hello, Cecilia. Hi, Dad. Good to see you all again.'

Kamal noticed the cold look his son gave him, but Cecilia pressed on with her briefing. 'Yes, Adam, I have just a few words of advice, but I shall re-iterate. I cannot stress enough that this mountain is first and foremost a place of great importance to the Kadazan-Dusan, who as you know, are the largest ethnic group in Sabah. These people believe the mountain is home to the spirits of their dead ancestors. The name Kinabalu is derived from the phrase *Aki Nabalu* which means the revered place of the dead, a place for their spirits as they go to their final destination in a world beyond our own, so the mountain links both the physical and spiritual worlds.'

'Gosh, I didn't know that,' Adam said, taking a sip of his coffee. 'Thanks, Cecilia, that's very helpful, I can now understand why the local people wouldn't appreciate climbers shouting or otherwise disrespecting the mountain.'

'Exactly. The guides, many of whom are Kadazan, always warn climbers to control their language, even if they fall and hurt themselves. Every December the tribe conducts a ritual called the *Monolob* to appease the spirits of the mountain and allow tourists to visit. A high priestess called a *Bobolian* makes an offering of seven white chickens accompanied by seven chicken eggs, betel nuts, tobacco, limestone powder and betel plant leaves. She leads a chant and the chickens are then slaughtered. In the past this ceremony used to be conducted before every ascent. One year, it did not happen and a girl slipped and fell to her death. The locals took this as a sign that the spirits were angry.'

'Bloody hell,' said Adam forgetting to be respectful, 'I hope they'll kill a few chooks for us then. Today is Friday and we are all set to go on Monday. What about the weather, is there a good forecast?'

'Yes, I think you'll have a good first climb and you'll have a good experience. I myself will go with you to the park headquarters and I can talk to some of the guides there. If you make a good impression on them, and they can see you are serious about wanting to learn everything, they will help you. But slowly slowly. Take one step at a time, as they say.'

'Thanks again, Cecilia, it's really good to meet you and hear what you have to say, and we'll see you on Monday.' Brent stood up and signalled to Adam to drink up. 'We've got a date with a speed boat and some water-skis at the club, we met some guys who were game to take us out and give us some lessons.' He picked up his rucksack, 'I used to ski on the snow, but never on the water. Can't wait to give it a go.'

'I'll see you at home, Adam.' Kamal looked pointedly at his son.

'Maybe later. I'll probably hang out with Brent this afternoon as we have to buy some supplies after the water skiing. Bye, Cecilia, your information was really interesting and I'll be sure to fill Mum in with all the native folklore. She's always been fascinated with all of that.' He turned away and followed Brent out of the hotel.

'And what about you, my friend?' Cecilia looked Kamal in the eye with kindly concern. 'Do you need any appeasement for your spiritual life?'

Kamal grunted. He pursed his lips, took off his glasses and polished the lenses. Without the spectacles his face looked vulnerable, almost young, and Cecilia could see where the son had inherited his good looks. 'It would need more than a few of chickens to sort my life out. Since moving back here, I am being plagued with demands. Rose wants the whole package.'

'Understandable, you have a daughter together. Are you sure Edie doesn't know?'

'Pretty sure, she's a rock that one, she's put up with me over the years and I honestly have never loved anyone as I love her. From the very first day I met her. All the others I've been involved with over the years have just been passing fancies, but I admit Rose has been important to me for a long time. I don't know, Cecilia, I just don't know what to do.'

'Things have a way of resolving themselves, you will see. The time will come when you will decide, better not to have a big confrontation, better to let the spirits take control. They will guide you.'

Kamal laughed, 'Honestly, Cecilia, Amelia is right, you spend far too long with your toothless hags up the river!'

'Don't mock, my friend.' She stood up and opened her handbag, checked her face in a compact mirror then smoothed the creases from her long black dress. 'I have learnt many things from those wise women, they know things that we could never imagine. Some call them *shaman* and they exist in all cultures, especially in countries that have rainforests. Now, give me a kiss and go home to your number one lady. She is a good woman, and neither of us need any wise woman to tell us that.'

Chapter 46

'How are you doing, mate?' Brent's baseball cap and the small towel around his neck were soaking with perspiration.

'Pretty good,' grinned Adam. 'It's been everything Grethe and Lars described, but I'm really glad I don't have to stop and look for pretty flowers every five minutes. I just want to get up there.' He breathed deeply, wiping the sweat out of his eyes, and turned to their guide. 'How long have we been trekking now, Gimbang?'

'Close to five hours already. We'll get to the Paka Shelter at 3,080 metres in about half an hour.'

'Adam, we should take a look at the Paka Cave,' suggested Brent. 'Well, the notes say it's not really a cave but a large overhanging rock next to a stream, but it sounds like a great place to have a snack; a bit of fortification before we head up to the base camp. It's going well, but frankly I'm glad those Kadazan porters have got our packs. Gimbang said he's been climbing this mountain since he was three, but I didn't see him slaughtering any chickens before we left, did you?'

'No, but remember, Cecilia told us it's done as an annual ritual now by indigenous rangers or priests at Panalaban. Don't worry, she assured us that it was all taken care of. In the olden days we would have been given a chicken leg to chew on the trip. Fancy a fruit pastille instead?'

About forty minutes after their snack, the group made it to their first day's destination at 3272 metres, the Panalaban Base Camp and the Laban Rata Rest House.

'Hey, mate, before you crash, take a look at this,' Adam was staring up towards the magnificent granite peaks of the summit towering above them. 'And look over there, the sunset is pure gold, the ridges running down towards the valley seem to be infused in clouds of orange flames.'

Brent and Adam gazed in awe at the scene in front of them, before finally entering the hut and flopping down on to their wooden sleeping pallets.

'Pretty to look at, especially now we've stopped climbing, but hey! We did it! A vertical climb so far, just as they said and pretty intense. Glad we had those energy gels and electrolyte drinks, the old ticker was going flat out there for a while, but now I need to have some dinner and get some sleep.'

Brent grunted, 'It's probably chicken-head curry, I wouldn't get too excited.' He was already starting to doze off. The air was thinner up here, he felt the strain on his breathing and the start of a headache. 'I'm glad we get tonight to rest before the big race to the summit, I'm definitely feeling the effects of the altitude. How about you?'

'Nah, I'm fine, could trot up there right now,' laughed Adam.

'Well, all in good time.' Brent swung his legs over the side of the thin mattress, 'I'd better get up before I really do fall asleep. I hear voices out there, more climbers arriving. There's going to be a rush for the summit tomorrow. But first things first, let's eat.'

They were so tired that it seemed as though they'd only just gone to sleep when Gimbang broke into their deep slumber at 2 a.m. It was dark and freezing cold. Both lads groaned as they struggled into their clothes and boots, donning warm jackets, gloves and hats.

'God! It's cold,' exclaimed Brent. 'The air is almost brittle, have you got your head-torch?'

'Yep, got everything, just raring to go. How's the breathing this morning? Are you feeling any better?'

'Yeah, I think so, the rest must have helped my body adjust to the altitude, but look over there, look at those white plumes of condensation over those guys' heads! They look like cartoon speech bubbles, like you get on a winter's day back in England. I wasn't expecting it to be so cold.'

'Yes, but it's not too bad today,' said Gimbang. 'Last year we had snow on the summit. Better to start early to get the sunrise, as later mist and clouds gather and often it rains in the late morning. Makes it all very dangerous. But today, you are lucky, it is just cold, but as soon as we start walking and climbing you will get very hot. How is the breathing and headache, Mr Brent? Feel better today?'

'Yes, I do, thanks. I was a bit worried there for a while, thought I might miss out. Don't want to get this far and not get to the top.'

'Many people get sick. Sometimes after they rest, they can continue, but sometimes headaches are too bad. Dangerous then, can be fatal. Better be careful.'

Adam looked at his friend with concern, 'You sure you're OK?'

'Yep, I'm sure, lead on, Gimbang. Onwards to Low's Peak.'

The small group set off with their guide at the front, still chatting on as they walked. 'Ah, you have read about this famous man, Mr Sir Hugh Low? His name is everywhere on this mountain.'

'Yes,' nodded Adam, 'we read in the literature that he was a government officer from Labuan in 1851. Quite an achievement back in those days when not much was known about the conditions. And he wouldn't have had these nice little shelters to have a rest or a kip in.'

'That is true, but although the highest peak is named Low's peak, the man himself did not reach it. There is also Low's Gully, an abyss a mile deep and of course you know there are plants and animals that all bear his name.'

'Yeah, we saw the Low's pitcher plant on the way up, it was pretty impressive.'

'Also, Mr Sir Hugh Low had big troubles to access the mountain back then, there were no roads just thick jungle, almost impossible to penetrate. He found it difficult to persuade native porters to accompany him because this mountain is sacred. It is a resting place of the dead. Even now there is still much of the park, like the northwest face of the mountain, which has still not been explored.'

'Yeah, we've been lucky to have you take care of us on our maiden trip and have all the facilities of the park and the shelters.'

The climb crossing the Panar Laban rock face to the Sayat-Sayat Hut was gruelling. 'This is no joke, Gimbang, how much further?' Brent gasped.

'One hour, usually, but use the roots of the leptospemum tree, I think you know these from your country? Same family as the myrtle tree? They provide a natural staircase up to the granite rock. Just concentrate, it's worth it.' The climb was more challenging than anything they had done the day before. The vegetation was stunted and contrasted sharply with the massive silver black dome of the summit. They saw scarlet blossoms of rhododendron stand out against the stark background. 'Luckily we have ropes now to assist us,' Gimbang heaved himself up and over the gigantic boulders. 'Take your time, we don't want any accidents.'

'It's quite exhilarating,' laughed Adam, 'just a bit different from the humid jungle we scaled in Santubong!'

'Yeah, and look ahead, isn't that a hut? That must be the Sayat-Sayat Check Point. We've been going an hour, just as Gimbang said. I could do with a full English breakfast right now.'

'Dream on, you might get a cup of Milo and some cold *bee hoon* noodles!'

'How did you know that, Mr Adam? Milo is very good for energy, and I cooked an egg in the *bee hoon* so I hope you enjoy it after I carry it all this way!'

From Sayat-Sayat Check Point the three traversed across the bare granite slabs that stretched endlessly ahead, an eerie moonscape of stone. Only other climbers with their faint torchlights could be seen, some ahead and some behind them. Brent was composing in his head sentences for his diary that he would write later that evening. He noted the vegetation at this high altitude comprised only stunted shrubs and tough grasses growing in shallow crevices. He felt the bleakness of the cold stone, the sheer rock-face, and the insignificance of himself and his friend in this landscape. He felt drawn to this mountain and wanted to share its stark beauty. Words tumbled about in his brain; how could he best portray this challenge? Maybe in the future he and Adam could support others to achieve their goals. Perhaps not as a guide like Gimbang, for he knew only Sabahans could be guides for the final stretch, being the most difficult and dangerous, but perhaps as providing inspiration through his writing? People who want a climbing companion for the earlier stages might be interested. As he trudged forward, ever upward, the air thinned and he saw the peak standing like a grey sentinel against the sky.

Gimbang stopped. 'This is the hardest part,' he explained. 'It is the steepest part of the whole climb. But we are strong, boys! Let's go, let's climb this Mr Sir Low's Peak!'

Adam watched the fifty-year-old guide, with his strong wiry body and hair tied back with a red bandana, bend into the ascent. He tried to follow suit, but as the incline increased, he dropped to his hands and knees. 'I've got this,' he shouted to Brent, 'this is how the orangutans would do it, keep close to the floor and scramble up.'

And finally they reached the summit of Borneo at 4095 metres high.

'Still bloody dark and still freezing,' Brent grumbled, blowing his hands and stamping his feet, 'but thank God, we made it safely and in time for the sunrise. Hey, Adam, over there. Look at the sky, it's awesome, a scene from Michaelangelo.'

Adam gazed at the glory of the new day. His eyes glistened with unshed tears with the wonder of it all. Brent and Gimbang joined him and they stood shoulder to shoulder watching the spectrum of colours as they changed, illuminating the sky in opal shades of blue, pink and violet.

'Wow, that was truly amazing,' Adam finally said. 'Seriously, it was like a slow-motion movie watching the sun emerge and grow like liquid fire. It seemed to get more immense by the second. I'll never forget this,' Adam said softly. 'But I'll be back. This is what I want to do. I want to watch the day unfold over this spectacular view of the mountains, the plateau and the valleys below. To look down at the whole of Sabah outspread below. It is truly unbelievable.'

Brent put his arm around his friend's shoulders. 'Yes, I'm with you, one hundred per cent.'

'You are good climbers, my friends,' grinned Gimbang. 'Congratulations on your first successful ascent. I know you will be back to do it again. For myself I sometimes climb this mountain three times in one week, it has become a very popular pastime for many people, but there are some people who require more assistance. They may have health issues, or are uncomfortable at climbing with a group. They need one-to-one guiding.' He consulted his watch. 'We have to go back now. Sign your names here in the book and then we should go down. It is not good to get caught in rain, it makes it more dangerous, many people slip. I hope your knees can take the strain. Sometimes my older clients have big problems with the knees, but you are young still, I think you will be OK.'

Later that evening, Adam and Brent returned to their accommodation at Poring Hot Springs on the south-eastern side of the National Park. They changed into their swimming costumes and made for the hot thermal pools to ease the aches from their legs and shoulders. The steamy sulphurous water, which had been channelled into several pools and tubs, was almost turquoise.

'This is the best,' Brent stretched out, letting his body soak in the Japanese-style baths. 'I can feel the heat permeating right into my bones.'

'Might help with the old legs tomorrow, that was pretty tough coming down. But it's just fitness, look at Gimbang, he is so fit, and he carried all our food as well.' Adam closed his eyes, letting himself drift in a haze of heat and exhaustion.

'We can do this, Adam, I think we can make a life for ourselves here, for a while anyway. I was thinking about it whilst scaling that granite plateau, and we might be the ideal companions for people less adventurous, or with reservations about their abilities. I think we could write about our experiences and invite people to come and we would be their companions, what do you think? Obviously, we can't abseil down Low's Gully as we previously envisaged, especially hearing about those soldiers that attempted it back in the 1994. But we could be climbing buddies, what do you think?'

'Hmmm, sounds good,' agreed Adam, dreamily, 'I could try and write stuff too, maybe for the Asian market. Must be some old grannies who would like to run up the mountain in their retirement?'

'Let's do it. We'll write some articles and send them off to England and some holiday companies. But first, we need to get to know the lower stages really well. Perhaps we should swot up on the flowers and birds and stuff as well.'

They closed their eyes as the buoyant waters rocked them into a dreamless state of bliss.

Chapter 47

My dear Joy,

It's been ages since I wrote, and I wanted to thank you properly for dealing with the letters and phone calls from that solicitor in Perth and letting me know about the death of my great Aunt Anne in Stonehaven. It seems that with her gone, all the people from my family have passed away now. Not that I ever knew anything about my father's people, so it's amazing what comes out of the woodwork when someone dies and there is property involved. Fancy me inheriting a house! That is a surprise. I can't see me getting back any time soon to take possession, but you say this solicitor, Mr Sutherland, has it in hand and a neighbour will keep an eye on it for me. A farmhouse? Why didn't my mother tell me anything about this, but on reflection, maybe she didn't know either as she didn't know much about my father? That was always a big dark secret. Gosh, Joy, it all seems so long ago now.

It was good to get your news as always, and hearing stories about being a head teacher in an Edinburgh school couldn't be more different to my work, tutoring my little boys to pass exams for common entrance to private schools. I do enjoy it.

Life here is pretty good at the moment. Christmas and New Year were so special with baby Clementine being the star of the show. I had no idea that being a granny could be so much fun. I adore that little girl, she has such soulful eyes, so knowing in such a tiny person. I do lavish her with dresses and cuddly toys, although I think Tara is secretly bemused, because she can't ever remember being so spoilt herself.

Kamal has been very attentive and keeps exclaiming how much the baby resembles himself, being so dark-skinned and inheriting his black glossy hair. No fair-skinned, blue-eyed blonde children in this family! Tara and Joe stayed for two weeks, and we had Adam and Brent for Christmas day. Also, Kate and Alistair Davidson and their daughter Felicity who had arrived from London for the holiday. I hardly saw anything of Adam. He spent every minute with the lovely Felicity.

I think I told you that Brent is now a father. Marie, his girlfriend, had a baby boy back in August. She had the baby in Australia, but she too came over for the Christmas period. It was so strange to see Tara and Marie at the yacht club, both with their babies in bassinettes under the casuarina trees. Just like me, so long ago, when I first arrived in Sabah. It made me quite nostalgic! Amelia and Michael were travelling so we didn't see them. They had gone to Singapore then Switzerland to catch up with their daughters.

So, I am happy. The decorations are down, everyone has gone, and the house has returned to its quiet, slumbering self, with only me and the cat and of course Moy Moy. I do worry about her. I feel she is getting quite arthritic. She was always slow, always so unflappable, and seemed to live life at her own tempo, but lately she takes even longer to do her tasks. I think it's time to look around for a younger girl to help with the laundry and the floor polishing. The infernal insects never let up and now we have an Asian hornet's nest up above the curtain rail, quite a big nest and very intricate with a little tunnel for the most giant wasp you have ever seen to enter and feed its young. Its abdomen is about the size of a small grape and it has these long menacing legs and huge alien eyes. I am terrified of it, and want the thing out. They give very nasty stings. But with Moy Moy unable to climb up on a chair, Kamal away in Kuching, Adam somewhere up that mountain, there is only me. The gardener is off having a holiday somewhere. I live in fear.

Brent has rented a house in Likas so Marie and baby Andrew are making a life for themselves there. Adam stays half his time here with me, and half up in Poring Hot Springs. He has really made friends with the local guides up in the Park Headquarters. He and Brent have climbed Mount Kinabalu countless times already. He has been studying books on flowers and butterflies. At school it was always Tara who had the passion for science and the natural world, never Adam. Now he can identify a bird way up in a flame tree, just by its song. He says the people that choose to climb with him and Brent are usually amateur nature lovers and like to put names to ferns or creatures they encounter. Of course, although they guide their 'guests' up the mountain, the professional Sabah guides have to lead the way especially for the final stages to the summit. It seems to work and all parties benefit.

Thanks to the lads' journal writing and advertising in British and American travel magazines they have had a steady flow of climbers and have made enough money to survive here. Kamal of course is cynical, it's as though he is waiting for them to fail. I think he has never really forgiven Adam for dropping out of university.

I must go now. Timmy the Third is meowing about something, probably his plate is empty. One of these days I will make it back to the bonny land, and see this house that is waiting for me.

In the meantime, love to you, from me.

Chapter 48

Without a prior booking with them, Brent was reluctant to accept the two Americans who had flown in. The two guys were wallowing about in the hot springs, drinking from cans of beer, when he and Adam had slipped into the same pool as them. 'Hey there,' the one with the shaved head had called out, 'we're over from New York, still getting over the jet lag. Are you the guys that take people up the mountain?'

'Yes,' replied Brent, 'but we're not official guides, you would have to book them separately, and porters for your kit. And you have to book and pay for a time slot as well.'

'Yes, we've done all that, buddy boy. We're raring to go on the fifteenth, which is in two weeks' time. By the way, I'm Caleb Van Zeller. I've done a lot of climbing in Colorado, used to ski a lot too. My friend here, Jake Brenner, has done a bit of climbing in Europe.'

Brent nodded to a languorous fellow, relaxing with just his blonde head sticking above the water. Adam's brow was creased in concern and he pulled at his small goatee and moustache that he had been developing since the New Year. 'So why do you want to use us as well, you sound quite fit and capable?' He eyed the dragon and octopus tattoos on Caleb's shoulders and back as the American pulled himself out of the pool and reached for his rucksack.

Caleb pulled out a bottle of vodka and poured a measure into the cup of his thermos and topped it up from a tin of coke sitting open by the bag. 'Cheers, guys. Perfect ending to the day in this perfect tub. Do you partake, gentlemen?'

Brent shook his head, 'Not for me, thanks, not the best when you are as dehydrated as we are. Water is the best thing after a gruelling climb.'

'This is my holy water,' Caleb laughed, 'the drink that has seen me through everything in my life, even skied with it flowing in my veins.'

'What about you, Jake?' Brent asked, averting his eyes from the small aluminium cup.

'Nah, not my thing, I like a beer but I can live without it, but a bit of hash, now that's when I get interested. You want a joint now? I have some here, won't take me a minute to roll up?'

'As my friend said,' Adam scowled, 'we've just come down from a hard descent and we still have to drive back. We're just in Poring to soak the bones for a while. We don't need anything, but thanks for the offer. Anyway, as we were asking, why do you want to engage us? You both sound pretty experienced.'

'We heard you have a good way with people and explain a lot whilst going up the trail. An old couple we met in KK thought you two were an inspiration with your knowledge of butterflies, birds and plants. That's what we want to know. What do you say, can you climb with us?'

Adam inhaled deeply and nodded slowly while looking for confirmation from Brent. They stayed on for another fifteen minutes making arrangements for the climb whilst relishing the heat and peace before returning to KK in their second-hand jeep. The morning's descent had been particularly challenging due to the heavy rain. The summit itself had been bitterly cold with sleet falling, the wet granite slabs black and ominous. Their clients were a mother and her teenage son. Both had fallen hard on the slippery path, the mother sustaining a gash on her cheek bone, and the boy had torn a chunk out of his leg. The descent was harder than usual with the two casualties but fortunately the guide, Ampingan, had first-aid supplies so was able to staunch the blood and tape them up till they could get to the hospital.

'I'll be glad to have a few days off,' said Adam, peeling a tangerine as Brent drove. 'The booking with those two guys might be a good thing financially, we don't have many clients lined up till next month.'

'Maybe, but I don't know, they seem like a couple of clowns if you ask me. We've said yes and we've taken the deposit, so we'll have to do it now. Do you want to come in for dinner with me and Marie, or shall I drop you off at your mum's?'

'I think I'll go home, thanks, if that's OK. I'm pretty knackered after the day we've just had.'

As the car sped through the dusky countryside, Adam stared out at the dark shapes of the trees and banana palms lining the road. He could make out soft lights coming from kampongs. The road was a driver's nightmare, what with the oncoming traffic bound for Renau and Sandakan and the enormous potholes in the surface.

'This bloody road is more of a danger than the mountain,' complained Brent, 'I hate having to commute up and down. Pity Marie wouldn't move up then we could live in one of those chalets near the Park Headquarters.'

'Or Kundasang,' offered Adam. 'She'd get good fresh vegetables from all the surrounding farmers. It's amazing what grows at this altitude.'

'Yeah, but she won't budge. She's happy in her domestic world of the yacht club and all the other mums and babies. Oh well, we'll just have to suck it up, as they say, at least while we are committed here. We have a few more clients in October, then maybe we could think of moving on. What do you think about trying Europe?'

'I've never been to a cold climate,' Adam stared out at the passing stalls full of woven baskets and bunches of bananas. 'My life has always been here in Asia, and a stint in Australia of course, and yet my mother is from Scotland. Funny that she never wanted to return there. I should go, maybe explore the Scottish hills.'

'They are bloody freezing,' and Brent shivered, 'just like the summit was today, but at all levels, not just the top!' He reached for an apple from the fruit bag they had between them and munched it as he drove. 'I don't suppose a certain Felicity might be an added attraction?'

Adam laughed, 'Yeah, London is on the way to Ben Nevis, isn't it?'

'Oh definitely, you could say that. I think she's unquestionably worth making a small detour for!'

The countryside grew dark, only the jeep's headlights picked up the dark shapes of the trees lining the sides of the road. Behind them the crickets sounded their nightly warnings in the impenetrable jungle. Brent changed gear as they approached a tight bend. 'I wouldn't have liked being Sir Hugh Low when he set out to conquer Kinabalu with his band of native guides. This road is bad but at least it's a road. We don't have leaches and wild animals and creepy crawlies to contend with. He must have been a very brave man, even if he didn't get to the top.'

Imagining the explorer hacking his way through the thick jungle, Adam remembered the forest in Pahang when he was a boy, and the unsettling feeling of being watched. 'Yes, we are lucky, we have a path and shelters, and every day is different.'

Brent slowed down as he drove through another village, and Adam could make out the familiar shapes of women preparing food, and of men sitting on plastic chairs smoking cigarettes. He saw soft light emitting from open doorways. Such a different world, he thought, from the harsh brutal windswept mountain I woke up to this morning.

Chapter 49

The monsoon was relentless. Lightning cracked over the ancient rooftops of the Old Bazaar in Kuching. Carpenter Street was lit with a spiteful surge of phosphorescent light. Booming thunder drowned out the sound of cars, only the sploshing of tyres throwing up spray alerted pedestrians to their creeping presence as they manoeuvred along the narrow street. Kamal was soaked. His white shirt was stuck to his back and his glasses were speckled with water and he shivered. He dived into a coffee shop.

'No umbrella? You want to buy one? I have one here.' An old Chinese woman dressed in a traditional *samfoo* outfit resembling pink flowery pyjamas grinned at him from behind the counter. Kamal appraised her gold teeth and he could see how she might have made her money, the kind who always had an eye for a deal.

'Just a coffee please and a pineapple tart if you have one.'

'I have. You want to play cards? Or anything else?' she added suggestively.

'Coffee is good.' Kamal smiled. He knew the girls used to ply their trade around here in bygone days, on the corner of Bishopsgate. He stirred his coffee remembering the early days when he came here on his own, back in the seventies. After work he would slip away from his colleagues and make his way to the Hunters Bar at the Aurora Hotel. For a minute he saw himself back then, surreptitiously meeting a girl called Sue; she charged forty ringgits, he remembered that. And there were others, but he had no recollection of their names. It was always the forbidden fruit that he enjoyed. He smiled at the audacious behaviour of Sue; she was a wild girl that was for sure. Kamal stirred his coffee lost in another time when he had Sue on his knee in a darkened night club. He could almost hear her high-pitched laugh, feel her pony tail swishing against his face, see her red lips and flashing eyes. But all that changed when he met Rose. He hadn't been looking for romance, but she was so damn beautiful and so insistent. He had no choice but to marry her, according to Sharia Law. Kamal sipped his coffee. How could he forget the early days of his liaison with the alluring girl who tempted him with her purity. He remembered how they used to meet secretly to eat satay and then go to the Rex Cinema after work. They would watch kung fu movies and it was as Bruce Lee punched and kicked his opponents in the Fist of Fury, that Kamal had simultaneously groaned in the darkness of the cinema, his hands exploring Rose's soft breasts and opened thighs. Lost in the past, Kamal blinked back to the present. The rain continued to beat on the roof, falling in sheets from the covered arched walkway. He was hidden by the watery curtain, but only for as long as the rain lasted.

'You know Kuching well?' asked the Chinese woman as she looked up from her abacus, her fingers clicking the black beads, no doubt plotting her next million.

'I've been coming here off and on for about twenty-five years. I used to work here.'

'I have been here all my life, my father and grandfather owned this coffee shop, also have one in Kai Ju Lane, but they had opium also. Long time ago. Upstairs, lah, they would smoke the pipes, lie and sleep, then come down and drink coffee. Coffee with butter in it, make it soft on the throat, lah. You like? You want to try?'

'Opium?' Kamal, in spite of himself was shocked.

'Ha Ha Ha, not opium, not here, lah. Not anymore. Police very strict now. No, but coffee with butter, you want to try?'

Kamal shook his head. He finished the last of his cup and rose to go. 'Not today, but thank you. The rain is stopping, I think I'll be on my way now.'

'I give you umbrella for half price, what you say? Maybe rain tomorrow?'

'Deal,' and he paid her the minimal price. He walked down towards the Hong San Si Temple and turned right into Wayang Street.

Rose was waiting on the threshold of the apartment. She had been listening for his footsteps on the stair. 'You're here at last, so many weeks I have wanted to see you. I am always waiting. You promised you would come to see me last month.'

'I'm here, Rose. We can be together for the weekend. Are you all set to go to the Damai holiday house this afternoon when Farah gets back from school?'

'Yes, of course, I have been looking forward to it so much.'

Kamal showed her his new umbrella, 'I had to take shelter, the rain was very heavy.'

'Why did you buy another one, we have so many already and the rain has stopped.'

'I know, but I liked the woman, she was a crafty Chinese business woman, I just wanted her to feel she still had bargaining powers.'

'Hmmm, quite pretty, nice orange and blue flowers. Maybe I'll use it.'

Kamal smiled. It was good to bring a gift.

Chapter 50

It was eight o'clock in the evening. Edie was entertaining her two friends, Kate and Amelia, to dinner at her house on Tuaran Hill. The night was velvet, somewhere an owl was hooting in the forest, and the bullfrogs down in the kampong were starting their nightly chorus. In the kitchen Edie spooned the yellow turmeric sauce over her *ikan molly*, a delicate fish curry dish. Red chillies garnished the edges of the plates and the rice was fluffy and fragrant.

'*Jabut makan!*' She called the ladies over to the dining room table which she'd set with candles and crystal glasses. 'Please sit down and pour yourselves some wine and I'll just bring through the masterpiece; I made it all by myself,' she gloated. She placed the steaming dish in the centre of the table. 'I have to admit though that Moy Moy and the new maid Pina did make the rice and the dessert. Pina is working out really well, and Moy Moy is teaching her how to cook and clean. Poor Moy Moy seems to be limping a lot these days.'

'That is so sad,' said Kate. 'Poor Moy Moy. Mind you, she was never the speediest of amahs even when she was younger.' She took a mouthful of fish and dabbed her lips with her napkin. 'This is delicious, Edie, really good; is this one of your mother-in-law's recipes?'

'It is and I think it's turned out not too badly. It's a pity Kamal is away, he really likes *ikan molly*, so does Adam but then Adam likes everything.' She looked at her wristwatch. 'Funny he hasn't called. He usually calls to tell me they got down from the mountain safely. They were escorting a couple of American guys up today and they were a bit concerned about them.'

'Maybe they're having a drink afterwards?' suggested Amelia. 'I shouldn't worry yet. Anyway, do you fancy going out to Cowrie Island with us next weekend. Michael's golfing friend, the one I told you about who has branched into tourism, has bought this island and he's built a fabulous, really exclusive resort. What do you think? Will you join us?'

'Isn't that the guy who used to be in town planning?'

'Yes, Tony Yong, what do you say? He sends a boat to collect his visitors and it's about a two-hour speed boat trip from KK. A total getaway.'

'Well, I think it sounds great. I can't see why Kamal wouldn't want to go; I think he really likes Tony Yong. What's that noise? Is it a car? Who could be coming up here at this time of night?' Edie tossed her napkin on to her chair and walked to the veranda in time to see headlights approaching the house.

A black car pulled up and two men in police uniforms got out.

'Mrs Shariff?'

'Yes. Can I help you?'

'Is Mr Shariff here?'

'No, he's in Kuching this weekend. Do you need to talk to him?'

'May we come in?'

Edie ushered the two officers into the sitting room. Her friends got up from the dining room table and came to stand either side of her. For a moment no one spoke, it was as though they were in a tableau. Only the sound of the overhead fan broke the stillness.

'Please,' began Edie, 'tell me, what is it?'

The taller of the two men, a Sikh, approached her. Just two small steps across the carpet. 'Madam, it is not good news. I am afraid your son is missing. He did not return from his climb up the mountain today. The guides alerted us. There is now an official search going ahead.'

Edie gasped; sickness rose in her throat. The policeman's words were flowing round her, the sounds were distorted as though coming from underwater. 'Helicopters will be used in the search. Local Kadazan people will be tracking the area and his friend is searching for him as well. Adam and an American man are both missing. No trace.'

Edie sank to her knees and retched, bright yellow remnants of her meal spattered her dress and carpet. Blackness engulfed her and she fell over on her side.

'Quickly!' Amelia gestured to Kate, 'Get Moy Moy, get a cloth and some water. Come on, Edie.' She wiped her friend's forehead with a tissue. 'She's fainted,' she addressed the other policeman, also an Indian, 'it's the shock.'

'Yes, Madam, I know, and it's quite understandable. Do you have a number for Mr Shariff so that we can inform him?'

'I have his mobile, but just a minute until we can get Mrs Shariff conscious again and cleaned up. Here's my friend now. Kate, can you wipe her forehead and try to get her to take a sip of water? Moy Moy, clean this up as best you can. Come on, Edie, can you hear me, can you get up?'

Edie's eyes flickered, 'I'm so sorry, I've made a mess, is it a bad dream? Tell me, Amelia, is it a dream?' Then she saw the policemen and immediately let out a scream and rocked on her hands and knees, 'Nooo! No, it can't be true, my Adam lost, he can't be.'

'Put the kettle on, Madam, make some sweet tea,' the policeman advised. Kate ran off to the kitchen, instructing Moy Moy to carry out the policeman's orders. On the way back to the sitting room, she spied the brandy in the cocktail cabinet. 'Amelia? What do you think? A spoonful might help?'

'Yes, it can't hurt. Come and sip this, Edie, just a small sip. I'm going to call Kamal and get him to come home as soon as possible. Where did I put my handbag?'

Amelia retrieved her handbag and took out her mobile phone then headed into Tara's bedroom and shut the door. She sat on the girl's childhood bed and dialled Kamal's number. The phone rang and rang, no reply. She tried again. Still no reply.

Should she leave a message? What could she say? Just: Get back here as soon as possible? She tried ringing one more time.

'Hello?' It was a woman talking.

Amelia exhaled. 'Where is Kamal?'

'Out just now. He's gone to get a takeaway.'

'Tell him to phone me, Amelia Low, as soon as he returns. Do you understand?'

'Sure.'

'It's an emergency.'

'Sure.'

Amelia returned to where Edie was sitting white and dazed, listening to the policemen updating her on what might have happened.

'Maybe we could call Brent?' Amelia suggested.

Edie turned to her; her eyes wide and unfocussed. The pupils appeared unnaturally black. 'Did you speak to Kamal?' was all she said.

'I left a message on his phone. I'm sure he'll get back to me soon.'

'I need him here, Amelia, I want Kamal,' and Edie started to weep.

Kate sat down beside her and put her arm around her friend. 'Shall we try and call Brent?'

Edie sniffed, but instead of answering she turned her head towards the two policemen. 'Is there a chance they might find him alive? He might have hurt himself and be unable to walk.'

'As I said, Madam, all efforts are in place to find him. Until we find a body, there is hope. But I must caution you, Mrs Shariff, you know the mountain is a very dangerous place.'

Edie lowered her head and rung the tissues Kate had given her into a tight ball.

'I am so sorry to have to bring you this news,' the Sikh policeman said. 'If we hear anything further, we will be in touch. But for now, we will leave you in your friends' kind, caring hands. I hope Mr Shariff gets home soon.'

As quickly as they had appeared, they were gone. It was as though the whole incident hadn't taken place. The dining table was still set with unfinished food, glasses half drunk, napkins in disarray. Moy Moy hovered, waiting for instructions.

'Clear everything away, Moy Moy,' Amelia commanded. 'Please store the food in boxes, and tell Pina to make more tea please, for the three of us. And bring sugar.'

'Yes, Mem.' Moy Moy padded back to the kitchen. Instead of doing as she was instructed, she walked to the back door by the laundry room and stepped into the starry night. The old Chinese woman looked down past the mango tree, down towards the sea. It was dark but she could see the faint glimmer of boats. It was peaceful out here. She listened to the cicadas. 'Where are you, my little boy? Adam? Are you frightened, like you used to be when you got lost? Moy Moy is waiting for you; Moy Moy won't let you be alone ever again.' Moy Moy winced, feeling the pain in her hip and in her back. 'Cancer,' the doctor had told her. If she passed away soon, she would keep her little boy safe in the next world.

'Moy Moy! Where is the tea, and what about boxing up the food, did you not hear me?' shouted Amelia.

'I hear you, Mem, Moy Moy is coming, no worries. Moy Moy is here.'

Amelia strutted back to the sitting room. 'Honestly, she gets more relaxed by the day, I found her out there looking at the stars. Oh! Is that my phone? Kamal?' She glanced at Edie leaning against Kate, still weeping silently. She took the call in Tara's room.

'You have to come home, tomorrow. Adam is missing on the mountain, feared dead. Edie is a mess. She needs you. We've had the police here and everyone has been trying to get hold of you. It seems that you have other things on your mind?'

'Adam? What?' There was no mistaking the shock in his voice. 'I'll get the earliest flight tomorrow. I'll be there as soon as I can. What about Brent? Are they both missing?'

'No, Brent is part of the search party, looking for them. There is an American guy with Adam and he's disappeared too. I was going to see if Brent would answer his phone, but Edie is not taking this too well. She needs her husband. I'll tell her you'll be back tomorrow.'

'Thanks.' And the phone clicked off.

Amelia sighed. So, there was truth in Edie's suspicions after all. Poor girl, best she stays ignorant of her husband's other life for now.

The night was interminable. The three friends sat together and snoozed and woke and Edie cried. Pina made toast and coffee and Moy Moy slept.

As the first rays of sunlight appeared over the rain trees, Edie's phone rang. 'Brent? Do you have news?'

'Nothing, Edie. We searched all over the mountain until it grew dark, and even then by torchlight, calling and calling. Eventually we had to sleep, we were so exhausted, but we will resume as soon as we've eaten some porridge. A helicopter team is going to make some circuits of the mountain. How are you, Edie? Crazy question, I know. Is Kamal with you?'

'No, he's not back yet.' Edie shook her head, clutching the phone. 'Amelia and Kate are here and Kamal is flying home today. The police came here to tell me but they have no news yet. Oh, Brent, what happened?'

'I'll tell you everything I know when I see you but I have to go now. The guides and porters are going to do another wide scan over the mountain. If Adam and the American have fallen or were injured, there are jungle guides who are preparing to search. There's an expert who did a great job rescuing some soldiers a few years ago, he's been alerted too. Everything possible is being done, Edie. I promise I'll talk to you later.'

Somehow the hours of the day ticked past, but the anguish of the waiting for news lingered. Amelia left to shower and change, as did Kate. Edie forced herself to do the same and get out of her soiled dress. For a while she was alone in the house. Nothing moved and the phone remained silent. She decided to look for Moy Moy who seemed to be more elusive than usual. She walked out of the kitchen, along the narrow path to her shack and knocked tentatively on her amah's door. There was no response. It was somewhere she would not normally enter but she pushed the door and went inside. Everything was clean in the wooden room, just as she would have expected. The possessions so few, just an old handbag that Edie herself had thrown out years ago was sitting by the bed. It was open, revealing a wallet and three bottles of tablets. A collection of dresses and cotton trousers hung from a clothes rail and a photograph of Adam and Tara was displayed on a shelf above it. Edie sat down on the thin mattress which was covered in an old batik sarong, and looked at the photograph of the dark-haired children in shorts and T shirts, aged about eight and six. Her tears welled up again, her beautiful children, and Moy Moy loved them too. Of course she did, she must be as heartbroken as she was herself. But what kind of tablets was she taking? Edie picked up the bottles and tried to make out the names. Definitely not aspirin. There was a small bottle of Tiger Balm beside the bag. Usually for pain of some sort. Poor Moy Moy, she must ask her if everything was all right. Just as she returned the photograph back onto the shelf, she could hear the slow shuffling steps approaching. Edie jumped up from the bed, guilty at having entered the shack without being invited.

'Mem? You get news? You come to tell Moy Moy?'

Edie shook her head. 'No news, Moy Moy, they are still looking.'

'Maybe they find today?'

'Maybe. We all hope so. Are you sick, Moy Moy? Is it your hips? Come and sit with me for a minute.'

'I think I tell you now, Mem, Moy Moy will die soon. Not good news. But I take care of Adam if they cannot find him. My spirit in sky will take care. Don't cry. I will go soon.'

'Oh, Moy Moy, you can't leave me now. I need you.' Edie held the older woman's soft podgy hand. 'Please tell me it's not true.'

'You take care of Moy Moy? You take Moy Moy to hospital when it's time?'

Edie sniffed. 'Oh, my dear friend, of course I will. You have been with us for years and years. I can't bear the thought of you suffering. Come, we'll go to the house and we'll get Pina to make us a drink of fresh orange juice. Tuan Shariff will be back in two hours. And maybe we will hear more news from Brent. We will wait together.'

Chapter 51

Brent finally arrived back into town after a week on the mountain. Before he had taken off his boots, Marie ran out to the porch and threw her arms around him, 'I'm so glad you're home safely.' Frowning, she studied the scratches on his face and the bruises and cuts on his legs, but she said nothing. His face was haggard and unshaven and his eyes were swimming with unshed tears. 'We lost him,' he finally said, 'I can't bear the thought of him waiting for us to find him. The guys on the ground are making their way through the dense jungle to see if he and Caleb might have fallen, but honestly even if they had, there is little hope they would have survived. They had no provisions with them, only a bottle of water each. The porters always carry the food.'

'Have you seen Edie and Kamal?'

'Yeah, I went there straight away and told them as much as I knew. They are pretty broken.' He looked round for baby Andrew and saw his son's blonde head above the bars of the playpen. 'Hello, little fellow, do you want a cuddle from your daddy? Come on then, up you come. Don't worry if you dribble over me, it's you that might need a bath after touching Daddy's sweaty shirt.' Andrew patted Brent's face and grinned as he showed off his brand-new teeth. Marie gave silent thanks to God as she watched the reunion of father and son. She was lucky. She knew that.

Up on Tuaran Hill, Edie and Kamal sat side by side on the veranda. It was to this old colonial house that they had brought baby Adam twenty-seven years ago, and it was where Edie had learnt how to be a mother. Was this where she was going to learn how to grieve for her beloved boy?

'They shouldn't have taken those Americans,' Kamal said. 'Brent had a bad feeling, he thought they were a bit arrogant.'

'I know, it seems that Caleb wanted to explore a little further after signing his name at the summit; he wanted to get some view for a photograph, and to see if it was possible to abseil, even though Brent and Gimbang had told him not to.' Edie pushed her hair back from her face. 'Brent tried to persuade him to come back. He said fog was coming in, like a thick grey curtain, obliterating any views. but Caleb just kept walking away from the group. It was Adam that went after him to check he would be all right. Brent said the American had brought vodka with him and against the guide's orders had drunk straight from the bottle and had then handed the bottle to Adam.'

'And,' Kamal said, 'that he drank it down like lemonade. I never knew that Adam drank, I always thought he was a good Muslim. He kept his secrets, that boy, and look where it has landed him now.'

Edie twisted her hands together, 'I never told you, my dear, but I promised Adam and I did keep our boy's secret. He hasn't drunk alcohol since leaving Australia. It was after he dropped out that he became totally dependent on vodka and from what he told me he hit rock bottom. He was very ashamed but after a big struggle with his addiction he told me he vowed he would never touch the stuff again. I have no idea what happened to make him take that vodka on the mountain. Maybe Caleb taunted him and the temptation was too great. I'm so sorry, Kamal.'

Kamal shifted in his seat. 'Where is Moy Moy? I thought she was going to bring us some fruit and toast.'

'Leave her, Kamal, she's resting. Pina will get it.'

'I don't pay her to rest, she should be getting the coffee and breakfast. I'll go myself and tell her to hurry up.' Edie's shoulders slumped and tears ran down her cheeks.

'Look at you, Edie, you're upset. You need coffee too; you have had a shock listening to Brent's account. I'll get that lazy amah to bring us something.'

'Please, Kamal. Leave her. She is very ill. I'll explain later, but for now, I'll get Pina to bring us a tray.'

Kamal fidgeted; he was angry with himself. If I had been here, he thought, could I have prevented the boys from going? They both claimed they had a bad feeling, but that was no reason to cancel. A bit soft. The sort of thing Edie would say. Now all this talk about Cecelia and *bomohs* and witch doctors. Why did Adam have to go after that irresponsible guy? And what is this about drinking? I never knew he had an addiction problem. And if he had, why be so stupid as to drink up on top of that dangerous mountain. And the fog. Who could have foreseen the fog? Came down like a screen, thick as a veil Brent said, and impossible to make out the stones and boulders, let alone the path to safety. I am resigned to Adam's fate but Edie still believes the boy might be alive somewhere. And that Cecilia, all the talk about spirits and white chickens, she is just feeding Edie's head with false hopes. Edie and Pina broke into his reverie carrying a tray of papaya and coffee. 'Are you going to see that *shaman* woman tomorrow?' he asked curtly.

'I am, Cecilia says this particular Kadazan tribal woman who lives in a remote village has powers and might be able to tell me if Adam is still alive.'

Kamal sneered, 'Yes, she will have powers through eating betel nut and drinking rice and snake wine. She'll be on some hallucinogenic trip, but if it gives you a sense of purpose, I'm sure that's what you will do.'

'And what about you?' Edie hardly recognised her husband. He had been brittle and edgy since hearing the news, his face was flushed and he had been drinking more than usual. Although they had cried together that first day and night, he seemed to be hiding his grief and frustration through the bottles of red wine that were starting to line up beside the bins outside.

'Please, Kamal, we need to be strong. The rangers and search parties still might find him, we mustn't give up hope. I feel he might still be alive.'

Kamal ran his fingers through his hair leaving marks like a ploughed field. He has such beautiful hair, she thought, it may be turning silver but he is still a striking man. 'Why were you in Kuching? I thought all those jobs were over now?'

'I had to go, just leave it, Edie, stop your nagging. You are perfectly aware that all our jobs require a personal touch and I had to see a client from Brunei who happened to be there. Now, what's all this about Moy Moy?'

The days turned to weeks, but there was no news. Tara and Joe and baby Clementine arrived to spend Christmas with her parents, but the holiday atmosphere was subdued. Clementine toddled about, chasing Timmy the Third, and her antics helped them smile and to break the awkward silences amongst the adults.

'What's wrong with Dad?'

'We all have our demons, Tara, and we are trying to cope the best way we can. I disapprove of his red wine consumption and he disapproves of me visiting the *bomoh* lady.

'What did the old woman tell you?'

'She said she can feel his heat at the foot of the mountain, which means he's alive. So, I am still hoping the search parties will continue to look.'

Tara looked at her mother's ravished face, the blue eyes that were almost colourless, and the old batik skirt she had taken to wearing. Tara could see how empty Edie had become. There was a listlessness about her, as though she was just going through the motions. 'And poor Moy Moy. I had no idea she was ill.'

'Yes, she told me on the morning after Adam was lost.'

'Poor Mum, I should have been with you.'

'I missed you, but you are here now. And little Clementine is loving her visit. Well, loving the cat anyway.'

The house seemed very empty after the small family left, the cot and the baby high chair silent without that little child filling them with happiness. The next few months brought the monsoon and the house and driveway were cloaked in mist and torrential rain. Edie nursed Moy Moy. Her amah had moved into Tara's old room, attended regularly by Doctor Kana. A whole chemist shop of little bottles containing pills for pain, for sleeping, for things neither of them knew what for, all lined up on the bedside table. Moy Moy hardly ate and her dark eyes had developed a white film over the iris. She squinted through her half-moon glasses when she wanted to make out what the doctor had prescribed for her. Each day she grew weaker. She was so thin. With persuasion she swallowed a single teaspoon of the broth from the Maggi Noodles packet that Pina made for her.

'Moy Moy is going, Mem. Open handbag and find my brother's letter inside. You tell him when Moy Moy is gone. He lives in Hong Kong.'

'Oh, Moy Moy, of course I'll do that.' Edie took the handbag and found the white letter with beautiful script. As she pulled it out, a small piece of tissue-like paper fell onto her lap. It looked like a receipt.

'Moy Moy, what's this?'

'Ah, you find it? Like me, I find it.'

'What is it?'

'Long ago I find it in pocket of Tuan's shirt. He come back from Sarawak. Send shirt to me for washing, I think he forget paper inside.'

Edie's brows wrinkled in consternation. She smoothed out the small square.

'It's a receipt for a pair of ruby and silver earrings.'

Moy Moy took her mistress's hand. 'I know Mem has no ruby earrings. I think, maybe I keep, better not tell.'

Edie's eyes were heavy with unshed tears but she struggled to smile. 'Why did I not appreciate you more, Moy Moy?' She continued to hold her hand, and leant over to pick up the lotion on the bedside table. She poured some cream on to Moy Moy's palm and with slow circular moves using her thumb she massaged the hand, tracing the veins and lines on the wrist.

Outside the rain beat down, the branches of the trees were blackened by the deluge, a crack of lightning filled the room. Moy Moy moaned softly before turning her face to the wall. Edie looked down at the hand cradled in her own. It had gone limp.

'You've gone, Moy Moy. Sleep well, dear friend.'

And then the tears came.

Chapter 52

'Edie, is that you?'

'Hi, Cecilia, you're ringing early. Is everything OK?'

'Edie, I had word from an old woman up near Kundasang. She lives in a remote village, quite far off the main track. She's heard about Adam.'

'Is he alive?' Edie gripped the mobile.

'She didn't say. She wants to talk to you. Shall we go to see her? I can drive you there if you like. It's about ninety kilometres from Kota Kinabalu and should take us about two hours. If we leave straight away, we could be at Kundasang about one o'clock.

'Kamal is coming home tonight. Should he come too?'

'No, better if it's just you.'

'OK, that's so kind of you, Cecilia, thank you. I'll get ready.'

Edie found Pina peeling potatoes in the kitchen. 'I'm going out with Miss Cecilia; tell Tuan I will be back late. Just make the dinner as I showed you, please.' Edie quickly grabbed a curry puff from the plate in the kitchen, nibbled it, then tipped the four remaining ones into a plastic box. She selected some litre bottles of water and packed her impromptu picnic into a rucksack. Pina added some apples and bananas. She had taken her new responsibilities very seriously since Moy Moy's death and Edie could see the girl was trying hard. Poor Moy Moy. Edie missed the old Chinese woman's gentle presence.

The drive up to the mountain was hard. They were held up by slow trucks, by traffic jams, and frequently had to reduce their speed at snake-like bends.

'He would have known this road so well,' Edie said, staring out at the villages and fruit stalls as they drove past. 'Do you think this woman has some knowledge that the police and rangers don't have?'

259

'Her daughter didn't say, just that she wanted to talk to the mother of Adam.'

Passing the giant cabbage statue in the middle of the Kundasang roundabout, Cecelia turned off sharply and veered down a track with fields on either side, mostly cultivated with salad crops. It was all very alpine and picturesque. Ashoka trees lined the potholed road, giving shade to some whitewashed houses.

'This looks nice,' Edie commented. 'Does she live in one of these houses?'

'Oh heavens, no! We are taking a turn here and then into the forest for about ten kilometres. Then we have to hike.'

'Cecilia, I don't have proper shoes, you should have warned me.'

'No worries, I brought you some jungle shoes, everyone wears them in the forest. They're like football boots made out of old car tyres. They're on the back seat, put them on.'

Edie wasn't so sure. She had expected to meet this woman in a nice coffee shop somewhere, not up some track with leeches ready to leap on to her legs. And she was wearing her batik skirt. The car finally came to a stop and Cecilia jumped out. Edie looked at the dense tree-covered trail. Would she learn something new? It was nearly a year since Adam had disappeared. Could he possibly still be alive?

'Come on, it's about two miles, let's get started.'

Edie noticed that Cecilia had dressed for the occasion. She was wearing long black trousers and had her hair tied up in a bun. Even without the false eyelashes and platform shoes she still looked like a dragon lady.

'I'm coming, but first I'm going to spray my arms and legs with mosquito repellent. Thank goodness I always carry it in my handbag. Poor Amelia nearly met her end with dengue fever.'

'You'll be just fine. Let's get on.'

The heat was sweltering and perspiration ran down their necks. They persevered, plodding through the dead leaves. The track was well used and Edie could make out footprints in the mud. There were flowers and butterflies, and all around them, the jungle orchestra made its own music building to a crescendo as the cicadas led the buzzing chorus. Would Adam have heard this? Would he have been lying injured and afraid? Could she dare to hope that he might be alive?

They finally came to a clearing and a wooden house built on stilts in the traditional Malay style. A rickety ladder was in place and a selection of plants were growing in pots around the wooden posts.

'Look! That must be her daughter up there,' pointed Cecilia, 'Hello! *Selamat malam!*'

'Does she speak English?' Edie asked.

'Yes, she will translate for her mother.'

'*Selamat Malam*,' Edie kicked off her shoes before attempting to climb up the ladder. 'That is quite a walk you have to do to get to your home.'

'Hello, Mrs Edie, my name is Ansayu. I am happy to meet you. Here is my mother, her name is Semitah.'

Edie saw an elderly lady sitting on the floor. Her legs were outstretched and she looked to be no more than four foot in height. Her skin was nutbrown and her hair was still black, despite her face having shrunk into loose cavities of flesh. She had no teeth, she didn't smile, and her eyes had the same knowing look that Edie had seen in adult orangutans.

'Please sit.' Ansayu herself sat down upon the dirty rattan settee. Edie sat next to her and Cecilia pulled over a chair. A young girl brought in a tray with a teapot and four glasses and placed it on a small table.

'You like tea?'

'Thank you, I do like tea.' It was surprisingly refreshing, though a little sweet.

Semitah put down her glass after finishing the drink. She began to speak. As she spoke, she addressed herself to Edie. Edie was only aware of the soft voice, the beady black eyes, and the silence surrounding them. Nothing seemed to move.

When the old woman stopped talking, Edie turned to Ansayu. 'What? What did she say?'

'My mother said that you need to know that your son has gone, he left for the spirit world. She felt his body, she knew where he was, she could feel him. He had fallen but he was alive, and she knew.'

'When?' Edie felt a lump in her throat. She turned to Ansayu, 'Does she know when, does she know where Adam is lying?'

'Yes, she knows. She has told me, and I have told the authorities. They are sending people into the heart of the forest. I think he fell and was injured but tried to get down and through the jungle. He would have died of exposure or starvation. That is why my mother had a feeling that he may have been alive

261

some months ago. My mother has been doing her smoke rituals and conjuring up the spirits of the forest, the python, the panther. She possesses magic powers that we cannot understand. She knows. The other man has gone too. Both gone. So sorry, but better you know.'

Edie knew. She had always known, but she had never given up hope. And now she needed to get home. This was too much. The forest, this old woman and her magic potions and ancient beliefs, and her beloved boy. He had always had a fear of the forest. Ever since he was little.

'Thank you,' she said.

It was a silent trip back, both women broken by the news, both weary after the hike to the village in the hot sun then again back to the car. Cecilia glanced at Edie who was staring vacantly out of the window. 'Is Kamal home?' she finally asked.

'Coming back tonight.'

'What will he say?'

'Not much, he'll say I'm mad to believe in what a *bomoh* tells me. He will try to make a fool out of me. Maybe I'll not say anything. I'll wait until the authorities give us the news.'

When Edie got home, Kamal had still not yet returned from work. Pina was hovering in the kitchen, the casserole she'd made was ready and her potatoes all set to boil.

'That smells delicious, Pina. I need to shower and change. I shall eat in an hour.' Refreshed and clean, Edie ate alone. The night was still, only the chichaks on the wall chirruped to each other. Pina had gone to bed. Edie poured herself a large gin and tonic and looked at her phone. No messages. She drank it down quickly and poured a refill. Carrying the icy glass carefully she went outside to sit on the steps leading to the garden. Timmy meowed and joined her, knowing that she would stroke his soft fur and that he would reward her with his deep melodious purr. They were still sitting there when the headlights of Kamal's car lit up the driveway. Edie didn't stir as she listened to the sound of the door slamming and his footsteps approaching the front of the house. Timmy leapt from the step and disappeared amongst the banana leaves.

'This is a nice surprise, waiting up for me?'

'You didn't make dinner. I thought you might have called me.'

'The plane was late, sorry. Why are you sitting out here? And you are on the gin.'

'Yes, I've had a couple. Do you want a drink?'

'Of course, it's been a long day. Not all of us can just swan about at home all the time. What have you done with your time today?' He stepped around her, avoiding touching her.

Edie stood up and followed him into the lounge. She sat down on the rocking chair, listening to him in the bedroom. He came out eventually, wearing a pair of shorts and T-shirt, and went to the cocktail cabinet to pour himself a whisky. 'Nice day?' she asked.

'It was OK, usual stressful stuff. What about you? Yacht club? How's Amelia?'

'No, I was with Cecilia actually.'

'Oh?'

'We drove up to the mountain to visit an old woman.'

Kamal sighed heavily and his face grew red, 'Are you so stupid? So deluded? What fairy tales are these hags telling you? It's always about the spirits with you.' He seemed to sneer at her as he took a sip of whisky.

'And what about you, and your mother's beliefs in the *hantu*? They are ingrained in you, so don't pretend you don't believe in the spirit world.'

'I don't. It's all superstition, it's time to move on, get modern. What is the matter with you? Always on about auras and spirits and clutching at straws. It is very unlikely that Adam is alive, it has been far too long. If he found refuge with native people they would have come forward. Stop living in a dream world, Edie.'

'I'm not living in a dream world; I am living a nightmare. Adam was alive for a while and the old woman said that he had been injured but that he has gone now.'

'And you believe her? She hasn't seen the body, she knows nothing. You and your ridiculous beliefs.'

'And the pot?' Edie asked. 'The pot we found full of bones in Kuantan all those years ago? You were uncomfortable with that. It seems to have brought us nothing but bad luck. It was around that time you started seeing that woman in Kuching. She has been like a black presence in our marriage, Kamal, and don't deny it. Has she been giving you trouble? She's been ringing me, I know it, always putting the phone down when I answer it. Does she think I'm stupid? And Adam, did he know about her?'

'Stop this, Edie, you've had too much gin. You pour half a glass each time, I've seen you.'

263

'And you're one to talk are you, you big liar. I may have had some gin, but before I sleep in Tara's room tonight, there's one thing I am going to do.'

'Oh, and what's that?'

'Just watch!' Edie switched on the light in the veranda and descended the steps to the garden. She fumbled amongst the plants growing in dragon pots at the side of the house. She located the one she wanted. It had a tree fern planted in it. The pot was terracotta with a round base and it hadn't changed much since the day it was found by her children on the beach in Kuantan all those years ago. Edie struggled to pull out the fern, wrenching the roots that were firmly embedded in the clay-like soil. She tipped the plant and soil on the grass, gasping for breath.

'Now what?' Kamal watched from the veranda.

'This is what I should have done years ago,' and she hurled the pot onto the drive. It hit the concrete with a dramatic crash and shattered in many pieces.

'More superstition, Edie, you are becoming more Malay than me.'

'Maybe. It comes from wholeheartedly immersing oneself in a country with a man who I thought loved me.' Dogs had started to bark in the kampong below. 'I doubt if it can fix anything, but it makes me feel better.'

The morning brought the sounds of bee-eaters and pitta birds squabbling on the overhead electricity wire. The rain trees' branches reached up towards a sapphire sky. It was going to be a hot day. Edie sat down to her morning coffee as usual on the veranda. She noticed the shards of the broken pot had already been cleared away. The gardener must have wondered what had happened. Of course he would never ask.

Kamal emerged from their bedroom. He was unshaven and his eyes were red rimmed.

'Paracetamol?'

'Maybe, though I doubt they will help. What's that noise? A car?'

Edie stood up and shooed the cat away from her legs. 'It's the police.'

The same black car that had brought the policemen last year parked and the same two officers got out. 'Good morning,' the Sikh policeman greeted them.

'Good morning, please, come in,' Edie ushered them once again into the lounge. 'Have you any news?'

'We have, and I am sorry, but we have recovered the body of your son. The body of Caleb Van Zeller is still missing, but we know it is Adam as we have his rucksack. I am so sorry to have to confirm his death.'

'Do you know how he died?' Edie knew already, but she had to hear it from an official source.

'We believe, from his injuries, that he sustained a blow to his head and had broken his left leg and arm after a bad fall. He might have dragged himself down from the mountain, perhaps hoping to find a village, but it would have been starvation, exposure or an animal that might have killed him. We will never know for sure.'

'But he did live for a while after falling?'

'We think so. The blows he sustained were not life threatening. I am so sorry to be the harbinger of such dreadful news. But here, we have his rucksack. All is in order, just as he had packed it.'

Edie stretched out her hand and took possession of the bag. She hugged it tight against her chest and squeezed her eyes tight.

'Thank you for coming, but please go now.' Her voice was trembling, and tears started to fall, 'Please, please just leave.'

Chapter 53

Edie woke up early to the sound of a cat meowing at her window. She pulled back the curtain and was met with a baleful stare. She rubbed her eyes, and grabbing her dressing gown went round to the back door to let her feline visitor in. 'And who are you?' Immediately he rolled over on to his side in a submissive manner, demanding to be stroked. 'Friendly, and obviously well fed. Were you just coming to see who is here? Come in then and you can watch while I switch on the kettle.'

It was comforting to have a cat on her lap as she sipped her tea. She hadn't given her own Timmy a thought since leaving. Closing her eyes she tried to suppress the memories of her veranda and her other way of life and the abyss that was always threatening to engulf her. She mustn't think about it. The cat meowed. 'Sorry puss, did I stop stroking your fur? I was miles away, but you'd better scram as I'm going to get dressed and go out. It's such a beautiful day.' She went through to the bedroom and pulled on her jeans and blue T-shirt, and frowning at the weather, decided to slip on her long silver-grey cardigan before stepping outside. Humming to the music on the car radio, she drove south. The roadside verges were alive with dandelions. There was a feeling of change in the air, the wind had abated and fields were rich green with new corn. She turned off at a sign indicating a road leading down towards the sea. Edie had visited this beauty spot previously with Robert Hunter, but that day had been wet and squalls of rain had prevented them from getting out of the car. Parking her car today in the small parking area, she walked down a narrow path lined with cloudy white hawthorn and strident yellow gorse. At her feet were clumps of bluebells and the last of the primroses. She found a bench conveniently placed at the viewing point. She sat down. It was all so quiet. The clarity of the sound of each wave breaking on the shore below her was sublime. It was as though she was letting the beauty of the place passively wash over her. There was no need to strive, to discover or to learn anymore. She felt at peace. Above her an aeroplane flew over, perhaps heading for Aberdeen. Edie stared out at the horizon, squinting into the sun as the North Sea glittered beguilingly. The smell of the hawthorn and coconut scent of the gorse was intoxicating. 'Oh, my beloved son,' she whispered, 'I wish I could have come here with you, to have sat here and shown you this beautiful land, and you could have learnt about my family and my grandmother. She too lost her son, so tragically, just as I did you. But she stayed on, she tended her garden, her chickens, and she lived a long time. But you, Adam you are part of the dust of Malaysia, your land of birth. Can I bear to be away from you?'

Edie's phone rang, a shrill interruption to her thoughts. 'Hello? Robert? Yes, I would like to see you. Please why don't you come to me for lunch. I'm out sunning myself, as unbelievable as that sounds. I'm sitting on the bench we drove to last month. I can't believe the colours of the gorse and the flowering currant trees. I'll call into Stonehaven and get something nice. I'll be home about one.'

Driving back, she thought of the word she had used, "home". Did she mean it?

Chapter 54

'That was a grand lunch, Edie, not what I'm used to at all,' Aggie dabbed her pursed lips with her serviette. 'Fancy me having such delicacies as smoked salmon and stuffed peppers in the middle of the day, and wine as well! Bob and I are accustomed to plainer fare. We like a bit of cheese maybe or a bowl of soup for lunch.'

'You're always welcome, Aggie, you know that. You've been such a help to me here.'

'Aye, the house is looking very nice and fresh and I see the tamarisk trees in the garden are starting to flower. I'd forgotten they were there. They do well with the sea winds.' Her lively eyebrows rose and fell as she accentuated her words. Edie sensed that the older woman was getting set to regale them with the latest update on an episode from her television drama but when no one responded, Aggie's bright eyes darted from the minister to Edie and then back again. A look of quiet understanding settled on her face and she stood up, laying her folded serviette neatly on her plate. She realised of course that she had gate-crashed this little luncheon, but they had been so insistent she stay.

'Well, now that was very nice, but I will have to be on my way. Bob will be wondering if I've decided to move in, I'm over here so much.'

Robert walked her to the door. 'You've been a wonderful support to Edie, just as you were to the two old ladies, and a good friend to me as well, Aggie. I'll see you again very soon.' He watched the thin figure scurry off down the path and a wry smile played on his lips. She must be in torment wanting to know what we are going to talk about, he thought. When he re-entered the sitting room, Edie had already cleared the lunch things away, but had taken the bottle of wine over to the chairs beside the fireplace. There was no need to heat the room today, it was warm, and the windows were open.

'I've re-filled your glass, Robert.' Edie placed the bottle on the side table. 'We should finish it whilst it's still chilled, then we can have some coffee.'

'So, my dear. You have a lot to tell me. I know a little about Kamal and your life in Malaysia, but you haven't told me why you have come here. Are you ready to talk about it yet?'

Edie lowered her head and began tentatively. 'His name was Adam; he was my boy. He grew up like so many youngsters, with the same troubles, the same aspirations, and the same potential of worrying their parents to death.'

The curtains blew in, stirring the air. Only the chirrups of sparrows and the constant cawing of the crows broke her narrative. Robert watched her face, the nuances of light and shade reflecting her feelings as she recounted her life in that distant land. He heard names of places he had only read about, characters that were becoming real to him as she laced her story with their antics. The afternoon was nearly gone, but still the light stayed outside. Edie got up to make more coffee.

'Shall I put a dash of brandy in them?'

'Maybe, I think we could both do with some fortification.'

Holding her mug of hot coffee in her hand, Edie seemed mesmerized by the swirls of heady alcoholic vapours emanating from it. 'I was given his rucksack by the police. When they finally left, I found the courage to open it and look inside. Kamal came to sit opposite me in the lounge. I found some small towels, a ski hat, gloves, all that he might have worn on the summit. The water bottles were gone, and all the snacks. But as I ran my hand round the inner pocket, I came across a clear plastic folder containing a small drawing book, and strangely enough, one lady's earring, a ruby droplet. I opened the book and saw a child's drawings. One of them depicted a family, a father, a mother and a young girl. The man was most certainly Kamal.'

'So, you were right in your suspicions all along?' Robert asked.

'It seems so. I was so upset that Adam had known about his infidelity, and had borne that secret alone. He must have suffered so much knowing that his father had betrayed us.'

'What was Kamal's reaction to your discovery of the truth?'

'He had the grace to blush. He just hung his head and let me rant and cry and accuse him of ruining our lives.'

'Did he explain?' Robert asked.

'Only that he'd married the other woman, but that he was going to divorce her. He said he still loved me.'

'And the daughter? How old is she?'

'He told me that the daughter's name is Farah and she's thirteen years old. Of course, Kamal has to provide for the child. He said he had been wanting to separate from Rose for years, but she was very hysterical and was threatening to hurt me. He said she was very unstable.'

'So, the mysterious phone calls were from her?'

'Yes. A woman will do anything. I just hope she hadn't tried any silly magic stuff that resulted in poor Adam's death.'

'I doubt it, Edie. From what you say, the American man, Caleb, was the cause of the accident. And if Adam had not drunk alcohol for a long time, the vodka would have made him unsteady and reckless. But it was an accident. You mustn't read more into it.'

'I know, I think I'm just tired. I've been going over it and over it. Being here, in this house, meeting you, hearing tales of another tragedy, the death of my father in Glasgow, has helped me to come to terms with my own loss.' She leant over and clinked her mug against his, 'Thank you, Robert.'

'And Kamal? How did he respond when you left?'

'He gave me this.' Edie went over to where she had thrown her handbag down. She retrieved a white crumpled envelope. 'Take it, read it.'

Robert gently opened the envelope and pulled out a photograph, a coloured photograph of Edie as a young woman. She had long fair hair, and was wearing a white coat. 'This is you?' He smiled, bemused.

'It is me. Please read the letter.'

My beautiful Edie,

I have broken your heart, a heart that has already suffered so much pain. Words of mine cannot heal your loss and cannot bring Adam back. I want you to know I have always loved you, from the very first day I saw you, and I have always kept this photograph of you in my desk. I would often look at it. I know that sentimental thoughts of mine will not repair the damage and loss of trust that you have suffered. I am begging you to forgive me. I have no right to ask you, but I want to grow old with you, Edie, just as we hoped we would do when we signed the paper so long ago in Johor Bahru. I understand your need to leave and return to Scotland. My life is nothing without you. You are my rock, and my other half. Everything else has been a mistake.

Robert stopped reading. He took off his glasses and rubbed his eyes. For a moment he saw another woman sitting on the chair opposite him. Much older and frailer. She had a Bible on her knee, and newspaper cuttings of obituaries in her hand.

'How did you cope, Isobel,' he had said to her, 'living with such a violent man? A man who hurt your children, who beat them till they bled and who had such a volatile temper you never knew when it would erupt?'

'Marriage is a contract,' Isobel had replied. 'In our day, when we married, we didn't know if he was the 'right' one, as they talk about today. We just got on with it. He was a hard man, old Jock; he could never contain his temper but he never hurt me, physically anyway. Maybe I should have left him but I didn't have the luxury of taking seven children and setting up home somewhere else. And when the news of our children's deaths came to us, one by one, the old devil actually broke down and cried. There is a soft spot in all of us; we each have our vulnerabilities. Some folk do terrible things and regret it. I could see that in old Jock.'

'And you forgave him?'

'No, I never forgave him. He allowed the temper to blind him. And that rage hurt my sons. But as the years went by, he grew more mellow. I used to think I was like a blade of barley in the wind. If you bend with the storm, the stalk doesn't break, and so it was with me. And Jock repented. Funnily enough in later life he spent a lot of time reading the book of Psalms. We'd gone through a lot together, poverty, disappointment and the sad demise of our family. In the end, when I laid him to rest, I wasn't sorry that I had stayed with him. I hope he found peace.'

Now Robert looked over at Edie, the granddaughter of that brave, resilient woman. How could he advise her? Edie was from a different generation, and hers was a marriage integrated into a different culture, a marriage that had been a sham for the last ten years.

'You're very quiet,' Edie broke into his thoughts.

'I was thinking about your grandmother, funnily enough. She too had a lot to forgive. She talked about barley and the wind, and I wondered about you living in the Far East. It's not barley you have there but bamboo. Very resilient, bendable and quite flexible, I believe.'

'You think I should go back?'

'It's a life, and it was your life, Edie. And it was an extraordinary life. You have your daughter and granddaughter in Singapore. Who knows what you should do, my dear? None of us knows, only you.'

'But I do love it here as well. I love this house, the bracing winds, the sea, the fields and the people I have met here.'

'And they will be here for you always. Your grandmother assured you that her home is now yours.'

Edie got up, a little unsteady. 'You are a terrible minister, encouraging me to see the world through a haze of wine and brandy. Drinking in the middle of the day, I'm almost as bad as you and my father were.'

'Never!' Robert laughed. 'Frank and I remain unbeaten on that score! Go home, Edie.'

'I can always come back.'

'You can always come back.'

EPILOGUE

Tara was cutting out animal shapes with four-year-old Clementine in their apartment in Singapore. They had a newspaper and thin pieces of sticks and slivers of bamboo arranged on the kitchen table. They were trying to make some kites.

'Mummy, I want an eagle,' Clementine demanded, handing the marker pen to her mother. 'Will my kite fly the highest?'

'It might, but mine is going to be a butterfly, so it might fly really high as well.'

'Granny, why are you making a fish kite?'

'Because you can get flying fish, and mine will have a long tail.'

'Kites can fly up to the moon, you know.'

'They can,' said her mother, 'and some can go up to the sun and get all burnt up.'

'When can we fly our kites?' Clementine asked, wielding the scissors in order to cut out the bird shape, her black hair falling across her face.

'We'll go to the beach this afternoon when the tide is out and there might be a good breeze.' Tara glued the sticks to the paper and attached a ball of string to each masterpiece. 'But first we have to let these dry.'

As promised, the three drove to the beach on Singapore's east coast and parked the car. The sun was low on the horizon and the wind was perfect.

Are you glad you came, Mum?' Tara asked. 'I've missed you so much. Did Scotland help you to come to terms with everything?'

'It did, but it's so good to be with you again.' She smiled and hugged her daughter. 'Now, let's fly these kites before the sun sets and it gets dark.'

For a magical five minutes, the papery kites fluttered high above them. The proud eagle, the whimsical butterfly and the sinewy fish flew and swooped and dived, much to the delight of Clementine. Flaunting their newsprint to the skies, they flew up to the moon, to the sun, and then one spiralled out of control and got tangled in the branches of a casuarina tree.

'Oh no!' cried Clementine, 'Granny, it's yours.'

'I can see that,' shouted Edie. 'You two should take care with your strings in case they get entangled and crash too.'

'I see a fish in the tree.'

A man's voice broke into their shrieks and laughter.

'It's a fish out of water,' the man said calmly. 'It's a fish that needs to come home.'

It was Kamal.

Edie gasped at the sight of him. She had not expected to see him, and certainly not here in Singapore. She turned to Tara who shrugged guiltily, as though to say he'd persuaded her to set up a meeting. Edie took a deep breath before stepping towards her husband. In a clear voice she said, 'I am home, Kamal.' Her gaze was steady. 'I'm back in this part of the world that I love, with the people that I love. And,' Edie paused for a moment, considering her words as she looked up at the fish stuck in the tree, 'that fish will fly again. Because you see, I am going to stay here, and I will be free, perhaps for the first time in my life.'

'That is ridiculous, Edie, I explained everything in my letter, of how I love you, and you cannot deny I always let you lead your life as you wanted. You know I am sorry and I'm asking you please to give me another chance.' His eyes were glinting with emotion.

'No, Kamal. No more chances. I loved you from the day I met you, but you have made a fool of me, and now I want my own life. I don't want to live with a man whom I can no longer trust. Not anymore. We all make choices in this life, and you made yours. When I was in Scotland, living in my grandmother's house, I was able to reflect on many things and I've gained a different perspective on how I want to live the rest of my life. I'm lucky as I have Tara and Clementine here in Singapore but I also have a home in Scotland.'

'So, this is the end?'

'Yes, Kamal, it is the end for us.'

'I'm sorry for everything, Edie.'

'Yes,' she said, 'I am sorry too.'

She watched him walk away, his footsteps crunching on the sand and gravel.

Edie turned towards the sea, aware that Tara and Clementine had retreated to their car. Alone she stared at the blackening sky and the distant neon lights of the city skyscrapers. The waves washed the shore, splashing her bare feet. Oh Isobel, she thought, I know you might have forgiven him, but I can't. Once I thought I had to stay and be strong for the children, but now I don't need to. Adam has gone and Tara has her own life. I am always going to be torn between my two countries, but that is not such a bad thing. And now I can make plans, a new life here in Asia, and maybe summers back in Scotland.

She heard the final crunch of gravel as Kamal's car reversed and finally roared out of the beach car park. Edie sighed deeply. It really was the end. She expected to feel sadness, but instead she felt relief and for the first time since Adam had died, she was at peace. She turned back to where her daughter and granddaughter had returned from their car and were standing under the casuarina tree. Their faces lit up when they saw she was laughing.

'Are you ready girls? Granny is going to get that fish down from that tree, and tomorrow we shall fly again!'

www.ingramcontent.com/pod-product-compliance
Lightning Source LLC
Chambersburg PA
CBHW060344030726
47497CB00003B/587